The Kafka Society

The Kafka Society

"A Jack Madson Novel"

RON FELBER

BARRICADE
BOOKS

Published by Barricade Books Inc.
2037 Lemoine Ave., Suite 362
Fort Lee, NJ 07024

www.barricadebooks.com

"Please do not understand me too quickly."

—Andre Gide

This book is for Mickey

Chapter One

"**O**kay, Madson," Grady, the rangy black guard sang-out to me. "Attorney's here, wants to see you."

I strode beyond the first set of bars. They closed behind me with a metallic clang and locked as the second set sprung open and I exited cell block F, ambling down the Tier's narrow corridor awash with catcalls from the inmates in the cell blocks we passed. "White Boy! Talk to your attorney 'bout me!" one shouted. "Fucking traitor!" screamed another. "*Vete al Diablo!*" cried-out another as the less boisterous amongst them held headlines up to the bars as Grady and I forged ahead. "MAD SON KILLS PAL!" was the *Post's* banner story. "JACK THE STRIPPER! Killer Shared Love Nest With Porn Star!!" clarioned the *Daily News.* The electronic media was no less hostile from FOX and MSNBC, on to the networks. And who could blame them, what with the full court press the FBI was throwing at me? Truth was, it had gotten so I wondered myself if I was innocent of the crimes I'd been charged with!

Fuck you bastards! You don't know who I am or what really happened! My anguished mind shrieked back at them, the disembodied voices suddenly conspiring around me like a gathering of dark clouds before a cataclysm. *So why don't you just shut your fucking mouths!*

1

"Nice fan club you got here, Madson," Grady commented neutrally.

"They'd sell tickets to my execution if they had 'em," I growled, and this must have tickled Grady because his cinnamon eyes twinkled as we continued our trek to the "Visitor's" conference room. The clamor was suddenly squelched as the room's steel re-enforced door opened and shut behind us like the portal to a vault.

"What have you done with Madson?" I could hear celebrity attorney Jimmy Bryant ranting while prison officials tried unsuccessfully to shut him up. "I warn you, there are laws in this state to protect innocent men like my client, but I don't expect you folks'd know about civil liberties, would you?"

And to me it sounded like a one-man carnival, Bryant trundling down the corridor—short and squat—dark blue suit and vest, with barrel chest and fiery red hair, higher ups from the Correctional Department scurrying along side him, reporters with tv camera crews trailing behind. Then, he stopped, turned on his heel, and waited as the barrage of questions rolled up like a tidal surge to greet him.

"When did you first..." "Mr. Bryant! Mr. Bryant!!" "What about the woman, Bryant?" "Yeah, what about Havana Spice..."

Bryant listened patiently, bulging blue eyes alert as a terrier's, until the question he'd been waiting for floated up from the mix.

"Do you believe Madson's innocent after all of the testimony given against him?" A female reporter from the *NY Times* finally managed to inquire.

"Young lady," he snorted, "do you have even the foggiest notion of what justice in America is about? The lives lost, the blood spilled, by those brave souls who founded this great nation? Well, if you did," he declared reaching into his shop-worn leather briefcase, pulling from it a late edition of the *Star Ledger*, "you'd know that leaks plastered over the front page of every newspaper in the state and repeated by network and cable television, has not only undermined the possibility of a fair trial, but risen to a point where it's trampling on the rights guaranteed all American citizens by the Constitution of the United States!" He held his hands up in the air palms-forward as if to stave-off armies of onrushing soldiers visible only to himself. "That's all I have to say! That's all I have to say *for now!*"

"Jimmy..." "Jimmy..." "Mr. Bryant..." "Mr. Bryant..." the reporters called after him, but it was no use. He'd said what he wanted.

With that, the second steel door opened and into the MCC's "Visitor's" room came Bryant. His eyes met mine head-on as the door shut behind him, then shifted to Grady.

"Well? Is there a reason you're standing there gawking at me?" he asked.

"No, sir, Mr. Bryant."

"Very well, then," Bryant shot back waddling toward us. "Mr. Madson has been delivered forthwith and I'm about to confer with him, so if you'd be so kind to leave us to our work?"

Grady pivoted toward me. I was sitting in a folding chair unmanacled as was the norm, unless you were being taken across the Square for a court appearance. With no Armormax between us, most lawyers preferred a guard around, but not Bryant who scooped up a metal chair, its back to me, and sat, short arms dangling over it, as we faced one another.

"Well, go on then! John Madson is no threat to me or any man, but I suspect you already know that!"

"Yes, sir, Mr. Bryant," Grady snapped back, and I thought it was kind of humorous as he blundered out of the room and Bryant leaned over the back of the folding chair, his oversized head jutting forward, blue eyes bulging. "You chew?" he asked, reaching into his side pocket, pulling out a plug of tobacco. I didn't answer still in awe of the presence a man so physically unimposing could carry along with him into a room. "Disgusting habit," he said taking a big chew. "Took it up after my family moved from New York City where they immigrated from Ireland, then on to Athens, Georgia." He snatched an empty Styrofoam cup from the tabletop and spit into it. "Athens! Calls to mind the Golden Age of Democracy: Socrates, Plato, Aristotle. But my childhood was nothing like it, not in Georgia, not in County Cork, neither. Poor as church mice my family was, plunged into Dante's seventh circle of Hell, replete with violence, social injustice, and ignorance!"

I sat up straight in my chair, the spell cast by his initial foray broken. "Is there a reason you're an hour late?"

"Sure is," he shot back. "It's for the media. Come early? Reporters think they're doing you a favor. Keep 'em waiting and they know you got somethin' to say. Then you say it, Jack. You say it in 'media speak' with lots of one-liners suitable for sound bites 'n headlines. You say it loud. You tell it straight. And you swear on your mother's cunt that, no matter how outrageous it may be, every goddamned word of it's true!"

I nodded, non-committal, to let him see I was no convert to the Jimmy Bryant Fan Club. "There a reason you changed your name from O'Brian?"

"You want to know why I changed my name?" he asked, a brogue suddenly emerging. "Sure, I'll tell you. My father was a drunk and my mother was a whore, simple as that." He shot a stream of brown liquid into the Styrofoam cup like it was meant to shoot a hole in its bottom. "Emerald Isle, they call it! If it was up to me, they'd sink the fucking island into the sea with every Irishman still on it for the way they treated my family. You know how much scratch I've lost betting on Irish heavyweights, Cooney to Morrison?" I shook my head again. "Enough to pay your goddamned bail five times over!"

"Somehow I'm not feeling much better about my chances now that I've gotten to know you better, Jimmy," I said like the wise-ass I am.

Bryant spit into the cup again; his fiery eyes turned sly as he sized me up, "You know, you're not so hard to figure out, Madson."

"Try me," I challenged.

"You grew up in Newark, New Jersey. Father was a truck driver and you lived like white trash," he said, staring hard into my face. "The other kids taunted you by day, your father abused you by night, wound up committing suicide, and there wasn't much to be happy about being you, was there, Jack? By the time you made it to the monks at St. Damian's, you understood two things: one, you could fight and tore through Golden Gloves like a man possessed. Two, you weren't half as stupid as others made you out and attended Georgetown University until the loans dried up and you became a D.C. cop."

"Not going to leave out my criminal past, are you?" I inquired through clenched teeth.

"I've got it all right here," he said patting his briefcase

with his right hand. "How after you'd had your fill transporting federal criminals, you headed back to Jersey. While there, you charmed your way into marrying the daughter of a Supreme Court Judge—Barton Crowley—and landed a VP spot at NuGeneration Holdings, a take-over house on Wall Street..."

"All of that, from the FBI?"

"No, *USA TODAY* along with thirty other internet reports," he added, his blue eyes locked with mine. "Seems you made quite a splash before Crowley sent you packing for Portland, Oregon. Stole bio-technology and sold it to the Chinese, faked your own drowning by way of a boating accident, then escaped to Mexico leaving a string of dead bodies behind you along the way! That was three years ago. So after the old man dies, you decide to test the waters back East."

"That's right."

"And within a month, you get yourself into a mess like this; the permanent kind, most believe, leading straight to Lewisburg Federal Penitentiary."

"You've got your facts straight, but not much else."

"Like 'motive'?"

"Yeah, like motive. Like whatever I did wasn't because I'm a murderer. It's because..." I hesitated, wordlessly grabbing at justifications as they fluttered like moths before my eyes.

Bryant studied my expression and laughed out-loud.

"What's so fucking funny?" I snarled, rising from my chair, ready to go after him.

"Rage," he said, simply.

"What?"

"That's what we share in common, you and me, Madson."

"Rage, *at what?*" I bridled, settling back into my chair.

"At the injustice of life," he ventured, "and that patch of psychic space we share deep inside us both. It's the reason I understand what growing up estranged turns a man into, how it makes you *feel*, how it makes you *act*. And just because my background is as sordid as yours, well, I'm not the man facing murder one, am I?"

"No," I admitted.

"That's because, unlike you, I've learned to control it. Anger's still there, but with me it's channeled. I don't run from life into the recesses like the goddamned vermin that infest this rat hole," he cursed, stomping a gigantic cockroach with the heel of his shoe. "No, I take it on direct! I beat the motherfuckers at their own game; in the courts with their own law!"

"Can't fault you for that," I agreed, our eyes searching one another's for a connection.

"Well, all right, then," he concluded, pulling a Lanier tape recorder from out his battered briefcase. "I know you, and you know me. So, let's put our pistols on the table. Can we do that now, can we cut the bullshit?"

"You said before that you keep the media waiting when you have something to say. So, do we? Do we have something to say?"

"That depends on you, Jack," he said switching his chew from one cheek to the other. "The notes I got from your court appointed lawyer are worth shit. My notes are no better. What I need from you now is the truth, the full story, because I know that if you blew Tom Dougherty's brains out, it was in self-defense, or at least for good reason. You're no murderer, Jack. A bit of an asshole. A misfit, perhaps. But you're not the type to murder in cold blood;

or blow up federal buildings; or any one of the multiple counts they've got you in here for. So will you do it, Jack? Will you give it to me straight, start to finish? Can you trust me enough to do that so I can help get you out of this Hell on earth?"

"Yeah," I said in a clear voice, the ardor of which surprised even me, "I will, Jimmy. I'm going to tell you everything, every last detail," I swore, "just the way it happened."

And just then, as Bryant leaned his bulldog frame to one side to flick on the tape recorder, he and everything else in that shabby, ill-kept room may as well have disappeared. It was me now. Just as it had been for the past three years.

After the murders. After the bombing. After my capture, my arrest, and imminent conviction.

Chapter Two

In lots of books I read where the accused tells his story, I notice once it gets to the details—like *what* really happened, *how* it happened, and *why*—the writer gets fuzzy when he reaches a high point in order, I suppose, to keep the reader in suspense. He might cut the scene or jump to another so you can't figure out if he's really the killer or just some poor gink someone's trying to pin the murder(s) on.

Well, I guess those are some pretty clever techniques for authors who aren't *really* killers and a lot of book reviewers seem to eat it up. But I'm no writer, and though I once penned a story or two for St. Damian's literary magazine, telling stories is not what this is about, so let me tell you straight up. Yes, I killed Tom Dougherty. Blew his fucking brains out in a tunnel located eight stories beneath the city of New York with a Glock semiautomatic. I also blew up the Federal Building and I guess you could say conspired against the United States of America, if chose to see it that way.

So now let me tell you everything those books won't ever delve into like how it *feels* to murder a man and what it takes for a run of the mill failed human being like me to transform into an enemy of the State so you can take it to the people who will judge what crimes I may have committed.

See, I was living at the Georgetown Inn in D.C., a place my pal, Eddie Lawler, owned and operated. Of course, it was family money bought Eddie the hotel. Truth was, his entire adult life could be described as one enormous bender he'd yet to desert—drinking, gambling, snorting cocaine off the hip bones of exotic dancers, some of it paid for, some of it on the house. So I suppose it was only natural that Eddie would have an affinity for someone like me who'd attended the University with him and could party with the best of 'em.

Long story short, Eddie had been putting me up *gratis* for near three months in a suite where I operated a one-man private investigation firm running down no-pay dads, insurance scammers, and divorce case surveillance gigs, if I had no other options. Why was I in D.C.? Let me answer that question with another: where else did I have to go after the NuGen fiasco, my run-ins with the Law in Jersey, and Barton Crowley's scorched-earth policy when it came to me, his profligate son-in-law?

Besides, there were other considerations like my daughter, Tiffany, fifteen years of age when I left, and now a freshman at New York University. Truth be told, I'd never gotten much traction in Portland anyway. What with the scandal at NuGen and the dog shit reputation that followed, I wasn't able to do much more than what I turned out to be reasonably good at: routine investigations, leading to petty outcomes, and fees that would make a monk denounce his vow of poverty, since I possessed neither the background nor the funds to post bond for a PI license.

As important, it was around that time that I was actually starting to believe I'd beaten back my addictions that like an unwelcome boarder seemed to have worked their way into my life. It was as if I'd suddenly emerged from a sodden fog of booze and amphetamines, to find memories of Tiffany impinging on my mind with the persistence of a cracked tooth discovered the morning after one of my infamous blackouts; or had it been only one morning and just one ten year blackout? Truthfully, I hadn't a clue.

But to me my past was irrelevant. What I needed to think about, I understood then, was the importance of my future, regardless of the things I'd done or left undone, and began to yearn for the company of my daughter, to crave a genuine relationship like I'd read about in books or heard about from acquaintances but never experienced myself.

Tiffany had become an obsession, but there was also the allure of Vicky Benson, an old flame from my university days, who maintained a legal practice on Constitution Avenue, and the fact that it was there that I'd worked as a deputy sheriff, transporting federal criminals from D.C. to Richmond State Penitentiary and back. Not much, I realize, but something. Enough for me anyway, stuck in Oregon as I was, dying for the chance to start a new life.

So, I guess you get the picture? Down on my luck, living case to case, not having quite kicked the alcohol and drug thing, okay? But it wasn't any of those that led me to this place where I am today. The morning all this went down I wasn't *hazy* about what had gone on. Uh-uhh, that morning, I had *no memory whatsoever* for anything that had happened during the past twenty-four hours!

See, it was about 10 am on a Sunday morning. I remember that because the sun was shining into my hotel window, but more than the warmth of the sunlight on my face, I could feel the warmth of the girl's mouth on me, kitten-like laps punctuated by deep-thrusting plunges that had my cock standing at attention like a five-star general had just entered the premises. The sensations; I mean, the things a pro like that can do to a man, well, like I said, she was a pro.

Laying on my back, staring deep into her sparkling green eyes—her long chestnut hair tossed across my thighs and abdomen—my body actually started to convulse. That's right! My arms, legs, and upper torso began to shake so violently, the stanchions of the bed started drumming against the floorboards like a scene straight from *The Exorcist*, until all resistance collapsed and she took what I gave her greedily into her mouth. There I lay trembling like a wet pup when, a moment later, I watched a mischievous glint creep into her eyes and the next thing I knew she was riding my rock-hard cock like a cowgirl on a wild stallion! And seeing her atop me, eyes clenched shut, so ardent in her desire, a tsunami of lust began building deep within me, and the overwhelming obsession to fuck that sex-beast from the sweat-drench sheets of my quaking bed to oblivion and back again!

Yee-haaa! Yeah, we were on an out-of-control amusement park roller-coaster and ravaging that girl—wherever she'd come from, whoever she turned-out to be—was all that mattered to me! This beauty, now straddling me like a woman possessed, with long hair flying, face flushed, and pink breasts matted with sweat, *was on fire*, her pussy tight and drenched, alternately swallowing and releasing my cock with shakes and rhythms I'd never dreamt existed!

"*Oh, yes!*" my Sex Goddess began calling out to the Heavens. "*Oh, yes! Oh, yes, yes, yes!*" she clamored, taking me deep into her burning flesh, until at the last possible moment, she slipped me, near mystically, from one orifice into a second, deeper corridor, crying out in unabashed ecstasy as I penetrated, *"Jesus, my Lord and Savior, I've just seen God!!"* And I was no more than a stroke and a thrust behind, *"Oh, baby, yes! Okay! Just like ... my, God, that!!*

And at that moment, it was like I'd just passed through the gates of a huge city in the desert, or was it a place on the moon? I couldn't know because the colors had the unreal pastel of the plastic in a child's playroom and the main street was the Vegas strip at midnight set flaming with light as a million light bulbs flashed onto the scene!

Then there was quiet. Not a sound except the panting of us both trying to catch our breaths, sunlight streaming through the drawn shades, bathed in the post-brawl aftermath of colossal morning sex. Floating on a magic carpet of bliss, the Mystery Woman's sultry green eyes remained clamped shut, basking in the remnant delights of multiple orgasms, her feline tongue licking idly at my ear. When her eyes opened, they were accompanied by a spontaneous grin that was both broad and beautiful.

"You-are-a-wild-man," she said, throwing a long shapely leg over me, pecking me on the lips, and dismounting with the professionalism of a championship equestrian.

I watched her enter the bathroom and run the shower. She stared into the mirror, played momentarily with her shoulder-length hair, then stepped into it.

To me, our entire encounter was just all too fantastic. This woman—twenty-five, twenty-six, maybe—was a fox of massive proportion, but there remained one not so insignificant problem, I was thinking as I climbed from the bed and poured two cups of water into the coffee machine.

The problem, I pondered, trying to marshal my scattered thoughts into some version of reality, was that I had no idea who she was, how she'd gotten in my room, or what we'd been up to the night before. All of these elements, part of an equation that to me—a guy famously prone to blackouts after nights of heavy drinking—seemed more than a little disturbing. *Blackouts.* Hazy periods unclear to me post-binge. But never like this. Never so profound as that morning!

I put on a white terry cloth robe and was sipping coffee from a ceramic cup with "GO HOYAS!" embossed on it when my Mystery Woman emerged from the bathroom, unabashedly naked, toweling her hair. Fully awake now, I realized this was as sensuous a woman as I'd ever seen: her shoulder-length hair was the color of chestnuts, her breasts were full and perfect, her body athletic, with movie-star features, and dazzling green eyes that shimmered when she bared her perfect white teeth and smiled. None of this, I knew, was going to make what I had to say any easier.

"I realize this is going to sound strange," I said uncomfortably, handing her the second cup, "but I'm not sure I remember much about last night."

She was done toweling her hair and had started dressing, slipping on a pair of Ralph Lauren jean, sans panties, while talking at the same time. "You told me this would happen," she said as she stepped into a pair of suede Tres Outlaw boots, then sipped at her coffee. "You said you wouldn't remember nothin', and I guess you was right. You don't know who I am, do you?"

"Sorry."

"Well, if you don't remember me from us fucking and sucking each other ten hours non-stop, I hoped you remembered me from my internet ads." She chucked the towel in my face. "Shit, you fucker, I'm Amber Starr, the 'San Antonio Hellion!' Don't you go to the gentlemen's clubs?"

"Yeah, sometimes," I confessed, fumbling with the towel, "but I still don't know who you are, or remember anything about last night. I can't explain it. Not any of it," I told her truthfully, my cautious eyes attempting to probe beyond the chill of her vexed expression. "Would you like a hug?"

"*No, I don't want no fucking hug!* Anyways, I guess I got what I wanted and you did too, so no hard feelings," she said, her stare dropping to my crotch, "just a hard cock, which I see you got already, but I gotta go model for Pulsin' Pussy energy drinks this afternoon, then dance at the Casanova Club 'til three in the morning, so no more monkey business. You?" she said appraising me. "I don't know what I was thinkin'! You don't have no money, do you, Jack?" I shook my head. "Figures," she lamented. "Well, anyways, you got an awful nice smile and seem like a good Joe even with that tough guy act you put on, *sooo,*" she said pecking my forehead as she tweaked the head of my cock between her forefinger and thumb, "you never know, Darlin', this could happen twice!"

It was then that Amber Starr, the "San Antonio Hellion," scampered from my suite at the Georgetown Inn, leaving me to my solitary amazement.

Chapter Three

O nce Amber left my suite, I drifted to the bay window
overlooking Wisconsin Avenue. I watched her hail
a cab and ride off toward Watergate, searching the
fogbanks of my memory for clues. *Blank* was the only word
that popped back from out of the vacuum. My mind was
indeed a total blank, I concluded, about to start dressing,
when from the corner of my eye I noticed my Mustang
convertible parked on the opposite side of the street. The
sight of it and the fact that I had no recollection of driving
it into a space front-end in, back-end four feet from the
curb, was startling to me. *Have you gone mad?* the sternest
voice of the many voices that comprised me was set howling.
No memory? No memory for even your car? And, in the shape
I was in that morning, it seemed as likely the Mustang was
dropped into the center of Georgetown by an alien space
ship as left there by me! Worse, as my bleary eyes came into
focus, I observed coveys of pedestrians collecting around
it, staring at the passenger's side, invisible to me from the
window. Whatever it was grabbing their attention couldn't
be good, I calculated, because after lingering there most
tramped away shaking their heads in disgust with more
than one, I suspected, already dialing 911.

Was it possible I'd become ill and painted the car's
passenger side with a fresh coat of vomit? Amber didn't

seem to know anything about it, but could it have happened after I'd dropped her off and gone on to park? Whatever the answer, one thing was clear: I better get it off the street, and soon, before a neighborhood shop owner had it towed!

Coffee cup in hand, I trudged to the elevator, into the lobby, and out the hotel entrance, slippers flip-flopping on my bare feet, white terry cloth robe flailing in the crisp December wind coming hard off the Potomac.

"Mornin', Mr. Madson," Lawrence, the ex-GU basketball star-doorman said, looking me up and down.

"It's my car," I explained. "I got to move it."

"I can see that, Mr. Madson," he answered, casting a dubious stare across Wisconsin Avenue to the Mustang and crowd it was attracting.

Hungover and queasy, I stood impatiently at the edge of the curb knowing I looked like a patient just escaped from some clinic for the socially depraved and not giving a shit about it. Traffic was moving in fits and starts, and it was during one of the loggerjams that I navigated my way to the opposite side where the Mustang stood out like an Amber Starr pictorial in a prayer book.

A white-haired gink dressed in sneakers with a Wizzards warm up jacket stood arm-in-arm with his hunched-over wife looking it over as I approached.

"That your car?" the old man asked.

"'Fraid it is," I answered passing from the near to the far side of the Mustang.

But if my demeanor was casual, then it did a 360 to something like horror when I saw it. My car wasn't covered in vomit. No, its entire passenger side was painted in blood. Human blood, I guessed, of a quantity that suggested someone had taken a bucket of the stuff and heaved it onto the passenger door, frontend, and window!

"You in an accident last night, son?"

"Not that I can recall," I sputtered, feeling suddenly weak at the knees; sensing for the first time that perhaps I was held in the grip of an imperative larger than myself.

"Joe," the woman said then, tugging at the sleeve of her husband's jacket, "I don't think this here is any of our business."

The old man seemed unable to take his eyes off me as she shepherded him from the car.

"You're right, Mamma," he agreed. "This ain't anything we need to get involved in."

They turned and pulled away, but it wasn't difficult to know what they were thinking when they looked at me: six foot one, a hundred ninety pounds, black hair uncombed, looking disheveled as a DWI plucked from county jail dropped-off at Wisconsin and M Street during morning's rush hour. I was stunned, mesmerized by the horror of the two thousand pounds of steel, and sheer volume of blood, that confronted me.

I padded myself down, searching for cuts or knife wounds that might explain what I was seeing. There were none. *Bloody nose* was the next possibility that streaked through my mind and I rubbed my nostrils vigorously, studying my hand to determine if last night's blackout was accompanied by one of my all-too-frequent nosebleeds. It wasn't. So, like a primitive I trudged around the Mustang, eyes glazed, as I peered into the passenger window, then in through the windshield. I touched the streak of blood on the door's painted surface, still red and slippery at center, turning the color of rust at the periphery as it dried. I stared at my blood-stained fingers rubbing the tips together as I watched the red liquid spread from one finger to the others, then brought my hand to my mouth for a salty taste when the revelation like an exploding supernova burst into my consciousness.

"*Eddie,*" I whispered, "*you son of a bitch!*"

And at that moment, I felt like a man trapped in a dark mine who'd suddenly come upon a probe of light and a way out! Who else but Lawlor—party animal, wild man, practical joker—could come up with a prank like this? Come out from behind the camera Ashton Kutcher, *I have been punk'd!* Blood? Yeah, sure! Cows blood, or chicken's blood, or whatever kind of blood Eddie could get hold of from the Inn's meat purveyor!

"Yeah, you got me this time," I found myself nodding as I opened the passenger door with my electronic key, but from out of that conclusion sprung another. The car's interior was not *covered* in blood but *splattered* with it. Splattered, as in spurting arteries, spewing like water from an unattended hose twisting of its own force. From windshield to steering column then on to the dashboard my wary eyes traveled, finally settling on the passenger's seat where a circle of blood six inches in diameter and one-quarter inch deep winked back at me as it congealed.

Then it occurred to me: Eddie had no key to the car, so how could he have done this to its interior? Probably, *no certainly,* he could not have done it. Not as a joke, or perverse prank, or at all! It was then that the urge to follow the trail of what I was seeing—from source to conclusion—gripped me. I was calling myself a private investigator these days, wasn't I? A detective follows the sequence of a crime from conclusion to initiation, but the front seat of the Mustang, my instincts were screaming, was not the conclusion *but the start.*

I pulled back slowly from the car's interior and turned to face its backend. It's the trunk, I theorized, that's where the body was taken after the victim was slashed or stabbed or brutally beaten. Then I drifted, locked so thoroughly in the moment that I couldn't tell you if my feet touched the concrete, passed the car's blood splattered body, and on to the trunk which popped open with a press of the key.

Pedestrians and workers from shops along Wisconsin Avenue had gathered around me by then: the manager of Starbucks, the sales clerk from Jasmin's, an upscale clothing boutique, the counterman from Jersey Bagels where I sometimes took breakfast, adding their number to the covey of onlookers who stood at its core. But I wasn't aware of any of that. No, it was the open trunk that I was transfixed upon as much as they were transfixed on me, this curious ghost of a man, half-dressed, still clutching a half-empty cup of coffee in his hand.

The open trunk suddenly became to me an open sepulcher. The body, I was convinced, had been there, but was risen up from its confines. Yet, like an open grave it beckoned me, egging me on to examine what was once in it but there no more, because even as I approached there was little to suggest anything different than what was there all along: a spare tire, grease-covered and thread worn; a gray, oil-stained sweatshirt with the words "Wrigley Field-Chicago" embossed across its front; an open tool box with wrenches and fittings scattered around it. But then, back and off to the side, I noticed a crumpled gunny sack of the type a merchant marine might take to sea. This, well, it wasn't mine, I recognized immediately, and edged closer, knees pressed up against the Mustang's chrome bumper, then reached deep into the trunk for it. My outstretched fingers grabbed hold of the sack's drawstring, fished it out, and started pulling it open.

I can tell you, I was not anxious to do this. It was only later in testimony taken from others around me that I learned how they, too, were fixated on what might be inside and how the braver among them drew closer to me as I slipped my right hand in while holding the sack open with my left, fingers finally touching and then seizing the object it contained in the palm of my hand.

It was round, but not perfectly round. It was also sticky so that my first thought was it might be an overripe melon because in addition to my sense of touch there was a sickeningly sweet odor that wafted from out of the rough hewn bag that had me gagging in what had become a kind of slow motion dream where, inch by inch the inside of my hand, now coated in the goo that oozed from the object I held, began to anticipate what it was, *exactly what it was*, and dropped it as if my palm and wrist and arm had suddenly been jolted with a thousand volts of white-hot electrical current!

The object tumbled from my hand down into the depths of the sack and the depths of Hell so far as I was concerned and I shrieked in horror and I shook my head from side-to-side and threw the sack back into the trunk because if the object itself was no longer held up into the daylight for me to see, its image, stark as a cobra, was scorched like the negative of an old-fashioned photograph into my brain.

It was a human head, severed at the neck, cut clean and sure, as if by a surgeon. A human head that was small, not that of a grown man, perhaps that of a child, that had been skinned, red as a pomegranate, without nose, eyes, ears, or lips!

I slammed the trunk shut like I was slamming the slab to a mausoleum trying, not to keep intruders out, but to hold in the roaring sense of evil that threatened to escape from inside.

It was a human head to be sure, I pondered, steadying myself against the car as I stared out into the blur of faces around me. *But whose head was it? What story did it tell?*

Chapter Four

I've seen dead men before, but not like this. No torso. No arms or legs. Not even lips, ears, or eyeballs. No, this was different from anything I'd ever seen or wanted to see again. And standing there, suddenly cognizant of onlookers circled around me, I confess, it made me claustrophobic; like a welter of intense heat had passed through me and despite the 50 degree air, I was suffocating, as if the oxygen had been sucked from the atmosphere, and I had to get away from that car and what was in it to keep from smothering to death!

"Someone call the police!" I heard the voice of a man in a suit call out over the cacophony resounding in my ears, but I'm uncertain whether anyone actually called because most stood milling around the car, informing newcomers about what they saw or what someone else might have seen, a fair number whispering amongst themselves about me, I imagined. When I tried to run for the Inn, a woman shouted, *"That's him! That's the man who owns the car!"* Next thing I knew, a truck driver, making a delivery to one of the nearby stores, grabbed me from behind.

But there was no man, or group of men, going to hold me back because panic had set in and I was convinced—real or imagined—that my life depended on making it to the Inn's lobby, if only to breathe again.

So, I threw the man off me (sent him sprawling on the pavement like a rag doll!) then lurched through the knot of traffic that had coalesced around what had become a crime scene, past the doorman's post, and into the lobby. From there, I caught a glimpse of Eddie Lawler who stood silently staring out of his office window while the normally laid-back Lawrence gave him an earful.

The scene was ludicrous and I might have chuckled over it if I wasn't locked in the shit storm I found myself: A 6' 11" African American ex-basketball star, animated as a cartoon character, hovering over Eddie, a dwarfish man who could pass for Danny De Vito's brother, standing just under 4' tall, nervously puffing a Marlboro Red, blowing smoke rings into the window casement.

"Okay, I get it, Larry," Lawler was saying as he turned to find me standing in the doorway.

"What you want me to do, Mr. Lawler?" Lawrence asked.

"Nothing. Take a break in the kitchen and get yourself a cup of coffee."

The huge black man brushed past me on his way out. I closed the door behind him.

"Really fucked the pooch this time, huh, Jack? Cops'll be here any minute," he said, snubbing the cigarette in an ashtray and taking a nip from a half-eaten donut. "I got one motherfucker of a hangover, so please tell me what the fuck's going on across the street from my hotel?"

"It's a head, Eddie. I got a fucking head in the trunk of my Mustang. Car looks like it took a bath in blood, and in the trunk there's a sack, and in that sack, I swear to Christ, there's a human head!"

"Whose?"

"How the fuck do I know? Brad Pitt's! Barack Obama's! What kind of a question is that?"

"Are you sure it's human? Could be…"

"Eddie, it's fucking human, *and it's skinned.*"

"*The fuck you say!*"

"Honest to Christ! Skinned! No ears, no eyes, no nose, no nothing."

"Bullshit!"

"I'm tellin' you, Eddie," I said earnestly. "I'm telling you."

Lawler puzzled over the information. He took a bite of his donut and washed it down with a swig of coffee, "Well, I gotta see this," he declared slamming the cardboard cup down onto the desktop, then marching from his office, and into the street. "Shit," he hollered, turning back to me, oblivious as he stomped through oncoming traffic, "the guys at Thursday night poker are never gonna believe this!"

With car horns blaring and Eddie cursing a blue streak, I followed him through traffic and the gaggle of curiosity seekers the little man shoved aside, realizing my first choice in terms of help may not have been the wisest.

"Open up! Come on, Jack! For Christ's sake, I want to see it!" he blustered, handing me his cell phone once I'd popped the trunk and he'd gotten his hands on the sack. "Now I'm going to pose with this fucking thing," he explained, plucking the head from the gunny sack, "and I want you to take a photo. I'm telling you, this is going to blow their fucking minds!"

"*What's he holding?*" a co-ed from the university asked disgustedly.

"Eddie," I pled, watching as he showed off the head

like it was a trophy and he was a proud Pygmy tribesman, "it's somebody's head, for Christ's sake! Whoever it belongs to was somebody's daughter or sister or brother. I mean, whoever's head this is had a mother just like you!"

Her boyfriend edged closer, *"It's a human skull!"* he heralded to everyone's astonishment. *"This sick bastard's got a dismembered body in the trunk of his car!"*

"Shut the fuck up and take the picture," he snorted. "No wait," he corrected pulling a Cohiba from the top pocket of his Armani shirt and sticking it in his mouth. "Now take it, quick, before I catch HIV from this goddamn thing!"

So, I snapped a photo. Okay, three photos, but when the counterman from Jersey Bagels announced he'd alerted 911, well, *that was it for me.*

"Look," I said slapping the cigar from his mouth, "you're going to put that head back where it came from or I'm going to shove it down your fucking throat!"

Eddie looked up at me like he'd snapped out of a hypnotic trance, his face flaccid, his large black eyes fluid like those of hound dog, "You didn't kill nobody last night, did you, Jack?"

"No."

"You don't know what you're like when you've been drinking..."

"I didn't kill anyone, Eddie," I said resolutely. "At least I don't think I did," I added, already dialing Vicky Benson's private number as I watched the crowd of one dozen grow to fifteen or more.

"Was it Amber who did him?"

"Did who?"

"This guy here, the 'headless horseman,'" he said

returning the head to the gunny sack and back into the trunk. "I mean, I couldn't help but notice Amber Starr left your room this morning."

"I don't remember a thing about last night, Eddie, nothing."

"You spent the night with Amber Starr and don't remember nothing about it?"

"Not 'till this morning," I explained, waving him off once she picked up and Eddie began unleashing a string of expletives at what was fast becoming a mob. "Hiya, Vicky? Yeah, this is Jack. I've got a situation here and I need your help *now...*"

I gave her the short version of what happened (was there another?) and minutes later my ex-girlfriend-lawyer, was on her way—Connecticut Avenue to Georgetown—with just two pieces of advice: one, *don't talk to anybody until she arrived*; two, *don't touch anything that could disturb the crime scene.*

I looked beyond the Mustang to Eddie, now talking animatedly to two Uniforms who'd just arrived, one of them already busy on his Motorola checking out my Oregon plates with NCIC. So much for not talking to anyone, and so much for not disturbing the crime scene meaning *playing with the fucking head*, I was thinking as I strode toward them realizing that, like most cops in town, they knew Eddie.

"You the owner of this vehicle?" the taller of the two asked.

"Yeah, I am."

"I'd like to see your driver's license and registration," he told me, then turning to his partner said, "Get CSI over here right away."

"I can get you the license from my wallet, but the registration's in the car. I don't think you want me to get it."

The tall cop who had a long pink face and looked to be in his mid-twenties shot a glance over to the blood-covered Mustang, "No, probably not. You okay standing out here dressed like that? If you're cold you can warm up in our car."

"I'm fine."

"Mr. Lawler tells me there's been a homicide. He tells me there's a sack in the trunk of your car with somebody's head in it, that true?"

"Yeah, there's a head all right so I suppose a homicide goes with it, but I know nothing about either."

He nodded, "Okay, you stay here while my partner runs your plate and I get rid of this crowd. He'll be back soon as he's done to take your prints and verify ID. "

"Not without an attorney, he won't. I called, she'll be here any minute."

"Suit yourself," he answered, "but one way or another, my partner's going to take your prints with the handheld and run it through IBIS."

I was about to tell him I'd once been a cop and understood my rights when the wail of nearing sirens cut through the mid-December air and four police cars and an ambulance pulled up behind us. A half dozen Uniforms exited their vehicles making a bee-line for me and Eddie, but it was the two men dressed in suits that commanded my attention. They left their unmarked car calmly, the first to exit likely from MPDC Homicide, but it was the second, who trailed behind, that had Fed written all over him. Of average size with features like cut granite and piercing blue eyes that looked sharp enough to do the cutting, he wore a tailored black suit sporting a *gravitas* that distinguished him from the other, a frail, wan looking man with pasty complexion, who seemed like a run of the mill local.

"Morning, Tom," Eddie called out trying to seize the initiative but his pal, the D. C. detective, ignored him. "Name's Will Harris," Eddie whispered on the sly, "we gamble together. Cooperate and maybe I can get you outta this mess."

"CSI is on the way," Harris told the cop next to me with a take-charge attitude that was surprising. "In the meantime, I want this area cordoned-off," he shouted over the thwomping sound of a police chopper as it veered toward us canvassing the whole of Georgetown. "And you guys," he added, speaking now to the three detectives that had gravitated around him, "I want you to start rounding up witnesses. Anyone that might have seen anything—surrounding stores, restaurants, neighboring properties—and the hotel; maybe one of the guests there's an early morning jogger. If so, we want to talk to him. Anything you want to add?" he asked turning to the blue-eyed Fed.

"Yeah, get hold of the tapes from every surveillance camera within a five block radius of that car," he said pointing to the Mustang. "I want you to talk to the managers, owners, security guards, whoever can get them to you. If they ask for a warrant, tell 'em the paperwork will follow. If anyone balks, threaten to take them in as a material witness. From the looks of things this scene is still warm."

"Eddie, you got no problem with that, do you?" asked Harris.

"Hell no," he answered. "The last thing I want is some lunatic prowling Georgetown."

"Okay, then, let's get this ball rolling!" the detective

exhorted in a booming voice that seemed not his own, his entire persona deflating to become himself again, a burnt out fifty-year old cop, as he drifted past me on his way to the car with the second investigator, the Fed, a half step behind.

"Jesus Christ, this place looks like a scene from *Saw IV* with all the blood been dumped on that Mustang, don't it, Don?" Harris wondered aloud.

"Yeah, and we don't know a thing about it!" Eddie interjected, angling in alongside them. "By the way, this here's the car's owner, a dear friend of mine. Name's Jack Madson. We went to GU together, Will. He's from out of town, came back to visit for ol' times sake."

By now the Mobile Crime Investigation Unit had arrived and was all over the Mustang. A team of technicians dressed in white coveralls wearing latex gloves and face masks scoured the terrain within the established perimeter. I craned my head around to see a bank of video cameras from CNN, FOX, and WYAN, the local station, set up while reporters were being wired for sound.

"Lt. Will Harris, MPDC Homicide," he said, extending his hand. Together we watched the ME transfer the skull with forceps from the trunk of the car to a hermetically-sealed container marked EVIDENCE. "Looks like we've got a homicide, know anything about it, Madson?"

"Truth is, I don't remember anything about the past twenty-four hours. I woke up this morning to find my car with a sack in the trunk and a severed head in it. That's it, that's all I know."

"Sounds weird, but I've heard weirder," Harris commented, eyes shifting to Blue Eyes who remained as yet unidentified to either Eddie or me.

"You want to talk weird?" Eddie blurted. "This here guy spent a smokin'-hot night with Amber Starr and don't remember a thing about it!" Eddie giggled, "Hey, Will, maybe he's a victim of date rape? Imagine bein' date-raped by the 'San Antonio Hellion' and forgettin' everything about it? *Now, that's what I call weird!*"

Harris gave about the most economical smile I'd ever seen, "Hey, Julie!" he called out to one of the technicians, "Blood fresh?"

She pulled her face mask below her chin, "Three to four hours, no more!" she hollered back.

Harris nodded and began walking toward her when the Fed stepped into the pocket, "These cops make you stay out here like this? You must be cold. Eddie, why don't you get us a quiet room where we can talk with Mr. Madson in private?"

"You can use my office," Lawler shouted over the sound of the chopper making its rounds again.

Then, as CSI scoured the area, Uniforms tried to keep pedestrians away and traffic moving, and scores of detectives branched out to question potential witnesses, Eddie, Harris, the Fed, and me, made our way to Lawler's office.

"You know, I don't think I got your name, Friend," I mentioned, not so polite, as we crossed Wisconsin Avenue.

"That's right," Blue Eyes answered, staring straight ahead as he walked. "This is local investigation."

"So why are you here?"

"I'm not your problem, Madson, but that severed head is. Given your situation, I'd say you're in about as deep as you can handle. Forensics lifted a print from the car mirror. We know your history."

I didn't answer; couldn't. My tongue was too thick to talk and my throat contracted like a noose had been drawn tight around it. *But it's okay,* I thought as my right foot stepped onto the sidewalk facing the Georgetown Inn. *It's okay now,* my booze-sodden brain was racing before they hauled me into the hotel lobby and I looked to my left down Wisconsin Avenue.

Vicky Benson's silver Jag had just pulled into a parking spot on M Street.

Chapter Five

O nce in Lawler's office like actors in a play each of us fell into a kind of order. Eddie and I sat in two uncomfortably avant-garde chairs shaped like the palm of a giant's hand while Harris sat behind Lawler's desk with Blue Eyes playing the role of the vigilant sentry standing back against the closed door, arms akimbo.

We'd no sooner gotten settled than Vicky Benson rapped hard on the door and entered.

"Hiya, Vicky," Harris greeted. "I don't think you know Special Agent Woods." He raised his eyebrows to show just how much that impressed him. "He's with Special Operations, Homeland Security."

She introduced herself as my attorney. They shook hands.

"There's been a homicide, Vicky," Harris continued, "but I'm guessing you know as much about it as we do." He gestured toward the bay window where we could see the Mustang, now impounded as evidence, being towed to a Forensics' hanger on L Street. "I was just about to ask Mr. Madson what he knew about it since the victim's head was found in the trunk of his car."

"Are you charging my client with a crime? Because if you are…"

"Easy," he assuaged. "The only crime he's been charged

with so far is illegally parking his vehicle on Wisconsin
Avenue."

"All right, have it your way, Will, but Jack," she
cautioned, "you're under no obligation to answer and I'll
let you know where to go and how far, *got that?*"

The gaunt man sucked what must have been a shot
glass full of bile back down into his stomach in a manner
that seemed not unnatural to him, "So, okay, Madson,
what's the last thing you remember about last night?"

"Dinner at *Clyde's*," I answered, feeling my way back
through those fog banks.

"What time?"

"Seven, seven-thirty."

"Before that?"

"Like I told you, nothing from dinner on."

"No, *before* that. Walk me through it."

"Hey!" Vicky objected. "He said he doesn't remember!
If you're going to badger him, I'm going to instruct my
client not to cooperate."

"Yeah, and I'm going to take him downtown as
a material witness and let the judge sort it out, but
right now I've got a homicide on my hands here in
Georgetown, Counselor! Who knows if it's the son of a
foreign diplomat or the daughter of a U.S. Senator, but
out there in that car is the head of a homicide victim,
recently decapitated, face ravaged beyond recognition,
without identification or any means outside a forensic
artist to reconstruct what he or she may have looked like!
Now, do you really expect me to fall in behind your line
of legal bullshit?"

"You know he told me that!" Eddie suddenly blurted.

"Jack told me first thing I saw him this morning he didn't remember nothin' about it."

"Shut up!" Harris shot back at the little man, grimacing as he sucked another ounce of acid back into his gut.

"No, it's all right," I uttered, the memory of that night drifting like a ghost from out of the fog banks. "The girl. It was after dinner while at the bar I met her."

"Amber Starr?" asked Harris.

"That's right."

"And?"

"We left *Clyde's* together, but then nothing."

"Okay, what were you doing before you met at *Clyde's*?" he urged. "Where were you then?"

"Drinking at *the Tomb's*."

"When to when?"

"From the time I woke up 'till the time I met Amber."

"Your girlfriend, the stripper, she like to play with knives, Madson?" Woods chimed in, stepping toward me from his post at the door. "Maybe the two of you together..."

"Never saw her before in my life," I swore, glancing over to Vicky. "Not even in the clubs."

"So where to now?" Harris complained throwing his hands in the air, exasperated. "I say we read him Miranda and book him 'murder one.' He's all we got. Besides, even he can't explain where he was last night or how that head landed in the trunk of his car!"

All eyes turned to Woods who stood studying everything about me with savage patience: facial expression, posture, the way I sat in my chair.

"No, I say he's telling the truth. I think he got blasted at *The Tombs* yesterday afternoon, and probably the past twenty afternoons, and may have been drugged—*rohynol, klonopin*—either would explain his loss of memory. I say we check him into GU hospital, have blood drawn, find out one way or the other. You okay with that, Madson?"

I turned to Vicky, who seemed unopposed to the idea, then gave a nod.

"Good. In the meantime, the car will be examined for prints—yours, and others—while Homicide checks for a DNA match in COPIS, and Forensics works on identifying the victim: age, gender, and anything else we can determine."

"We put an APB out on Amber Starr," Harris added. "I doubt she'll be hard to find."

"Miss Benson?" the Fed checked.

"For starts I'd like to see the court order authorizing you to search Mr. Madson's car..."

"Granted by the county judge twenty minutes ago telephonically."

"And if you don't mind, I'll take my client to the hospital. I'd like to be with him when blood is drawn, *before and after.*"

"I see no problem with that. You can follow my car there."

Then, the actors dissembled from the stage. Act I was over, but not the play. We each moved toward the door, Eddie, Vicky, me; and Harris with Woods.

"Oh, and Miss Benson?"

She turned to him.

"Jack Madson is someone you've known for some time, correct?"

She nodded.

"Well, maybe you know this, and maybe you don't, but

you should be aware of Madson's pedigree: technology stolen from a venture capital firm in New York three years ago with a string of suspicious deaths thrown in for good measure. Just a suggestion," he said with a grin and a wink, "but you should choose your friends better."

Then, Special Agent Don Woods turned his back and left Lawler's office with Harris.

What I told no one, including Eddie and my ex-girlfriend attorney, was the bone of a lead Amber Starr had thrown me to chew on before she'd left my hotel suite: the name of the strip club where she worked and was performing that night.

Romeo, no, I was thinking. *Cupid, no,* I strained trying to reconstruct our conversation. *Caligula, no, no!*

It was Casanova.

"The Casanova Club," I whispered to myself before leaving Eddie Lawler's office for the streets of Georgetown.

* * *

That night back in my hotel room after spending two hours at the hospital and three more downtown with Harris and company, I poured myself a stiff drink. Glenlivet, no water, no rocks, it barely hit the glass, so anxious was I to throw it down!

Then, I poured myself another—four fingers deep—and collapsed into the divan set off in the adjoining room in front of the widescreen television. Woods was right about the drug, traces were still in my blood stream; a club favorite known as GHB, or G-Juice, and identified by the Doc at GU as *gamma hydroxlntyric acid.* Tasteless, colorless, and deadly potent, it was officially used to treat severe cases of narcolepsy but was as often concocted in street labs to facilitate criminals in the commission of rapes, robberies and, in my case, a brutal murder.

I took a pull from my glass thinking long, careful thoughts, savoring the scotch with lusty pleasure as it past, lips to mouth, warming my insides still knotted after my morning from Hell. Sure, I'd fallen a good distance from my high-flying Wall Street days, but now, with evidence to support my "black-out" alibi, even Woods would concede I'd comported myself like a stand-up guy who was not yet a shoe-in for membership in the Maniac Axe-Killer Club.

But all cops harbor their suspicions, I pondered, staring blindly at the tv screen. Woods, more than the others, had taken an instant dislike to me and made no pretense about it. Fair enough, I didn't like him, either, but there was something in him—perhaps the intensity of those cool blue eyes—that seemed to resonate, 'I am a man who lives for the hunt, Partner, better to leave me be.' Tough, durable, and predatory, he was obsessive in his attention to detail and reverence for protocol. The kind of guy who'd eat his M&Ms with a knife and fork, the federal marshals I once worked with used to say about cops like that. But one thing certain, the prospect of having a Special Ops hound like Woods on their trail would scare the shit out of any one of them!

Still, I took comfort in the fact that I'd taken everything they threw at me dishing out as good as I took and come out of it unscathed. The 'let's get to know each other' bullshit over cold coffee and stale cigarettes, the interminably stupid questions that hung on you like skeins of slime as you sat there sweating, some of them surrounding you, others hidden behind that section of mirrored wall, just waiting for you to utter something they could twist into a confession. But here I was content as the Buddha, a glass of first-rate booze in hand, sitting on my divan released without legal restriction.

Then, with a mind as vacant as the blank tv screen in front of me, I got up to freshen my drink when the phone rang. *Screw it!* was my first impulse, but its ringing was persistent, and in the course of my trek back to the divan I decided to retrieve it.

"Yeah?"

"Jack?" a man's voice asked.

"Who wants to know?"

"This is Tom Dougherty."

"Dougherty?"

"Yes, Tom Dougherty from St. Damian's. Come on, Jack, you couldn't forget your best pal from high school!"

I hadn't. Tom was a good sort. A bit of a two-face, but we'd had a lot of fun together back in the day learning to become All-Star Catholics at that inner-city all-boys prep school.

"Sure Tom, but Jesus, it's been a while, hasn't it?"

"Afraid so, and believe me I'm sorry I didn't contact you after…"

"That's all right," I said cutting him short. "You don't owe me any apologies."

"Yeah, well, I heard you were living in D.C. and I'm here on business so I thought I'd give a ring see if we could take dinner together, or a drink."

"Oh, I don't know," I stammered, rubbing the palm of my hand over my face, "it's been a rough day, Tom."

"Fine, so you tell me your story, I'll tell you mine. Come on, Jack, one drink at *Billy Martin's!* Tell you the truth I could use somebody to talk to…"

I hesitated mostly because the Tom Dougherty I grew up with and had last seen ten years before never needed 'somebody to talk to.'

"Okay, one drink," I agreed, returning the receiver back to its cradle wondering what interest Tom Dougherty, family man, Stanford MBA, and Assistant FBI Director-Eastern Seaboard, could possibly have in talking to me.

Chapter Six

That night I met Dougherty at *Billy Martin's*, an upscale chop house on Wisconsin and N frequented by Washington establishment-types dining with pals or taking drinks with pay-by-the-night call girls. The atmosphere as I entered was replete with the aroma of sizzling steaks, glitter of expensive silver, and practical reserve that bespoke men who made fortunes at night while they slept.

My eyes swept over the neatly arranged tables and high-backed chairs set up and down the polished mahogany bar. Tom's eyes lit in recognition and he half-rose from his seat like a guy desperate to see a friendly face even if it had been a decade since he last saw mine. I offered a polite smile and walked toward him acutely aware that I was wearing tattered jeans, a sweat shirt, and faded New York Yankees warm-up jacket, and he was dressed in a Burberry's pin-striped suit, custom-tailored white shirt and D'or tie with wingtip shoes. Worse, he looked five years younger than me having found his way to the Bureau gymnasium five days a week, I guessed, while my time was spent wasting away in Oregon or, lately, at the Inn eating sporadically and drinking often.

"Jack," he welcomed, clasping my hand in both of his as he ushered me to the opposite side of the table, "thanks for coming."

"I was just thinking, last time I saw you was at a fight in the Garden, Klitchko versus Jackson."

"That was a long time ago," he agreed settling back into his seat. "So, how have you been? I hear you're doing some work as a private investigator here in Georgetown."

"How's Annie and the kids?" I deflected.

"Oh, you know Annie," he answered sipping from the cup of black coffee. "Stay-at-home Mom, teaches Bible classes on Sunday mornings, still the Rock of Gibraltar. The kids? Matt's in his second year at Princeton, wants to study medicine; Elise is a senior at Marymount; and Danny's a fourth grader over at St. Joe's, down the street from our home in Mendham."

"Horse country," I remarked.

"Some call it that, but it's Peapack, the town over, where Jackie O kept her stables and the U.S. equestrian team holds its try-outs. Mendham? Well, that's mostly lawyers and Wall Street financial types."

"I stand corrected. I had you pegged as 'one-percenters' only to discover it's more like the 'point-five percent' crowd."

"Come on, Jack. I know you've fallen on hard times, and I want to help."

"I thought it was you needed someone to talk to," I retorted.

"Those two ideas are not mutually exclusive. Maybe there's a way we can help each other."

Tom's amber eyes leveled with mine, and if I hadn't noticed it before, his youthful appearance may have been as much illusion as first impression. The skin around his eyes though smooth and without circles could as easily been the work of a first-class surgeon as the result of clean living, but it was the eyes, along with his prematurely white hair, executive cut, that seemed wizened, derived from some inner core that upon closer examination appeared effete, perhaps even haunted.

"Nice sentiment, but I doubt you can help me, and I'm goddamned sure there's nothing I can do for you."

He nodded as if to say 'don't be too sure, Old Chum,' then took another sip from his cup, and if I half-expected him to switch tracks and ask the inevitable questions about ex-wife Jennifer, and Tiffany, my eighteen-year old, Tom surprised me and waved down our waiter instead.

"How about a drink for my friend here, Tony? What'll it be, Jack, Scotch?"

"Glenlivet-rocks."

"For you, Mr. Dougherty?"

"Just a refill," Tom answered, running his two middle fingers around the rim of his cup.

"Yes, sir, Mr. Dougherty," he replied crisply as I watched Tom watch him leave.

"So, you wanted to see me," I said cutting to the chase, "seemed like it might be important, is it?"

Tom's head sank like a weight hung from the nape of his neck had just been lowered. He considered his words like he was picking out a tie from amongst the one hundred fifty in his closet and looked up. His expression was tortured.

"I don't know how to begin, Jack, I feel so humiliated by what I've done, so I'll come out and say it. You know Annie and I are *Opus Dei?*"

"No, I didn't know that. Neither of us was very religious in high school."

"It was Annie who inspired it," he answered

instinctively, "and, Jack, I tell you, it's been the most wonderful thing that ever happened to either of us. Taking this leadership role within the Catholic Church changed both our lives and saved our marriage. Before that we just seemed to *exist*, but now with this spiritual mission, we're alive, vibrant again, in union with the Body of Christ, and so is our marriage."

"You had a problem?" I reminded.

"Right," he said, nodding grimly. "You see, it's that life we've been living for these past ten years that makes what I'm about to tell you so sick, *so repulsive*. I took a misstep, Jack. I fell from grace and—I hardly know how to say it—but I've betrayed both my God and my wife. I had an affair with another woman. Paid-for sex with a 'party girl,' I guess you'd call her, and now she's threatening to go to Annie with it."

"Blackmail?"

"I realize you must think I'm the biggest fool who ever walked the planet, especially given my position at the Bureau, but she may have video-taped us doing ... having sex together. An AVI surveillance camera similar to the ones we use for sting operations. Talk about a man being 'hoisted by his own petard,'" he wondered aloud, "*how could I have been so stupid, Jack!*"

"What kind of money is she asking?"

"One hundred-fifty thousand."

"How often did you meet?"

"Just five, maybe six, times."

"Where?"

"She had an apartment in New York, forty minutes from Mendham. A penthouse in a building called the Eleven80. Sometimes we'd meet there, sometimes in a hotel—the Warwick or Plaza—and, God help me, Jack," he pled taking hold of my wrist, "she's calling my home. My home! Where my children sleep and my wife spends her days and nights! When Annie answers, she hangs up, or sometimes stays on, probably just to hear her voice, and when she does, you can't imagine the terror that comes over me not knowing what she might tell Annie every time the phone rings!"

"Easy now, pal," I cautioned, convinced that perhaps he truly had changed from the condescending loner of our adolescent years to a man whose life—absent the intervention of a clever hooker—may well have undergone *metanoia*, the 'change of heart' the monks at St. Damian's had instructed us was finally necessary to become 'born again.'

I watched Tom's hand shrink back beneath the table as Tony arrived with my drink and a carafe of steaming coffee.

He put the drink in front of me and freshened Tom's cup, "Can I get you anything else, Mr. Dougherty?"

"No, not just now," he answered, a fleeting grin passing over his face as he watched Tony leave, then turned his attention to me. "Not much of a re-union, I'm afraid, eh Jack?" he asked sadly.

I drew deep from my glass, a tall one with just one cube of ice, "Shit happens," I observed licking the remnants of scotch from the edge of the glass. "Fact is, I don't know what I can do to help, but if you want an opinion, I'd pay her and be done with it."

"But how could I know if she's given me everything—the video tapes, I mean? How could I be certain she doesn't have copies, or photos, that we don't know exist?"

"There is no 'we,' Tom," I said, staring him dead in the eye, "there is only 'you.'"

"But my family, Jack; my career at the Bureau; my stature within the Church, don't they count for anything?"

"Yeah, those things, too, but no matter what anyone does short of murder, you'll never know if she's given you everything. Best to pay and fess up to Annie, it's the only way to put this behind you, but whatever you decide, I'm not the guy to do it. You don't know the half of my problems, but if you drifted once, I've spent the last five years of my life playing the wrong side of the equation!"

"And you're trying to get back on track?"

"Maybe I am," I admitted polishing off the last of my drink, "but what's that to you?"

"That's where I can help, Jack. Jesus Christ didn't spend the few years he had on this earth with priests, or ministers, or rabbis. He spent them with sinners. Men like Saul, the persecutor, and women like Mary Magdalene, a common harlot. It's never too late to change." He reached into the inside pocket of his suit jacket, pulled a white envelope from it and handed it to me. "Inside that envelope is five thousand dollars. Consider it a stipend to handle my situation the best you can and in the most discrete way possible." He plucked a Mont Blanc pen from the pocket of his white shirt and scribbled on a cocktail napkin embossed with the Carriage House logo, "The woman's name is Havana Spice. She's twenty-six years old and originally from Cuba. In addition to being a 'call girl,' she stars in pornographic movies, do you know that name, 'Havana Spice?'"

"I stay away from pornography. It makes you blind," I said, turning the envelope back to him. "What's more, I have no interest in taking your case."

But Dougherty would not accept the envelope and we were left in a stalemate with him holding one end and me the other.

"You need a PI license to practice in the District, Jack. That means a clean record and eighty thou up front to post bond. I could have your record wiped clean and the bond waived. I could do that, Jack, and I will do it, if you talk to Havana Spice on my behalf."

Tom pushed the envelope forward. I looked him in the eye and took hold, stuffing it into the back pocket of my jeans.

"You know how to handle people like her, you always did. Me? I'm just a numbers guy, a pinhead economist lucky enough to get promoted. You remember what you said when we met as freshman, standing in line for orientation in front of St. Ann's Abbey, Jack? You said, 'you're a guy that could convince somebody the sun is 1750 miles from the earth, but not be able to give them directions to the school library.' That's what you said, and you were right. Talk to her, Jack. Convince her to turn over what proof she has and get off my back, forever."

"You'd pay?"

"Gladly," he said without hesitation. "Call what you're doing a favor … an act of good will for a friend. As for the money, take what you need for expenses and keep the rest yourself. If you need more, it's here for you. You know, in addition to my work at the Bureau, I've been very fortunate with my investments over the years so I'm not without means to support my family, to tithe the Catholic Church, or to help you."

"Okay, Tom, I'll do what I can. I'll talk to her, but let me ask you one question that you can answer with as little detail as you like: the sex you had with Havana Spice, was it 'unusual?' Were there other parties involved?"

"No, nothing like that! Yes, we had sex, oral sex, too—her with me—but she wouldn't let me in the 'back door,' not that I didn't try. Said she was saving it for a 'special someone', like to her that was the last thing she had to offer a man. As for *manage a trois*, give me a break, aside from Annie, she was the only woman I'd ever been with!"

"Fair enough," I chortled, a flash of the hundred questionable women I'd been with streaking through my mind. "Let me see if I can get her to turn over what she has on you, videos, photos, whatever. It may cost you, but in the end she'll understand that everyone has their skeletons, even Cuban porn stars."

"Thank you, Jack," he said reaching over the table to embrace me, "I knew I could count on you."

With that, Tom handed me his business card, white with glossy black print, 'Thomas W. Dougherty,' it read, 'Assistant Director, Federal Bureau of Investigations—Eastern Seaboard.'

Chapter Seven

I hung on at the Carriage House for another Scotch savoring my new assignment touching the wad of cash in my back pocket to confirm it was really there! Five grand was the kind of money I hadn't seen in half a year and after taking down my second scotch-rocks I could almost convince myself it belonged there. Still, just how deep the shit was that Dougherty had stepped into was as difficult to gauge from my vantage point as the chance I had of shutting down Havana's extortion scheme.

So what was *her* vantage point? I left Billy Martin's place for Wisconsin Avenue overflowing with late-night wassailors, ruminating on the subject. Money was, of course, the first consideration, but did a woman like Havana need it? One would imagine her living like a rock diva with income streaming in from adult videos, "live" websites, and a stable of high-tone John's not so unlike Tom, *but who knew for certain?* Pirated internet porn, along with an inexhaustible supply of willing amateurs had sent the multi-billion dollar adult film industry into free fall. So far as Spice's extra-curricula activities, perhaps she'd hooked-up with a parasitic pimp who was siphoning the life blood from her or turned into a smack freak working claw and nail for her daily fix?

Either way, a fellow high up in the food chain as

Dougherty presented an easy mark for a blackmailer once they'd bored their way into his life, except in his case there was more to it than currency. Arguably the most powerful law enforcement official on the east coast, extortion need not be limited to a commodity so mundane as cash. The price beyond the $150,000 Spice demanded may have been the opening gambit in a larger power game played for stakes of catastrophic proportion, say, by organized crime, or terrorists using Havana Spice as their pawn.

Once back at my suite with the speculations swirling through my brain giving way to adrenalin, it was all business for me. *Time to do your homework!* I commanded my torporous inner self, a twenty-first century Ahab roaring to the least of the Pequod's crew. The image stretched my lips into a half-grin as I sat down at the desk in front of my Dell XPS laptop surfing the net for information about these latest entries into the surreal pageant I called my life.

The first was *Amber Starr* and, yes, indeed, there she was, the San Antonio Hellion, true to form, breasts bared and wearing a G-string, smiling like the preacher's daughter just won the chili dog cook-off at the July 4th county fair.

You, My Dearest, are probably doing your choke-the-chicken act for an audience of D.C. detectives and a very uptight Special Ops hound tonight, I mused, my interest turning to the second entry into the Jack Madson "Super Sleuth Sweepstakes" as I googled the name *Thomas H. Dougherty* and watched the 3042 hits it generated pop onto the screen:

'Dougherty Briefs President On NYC Terrorist Caper!' from the *Daily News*; 'FBI Higher-Up Backs Patriot Act Expansion,' courtesy of the *New York Times*. Then, retrieving hits deeper into the run, 'Tom and Ann Dougherty Meet Pope Francis, Gain Private Audience,' from the *Christian*

Science Monitor; and 'Dougherty Named "Man of the Year," Donates $1.5 Million To Catholic Charities,' the cover of *The Advocate* monthly magazine.

On and on, dozens of articles, headlines and photo ops of Dougherty receiving citations and awards with everyone from Obama to the Joint Chiefs of Staff, Pope Francis to China's Xi Jinping!

Yeah, my friend, you've come a long way from our days battling for survival at St. Damian's during the Newark race riots tore through the city, our school, and us, and goddamnit I am proud of you! I reveled, googling my third entry, *Havana Spice*, the twenty-something hooker/porn star who threatened to reduce what Dougherty had accomplished to a pile of rubble unless I did something about it, and the number 3057 totalled up on the laptop's screen.

Eight more entries than Tom, I calculated with an ironic chortle, *and it's no mystery why*, my voracious eyes, and the little man down below, concurred. I clicked through the on-line promos to the website, *Naughty but Nice, Havana Spice*: 'Havana Does Candi Kaye' was one of her epics; 'Spice Likes Donny "The Dong" Lewis,' was another; and, finally, the one that started it all, 'Jessie The Dwarf Demolishes Young Cuban Lesbo,' with the tag line, 'A sixteen-year-old's tale of pain, suffering, and ultimate vindication at the hands of a giant-cocked "little man" with a fetish for spanking under-aged nymphos!'

No imminent Oscars here, no meetings with the President, no private audiences with the Pope, I ventured, *but she certainly was fetching, even breathtaking*, I found myself thinking. Havana Spice had long black hair, large raven eyes, voluptuous lips, high cheekbones, and tanned body, trim and yet sensual as ever the female form might achieve.

Yet, despite all of that, there was something about her that had me harkening back to my old flame from times past, Tomi Fabri, perhaps the only woman I ever *really* loved. Dead four years now, I remembered that same quality in her, and it was *honesty*. A 'take me as I am' bravado that shone through everything she did or said, the way she smiled, the way her dark eyes glimmered bright as the north star against the blackest crystal clear sky. Also, I sensed a great sadness and vulnerability in those eyes and in that face, *but that was Tomi Fabri*, I caught myself thinking before taking the comparison too far, *and unlike Havana Spice, Tomi Fabri was not a whore, nor was she a blackmailer!* Nevertheless, this was a major league temptress, I went on to concede, absorbing not just the face and body of Spice but the aura that surrounded her, one I doubted many men, even Tom Dougherty, who wore his sense of self-discipline like body armor around him, could easily resist.

And it was then while shutting down my laptop that I felt a sense of outrage rise up from my gut at what had apparently happened to my friend of thirty years. Here was a guy played by the rules for the better part of his life and fought hard to make something of himself. Sitting tired and lonely in a hotel room, downtown D.C., he goes to a bar where he meets an attractive young lady. They share a drink, and maybe she slips him a *rohynol*. Half-hour later, they go to his room where they may or may not have sex, and by morning next she's got this one-woman-in-his-existence wonk eating out of her hand while she video-tapes him in compromising positions for purposes of blackmail!

I snatched my cell phone from off the desktop and dialed a number with a 201 area code glancing at the digital clock on the nightstand next to my bed. *Two a.m.*, irrelevant to a man like Johnnie "Lights Out" Giambi my mind projected, probing beyond the tumult of the onrushing storm, to an image of him alone watching early morning television or tossing tormented amidst tangled sheets in his bed.

Giambi had been an up-and-coming UFC contender until he ran into Harold "X Man" Fenderbass and his scumbag trainer, Louie Resto. Resto, it was later proven, had soaked his fighter's gloves in liniment prior to a championship bout in Texarkana. That night, virtually blind, Johnnie took a brutal pounding that left him minus his left eyeball.

The phone rang six times.

"This is Jack Madson," I said once he picked up.

There was a moment's silence during which I imagined him rubbing his one good eye while sweeping his hand through his shabbily-cut black hair.

"Jack, is it day time already?"

"No, Johnnie, it's somewhere in between, but I need you to work on a case for me pronto."

"What case?"

"Blackmail. Woman named Havana Spice. Porn star been doing some sex-on-the-side with a buddy of mine.

"So?"

"I need anything you can get on her. Talk to your pals at NYPD. Get her rap sheet. Find out if she's backed by a pimp or group of incorporated pimps, your guys will know."

"Love! Now there's a headache, ain't it, Jack?

"Like I said, he's a friend."

"You comin' back any time soon?"

"Maybe tomorrow if the cops don't stop me."

"Oh, shit…"

"Believe it or not, I woke up to find a dead man's head in the trunk of my car this morning."

"Jesus, Jack! A fucking head?"

"No worries, Johnnie. You just take care of what I said and, promise, I'll see you in New York tomorrow."

"Okay, I'll do it," the ex-MMA contender stumbled. "I'll do just like you say."

Soon as I hung up the phone, I threw down three Oxycodone and an Ambien, put on a clean pair of sweats, and crashed for the night. I say 'crashed' but rarely was it like that for me, did I mention I was what most would call an insomniac? Well, it's true. If during the course of the day I could achieve what I'd come to call the 'proper balance' between drugs and booze, I could sleep good as most, but if not, well, it made for an interminable night.

For me that night it was easy, at least at first, and soon as my head hit the pillow I was out like a light before like a wave this dream, *that goddamned dream*, swept inexorably into my head. It was always the same and it came always like a slow steady wave surging forward penetrating all the scar tissue that like a sea wall I'd constructed to contain it.

I am a child in that dream (is it a memory?), thirteen years old, in the Newark house where I was raised. It is noon and I am home from school because I have a cold and my Mom is tending to me. I am sleeping but awaken alone and during the haze that follows, hear my father dressed, I know, in his Pabst Blue Ribbon uniform, stopped-by with his beer truck, for lunch. At least that's what I'm thinking but instead of eating he walks directly into the tiny cubicle he calls "his office," removes some papers from his desk drawer then goes down into the basement and burns them.

By that time, I am downstairs in time to see him laboring with angina as he climbs the stairs from the basement, blue uniform sweat stained around the underarms, the sulfurous smell of burned paper clinging to him. Quietly, wordlessly, like a cold wind, he moves past me, Remington 10 gauge in hand, on his way upstairs to his bedroom.

And that's when I hear it. The sound I've re-lived every night like the crack of a whip, on some occasions, and like the thunderous roar of an explosion muffled by the flesh and bone it had torn through, on others.

"Daddy!" I scream flying up the staircase as fast as my legs will propel me.

I try the door. It opens and in the darkened room with all the shades drawn except one, there on the bed lies my father, making hoarse breathing noises. His eyes are closed, and in that first instant as I see him there in the half-dark, nothing looks wrong. I put my hand under Dad's head. My hand slips under easily and when I bring it out again it is wet to the arm with blood.

Sometimes lying awake at night like that night afterward at the Inn, I pretend not to know why I drink or why I can't sleep at night.

But in my heart I know it's because when I sleep, I dream, and when I dream I see my father that way all over again.

Chapter Eight

The next morning I woke up at 9:30 a.m., got out of bed, walked to the bathroom and promptly vomited. As much a daily ritual as a monk's Horarium, I rinsed my mouth with Scope, popped two Adderall, cracked a Metidate capsule, and ground the tiny green, white, and red beads until they dissolved beneath my tongue. Seconds later, I could feel the drugs pulsing through my veins like a live electrical wire.

Standing in front of the sink, I finally worked up the nerve to look at myself in the mirror. It wasn't pretty. Blood-shot eyes, black hair matted thick as an animal's fur. *Fair enough*, I thought, studying the countenance of my Secret Sharer, *what did you expect, Johnnie Depp?* I threw cold water onto my face, and trudged back into the bedroom for my "morning medicine," a single shot of Jameson's in a Dixie cup I kept by the side of the bed.

I took the whiskey down bravely then sat on the bed's edge attempting to measure the modicum of sleep I'd managed, first by length (three to four hours), then by quality (poor to horrific) having spent those hours of repose in the dungeon of the Devil, himself, locked in the no man's land between consciousness and delirium, its walls undulating, its floor heaving, surreal as a Fellini nightmare.

It was one thing to blow on the embers of a childhood tragedy, it was another to feel the promise of an answer, and at that moment, I had an insight into the nature of obsession, itself. Obsession, I'd come to realize, was an empty mansion built inside your head that one is compelled to explore, room by room, in search of the unfathomable until, exhausted, we're sent back to booze, or drugs, or sex so that to a man obsessed, sleep becomes its own private haunting.

So there I was sitting on my bed, empty Dixie cup in hand, with the amphetamines working their magic, thinking *now is the time to break loose from the strangle hold this scaly freak has on me and straighten out my life!*

I picked up my cell phone and poked at the name 'Vicky Benson.'

"Hiya, Vicky, this is Jack."

"I know, how are you doing?"

"Vicky, I need to go to New York to help an old friend."

"You help a friend! Do you know the kind of trouble you're in? If either Harris or Woods wake up this morning with the notion that you had something to do with that head in your trunk, they'll take you down in a heartbeat. Frankly, it was only the blood test that kept them from doing it in the first place!"

"Harris is a twit just wants his pension. With Woods it's something different, not sure what, but have you ever seen Homeland Security involved in a 'John Doe' homicide?"

"Does it matter what I've seen? Jack, it's a mistake to leave the District now. It sends the wrong message!"

"So what am I now, a politician? Give me a fucking break, Vic, my question's simple: legally, can I leave D.C. to go back home and visit, yes or no?"

"Fine, Jack, there's nothing to prevent it except common sense, but let me ask you a question, is it an old friend or your daughter Tiffany, you're going to see?"

"Not sure. Maybe both."

"Either way, I don't advise it, as your friend or your attorney."

"Well, either way, I'm going, but I guess you already knew that."

The call ended without fanfare. Vicky was a good attorney and a better lover. Not in bed necessarily, though we'd had plenty of that, but in life, meaning that if she wasn't in love with me, I still occupied a warm spot in her heart that I knew would get her over whatever umbrage she felt about my disregard of her personal advice.

Next, was a call to the Elysee, a favorite hotel from the days I was knocking down a million per annum on the Street, for a two-day reservation. After that, it was on to Avis where, with Mustang impounded and pockets fat with Dougherty's money, I rented a black Porche 911 convertible, and I was on my way!

The drive from D.C. to New York takes about five hours but it felt like half that so occupied were my thoughts with Dougherty and, yes, the odd chance possibility that I could muster courage enough to visit my daughter who I hadn't laid eyes on in some fifty months. Beyond that, "Tommy Gun" by the Clash, "Pretty Vacant" by the Sex Pistols and "Blitzkrieg Bop," a Ramones classic, blaring over Boise speakers, Jersey Turnpike North into Manhattan, kept the Porche's interior pulsing with sound and my mind suitably numbed to the reality of what lay in store for me in New York.

Later that night, I met Lights Out at the Monkey

Bar, the two of us surrounded by murals depicting Cole Porter, Benny Goodman, and a teenaged Sinatra, all icons of the Swing Era; not to mention members of the Lost Generation like Hemingway, Fitzgerald, and Tennessee Williams, who it seemed met his Maker after choking to death on a champagne cork while celebrating in his suite on the eleventh floor.

I told Johnnie I liked the place and Lights Out agreed looking around the room like a kid just landed in the basement of FAO Schwartz. Then we got down to business, me, with my scotch, and Johnnie with a Diet Coke.

"Havana Spice's real name is Noemi Machado," he began, one eye wide with excitement, the other sewn shut forever. "Cop friend of mine printed her rap sheet," he said passing it across the table. "Prostitution, loitering, and a heroin bust three years ago."

"Your pal mention anything about blackmail?"

He shook his head, "Not a word."

"What else you got?"

"Her family came over in the late-nineties. Father was a freedom fighter goin' back to the sixties. She was twelve when they left. She's twenty-six now with a eight-year old kid named 'Savito.' Father's dead. Mother still in Cuba."

"She connected?"

Lights Out stole a sip from his glass of Coke, barely able to contain himself, "She hangs with a biker named Ronnie Riecher. Guy's a fucking monster, six-seven, two-hundred sixty pounds, works as a bouncer at Red Hot 'N Twenty-One, a strip club on Rt. 22 in Jersey. She dances there between internet gigs. Some say Reicher's her boyfriend. Everyone says she swings both ways, but anyone ever saw her videos knows that."

"So what do they make of her, these cop pals of yours? They must have picked up something off the street."

"She ain't on the street, Jackie. This one's a five-thou-a-night kinda broad." He closed his one good eye and cocked his head dreamily, "Fucking Havana Spice must be like sticking your cock in a jar of honey! They say she's *that* fucking good."

I savored the last of my drink then sucked on an ice cube, "Anything else I should know before paying Hot Twenty-One a visit?"

"Just that the guys hang-out there are tough as they are crazy. Hell's Angels crawling like ants on an ant hill stoked to the gills with crystal meth, which I'm told is their business and their hobby. Crazy bikers high on crank twenty-four seven don't add up to nothin' good."

"Yeah, I get it, Johnnie. Got plans for tonight?"

"I never got no plans, Jackie, you know that."

"Here's the key to my room," I said turning over the plastic card key. "Go to 'On Demand,' you can watch a re-run of Golovkin-Mayweather, it's a cluster fuck."

"Thanks, Jack, but what about you?"

"I got some personal business to tend to."

"Don't involve no cut-off heads, I hope."

"Not this time," I said signing the bill and standing to leave.

"Oh, and Jack, there's somethin' else about Havana you might want to know."

"What's that?"

"Every week she sends her Mom money. Sometimes

a thousand, sometimes five hundred, but every week like clockwork a wire transfer goes off to Cuba."

I shook my head, "Go figure," I told him. "In the meantime, make sure you tune-in that fight, and take a beer or two from the mini-bar while you're at it. They won't be missed."

Chapter Nine

What is courage? According to a quote from Norman Mailer, courage requires that a person deal with "forces larger than himself." Well, I suppose it depends how you define "forces larger than yourself" to know whether there's a spark of courage in me. If, by that you mean, 'fighting big guys who want to kick your ass,' then I am a man of formidable courage because I never backed down from a fight and can truthfully say, 'I fear no man.' If, on the other hand, you mean non-physical encounters, the kind that require confronting 'emotional forces,' then history proves I am indeed a shameless coward.

To my chagrin that day such were the forces I was bolstering myself to meet as I sat in the Porsche, watching my eighteen-year old daughter, Tiffany, leave NYU's Tisch School of Arts building, chat with classmates out front, then make her way toward Mercer Street residence hall.

Tiffany, fetching these days with auburn hair, pretty face, hazel eyes, and long legs, seemed cheerful as she strode along with another girl, backpack slung over her shoulder talking animatedly, I imagined, about the photography class they'd just attended. Of course I did nothing to attract attention. Coward that I am, I followed safely ensconced behind the wheel of my Teutonic sports car, feeling strange, even predatory, as I observed the little girl I'd left behind four years earlier.

Once arrived at Mercer hall, the girls walked into the lobby and separated, her classmate to retrieve mail, Tiffany to ride the elevator to the apartment she shared with another coed on the sixth floor. *Could I do it? Did I dare see her?* I anguished trying to stir even a shard of will from amongst the scattered wreckage that was our relationship. With her mother committed at Greystone Psychiatric Clinic, there seemed little hope I'd go unblamed for whatever misery she'd gone through as a result of my leaving. Fact was, she probably held me responsible for all of it: the divorce, the press that followed my faked death, even her mother, Jennifer's, mental collapse.

I parked the car a half block away and got out. The air was December brisk and maybe forty-five degrees but without jacket I was still sweating like a swamp rat, the thick tar-like kind that hangs on you like oil. The odor that accompanied it was not unfamiliar to me. It was the stench of inadequacy, the feeling that somehow an emotional amputation had occurred, and I was not like other men who could live and work and love, I understood, trundling into the residence hall and entering the elevator for the sixth floor.

I exited, walked toward '612' then stood staring at the black doorbell at the door's center above the peek hole. Finally, I pressed it, terrified at the possibility that once she recognized me the door would not open. But it did. And in the subsequent seconds that seemed like full minutes to me, there we stood, Tiffany and me gazing at one another like aliens from two distinct worlds, until recognition set in and she rushed to close it.

"Oh, no, you don't! Not this time! I'm not letting you in my

room or in my life ever again, Jack!" she screamed, shoving
the door forward with the full weight of her shoulder as I
moved in to block it from shutting.

"I just want a second to talk, to see how you're doing!"
I pled with equal vehemence, and bulk enough to step
inside despite her efforts.

"Get out! Get out now!!" she shrieked, holding her head
like it was about to explode.

I stepped toward Tiffany trying to comfort her, but
like everything I seemed to do when it came to this kind
of courage, it was misinterpreted not just by her but by
her roommate, a pale young woman with short black hair
who, stunned by the ferocity of her protests, took me for a
stranger trying to assault her.

Before I could explain myself, she left the room, and
came flying back pointing a can of mace in my direction,
screaming near hysterical as my daughter.

"Leave her alone, you understand? Get out of here!" she
screeched, edging toward me before letting out a blood-
curdling cry for help. *"Police! Police! Somebody call campus
security!!"*

Did you ever see the original "Frankenstein" and the
look on Boris Karloff's face when he's trying to befriend
the little girl by the lake and the angry mob of town's
people set upon him? Well, that was my expression
at that moment—panicked, bewildered, totally
discombobulated—as I noticed students beginning to
cluster at the entrance to Tiffany's dorm room and fled
back out into the hallway making a B-line for the stairs.

*"You left us! You left my mother and me thinking you were
dead! Do you know what that feels like? Do you know what that
fucking feels like??"* I could hear Tiffany's wails ringing out

through the hallway after me as, like a would-be rapist, I scrambled down the staircase and into the lobby, brain throbbing, lungs on fire, finally bursting from the building like a swimmer breaking water.

Once in the Porsche, I popped the clutch, burning rubber as I made my escape, thankful to the point of tears to be away from my daughter, my failure, and my humiliation, headed back to the Elysee where a stiff drink waited.

Later that evening, just prior to leaving for Red Hot 'n 21, I gathered my thoughts and my will regarding what happened earlier that day over a glass of Glenlivet at the Monkey Bar. My chances at reconciliation were nil, I conceded, at least now and for the next fifty years when, afterward, with me bedridden, or in a wheelchair, *or iron lung*, she might take pity on me.

So, okay, that was a situation I'd be forced to accept: whether I wanted to or not, despite the love I obsessed over and the forgiveness I wanted so desperately to ask for, Tiffany was inaccessible to me. Reality was, I'd have to stay away. I would have to somehow build a fence around my heart or risk going mad with grief. My daughter, it seemed, *had made herself dead to me*, a fitting reprisal since that was exactly what I had done to her four years before.

"Tough day, Mr. Madson?" Frankie, the barkeep, at the Elysée inquired.

My eyes lifted from my glass, "Nah, just fine," I answered with the flash of a grin.

"Well, your money's no good here tonight," he said as I started to sign the check.

"I appreciate that Frankie, you're a prince of a guy," I uttered getting up to leave.

"And, Mr. Madson," he added, "I don't know what's going on in your life. Maybe finances, maybe a woman, but I see a lot of people come in and out of this place and for my money you're worth the lot of 'em. You should remember that, Mr. Madson, it may be nice to think about some day when everything ain't 'just fine.'"

"You're a good man, Frankie," I said by way of 'good-bye,' then left to collect my Porsche, calculating the odds of getting through to Havana Spice.

It was later that night that I had my chance to chase down Dougherty's nemesis at Red Hot 'n 21, a bikers' meth den in Jersey where Havana was headlining. By the time I got there, the lot was packed with vehicles ranging from lawyers' Mercedes SLS convertibles to Dodge Ram pickups driven by plumbers, carpenters and other home repair types. A 5'X8' mobile marquee posted outside the rambling two-story strip club read, 'HAVANA SPICE XXX STAR, TOTALLY NUDE!! ONE NIGHT ONLY!!'

I parked my Porsche feeling better about myself compared to the dismal schmucks I imagined populated the place, then walked across the broken rocks of my ego to the club's entrance. Two Hell's Angels tattooed multi-colored to look like the cover of a comic book super hero greeted me, tough and surly.

"No cell phones," the one said while the other padded me down and nodded his 'okay.' "Fifty bucks cover tonight."

I pulled two twenties and a ten from my wallet, twice the normal cover, "So I get my sex now or later?" I asked handing it over.

"Only with yourself, partner," the Angel snorted stamping the back of my hand with the 'Hot 'n 21' logo while I took-in the ambiance which registered 'post-modern skank' as I entered.

On the circular bar was a walkway with stripper poles where five nude women who's eyes let you know they were eons away gyrated to the thumping rhythms of Motley Crue's "Shout at the Devil" wearing cowboy boots and hats while Havana's video "Havana Spice, Breakfast of Champions" showed on large screen tvs to the left and right of them. As for the rest, it was standard fare: lap dance booths, massage chairs set in a darkened annex behind the bar, and VIP rooms upstairs where high rollers who wanted more than a dance could drink champagne while getting their cocks shook by twenty-three year old Russian émigrés.

The difference between Hot 'n 21 and places like it wasn't the girls—coke whores and dim-eyed wild child suburbanites—it was the management and clientele that populated the place, some regulars from neighboring towns, but more often bikers, Hell's Angels to be specific, with names like Slasher, Wildcat, and Sabu, all of which was going to make for a memorable evening.

I edged my way through the crowd toward the bar to order a drink, but before I got there an Angel the size of a mountain with long hair and long scraggly beard stopped me dead in my tracks.

"Drink this," he said.

I looked into his bulging, red-veined eyes, raging with meth-induced intensity, "No thanks, I'll get my own," I hollered over 2 Live Crew's "Pop That Pussy" blaring from surround-sound speakers.

"*Drink this*," he rumbled again, his bug-eyes shifting to a silver tray he held, lined up and down with shot glasses full of a lime-colored liquid.

I stared at the drinks then back up to him as he took one down himself, "Mel-lon shots," he confided handing one to me.

"Excellent," I answered, grinning weakly as I tossed the shooter down then watched his gargoyle head bob approvingly before melting away into the crowd.

Once at the bar, where a naked coed-type poured me my scotch and a cowgirl sat legs spread with her privates in my face, several facts became clear to me. *One*, everyone in this place, except me, was swimming in crank. *Two*, the biker whose name I later learned was "Tooty" had become obsessed with pouring shooters down my throat leaving me blasted as anyone there. *Three*, Havana Spice had yet to arrive, but when she did the three hundred or so bikers and porno hounds were going to go ape shit, such was the level of testosterone that hung in the air of the room that night.

Attempting to divorce myself from the pink set spread-eagle before me, I glanced over to one of the mega-sized posters that hung on near every wall and studied the life-sized photo of Havana Spice. Dazzling smile, with tanned body and large supple breasts, it was a photo that exuded sexuality, like I could *smell* her scent, *feel* the white heat radiating from that photo across the room. *Hot, yeah*, I was thinking, *one smokin' hot broad, this Havana Spice*, I could not help but concede, when from the corner of my eye I noticed the back door open and through it walked Spice surrounded by three body guards led by Ronnie Reicher, the 6'7" Angel that Lights Out had described.

Reicher was a monster all right, but Havana was sexier than any photo could do justice, a natural born beauty together with a natural born killer, I couldn't help but contemplate as I watched the Angel security team organize itself into a phalanx before Havana made her move toward the stage, noticing that she'd come into the club wearing nothing but a G-string and a waist-cut black satin robe, meaning she was ready to perform.

Now I realize I could have pondered strategy hours on end but I had a specific mission in mind that night. So, despite the odds of getting shoved to the side without so much as eye contact, I decided to take the chance to introduce myself, get a business card into her hand, and inculcate within her a motive to contact me afterward, before the others saw her. That in mind, and looking more cop-like than, say, ninety-nine percent of the scumbags there, I strode to the periphery of her entourage, stood toe-to-toe with Reicher, flashed a badge from my Federal Marshal days, and reached beyond him to hand Havana my card.

"Lt. Will Harris, MDC homicide," I bluffed. "Miss Spice, I suggest you contact this man first thing tomorrow."

Havana didn't know what to make of it, though she accepted the card, while Reicher looked just plain pissed-off.

"Who the fuck are you," he spat back hovering over me like the giant he was, "some kind of paparazzi?"

"That card is from a PI named Madson. He'll explain everything when she calls."

"Yeah, or what, faggot?"

I straightened up square, ready to take a punch or throw one, I didn't care which. "Or there'll be consequences. Ms. Spice," I said turning back to her. "Call, it's important."

The big man studied me momentarily and saw something I guess he didn't take to, *"Get the fuck outta here!"* he roared lifting his massive right arm up and slamming me past a half dozen paying customers and into a concrete wall.

"Yeah, and fuck you, too!" I pledged picking myself up from the floor and flying back at him, landing two sharp lefts to his kidney then coming up and over the top with a right hook Jack Dempsey might have admired, placed perfectly over his left ear and to the temple.

Reicher's legs actually buckled, and for an instant I stood there admiring my handiwork, but only for an instant, because once he came to his senses, a fierce rage such as I had never witnessed sprung from out of him as he surged back at me.

Brave, yes. Stupid, maybe. But let it never be said I am a classic personality because reveling both forces, I stood spitting-mad ready to have a go at him, already taking on a boxer's stance, left foot forward, right foot back, to launch a lead right or counter left depending on how he played it.

But it was not to be because within seconds I was pinned down by three of the gorillas Hot 'n 21 employed as bouncers while Reicher was set upon by Angels from his own security team, over-sized arms and massive shoulders pinioned, still lurching at me.

"Fuck you! Fuck you, hit me? Hit me, you motherfucker, I'll kill you!!"

But that was him, not me. Mentally cool and physically sound despite what felt like two cracked ribs, it was at that moment I managed to make eye contact with Havana and accomplish the third element of my plan.

"Call that number," I shouted to her beyond the bedlam that ensued and music pulsing over the sound system just before they wrestled me out the door, *"it's about Tom Dougherty!"*

And in that meteoric moment with eyes locked while I was being carted outside and she was being escorted by her

Hell's Angel handlers to the stage to an avalanche of hoots and whistles from patrons, fans, and perverts, I noticed something that, if only for a nano second, glimmered in her eyes. It was fear.

But fear of what? Fear of who?

Chapter Ten

Don't ask why but there was something about Havana Spice that didn't sit well. Questions I had that attempting to answer felt forced and artificial. Like why would a Class A piece of ass like her perform at a Jersey dive when she could have been working across the river at Larry Flynt's, the VIP club, or any one of a dozen nightspots, classier, and better paying? For that matter, what was she doing surrounded by Reicher and his gang of crank-heads to begin with?

Could be the answers were simple: Spice had the hots for Reicher, liked drugs and the Angels' brand of non-stop partying, and took the gig as a favor to them. Maybe, but something in the way she entered the club that night, Reicher calling the shots and her just falling in line, for her own protection, no doubt, but as likely to keep her from others as a prisoner might be moved from one location to another by cops who, yeah, wanted to safeguard their charge but needed to hold him captive at the same time. Whether driven by logic or instinct, I waited outside Hot 'n 21, intent on nailing down an address where she lived, with whom she was living, and under what circumstance. Lucky me, Havana's "show" turned out to be more like an "appearance" and within an hour, she exited through a back door and into the parking lot. Moments later,

Reicher pulled up in a late-model red Corvette. Spice entered from the passenger side, then they drove east on Rt. 22 toward the Holland tunnel.

I tailed them into the city and onto Canal Street which wasn't difficult since the 'Vette's license plate read 'HAVANA' with more than one passing car hitting a horn on sight. Several blocks later, Reicher dropped her off in front of an acupuncture clinic on Mott Street then went to park as she entered. Of course, I waited for Reicher to follow, remembering something a DEA buddy assigned to infiltrate a heroin ring run by the Flying Dragons once said, "Chinatown is like an Escher drawing," he told me, "worlds within worlds within worlds."

Patient fellow that I am, sixty minutes into the stake-out it became apparent Reicher and Spice were not coming out any time soon. And it was then that another ghost of a remembrance swooshed through my mind leaving behind its vaporous contrail for me to ponder. My former DEA pal had also given me something to chew on regarding the problem of entrances and exits in the construct of Chinatown: underground tunnels used to make quick escapes from police raids on gambling dens, criss-crossed its underbelly like wormholes allowing gang members to enter on Mott Street and miraculously reappear five blocks away on East Broadway.

For that matter, an expert on the vanishings of major players in the shady underworld of Asian heroin, he'd also opened my eyes to New York's undercity that stretched no less than twenty-five miles counting abandoned tunnels, subways, and sewers, housing no fewer than five thousand "mole people" as he called them. These were men and women, minds often fractured with schizophrenia, who lived beneath the city, surviving in structured societies akin to tribes with their own mayors, cultural mores, even schools.

Such was the amalgam of anxiety, folklore, and information that roiled like molten slag in my gut as I left the Porsche to search them out, understanding that Reicher and Havana were probably any place but the simple two-floor storefront marked 'Acupuncture Clinic.' That is not to say I believed they'd escaped through the tunnels. No, they were still there, I suspected, perhaps in an upper floor or closed-up space behind a false wall where most everything in Chinatown—gambling, prostitution, drugs—happened ingeniously hidden behind the façade outsiders assumed to be real, worlds within worlds within worlds.

An Asian woman wearing an emerald-colored satin dress stood with her boyfriend, a teenager with straight black hair cut long and face like Jo-Jo The Dog-faced Boy. The woman, an Asia stunner, looked at me solicitously from behind a waist-high counter as I entered. Behind her was a mirror—two-way—that substituted for a wall. To the left of that was a door that led to I don't know where.

"You come for acupuncture?" the woman whose name I would later learn was Chok Por asked.

"No," I answered tempted to flash my badge but deciding against it, "I'm with Havana. She asked me to meet her here."

Chok Por pursed her lips studying me carefully and I wondered what she saw. The adjectives 'big,' 'serious,' and 'reckless' must have passed through her subconscious, I guessed, but what man really knows how he appears to others?

"Havana no here," she answered slyly, her boyfriend, Jin Lee, a Dragon soldier, I would later discover, silently staring, toothpick dangling from his mouth, whether hyper-zoned-out or hyper-focused I could not determine. "I saw her come in here with Ronnie Reicher not thirty minutes ago."

Again she shook her head, "Sorry, nobody name Havana here tonight."

"Okay, they told me not to, but I guess you're going to make me say it, I work for Mr. Dougherty," I gambled pulling out my badge and ID.

"Jin Lee," she said turning in something close to a military pivot, "open door for..."

"Jack Madson," I grinned extending my hand.

"Nice meet you, Mr. Madson," she nodded accepting my hand cordially, "welcome to the Casanova club."

Now, I'm not the most intuitive guy, but as I passed through that door and was confronted by two elevator banks leading to the Casanova club the vibe emanating from that strange and solemn corridor rolled over me with the force of a tsunami.

My first reaction once we were plunged one, two, three stories down into the depths of the underground was *Christ, I could use a fucking drink right now*, but by the time we exited at the eighth—designated not by number but the face of a smiling satyr—I began to appreciate the magnitude of the invisible world I was about to enter.

The moment the elevator door slid open a smiling greeter dressed in a powder blue tuxedo rushed to embrace me.

"Mr. Madson, so good of you to join us this evening!"

Tall and thin with a mustache reminiscent of Salvador

Dali, he angled back toward his lectern, studied a computer screen, then looked up to me eyes flaring.

"Did you have something 'special' in mind? We have an indoor pool, nude Jacuzzi, steam baths, seven orgy rooms, each to your sexual preference, game room, romp room for group sex, S&M dungeons..." he enumerated, voice trailing off then stopping abruptly as he noticed my prosaic gaze. "Or, perhaps, you'd like someone to walk you through the club and then decide?"

"I was thinking of something more in the way of a drink, Chandler," I said noticing the gold nameplate to the left of his lapel, "you do have a bar?"

"Nine of the best stocked bars in the city, sir."

"Could you take me there?"

"As you wish," he said with the same crisp military cadence Chok Por, eight floors above us, had used, "please follow me."

To the left of Chandler's lectern were oversized pewter doors with ornate Doric handles leading into the main floor that made you feel like you were entering the Kingdom of Oz. Two impeccably dressed young men who looked like bodybuilders held them open as we entered what seemed a parallel universe, surreal in the way a Gaudi palazzo captures something of what we recognize as our world while understanding it is not. It was as if I'd been staring intensely at a painting in a Chelsea art gallery and the artist walked up and said "forget about that, Jack," then tore the canvas from its frame, "this is the world I want you to step into!"

Then, to my horror and delight, I did. The huge circular bar, tended by a half dozen men and women wearing pink cut-away tuxedos covered in sparkling gems, was set in the center of what looked to have been an abandoned freight terminal, active in the 1920s, now reborn as a multi-level sex club with a Romanian trapeze act hurtling above us, gambling tables planted like studded diamonds around its main floor, and live sex shows performed in velvet-roped cages in front of porn aficionados.

As Chandler vanished into the crowd with the brush of a hand on my shoulder, I could see nubile blonde boys dressed in diapers with numbers scribed on their bottoms at the "play station" nearest me undulating to techno-trance music for an audience of cigar-smoking Ugandans bidding for their favors as at an auction. At another, four lesbians—Black, White, Asian—performed cunnilingus on one another while the two beside them, kneeling on all fours, went at it with a strap-on to the delight of American business types who drank, gambled, and blew coke from the mirrored counter top watching. And there were other stations, one, where eight or ten (I lost count!) young men and women writhed in a tangle of flesh in an all-out orgy; another, billed as "King Cobra," featuring a black stud, alternately servicing or being serviced by half-a-dozen young women, while a cadre of Chinese mobsters bet furiously on the number of times he could climax during a sixty-minute interval!

"Glenlivet-rocks," I ordered staring down at the reflection of the trapeze artists on the bar top trying to re-focus on where I was and why I'd come in the first place.

When my drink arrived, I downed it, tapped on its rim for a re-fill, and turned to the woman next to me.

"Ebony Jones," she said extending a large, long-fingered hand in my direction.

"Pleased to make your acquaintance," I said, accepting the handshake, suddenly aware this was no woman at all.

I looked down at the bar, happy to locate my refilled glass, taking a discerning swig. Ebony was black as midnight, 6'1", and dressed to kill in a tight, snow-white evening dress with a slit that ran from the floor to her testicles, with hair up and a high-cheek-boned model's face made-up like Charlize Theron on her way to snag an Oscar.

"You never been here before, have you?"

"No."

"What's your name?"

"Jack."

"You don't find me attractive, do you, Jack?" she wondered aloud with what could have passed for naïveté in Indiana.

"I don't know you, Ebony. Besides," I said with a shudder, "I don't even know what to call guys like you anymore. Transvestite? Transsexual? Transgender?"

"Call me, Thirsty," she suggested, then after a moment's thought, "You know, you sexy in a Clint Eastwood kinda way."

"Eastwood's ninety, Darlin'. How 'bout Brad Pitt? I always liked him."

"No, no, you too dangerous lookin' for that!"

"You think keeping up with Angelina Jolie is easy?"

"Buy me a Cosmo 'fore I die of thirst, Hot Rod."

I signaled the bartender, a petite hotty whose sparkly pink tux had a neckline plunged down to her naval.

"Cosmo," I ordered turning back to Jones, now smiley and talkative. "So what *is* this place?" I ventured. "Do you work here?"

"Me? Nah, I'm an ornament they keep 'round for their amusement. This place, five miles of underground rail and freight terminals, was converted to Casanova's six years ago," she explained parting her legs to flaunt the not unsubstantial bulge in her panties. "They bought it from the MTA. Part of some architect's dream to build an underground park with swings, gazebos, even gardens. But that never happened so they turned it into the Casanova club."

"Who is 'they?'"

She giggled not unattractively, "'They' is 'them.' The ones you never see or hear about. The people that control things: the city, the country, the world, for all I know. So what you here for, Jack?"

"I'm looking for Havana Spice. You wouldn't know what floor's her 'sexual preference,' would you?"

"Havana? She ain't got the swag for no 'sexual preference.' She upstairs workin'."

"Working? She just came back from dancing at a strip club in Jersey."

"Health care, car insurance, Havana pays taxes an' lots of 'em. Even stars like her got bosses send 'em out hustlin' what with the porn industry blow'd up by the internet an' all."

Ebony's drink was served. She took it in hand, studied it as if to check for floating bacteria, then threw it down like a linebacker.

"Here," I said slipping a $100 bill into her long-fingered hand, "buy yourself something sexy at Victoria's Secret."

"Wouldn't be caught dead in that trash, Hot Rod, but thanks just the same," she said, shoving the hundred into her brassiere. "You know, Jack," she added with no small degree of prescience, "I bet you're the kinda guy shit happens to."

"True that," I agreed downing my drink, and heading for the 'private' rooms set one tier above.

From the main floor I marched up a spiral staircase staring down at the panorama of depravity that ground on below and it was like the circus come to town, I speculated, starting my trek through the dimly lit corridor punctuated every fifty feet by doors, closed, half-closed, and sometimes wide open. Inside, private sex parties were in full swing with generous supplies of crystal meth, cocaine, and heroin as I crept along the hallway replete with the passion-ripped screams of sexual ecstasy accentuated by alternate sounds — often disconcerting — of whips cracking, music playing, and arguing between men and women.

Through those open doors I glimpsed every sexual possibility a man could imagine from three young women on a solitary man, to interracial straight and gay sex, to manifold variations of bondage, S&M, even staged rapes (perhaps not staged) performed for the titillation of Asian, African, and Eastern European high rollers. One thing all had in common was youth contrasted by age. The young women, men, and boys, were all extraordinary in their good looks. The men, and an occasional woman, were nearly always middle-aged, and lousy rich, if not physically attractive.

If a door was not open, it was unlocked — apparently house policy — and available for me to peer into looking for Havana doing what it seemed Havana did best. Still, it didn't take much time or many doors for me to begin feeling significantly discounted from the man I imagined myself. The atmosphere of the Casanova Club seemed corrosive, like each of us—patrons, visitors, even a private investigator like me—had crossed a line of demarcation into a tainted place that left our bodies and perhaps our souls filmed-over with a nano layer of spiritual decay.

Halfway down the corridor I could make out the image of a small boy wearing a T-shirt, jeans, and high-top sneakers intently working a Game Boy handheld. As I moved closer I recognized he was a mulatto child, black and Caucasian, or perhaps Hispanic, with large brown eyes, short ginger hair and a look of total concentration as he played Angry Birds 3.

This, I felt certain must be Havana's child: eight or nine years of age bearing a striking resemblance to his mother, the boy Johnny Giambi had told me about.

"Is your mother inside there?" I whispered pointing to the closed door.

He looked up from his Game Boy and nodded.

I put my index finger to my lips, "Savito," I said in a low voice, "I'm going to open the door and say 'hello' to your Mom, is that okay?"

He nodded.

And it was then that, ever so gently, I turned the door handle, slowly pushed forward, and stepped inside to find Amber Starr doing Havana Spice on a four-poster Victorian bed while Hell's Angel, Ronnie Reicher, shot "live" for an internet porn site with a Sony Cam Corder.

"My, my," I observed perusing the bed and the two women, arms, legs and faces intertwined, "what would Dr. Phil say about this?"

"Jack Madson!" Amber declared looking up from between Havana's legs.

I reached for the Remington six-shooter jammed

inside my belt, a relic from my Tex-Mex days with the Blunts four years earlier.

"You never said you were a cop!" she accused looking as cheated as a child who'd had her favorite lollipop snatched.

"I'm no cop," I answered, pointing the gun at Reicher who stopped the camera and turned.

"*You have no fucking idea the trouble you've gotten yourself into*," the giant muttered staring at me like the crazy man he was when Amber suddenly leapt from the bed, head in hands.

"All this bickering!" she shouted. "It gives me a migraine and now I don't feel like doin' it no more, with either of you!"

That's when I felt the blackjack hit me from behind. I took the blow decently. Even had the presence of mind to turn and throw a punch but it was no use.

The last thing I saw was Reicher, all 6'7" of him, Amber Starr, and Havana Spice standing over me: one laughing, one gaping, and Havana looking worried like maybe she actually gave a damn until our eyes met and a soulful simper curled the corners of her lips. *That smile will be the death of me* was the last thought that crossed my mind.

The son of a bitch that slugged me? Never did get a look at him.

Chapter Eleven

"*And it shall come to pass in the last days, says God, that I will pour out of My Spirit on all flesh,*" the voice raved on.

"*Shut the fuck up!!*" another man's voice rang out from the other side of the concrete chamber.

"*Blood and fire and vapor of smoke, the sun shall be turned into darkness. And the moon into blood, Before the coming of the great and awesome day of reckoning...*"

My eyes cracked open and it was like raising the blinds in a dark room. I squinted from the light to find kneeling beside me an emaciated street person dressed in an ill-fitting white shirt and tattered black pants ranting as he quoted, line and verse, from the invisible Bible in his head, blasting his words and breath that stunk like kerosene.

"*Shut up you fucking nut case 'fore I strangle you with my bare hands!*" the enraged business exec, hung-over and spent after a night of debauching, screamed from across the holding cell making several false starts toward him like a bull sizing up a matador then thinking better of it.

Gradually, getting a sense of my location, I staggered to my feet as the Bible-totting madman launched his counter-assault.

"*If there is a man who lies with man as those who lie with woman both have committed an abomination!*" he shrieked back at him while four or five others spending the night in the drunk tank skulked around trying not to be noticed.

"Leave him alone, won't you? Can't you see he's got mental problems?" The protest lurched from my mouth, the pain from what I guessed was a concussion slamming through my head like a cleaver.

But for the wild-eyed exec, down off his cocaine high, with tie hanging like a noose from his neck and Brooks Brothers suit rumpled and wet with urine stains, this was all too much to countenance and in something like a single motion, he let out a mind-shattering scream, then charged straight ahead, not at his Doomsday accuser, *but at me!*

Now there were several options to take at that moment not the least intelligent of which was to step aside, hold his head down, and send a kneecap smashing into his face. But stunned at the suddenness of his attack, I watched in disbelief as the squat, two-hundred-twenty pound madman plunged like a rampaging boar past the old derelict, then plowed into my legs full force, laying me flat-out on my back, head slamming against the concrete floor.

"Is this a fight? Am I in a fight?" I was still asking myself, a question twice answered as I lay there gasping for air. Once by the vinegary odor that oozed from the sinews of his body swimming up my nostrils with the salience of industrial acid (the surest sign of madness I knew!); the second signaled by his actions, as Mr. Exec, bearing the strength of five men, mounted me, left leg over my chest, in what I understood was going to be a moment-to-moment battle to survive. Hopped-up on drugs as he was, if Mr. Wall Street knocked me unconscious, I knew it wouldn't end there. No, he would keep bashing until he'd pulverized the life out of me!

"I watched the lamb open the first of seven seals. Then I heard one of the four living creatures say in a voice like thunder, "Come!" I looked, and there before me was a white horse!"

Funny how things work, but pinned on the floor with a turbo-charged lunatic sitting on my chest as I struggled to block fists large as ham hocks from knocking me unconscious, another deeper part of my brain was also at work trying to remember a jiu jitsu move Lights Out once taught me. In it, the downed fighter once mounted, throws his right leg over his opponent's back while throwing the full weight of his body against his attacker's ribcage to create enough momentum to reverse positions which I managed to execute, delighted to find myself atop the crumpled exec laying on his back, red-faced and squirming, as I dug my knees into his armpits to secure my position. And what was I thinking as I prepared to send this cocksucker back to his financial bankers, attorneys, and investors in a body bag? I confess to you now, it was about my father's suicide and the strap he used on us for any reason he felt like after a few pops at the neighborhood bar; it was about my fucked up marriage; and my work at NuGen. Yeah, it was about all of that, and more!

It was then, and only then, with position secured atop him, that the ice pick stabbing at the inside of my head, the pressure that had been thrust forward with the force of a freight train into my eyes, and cheeks, hands and fingertips, subsided. I was a brain full of blood and the light went red, *yes, it was red,* as I pummeled him with closed fists until the left side of his face cracked open, then his eye socket, and finally his skull, until his eyes rolled around like pennies in a doll's head!

"When the Lamb opened the fourth seal, I heard the voice of

the creature say, "Come!" I looked, and there before me was a rider named Death, and Hades was following close behind!"

It was then that I felt hands grabbing me from behind and the choking squeeze of a hammer lock around my throat.

"You got 'em?"

"Take him!"

"Take him down now!!"

Voices, disembodied, rang hollow in my ears as if emanating from some lost dimension where the only sounds capable of penetrating the icy veil of fury that possessed me; that wormed their way through every orifice and into my body and the air that I breathed, was hate.

"I'm going to kill you, you cocksucker!" I heard myself screaming as four guards restrained me and a paramedic injected a sedative into the upper bicep of my left arm.

"Feel 'im, don't ya, Boys?" the wiry old derelict shrieked hopping up and down with a satyr's glee. *"Yeah, He's here all right! Right as rain! The Devil's here amongst us sure!"*

"Kill you, kill you ... you cocksucking bastard..." I could hear my voice echo inside my head—light years removed from the Doomsdayer's ranting—fainter, and then fainter still, as the steel door to solitary opened and I was shoved through into what to me was simply a space; a vacuum in time I would occupy until someone—loyal friend or devout enemy—discovered I'd been arrested and petitioned the magistrate to either drop charges or set bail.

Chapter Twelve

'Does not play well with others' were the words they'd print on the back of my prison jumpsuit, I thought, feelings of anger and self-loathing inching up, belly to throat, like a ringworm until I was all but choking on it. "Let me out! Let me outta here, you Fuckers!!" an amateur might be screaming up at the ubiquitous closed circuit camera above, but I knew all about the cadre of cops horsing around in the Booking area as they observed. No point to any of that. Monitoring prisoners had been my forte not so many years ago. Besides, if they decided to throw me into the Metropolitan Correctional Center, appearing relatively sane and having beaten up on an overly aggressive Wall Streeter would give me the street cred of a lifer.

Small consolation to me, I rued, locked up in "the hole" as I was, set apart from the drunks and psychos, pathetically alone, the heat that had so boiled my blood minutes before beginning to dissipate. Clearly, there were multiple purposes to solitary confinement, I postulated as the reality of spending hours, and perhaps days, with myself set-in. The obvious was to sequester guys like me so no one else got hurt, and to protect those same prisoners from the population should groups of inmates set out against them. The less obvious was to give a man time to cool off and let the reasonable side of his nature usurp control from the demons that possessed him. But there was a third, which was to allow him respite to consider everything that happened, and maybe even *why* it happened.

Sitting on the concrete floor, feeling spent as a snubbed cigarette, legs splayed out in front of me, I stared blankly at the hole in the floor where all varieties of human effluent—piss, shit, vomit—eventually found their way, my mind drifting to an experience, strange even for me, that happened a number of years back. Still married at the time and nurturing a modest business involvement with father-in-law Barton Crowley and his Mafia cronies, I came to know Salvatore "Bill" Bonanno, son of Godfather Joseph, who practically invented the American Cosa Nostra.

Our relationship began slow, a lunch about an equity position in a company NuGen was acquiring, but quickly blossomed into a friendship as deep as any I'd ever experienced. Bill was in his seventies and I was in my thirties, and given the chasm my father's suicide had left in my life, I guess you could say we shared a kind of father-son connection.

Long story short, Bill, Tiffany, and I are having dinner at *Anthony's*, a restaurant he owns in Tucson, when my seven-year old daughter listening intently to our conversation, looks up from her plate and asks, "Have you ever killed a man?"

Well, how can he answer a question like that? So, I say, "Tiffany, that isn't a nice question to ask Mr. Bonanno." And she says, "Why not? That's what the two of you were talking about, isn't it?" Another question for which I had no answer, so I smile a 'kids will be kids' grin and shrug to our host who, to the contrary, is impressed by my little girl's candor. "No, no," he says very serious, "your daughter has asked a good question and I think she's old enough to hear the answer. The answer is, *I never killed a man who didn't deserve it.*"

Now let us jump ahead several years to a time before my technology thefts from NuGen, faux suicide, and divorce from Jennifer, to a business meeting I attended held in a 14th century castle in the French Alsace without cable, cell phone reception, or internet. British guys are blathering, Germans are interrupting, and the French talking about what will be served for dinner, when after three days, I finally manage a connection on my Blackberry to receive one solitary message. It's from my father-in-law, Barton Crowley, and the message is this, '*Your pal, Bill Bonanno is dead.*"

Now, understanding I'm stuck in France with no way of escaping what promises to be a $500 million score for NuGen to attend Bill's funeral, instead of leaving, I say to myself, 'Well, that's a lot of money and Bill would surely understand *that!*', and elect not to go.

Still, upon my return to the States, there must have been some lingering guilt because at exactly 3 am, with Jen sleeping fitfully beside me, Salvatore "Bill" Bonanno returned to pay me a visit.

Sound asleep on that blustery November morning, I feel the unmistakable presence of someone sitting at the edge of the bed; *actually feel* the mattress depress with his weight as he sits beside me! At first, I ignore it (I was sound asleep!) but eventually look up to see him sitting there staring at me, strangely disoriented like a messenger delivering a missive he, himself, did not totally comprehend.

"Bill!" I whisper, delighted to see him.

He nods, "How are you?"

"Fine," I answer.

"Tiffany?"

"In the next room, sleeping."

"Family," he says resolutely. "You know that's all you got in this life. You need to treasure your wife and daughter, Jack, that's the main thing."

"Yeah, I know, but it's not easy. Crowley, he's not too supportive. In fact, he hates my guts. Jennifer? Her father's daughter, pure and simple. But Tiffany, she's another story. She's my hope, Bill. She's the one I'm hoping makes this shit storm I'm going through–the bills, my fucked up marriage, the job at NuGen — all of it, worthwhile."

"Be patient with them, Jack, they're only human. They just see pieces of the puzzle, not what those pieces mean. You don't neither. But at least try, and someday you'll see all of it, what the pieces mean and what they look like put together. So be patient, Jack, be kind."

I look up to him then, *study him,* trying to figure out if this is a dream or a ghost or what, and I swear to Christ, he is so fucking real I could tell you the clothes he's wearing, how his hair is cut, fuck, I can tell you the aftershave he's wearing! But even at that hour, and half asleep, I know there's something wrong, out-of-synch, about what's happening so I prop myself up on an elbow and just say it.

"You know you're dead, don't you, Bill?"

"I guess so," he answers, looking suddenly distracted, as he rises slowly from my bedside.

"You know, you're always welcome, but *why are you here?*"

"To see you," he says, "make sure you're all right."

"Well, I am, I'm all right, Bill," I tell him honestly,

watching, fascinated as he looks around the room as if lost or being called back to wherever he came from, his physical presence deteriorating into something like an image on an old fashioned black and white television screen with poor reception and static, fading in and out.

"I gotta go now," he says uncomfortably, beginning to walk away to I cannot imagine where.

"Bill," I call out.

"Yeah?" he asks turning halfway toward me.

"What is it like being dead?"

He thinks for a moment and it's like watching a man about to enter a bath, assessing the water's temperature, is it too hot? Is it too cold?

"It's like I have to think about my whole life, everything I did, every act, big or small. Nobody says it's good. Nobody says it's bad. But I have to explain it, Jack. I have to account for my life in its entirety," he answers fatefully. "Guess we'll just have to see," he adds with a shrug. "In the meantime, you take care to take care, my friend. I'm going to miss you."

Then, he turns and starts to walk away, but for me it isn't over. It can't be. See, I sense there's this residue of something vaguely terrifying that's left behind as I turn to Jennifer, sound asleep beside me, and picture Tiffany, lying beneath her blankets in the next room, then project to some other early morning when all of us are asleep, and he returns again, and a chill passes through me stark as the bleakest winter's night.

"Bill!"

He cranes his head around, floating now, as he recedes back to whatever invisible dimension he emerged from out of.

"You know, I said you could visit here anytime, but I don't know the rules of this game, so you can visit, but only if it's 'all right.' Only if it's 'all right' for you to see me, understand what I'm saying?"

The Mafia chieftain gave a curt nod. He turned around again, began walking, and vanished into thin air.

There is a line from Milton's *Paradise Lost* that passed through my mind just then: *Millions of creatures walk the earth unseen, both when we wake and when we dream.* It was a phrase that caused me to ponder those millions of creatures who walked the earth unseen; and the nature of 'good' and 'evil,' what I'd witnessed during the past forty-eight hours, along with my own life, and it scared the shit out of me!

So why do I tell you about this event? Well, let me tell you, sitting on that concrete floor in solitary, staring at that hole in the cement with its connecting pipe that traveled thousands of feet beneath the ground through the bowels of the 13th Precinct police station down into the depths of the New York City sewer system, I imagined myself a wad of shit swirling down that black hole and through those pipes into the command center of Shitdom on my way to perdition, and it wasn't pretty.

Like Bill Bonanno on that chilling November morning, half-there and half-not-there, I agonized over the things, good and bad, that I had done: every crime I'd committed, every indecent act, every vile deed because, truth was, I had come close to beating a man to death that day—and would have—had those guards not pulled me off him! And I promise you, that morning, I did not feel like I understood any piece of whatever 'puzzle' may have existed, or even the possibility that there existed a total picture of life or one's destiny at all!

Why am I the way I am? I solemnly asked staring dead into the ubiquitous eye of the surveillance camera hanging above, trying to shut my eyes and sleep, but for hours afterward, the faces of the people I'd encountered—Havana Spice, Reicher, Dougherty, Eddie Lawlor, the patrons at the Casanova Club and, yes, even the head, skinned and hideous—swirled in a kaleidoscope of hellish realities that like a *venus flytrap* had suddenly ensnared me. *Why could I not defeat the rage and addictions that kept me from becoming the kind and good man I wanted to be?*

"Hey you, Madson!" the Sergeant on duty barked, jarring me back to this particular reality, the miserable one, in my jail cell. "Wake up! Bail's been posted. You're gettin' out."

"Man or woman?" I asked not a little disoriented, thinking maybe Eddie? Maybe Vicky, my attorney?

"Guy with one eye missin'. Some of the cops think he's *somebody*, one or two even asked for his autograph."

"Johnnie "Lights Out" Giambi," I whispered. "You saved my fucking life."

Chapter Thirteen

Getting out of that closet of a cell felt like Christmas morning to me as the Sarg hit the green button on the control panel and the door marked #3 popped open like the lid to a coffin. From there I was escorted down the narrow corridor that separated the Precinct's holding cells from Booking and as we waited for the Uniform to buzz us in, I could already see Lights Out talking to a detective I recognized through the square of bullet-proof glass set into the heavy-gauge steel door that separated us.

His name was Owen "Big O" Ewing, a tight end receiver for Notre Dame back in the day, whose career fizzled after a knee injury and two unspectacular seasons with the Jets. 6′3″ and a solid two-fifty, Ewing's signature afro was now close-cropped and grayed at the temples, but the physique was still there, trim at the waist and muscular, along with a high-cheek-boned countenance and quick smile that landed him in bed with the likes of Julia Roberts, Halle Berry, and a cartload of others I couldn't work up the energy to remember.

But now, at forty-seven, married, with two daughters, the "Big O" seemed less superstud than tired NYPD detective, trying his best to be patient with Lights Out who he knew meant well, while remaining plenty pissed-off at me.

"No, no Officer," I could hear Lights Out trying to communicate in plaintive half-stutter, one eye struggling to connect with the looming black man's less than congenial gaze, "Jackie's really not like what you say! See, he's just, you know, excitable, and when people give him a lot of shit, he don't react well. Hey, even the screw on duty says the other guy went after 'im, so what could Jackie do but fight back or get his ass kicked?"

"Look, Johnnie, I got no problem with you," Ewing tried to reason, "but you've got to believe there's more to your friend's problems than just this scuffle. Remember, we found him passed-out on the sidewalk outside a bar this morning and it wasn't from having one too many margaritas!"

"Beg pardon for breaking up this little soiree, but somebody better fetch me my 'personals' because it looks like I'm goin' home," I interrupted casting a humorless smile in Ewing's direction.

"Jack, you okay?" said Lights Out flying to me. "From what I hear you did a fucking job on some guy!"

"I'm fine, Johnnie," I answered, eyes still locked on Big O who seemed less enthusiastic about my imminent release.

"Yeah, you may be fine," Ewing retorted, staring back with equal vehemence, "but I can't say the same for the guy you tore into this morning: shattered eye socket, two cracked ribs, and a concussion. Turns out he's a VP over at Goldman Sachs and personal friends with the Obamas. He's already talking about a multi-million dollar law suit against you!"

"Tell him to get in line," I muttered, then exploded, "Listen, Lieutenant, I'm just coming off two insane nights

I'm still trying to piece together and another twenty-four hour stint in your drunk tank that hasn't left me in the best of moods. So far as I know, protecting yourself against a strung-out coke freak is still a legitimate in this town and I've got at least one guard and three prisoners will tell you Joe Wall Street, the Obama family's buddy, got exactly what he asked for! And one more thing, don't throw names like that around at me 'cause anyone's been anywhere knows a fifty grand campaign contribution gets your picture taken with the President. Two-hundred-fifty gets his whole fucking Cabinet singing Handel's *Messiah* in the background. For sale, all of it, the best democracy money can buy! So don't be threatening me with the Obamas, Goldman Sachs, law suits, and what passes for justice in this country! You're an ex-ballplayer, you know something about the physics of *machismo*. Guy hits you, you hit him back twice as hard, law of the fucking jungle!"

Something about cops and me, I could not help but puzzle because it was apparent those remarks did not set well with Big O who rushed toward me, a heaving mass of sparks and fire, then eschewed the idea, "Listen, you stupid son-of-a-bitch! A man called to make an inquiry about you three hours ago. Lt. Don Woods over at Homeland Security, you know him? Well, he sure as hell knows you! A little matter of a guy's head found in the trunk of your car? A little matter of you being asked to sit tight in the District since you'd been identified by the D.C. cops as a person of interest! Not to mention the fact that you half-beat-to-death a personal friend of the President's! Now you're going to give me a boatload of shit about the accommodations at my precinct?"

"Some men are born great, some aspire to greatness,

others have greatness thrust upon them," I answered, grinning like the wise-ass I am, paraphrasing Shakespeare.

"Funny guy, huh?" he spouted, turning to Lights Out, who seemed perplexed at most everything going on around him. "You know your buddy tested positive for opiates last night, Johnnie?" he asked accusingly. "Heroin, John, you got that? Your buddy here's a junky or on his way to it!"

Lights Out stared back at the ex-football star undeterred in his defense of me, "Now wait just one minute, officer. Jack Madson don't take no drugs!" he strenuously objected, then thinking better of it, "That is, he may do drugs, *but heroin ain't one of 'em!*"

Lt. Ewing studied Lights Out for a half-second, began shaking his head, then looked back to me, eyes narrowed as he leaned back on a heel, arms akimbo, "Let me ask you something, Madson, are you CIA?"

"Why ask that?"

"Because your pal Woods instructed me to release you. Said it was a national security matter. There are no charges. There is no bail, you're free to go."

"Much appreciated," I answered, non-committal to any of what he'd told me, as I strode toward Booking where my wallet, belt, and Remington, unregistered in the state of New York, were turned back to me by the Uniform behind the desk.

"Go back to D.C. where you came from, Jack Madson," Ewing called-out after me. "Or, better yet, Oregon, or some other leafy place. I want you out of my Precinct! I want you out of New York! *Are you hearing me, Mr. Madson?*"

Chapter Fourteen

O nce out of jail, I found my rented Porsche waiting
for me outside the station, fresh out of the NYPD
lot where it had been towed courtesy of New
York City's finest. From there, Johnnie drove it back to
his place over the Manhattan Bridge into Hell's Kitchen
where he rented a one-bedroom flat over a boxing gym
called Bronco's. The ride, itself, was quiet, then again,
few suspected Lights Out was going to be working the
talk show circuit any time soon. Besides, my head was
splitting from my encounter at the Casanova Club along
with twenty other traumas inflicted on me during the
past three days.

To keep things simple, Lights Out checked the car
into a paid-for lot. Then we walked over to his place and
took the flight of creaky wooden stairs to the second floor,
where he turned the key, and we entered.

The dilapidated couch, set in a cramped room with
a B&W television set, called out to me like the Sirens of
Lesbos, a temptation I did not resist, collapsing into it as
Lights Out forged on into the kitchen returning with two
bottles of Sam Adams.

"I know you like the expensive stuff, Jack, so I picked
up a sixer, want one?"

"Like a baby craves his Mamma's left tit," I answered,

taking the bottle from him and chugging the better half of it.

Lights Out sat across from me in what a decade earlier might be described as a cushioned chair.

"You're not really in the CIA, are you, Jackie?"

"Can't spell the name, John, trust me, I don't have a fucking clue where Ewing picked up on that."

"Said it was a guy named Woods, you know him?" he asked taking a swig of beer.

"Yeah, I know him. Let's just say there is a multitude of shit I haven't yet fathomed," I muttered, sleep beginning to fall over me like the veil of winter's night.

Johnnie seemed to notice something that bothered him. He stepped over to the couch and examined a deep bruise on my neck tracking down to my right tricep.

"That's a nasty one you got there, want some ice for it?"

I shook my head.

"From that fight with the coke head, huh Jackie?"

"No, no," I sighed taking down the last of my beer. "It was another fight. Remember Reicher, the pituitary case calls himself a Hell's Angel?"

"Havana's boyfriend," he confirmed.

"If you say so. Anyway, it's from my fight with him at Red Hot over in Jersey. Threw me against a wall. That's where it came from."

Johnnie studied the bruise like a midwife examining the after-birth of a monster.

"Jeez, Jack, anyone ever tell you that you fight a lot for a guy don't get paid for it."

I closed my eyes, a condition most anyone could convince me was permanent the way I felt that night, "So I've heard."

"You're gonna fight him again, ain't you, Jack?"

"Not planning on it."

"Well, if you do, remember to close the distance, get inside those long arms, and take him to the ground. 'Ground 'n pound,' you'll remember that, won't you, Jack?"

"I'll do my best," I promised, then struggling, pried my eyes open. "You know, I appreciate you coming to get me out of the slammer like you did, even if there were no charges. You didn't have to do that and I appreciate it. I just wanted you to know that, Johnnie."

"I owe you, man! Think where I was five years ago after X-Man and Resto got their claws into me. No money! No eye! No career! But you took care of me, Jack. You paid my medical bills, got me work and a place to stay here at Bronco's. Shit, you're the only real friend I got."

"Well, thanks, John. You know, I'm not feeling 100% so maybe I'm going to close my eyes and sleep for awhile."

"Whatever you say," Lights Out pledged then, leaning over the side of the couch, whispered, *Sleep well, my Brother.*"

When I was a kid, after my father's accident, I had different ways of occupying myself while I lay awake when sleep would not come. Often, I would think of a trip my Dad once took me on fishing in Idaho, just the two of us. At those times I would visualize that stream and fish its entire length in my mind, fishing all the turns of its bank, sometimes catching trout and sometimes losing them. Over and over again, I'd fish that stream, starting where it emptied into the lake and fishing back up stream, trying for all the trout I'd missed coming down. Some nights, I made up streams, some of them wildly exciting and it was like being awake and dreaming at the same time.

But some nights, I could not bring myself to enter into the exercise of trout fishing at all and on those nights I was left cold-awake, alone with thoughts, my school and the nuns who taught there, the homework done or left undone, the ritual boxing sessions with my father when he'd get down on his knees, put on fourteen ounce gloves he claimed once belonged to Jack Dempsey, and we'd have at it! And when we boxed, I would try especially hard to impress him, if not with the punches I landed, at least with my ability to take his blows registered with the force of wrecking balls, until afterward with both of us slick with sweat, he'd clap me on my shoulder often breathless, himself, and say, "Well, I suppose you're not the worst kid, are you?"

Still, during those hours spent on Johnnie's couch that nasty jokester, my subconscious, must have had something more ambitious in mind because it was that night that Havana first entered the lexicon of my dreams. No, it wasn't sexual in nature, I didn't need dreams for that! It was Freudian or Jungian or some such crap, because in my dream, though Havana was wearing not a stitch, she was lying supinely on a wooden raft, propped up on an elbow, floating on a subterranean river. It was very dark, except for flaming torches as one might imagine in a medieval dungeon that clung to the stone walls beyond its banks to half-light the underground. And, on those banks I observed people—most of them children eight, ten, twelve years old—shut up like animals living in wooden cages!

Then Havana looked straight at me, eyes piercing through time and space, as I lay there on Johnnie's couch and, expressionless, dipped her hand into the water, and the river began to boil in a frenzy of activity beneath the surface. Then, she pulled it out again, but now her hand (her entire arm!) was skeletal, bone and nothing more, the skin eaten away, it seemed, by unseen schools of flesh-eating piranha. Yet still Havana continued to stare, a frightening, helpless look, and the dream just went on like that repeating itself like some closed-loop DVD trying to communicate something, *some thing*, as near to me as it was five galaxies removed from any notion I'd yet conceived!

But in that domain of half-sleep there existed a kind of logic that by morning's light would inevitably drag me from my psychological diversions down, further still, into the depths of that awful morning my father died. That night at Johnnie's was no exception and like my trout excursions that, too, I re-lived moment-to-moment with equal specificity. The beer truck pulls up to our home. My father enters, gathers his papers, and stomps down into the basement. My nostrils fill with the smell of the fire that consumes them as I encounter him, speechless, climbing the staircase headed for the bedroom. Next comes the blast that rips through the silence of my wonderment, and with it a dismal sense of foreboding that like a wrenching fist grips my internals as I fly up the staircase into his bedroom and spy him on his bed wanting so desperately to believe he is only napping, edging cautiously forward to discover he is only half-alive, the bottom part of his skull blown apart, lungs emoting strangely terrifying noises as if drowning in his own blood as I reach out to touch him … *Dad … Oh, Dad … what in God's name have you done?*

Do I have to tell you I woke that morning with a soulless shudder in the deepest grips of a cold sweat? And even moments later when I noticed Lights Out hovering over me with two steaming mugs in hand, it was Havana's chilling image lying on that raft that remained branded in my brain. *What did it all mean? What the fuck had I gotten myself into this time?*

"Morning, Jack," Lights Out beamed, "sleep good?"

"Not bad," I lied still blinking myself back to his single bedroom flat in Hell's Kitchen.

"This ain't no Elysée, but I brought you a cup of coffee with a shot Jameson's, your favorite."

"Thanks," I said sitting up, taking the mug from him.

Lights Out plopped himself in a chair across from me, "So you plannin' on hangin' around here long, Jackie? You know, seein' how you're fighting all the time, why not take some training here at Bronco's, guys'd love to see ya."

I blew into the mug, watching a cloud of steam rise then dissipate into the air. "Not this time, Johnnie. I figure New York's seen enough of me and I know I've seen enough of New York! I've got one last call to make across the river, then I'm off, back to our nation's capitol."

"Sorry to hear that, Jackie, but one thing sure. If things go bat shit and you need a place to stay, you can count on me."

I nodded rising from the couch and it was like stepping into another atmosphere, "I'll keep that in mind, John," I promised grimly, taking a swallow from my mug of Jameson's and coffee, "Before this is over, I have a feeling I'll be needing all the help I can get."

Chapter Fifteen

I parked my Porsche across the street from St. Ann's abbey, then crossed Martin Luther King Boulevard, memories strong as ocean currents tugging me back to the day four years earlier when, shot through the chest, I came to Jeremiah in search of sanctuary. *Not great days,* I remembered grimly, veering toward the two iron-re-enforced oak doors that marked the chapel entrance. *My life was in shambles at that time but let's see if Jeremiah's still chapel curator. More to the point, let's see if he'll see me at all since the last time I was arrested at gunpoint causing no small embarrassment for the monastic community renowned for their quiet commitment to educating promising young men from Newark's inner city!*

When I entered the chapel and saw Jeremiah, arranging flowers at the altar, a flood of faces, voices, even smells, of one-hundred-fifty teenage boys from my high school days stopped me dead in my tracks. *Omni tempore silencio studere,* I recalled Fr. Mark, the school's headmaster, proclaim thirty years before from the pulpit that rose up in front of me, "at all times cultivate science." Of course there were many more dictums, all based on the teachings of St. Damian, who expounded the virtues of a "deeper reality" hidden beneath the veneer of societal norms, its truth uncovered through the rigors of monastic life and *conversatio.* Translated literally, it meant "conversation of life," but to the monks at St. Ann's it was a path to salvation achieved through a "constant dialogue with the world around us" and "continuous search" for the inner Truth they believed lay fallow within each of us.

But it was Jeremiah who set us all on our asses when in class one morning he bared a silver medallion from around his neck. Embossed with the image of Maat, the Egyptian goddess of Truth, depicted as a naked woman with neck and head replaced by a giant feather, it bore an inscription: *The difference between the truth and a lie is the weight of a feather.*

"This is something St. Damian would appreciate," Jeremiah explained to us then, "because, like the Egyptians, he learned while fasting in the desert that before a person can defeat Satan, he must first conquer himself. *Vade retro Satana non quam suade mihi vana!* he shouted at the Devil who tempted him with pleasures of the flesh. "Great Liar, do not tempt me with thy vanities!" he warned, then threw himself into a thicket of thorns until, after three days, exhausted and torn, Damian, finally watched Satan retreat whispering a prayer to himself, "Jesus Christ, my Lord and Savior," along with the revelation, *"The greatest lies I tell myself!"*

How far from that exalted theology were we then when Mike Higgins turned Fr. Genarius' prized fish collection into floating skeletons with a shot glass full of phosphoric acid in chemistry class; or Lamar Peterson unscrewed the hinges to the massive door at the entrance to St. Ann's that Fr. Boniface flung open with reckless abandon each morning; or the dead piglet spared dissection in Biology class by Tony Spirito strategically placed in the Abbott's briefcase prior to a budget presentation to the school's Board of Directors! Oh, yes, we were *at all times cultivating science*, at least when we weren't pilfering liquor from the neighborhood stores and selling it wholesale out of our lockers, or printing phony IDs to get us into the local go-go bars where black girls shook their asses and showed us their titties! And, of course, there was *conversatio*! Indeed, we were engaged in *constant dialogue with the world around us* starting with every bouncer who'd turn a blind eye to the disconnect between our fifteen-year old faces and the twenty-one year old birth dates on our IDs, every pimp who introduced us to sex with his stable of whores, or the drugs they sold, heavy as heroin or light as hashish!

I shook my head at the strangeness of American life today, where violence lives like an electronic hum behind the silence of even the sleepiest Sunday afternoon and madness seems around every corner. But the meaning of my reverie was as elusive as ever, and like a storm passing over a deserted island, the dark nostalgia blew out and over me as my thoughts returned to the chapel and a sight as charming as it was hopeful: the old priest, Jeremiah, genuflecting as he stepped back from the altar and tabernacle that he believed housed the body and blood of our savior, Jesus Christ!

Of course he couldn't see me with his back turned and I wasn't sure that he'd notice me in a pew praying in the chapel's half-light. But pray I did during the moments before I re-introduced myself after a four year absence and another twenty before that.

I prayed for Bill Bonanno. I prayed that he'd be forgiven for whatever sins he may have committed, for whatever lies, or violence, or corruption he may have perpetrated. Most of all, I prayed that before he died he understood in his own mind, and heart, and soul that false pride—pride in a way of life that he called one thing, but was really another—was perhaps the only real sin and that all others sprang from it. I prayed for my friend, Eddie Lawler, that he would find something or someone who would give meaning to his life and that he wouldn't drink and whore and gamble so much though I realized he really seemed to enjoy it. Then, I prayed for the victim of the horrendous murder who had somehow entered my life. I prayed that he hadn't suffered terribly and that death came swiftly, and that he died without knowing the horrors of the fate that had befallen him, that he never saw his murderer, never saw the brutality in his gaze, or knew the hideous nature of his mind, that somehow, miraculously, he died innocent. Finally, I prayed for myself, *"Dear God,"* I pled, *"let me find Truth."*

When I opened my eyes again, it was like some species of bi-location because standing in front of me was Jeremiah smiling, "Good to see you, Jack," he bade as if none of what I described had happened four years ago. "How are you doing, son?"

"Fine, Father," I managed to answer. "I was in the area and thought I'd stop by."

"Come, get up! Let me take you around. You know there've been some changes since the last time you came to visit."

"Didn't know that," I commented as I followed him out to the Boulevard where he paused center-building and took a step back.

"We've been working closely with one of our alumni, you know him, Tom Dougherty."

I nodded as cars flew by and the wind blew Jeremiah's thinning white hair back and to the side exposing the pink of his scalp.

"Tom and his wife Ann have been active in helping find homes for orphaned children from around the world. Some of the older ones come here to be educated living in dorms just like the kids from here in Newark. The countries may be different," he explained, hollering over the sound of cars and trucks passing, "but the problems are the same whether here, or Columbia, or Kosovo. Tom and Ann started the Dougherty Foundation, put a hefty check behind it, and now we have our new wing," he said tracing the building left to right with his forefinger. "It houses twenty-five kids, all full-time students, sequestered from the poverty and political turmoil of their native countries, now part of our community. Orphans most, they'll be educated right here in the Abbey with us."

"Sounds great," I couldn't help but admit despite the pang of jealousy that even I noticed had crept into my voice.

"It's cold out here," Jeremiah bellowed, bracing his slight frame against the wind as it gusted, "let's go into the rectory where we can talk."

I followed him as he ambled up the five brownstone steps leading into the residence where twenty-seven Brothers lived, worked, and prayed each day noticing how the bend in his frame, straight and tall when I was a student, had become more prominent, a sturdy tree whose branches heavy with the strain of living had finally bent to its master, time.

The monks, themselves, had taken a vow of poverty upon ordination so that basic necessities—medical procedures, dentistry, even food—were derived from whatever tuition students or their parents could scrape together, contributions from the congregation at St. Ann's, or tithes from successful alumni like Dougherty. Still, whatever face-lift the school underwent had indeed transformed a ravaged campus into a modern, albeit unique, institution. From dormitories to classrooms, all of it, first rate.

Finally our tour through the narrow hallways of the monk's residence concluded when Jeremiah stopped at a heavy wooden door with black iron handles that had somehow escaped the scope of Dougherty's renovations.

"This is my room," he chimed opening the door to a cubicle with bed, bookcase, and crude wood desk. "Please have a seat," he offered waving his hand at a chair, then plopping himself down at the edge of his bed. "I'd offer you something to drink but I'm afraid I have only water or church wine…" he said, rising half-way, ready to retrieve it.

"No, I'm not thirsty, Father, I just wanted to see you. First, to apologize for what happened last time I came by. Second, to tell you I'm back on my feet again and ready to make a go of it."

"Oh, that's good to hear!" he beamed, clapping his hands together not totally unlike a delighted child. "I've prayed for you, Jack. I haven't stopped, you know, not since you graduated."

"Thanks, Father, maybe it helped. At least I hope so. Say," I said looking around the room searching my mind for a way to steer clear of my fucked up life and current situation, "looks like a lot of good things have happened to the school over the past couple years!"

"As you know, we take a vow of poverty, but money is still a necessity. Tom and Ann Dougherty have been very generous and, yes, I realize there are tax advantages that make contributions attractive to them, but it didn't have to be St. Damian's and without the dollars their foundation provides we might not be here at all."

"What's it been, a hundred-seventy years?"

"One-hundred-seventy-five since the Abbey was founded. Nearly one-hundred-fifty since the school first opened."

"Well, I take my hat off to them. I guess not everyone from St. Damian's turned-out like me."

"Don't be so hard on yourself. Remember, salvation can only happen when you're ready to accept Him, no sooner, no later." Jeremiah's eyes narrowed as if to bring into focus what might have seemed a blur, "You look tired, son. Are you sure everything is all right?"

"Absolutely, I've got a profession now. I'm a private investigator, Father. So, no, I don't have every nut and bolt locked down, but I'm making my way toward something with a future."

Jeremiah's eyes had never let off me and I wondered then who'd make the better detective between us as he nodded slowly, then stopped like he was a wind up doll whose spring had just run out.

"You know, I have a theory about salvation, Jack. It's that every person is really *two people*. Inside each of us, two separate identities exist side-by-side like Siamese twins. Together they go through life in harmony, but not always, meaning there are exceptions. And for those individuals, life is more contentious, Jack, but it's also more profound. For Dougherty, it may be easy. Dougherty #1 and Dougherty #2 may well agree on most everything: the fact that Ann would make a fine mate, so they marry; the fact that Jesus Christ is their Savior, so they become devout Catholics.

But to others, like you, it's different. For you there may be no agreement between the Two Selves at all. Jack #1 may love the family's pet dog. Jack #2 may despise it. Jack #1 may want to find a nice girl and settle down, Jack #2 might expend every fiber of his being trying to prevent that from happening; Jack #1 may be 'good,' but Jack #2 may be the Devil incarnate."

"What are you saying," I asked, a wave of heat jumping the distance between us, "that Tom is a good man and I'm some kind of monster? That Dougherty is stinking rich, wrote a check for twelve million to the school, and I didn't, so that makes me some kind of pariah?"

"No, son, that's not what I'm saying," he argued. "You can't buy salvation! Tom doesn't know that and so we pray for him. Besides, Dougherty only recently found his faith again and that's my point. Jesus Christ will never give up on you!"

"Well he wasn't so religious when we were here together," I persisted. "Pulled off every high school prank I did, though I was the one got demerits for it! Hell, I thought Tom was in a good way with the Church for most of his life!"

"Tom and Ann re-dedicated themselves to Catholicism while on a tour of the Vatican. It was the miracle of the incorruptible corpses that inspired them. Ann at first but then Tom who found the experience so overwhelming he underwent 'spontaneous conversion,' as it's called. They've been devout believers, *Opus Dei*, from the moment they laid eyes on the Incorruptibles, entombed behind glass for everyone to see, believers and non-believers alike."

"Incorruptible corpses?"

"St. Bernadette of Lourdes, St. Vincent de Paul, Pope

Pius IX, some go back centuries but once exhumed it's obvious to everyone the bodies have never decayed, most looking as if they're simply resting, even today, ready to awaken at the Lord's bidding."

"Chemicals?"

"None."

"Mummification?"

"No, these are miracles, Jack! No one can explain it. No one ever will. But the real miracle isn't their incorruptibility, it's their affect on those whose lives they've transformed. That transformation may not seem near to you now, Jack, but it will happen as dramatic and even more meaningful than what happened to Tom and his wife. You see, the wondrous thing about my theory is that these Twin Selves are more resonant in some — like St. Damian — and that because God allows us to choose our own destiny; he must give the Devil equal opportunity in a kind of contest, each vying for your eternal soul. Satan needs to 'win' you. Jesus Christ wants you to come to Him. And if you come to Him, it won't be like the others for whom the struggle is easy because you have a large soul, Jack, you *feel* more than others. That's not a curse, son, it's a blessing. Remember," he said speaking in a voice that seemed prophetic as Damian, himself, "it is always lightest before the dark."

"No," I corrected, "the expression is 'it's always darkest before the light.'"

Jeremiah shook his head, eyes blazing, "No, I said it the way I wanted."

Then, raising his right hand up into the air, Reverend Jeremiah Cullinane blessed me.

* * *

Once broke free from the Abbey's gravity, and with Jeremiah's quixotic farewell still fresh in my mind, I decided to wait-out rush hour before heading back to D.C. I snagged a burger at Pistols, an appropriately named diner not far from the federal courthouse that loomed with its Greek columns, a monolith to some civilization that had long since deserted Newark, New Jersey.

It had been nearly two decades since I'd basked in the ambiance of the city's downtown and little had changed. Run by "Tony Boy" Bontempo and his dad, Ritchie "The Boot," back in the day with graffiti like "Frankie Valli Sat Here" carved into the wooden booths at diners like Pistols, the wood had been replaced by plastic with graffiti like "Suk Dic Mutherfukr" spray-painted onto its exterior, and the Sicilian Mafia switched for street gangs with names like the Crips and Latin Kings. Still, Newark—like most of America's industrial cities— remained a shithole, only worse, with most of its jobs and industrial base now shipped to China and anyone with a brain in their head fled to the suburbs.

After traffic subsided, I hopped into my Porsche, popped a handful of Adderall tabs to fortify myself, and headed back to D.C. Once on the Jersey Turnpike, it was a straight shot south on I-95 and cruising that crisp, star-filled December night at an eighty-mile-per-hour clip, I finally felt relaxed enough to chill, the Bose sound system blaring "Psycho," by the Sonics, The Scorpion's "Virgin Killer," and "Stop Breakin' Down," a smokin' hot Stones' cover. As one would expect, between the pounding vibe of the music and hypnotic optics of oil refineries, semi-trucks, and billboards raced past in a blur, I found my subconscious sharing information, attempting to digest the chain of events I'd been living through during the past three days. Not unlike an observer watching a political debate, it seemed my role to evaluate the back-and-forth between them. *'No, that couldn't possibly be true!'* I found myself objecting, or *'Yes, of course, what did you think he meant by that, anyway?'* But by the time it all ended, the multiple parts of myself had cobbled together some basic facts and a path forward.

First the bad. My attempted reconciliation with Tiffany had been a disaster: *better leave it alone for now.* Next was Havana Spice. Given her proximity to Reicher, I never did get to talk to her about Dougherty, but had at least managed to deliver my card and got her calculating the wisdom of blackmailing a man so well-connected as Tom: *I would follow-up with her once back in D.C.* Finally, in addition to legal problems back in the District, I'd added a brush with the law in New York to my resume. True, charges had been dropped, but the incident may have piqued the interest of a cop additional to Don Woods at Homeland Security, Lt. Owen "Big O" Ewing, NYPD: *this I would try to forget ever happened!*

Now the good. If Havana Spice was trapped in some kind of coercive relationship with Reicher and the Angels, she had my contact information and might reach-out to me: *this I would encourage through an intermediate like Amber Starr or in person, after doing research on Reicher such as, were there any outstanding warrants for his arrest?* Another positive was the connection I'd established between Havana, Amber, and Reicher with the Casanova Club, a focal point it seemed for all things perverse. Dougherty and his boys at the FBI had apparently already infiltrated its network of patrons, all prime targets for blackmail by the club's ownership, and, yes, *I would be investigating to uncover just how deep into society's flesh their tentacles extended.*

Still, with the debate in my head all but settled, I was left with one question that stuck like a soup bone in the pit of my stomach and that was, *why had Woods instructed Big O to release me without charges?* National Security? Now there was a joke! No, it had to do with something else, I reasoned, perhaps the head in the trunk of my car, or Eddie, or Vicky, or—was it too large a leap—my father-in-law Barton Crowley, now deceased?

I switched on my cell, gave the voice command, "Tom Dougherty," who two rings later, picked up.

"Jack?" he asked in an urgent whisper. "I'm here at home so make it brief."

"Okay," I answered. "I'm on my way back to D.C. I met with Havana and her boyfriend, all six-foot-seven, two-hundred-sixty pounds of him. We don't get along."

"Jesus, Jack, is there anything I can do to help?"

"You can keep your cock in your pants from now on, for one thing, but it seems there's more to your girlfriend than meets the eye. The crowd she hangs out with isn't very savory, but I think we can get them to back off. One thing about bullies like Reicher: good on offense, lousy on defense once someone has a mind to go after them."

"I see," Dougherty answered tensely, "and you think you can make this nightmare go away?"

"I do. The message is delivered. Let's give it some time, see how they react."

"Thank you, Jack, I can't tell you how much this means to me."

"And one last thing: money, I need some. Your friends

travel in rarified circles, Tom. Hanging with them ain't cheap."

"Would another five thousand help?"

"That should do it. Have the money dropped off at the manager's office, Georgetown Inn. The owner's a friend of mine named Eddie Lawler."

I clicked off my cell, then reached into the pocket of my N.Y. Yankees' warm-up jacket for a pack of Wrigley's left over from the night before. Once retrieved, my eyes fell on the scrap of folded paper that clung to it.

I flattened it with my free hand, noticing the watermark that leaked through its heavy bond along with four typewritten words, bold and in caps, **"YOU SHOULD BE DEAD!"** the note read.

Chapter Sixteen

I arrived back at the Inn around midnight. Traffic could be a bitch around the Beltway and the approach into Gtown and I'd managed to avoid both. Once in my suite with the Adderall worn down, I managed a decent night's sleep, and gave Vicky Benson a call to see if she'd join me for a sandwich over at the Tombs, a nearby rathskeller where kids from the university hung out.

Anxious and concerned like the good attorney-ex-girlfriend she was, she agreed and by noon, perked up with four tabs of Focalin, I managed to drag my heavyweight-sized carcass to the 1789 and down the flight of stairs leading to the Tombs.

Vicky stood nervously waiting at the tavern's entrance along with a kid who looked to be about fifteen and according to all available evidence worked there as the greeter.

"Jack," she said urgently as I approached, "I just tried to call you!"

"Well, here I am," I offered casting her a raffish grin. "Noon, I got it right, didn't I?"

"I know, it's just that I worry about you. I swear, I don't know why, but I do." Her expression changed to something between somber and annoyed. "Come on, let's get some lunch!"

I followed behind her and the greeter wondering what someone who hadn't known Vicky for twenty years like me might think when they first saw her. 'Something less than a stunner, but something more than a Midwestern farm girl,' was the phrase that came to mind. Vicky was big, maybe 5'11", possessed a credible figure, buxom with broad shoulders narrowing at the waist, shapely legs, and a longish face with complexion white as alabaster that could, given the right occasion, break into the most genuine smile I'd ever seen. Her eyes were bright and engaging like they could reach out and grab you, her full red lips parting to reveal teeth that sparkled to match the glow in her eyes. Yes, Vicky had a smile to remember. Probably, it was her most salient feature.

Navigating the clusters of students—boyfriends with girlfriends, some with their parents—we stopped at a table not far from the bar where Johnnie Appleseed pulled a chair out for Vicky and we sat, intimately, shoulder-to-shoulder rather than across the table from one another. It was the least I could do.

"So tell me everything and I'll do the same," she suggested leaning toward me hands folded center-table.

"I got arrested," I began sadly.

"I know."

"Lights Out?"

"Yes, he called yesterday thinking, correctly, that I'd want to know. Jack," she wondered wincing, "how could you be so foolish?"

The waiter arrived, cherubic face scrubbed and smiling, "Can I get you folks something to drink besides water?"

"Yeah, a beer—Sam Adams," I said, then looked to Vicky who didn't seem to be having much of an afternoon.

"*Jesus,*" she muttered, "*get me a Cosmo!*"

"Right away," the student-waiter agreed already in motion.

"It wasn't what you're thinking," I tried to explain, face not six inches from her as I sat forward in my chair. "I followed Havana Spice, the porn star blackmailing my high school pal Dougherty, from where she was working in Jersey to a place in New York called the Casanova Club. Now, that's something to talk about! Anyway, once there I find her in bed with a girl, that would be Amber Starr, being broadcast "live" via Camcorder to a website by a biker named Reicher. See, I'm there to talk—Havana and me—so I can get her to back off blackmailing Dougherty, when somebody hits me from behind, sticks a hypodermic needle into my arm, shoots me up with heroin, then leaves me unconscious on the street for NYPD to discover."

"And you wonder why I worry about you?" Vicky gasped, shaking her head side-to-side as our drinks arrived. "I don't know where to begin, Jack! And what's this Johnnie's been telling me, they dropped all charges, vagrancy, drunk and disorderly, carrying a gun without registration, not to mention another fight I understand you were involved in while incarcerated!"

"Guilty as charged, *no lo contende,*" I pled lifting my hands into the air and taking a long gulp of beer. "How about from your side?"

"Of course, Woods has been asking about you. So has Will Harris. Was it Woods who got NYPD to drop charges and have you released? Why would he do that?"

"I don't know," I answered glancing over Vicky's right shoulder as she sipped her Cosmo, "why don't you ask him?"

"What are you talking about?" she wondered, noticing the trajectory of my stare.

"He's right here now. He's being taken to a table with what looks like his wife and son ... and now he's seen us ... and now he's on his way over."

"Hi folks," Woods greeted as he approached, "lucky I turned this way or I might have missed you."

Dressed in a three-piece suit, Woods never looked more like a cop, clear blue eyes as focused as they were detached, smiling that 'I know something you don't' smile that cops love so much, his compact frame shifted back on one heel to accidentally on purpose reveal the Glock semi-automatic he carried in a shoulder holster.

"Would have been a tragedy to miss him, wouldn't it?" I asked Vicky whose eyes were already telling me to knock off the sarcasm.

"Look, Madson, maybe we got off to a bad start. I'm willing to admit I might have been a little rough on you, so what say we start fresh with me telling you I never thought you murdered that kid in the first place. Remember, it was me who had you take that blood test. Without proof of GHB in your blood stream you might still be pacing the length of a jail cell."

"Did you say 'kid'?" I asked.

"Yeah, just to show you there's no hard feelings, let me share some info from the coroner's report. The head belongs to a fourteen-year-old Asian male who's essentially 'no one.' No prints. Facial features cut-off, tissue around the skull peeled away. No DNA matches. No teeth in his head to cross-check dental records. Nothing, except one thing. The presence of chemicals in the fluids that were still secreting out of it, since Forensics believes all this happened something like four to six hours before you discovered him 10 am that morning."

"So that would mean…" Vicky began.

"That would mean your boy here couldn't have done it since he was busy shagging Miss Amber Starr who gave us a statement to that effect."

"Chemicals?" I asked pointedly. "You said Forensics found chemicals in the boy's secretions."

"That's right, a laboratory's worth starting with a proprietary formulation called Formalin and ending with trace elements of a dozen others: phenols, aldehydes, methanol, quaternary ammonium."

"Those are fixatives, chemicals used for embalming…"

"Bright boy!" Woods said, blue eyes twinkling.

"But that makes no sense. Clearly, the corpse was dismembered, brutally from all indications, and that would take hours," Vicky puzzled. "So if the boy was murdered between 4 and 6 a.m.," she looked directly up at him, "You're not suggesting he was injected with chemicals then killed and dismembered?"

"I'm not suggesting anything, just stating facts from the pathology report. But you're right, Madson, each of those chemicals act to fix cellular proteins so they can't act as a nutrient source for bacteria. The end result is that the tissue decomposes more slowly creating the appearance of blood flowing under the skin which, of course, it can't since they're dead."

I shook my head fatefully, "Monstrous son-of-a-bitch this killer, any leads?"

"None that I can discuss."

"But that's the end of it for my client? Miss Starr's statement and the presence of GHB in his blood stream exclude Jack from any list of potential suspects, am I right in assuming that?"

"Like I said, I don't think he had anything to do with it, at least not directly, though your client seems to have a knack for getting himself in deep with the law. I got a call from Owen Ewing at NYPD yesterday," he said fixing his icy blue eyes on me. "I guess you're the type of guy who can't just stay home and watch a movie, are you, Jack?"

"I was wondering when you were going to bring that up. Am I supposed to feel indebted because you got those charges dropped, or should I just ask now what you want in return?"

"Look," Woods said glancing to a table where his wife and son sat talking, "I came here to take a tour of the campus with my wife and son, not to get into it with you, so let's just say I did it because I thought 'here's a guy who could use a break.' But since you brought it up, let me give you some free advice. I know why you were in New York, and I know who hired you to go there, and if I were you, I'd steer clear of Dougherty. He's friends with ex-CIA, organized crime, and worse. Way out of your league, partner."

I rose up in my chair feeling the flat of Vicky's restraining hand on my thigh, "Well, you're not me, Woods, but I'd like to hear how you came upon that information, was it a parabolic mike at Billy Martin's Carriage House, a wireless tap on my cell?"

"How I know what I know is none of your concern, Madson!"

"Maybe not, but now let me give you some advise, stick to solving this murder and get off Tom Dougherty's back! You think I don't know about the rivalries that go on between agencies? Tribal, that's the way I'd describe it between the FBI, CIA, Homeland, and the others. But for the record, Dougherty is a friend of mine, someone I've known for thirty years, got that? So if the cabal I'd bet you're trying to hatch has anything to do with me helping you go after him, you'd best keep that in mind!"

"All right, Jack, have it your way. Nice talking with you, Miss Benson," he said with a gracious nod, "Jack, I'll be seeing you around."

Chapter Seventeen

Once Vicky left for her office and Woods and his family departed, I hung out at the Tombs talking up a young coed who found me interesting the way an amateur archeologist might peer into a magnifying glass at a fossilized bone, though I'd made less likely hook-ups based on no more than that. But romance was not on the menu and from there — stalwart in my commitment to spend every cent left of Dougherty's advance — I launched into an improvised version of the "Georgetown Crawl," touring bars up and down M Street until, sodden and exhausted, I began to ruminate over the rubicon that set me drinking in the first place!

The obvious one I mulled over while sitting at Clyde's dealt with Woods and how, and why, he'd burst into my life. I didn't like the son-of-a-bitch from the moment we met and it had gone downhill from there. Crisp and ruthless with a mind sharp as the needlepoint-pupils of his blue eyes, Woods had managed to mask career ambition in the great coat of patriotism, but I wasn't buying, and when he brought up Dougherty's name at the Tomb's the coincidences came together like chain lightning. The reason I wasn't taken into custody after reporting that kid's head in my car, why I was released from the slammer in New York, and how he knew I was working for Tom

Dougherty, all pointed to one thing: being a long-time pal of Dougherty's, Woods and the boys at Homeland had identified me as someone they could use to nail him which meant they'd be approaching me to "cooperate" not far down the pike.

What theory or sting operation were they trying to prove or lure him into, who could say? But for me all of that was irrelevant! Operating as Assistant Director of the FBI for the most target-rich region in the country, how could he help but attract high-powered enemies along with his high-powered friends? After all, wasn't it CIA guru Allen Dulles who once declared 'great men deserve great enemies?' More, even to an outsider like me, it was obvious that Dougherty was being set up by Homeland Security, the new agency on the block, in some kind of internecine turf war with the FBI, or who knew what other Intel organization?

Still, I was relieved to have been dropped from the list of suspects in the murder of that poor Asian kid, I concluded, before moving on to the next rubicon that like Caesar's river of no return awaited me at Chadwick's, then Cabanas, and The Third Edition, where I pondered the riddle of Havana Spice.

True or untrue, I always fancied myself the possessor of at least a modicum of ESP. By that I mean, any reasonable detective — like a gypsy fortuneteller — need not tap into the supernatural to discern the future, but into the details. How someone walks or talks; if they smile, when do they smile; if they speak, what are they telling you behind the words; eyes, too, often tell a savvy investigator what emotions, if any, a person is feeling when a particular topic is broached; and dress, let's not forget that! The way a man or woman dresses can be an encyclopedia about who they are and how they see themselves fitting into the world that surrounds them.

When it came to Havana, all these intimations hit with the force of signals broadcast from a fucking radio tower! 'And what are they saying?' I asked myself, waiting for the proper description to emerge from my subconscious. The answer came to me in one word, 'danger.' Danger for whatever reason: perhaps the gentle intelligence exuded from the face of Savito, her nine-year-old son; or Lights Out's info about the hefty percentage of income she sent back to her parents in Cuba; or was it the hope in her eye when she saw me that night at Red Hot 21, I wondered, praying that someone had finally uncovered the private hell she'd endured since first arriving in the U.S. at the age of sixteen?

Still, it came down to two simple questions, each left unanswered, but certainly not surrendered from the closed fist of my resolve. *How was I going to circumvent Reicher, and his band of Merry Men, to uncover Havana's motivation in attempting to blackmail Dougherty? What was there about this woman that so totally infatuated me?*

Later that night, moving on to Mr. Smith's (where I heard jazz) and Blue's Alley (where I listened to a Howlin' Wolf sound-alike) and Garrett's (where I sat drinking double scotches), I remembered the death threat lying silent as a cyanide capsule on my desktop. **'YOU SHOULD BE DEAD,'** it read. A simple statement that carried with it implicit messages like, 'I *could have* killed you, but didn't this time'; or 'You *should be* dead, but I need you now and harbor a torturous demise for you later; or '*You* should be dead, but make no mistake others will die in your place.' In the end, the only thing certain was that, for whatever reason, there was somebody—perhaps Reicher, Chok Por, Jin Lee, her Flying Dragon boyfriend, or even Special Agent Don Woods—who wanted me to back-off my investigation of Havana Spice and the Casanova Club.

Already late evening, with absurdities eating into my every supposition with the ferocity of ants, I knew that like Caesar standing at the edge of the Rubicon, I was headed toward a point of no return with this solemn vow on my lips, *I am going to figure this out. I am going to succeed. I am not going to fuck this up!*

By midnight after a nightcap with Eddie Lawler, I returned to my room, gulped down three Ambien with a beer, then tuned into Channel 8 News in time to watch Michelle Leigh report "live" from a location in front of the Inn. She spoke of the "ongoing investigation" and discovery of a "human head," now identified as that of "an adolescent Asian male," but with the first snake of *zolpidem* winding its way through my brain, her words dissolved into the air like snow flakes on a warm winter's day and to me it was near-comical: "The head ... *was dead* ... the boy ... *named Roy* ... suspects include ... *you dirty dude* ... Madson released ... *a cold-blooded beast,* my addled brain re-worked her words so that smiling, at this late and empty hour, I passed out on the couch fully clothed eyes glaring at the death threat that lay on my desktop, wondering if, in fact, some time soon I would be dead.

The knock came hard on the sturdy white door that marked the entrance to my suite and, I must say, I had no idea what time it could have been or even where I'd been sleeping. I spied an open bottle of Jameson's on the top of the dresser as I lumbered to the ante-room, wishing the banging would stop so I could steal a nip along the way but soldiered on instead throwing the door open with a guttural growl.

"Yeah?" I demanded.

"Jack! My God, you look like you're risen from the dead," Dougherty said, shaking his head. "I came to drop-off the money, aren't you going to invite me in?"

"Yeah, sure, give me a sec to straighten up," I muttered, making my way to the bedroom. "There's a coffee machine if you want some. I sure wouldn't mind a cup."

"No, I don't suppose you would," he called back as I plucked the bottle of Jameson's off the dresser top and headed for the bathroom.

I could hear Tom fiddling with the machine while I downed two Adderalls with a pull of whiskey letting the water run to cover any hint of what had become my morning ritual.

"I met your girlfriend the other night," I said drying my face with a towel. "Also met her 6' 7" boyfriend."

"So you said."

"Yeah," I asked tossing the towel into the sink and re-entering the ante room, "did I also mention I got hit from behind with something felt like an anvil and spent the night in jail?"

Dougherty poured two cardboard cups full with black coffee and handed me one, "Never said it would be easy, but there's $7500 in that envelope," he said motioning toward the desktop and a white envelope set beside the paper on which the death threat was written.

"Keep this up and I'm going to have to start paying taxes," I quipped, wondering if Dougherty had been reading my fan mail.

"No worries. It's cash, one hundred dollar denominations."

"And how about the rest of it, Tom? The kid's head they found in the trunk of my car, did that information cross your desk over at the Agency?"

"I knew about it, sure. Even FBI men watch the news."

"Why didn't you say something?"

"Why didn't you?" he asked smiling comfortably. "Besides, maybe I did, just not to you. Maybe that's the reason MPD let you go in the first place."

I took a sip of coffee, shaking my head before the cup left my lips, "No, Tom. The reason they never took me in was I had nothing to do with that kid's murder!"

"Do you think I don't know that? I knew about your situation before we met at the Carriage House but wasn't going to be the one to bring it up. Come on, Jack," he argued tossing his cup into the waste paper basket, "we've been friends for thirty years! If you needed help, I figured you'd ask for it. Anyway, I had my own problems to sort through, though I can tell you, you've made no friends here in the District since you arrived and that can be dangerous in this town."

"What's that supposed to mean?"

"It means there's been a highly publicized murder—a grisly one at that—with little or no evidence since the boy's remains were sanitized: no surveillance tape, no witnesses, and no suspects to tie to it other than you and maybe that stripper you spent the night with."

"Yeah?"

"Politics!" Dougherty erupted. "This is Washington, D.C., my friend. Nothing here means anything unless it's interpreted in the context of politics. A man like Woods won't rest until someone—innocent or guilty—wears this atrocity like a laurel wreath at Marathon. It's the nature of the beast, Jack, but I've got your back so whatever poor sap hits the jackpot, it won't be you."

I took three steps toward the trash can and deep-sixed my cardboard cup, "Maybe," I offered speculatively, "but I'm not the only one who has enemies."

I watched the expression on Dougherty's face transform, there was no other word for it. He was singed by the comment, "What makes you say that?"

"Vicky Benson, my attorney, and I ran into Don Woods over at the Tombs today. He was there with his wife and son, but stopped by our table to share some info about the coroner's report, *and about you*. It was my impression he's as interested in you as in the murder, but like I said, it's just an impression."

"What did he tell you?"

"Nothing, really. Only that you're a high-flyer and 'out of my league'. From my side, I told him he was an overly ambitious asshole and that if he was looking for someone to help set you up, he'd come to the wrong man."

"Yes, of course," Tom agreed, relief like a bright light suddenly illuminating his face, "I'm sorry to have asked. But just to demonstrate the point I was trying to make," he explained planting his right hand on my shoulder, "Woods is divorced. A childless marriage at that. He has no wife or son, go look it up on the internet. And that's the problem with this town! Do you know what we say at the Agency about the charlatans over at Homeland and the CIA? We say 'the only way to uncover the truth is by comparing their lies.' You see, they're not men like you and me, Jack. These," he struggled to find the word, "*caricatures* don't live in what you and I would judge to be reality. No, they live in a world built upon the lies they foment, so much so, they can no longer recognize what is real. What is it they say about the difference between neurotics and psychotics? 'Neurotics build sand castles in the sand and psychotics live in them.' Well, that is what's at the core of the American dilemma. It's Kafkaesque, this society we've invented for ourselves. Like Joseph K in *The Trial* or Gregor Samsa in *Metamorphosis*, we tell so many lies that one morning we wake up to find the tables have turned. The truth becomes an estrangement and it's within that house of lies that we're forced to live!"

I must have been staring strangely at him because when Tom looked into my face, his manicured hand withdrew and he fell back a step.

"Sorry," he apologized, his sharp, amber eyes shifting from me, "because you're right. It was wrong of me to bring up your situation in that context and I'm sorry. What I was trying to say is that we're friends, dear friends, for a lot of years, Jack, and frankly speaking—outside of Ann and the children—I don't have many. Acquaintances, yes. People who call themselves friends to gain power within the Agency, that goes with the territory. But true friends, like you? They're few and far between and that's why I'll use whatever influence I have to get you the fresh start you deserve."

I studied Tom then and it was like a time machine had catapulted me back to my high school days. Suddenly, his prematurely white hair was black again; his custom-tailored Brooks Brothers' suit was a blue blazer with the St. Damian's Prep insignia embossed on the front left pocket; his angular, suntanned face became round and ruddy with eyes twinkling solicitously, near-impossible to resist.

So, yes, I embraced him. I embraced his success, his near-fanatical Catholicism, his position at the Agency—and all that went with it— his wife, Annie, his three kids, even their German Shepherd show dogs, Blondi and Prinz.

"Okay, Tom, let's do like you say. I'll do my damnedest to convince Havana Spice and her Neanderthal boyfriend it's in their best interest to move on to another mark, hopefully some crooked politician and not a prince of a guy like you, fair enough?"

"That's great, Jack, so long as you know how indebted I am to you for helping," he pledged breaking loose from me, "but now I'm headed to the Hill for a *tet-a-tet* with Bob Mathers, Chair of the Foreign Affairs Committee."

"I know Mathers," I noted as much to myself as to him. "He was a business associate of my father-in-law, Barton Crowley. Made a killing steering defense contracts to his pals at Becton Dickenson during the Gulf War."

Dougherty slipped into an overcoat, "Don't believe everything you see on FOX News," he cautioned, stepping into the corridor. "And, Jack," he added, his smiling face peeking back through the half-closed door, "only suckers pay taxes."

"Thanks, Tom," I answered with no small degree of irony, but it was too late, he'd already disappeared, the door having closed behind him, my eyes and my brain now drawn in equal measures to the desktop where the death threat lay face down across the room from me.

Like the pull of an ocean tide, the note tugged on the steel hook of obsession planted in my brain so that I followed as much as walked to the desk. There I sat pushing the white envelope to one side as I removed a magnifying glass, tweezers, and plastic baggy from its upper drawer placing them beside the note and my Dell XPS laptop.

Careful not to disturb existing fingerprints, I used tweezers to unfold the 5″ × 7″ scrap of paper spreading it out on the desktop. The words, bold and in caps, typed on customized lavender paper, had been laser printed, I surmised, based on the sharpness around the edges. The paper, itself, was unique not only in color but in the weight of its bond which a good guess would put at 24 pound.

More than any of that, it was the watermark that shown through the paper like a penumbra that most intrigued me, but try as I might—held up to the light, turned at angles, even inverted in a mirror—could not identify. Oval at top and flat at bottom, about 1.5″ in length and one-third of that in diameter, there was a reddish-brown tint to it that, once magnified, revealed two tiny black eyes with .5" antennas protruding above them!

I flicked on the laptop and began searching the internet for purveyors of custom stationery in the D.C. area A to Z: Dempsey & Carroll, who famously supplied writing materials for presidents Reagan to Obama; Kinokumiya, who specialized in Yuzen patterns from Japan; Il Papiro, Smythson, Strathmore, there were dozens in the District and hundreds, perhaps thousands, worldwide capable of customizing stationery of this type. But the watermark, itself, intertwined into the paper's cotton fiber like a DNA imprint, pointed to something as blatant as it was chilling. This image, once identified, seemed to me a billboard written in neon or an internet pop-up flashing on a computer screen, 'Here I am, Jack, you stupid motherfucker! See if you can catch me!'

It was at that moment that the telephone in the next

room began to ring. That was not common for me at the hotel, I thought, noticing that it was 7 p.m. Ten years ago as a Wall Street up-and-comer calls came to all places and at all hours, but not lately. At the moment, however, what impressed me most was my quiet expectation that the phone was going to ring the very second the killer's message registered clear to me. Then, it did.

"Madson," I answered grabbing the phone.

"Jack Madson, the private investigator?" the woman's voice came back in a throaty whisper.

"None other, who is this?"

There was a long silence, then, "It's me, Havana. I had your card and you're the only one I could think to…"

"What is it? Are you in some kind of trouble?"

"They're going to kill me, Mr. Madson."

"Who?" I stumbled. "Who is it that's trying to kill you?"

" 'Them,' *they* are. At first I thought they were going to use Ronnie, but even he's nervous as a cat, so now I don't know who'll do it. I just know that I'm a dead girl if I hang around here much longer."

"Call the police."

"I can't do that."

"Call 911."

"No, I can't."

"Do it!"

"You don't understand. They are the police. They are the cops, and the judges, and the juries. They're everything, can't you see that? No, Jack, I need you! You're the only one innocent enough to help, to have a chance…*Oh, Dios mio!*" she began sobbing, desperate and scared. "*Eleven80, penthouse, please hurry!!*" Havana uttered a millisecond before the line went dead.

Chapter Eighteen

*H*ere *was* a *fix to be in!* I calculated, slamming the phone down, already decided to leave for New York. *But how?* Near anyone would call the cops, but 'near everyone' didn't know what I did about Dougherty and the FBI, Woods at Homeland, and Havana Spice, caught between warring intelligence agencies and an underground empire whose global influence I'd already calculated, could leave them inextricably linked. And like Havana, I now found myself walking that same alley between two theaters, those separate playhouses of cynicism and paranoia, finally deciding to give Johnnie Giambi a call.

"Johnnie?"

"Yeah, Jackie, it's me."

"I need a favor," I began before asking him to run interference for me at Havana's place since the ride — even in a Porsche doing ninety—would take no less than four hours.

"No problemo," Lights Out was quick to respond and we agreed to meet, him first, and me, fast as my car would get me there.

I threw socks, underwear, toothbrush, script container, a plastic baggy containing the death threat, and my Colt 45 into a gym bag, then made my way to the Porsche and New York's West Side where Havana Spice resided.

It was after midnight by the time I pulled up to the thirty-five story art deco hotel reborn "Eleven80," a luxury high-rise on West 34th near Penn Station. The streets were deserted with a cold December drizzle falling from a shroud of clouds that enveloped the tri-state area as I parked in front of the building that rose up before me somber as a megalith. Built in the 1930s by real estate mogul Abraham Lefcourt, it featured terra cotta panels and copper spandrels decorated with geometric floral motifs and must have been something special back in the day, until it went into foreclosure and Lefcourt departed this world from out of a sixteenth floor window.

The lobby, too, seemed weirdly surreal like Lefcourt had been taking LSD with his coffee during the days leading up to its design. Avant-garde, to be sure, but straight out of *The Shining*, I was thinking as I drifted through the high-ceiling lobby, now empty as a mausoleum, sans doorman, security guards, or any living soul.

I marveled at its emptiness then, standing solitary as the lone survivor of a cataclysm, afraid of what awaited me, wondering why I was still alive. Wide-eyed and unsettled, I boarded one of the five elevators that stood doors open to the left and right of me. Up the first set of ten floors, then on to the second, and third, the lift ascending past 320 luxury condos, still higher to the one marked 'penthouse,' the place where Havana Spice lay her head each night. And during those moments I cannot adequately describe the sense of foreboding I felt. 'Dread,' there was a word. Or 'burdened,' like a hundred pound weight was laid upon my chest causing me to breathe differently, short and tight, as if the air was thinner by half, and my lungs shrunken to one-quarter the size they had been. 'Sick,' was another word that might begin to describe the sense of gloom I was feeling. Or 'perversion,' or perhaps, to use a single word that captured all of these sensations, 'EVIL.' The stomach-churning realization that had some primeval filament buried deep in my brain crying out, *"Better to deaden your senses now, Bucko, 'cause it's going to be one helluva ride!"*

And, I assure you, these warnings were not misplaced, I understood, leaving behind the elevator's sodden basement environs smoldering with the smell of rats and roaches for Lencourt's highest level marked by the fetid stink of, *was it fire?* And so I continued my sojourn through the last of Eleven80's deserted corridors. Door upon closed door, I marched forward, a lone troop on a long patrol, until finally I came upon the entrance to the place that the long-forgotten synapse in my head had warned me about.

The door to Havana's penthouse suite was agape and just then I wondered, 'Is it possible? Is someone speaking to me?' because I swear I heard a voice, or was it simply a powerful thought throbbing like a twitching vein at my temple, inviting me to make my way forward. *"Come inside and join us,"* the Beast beckoned, a monster to be sure with coiled tail and cloven hoof. *"You know this is where you belong, don't you?"*

And with that offer, I entered with marked trepidation, I can tell you, because what my mind did not want to absorb, my eyes did. Blood intertwined with ripped white chunks of spongy tissue, and hair—long and blonde—still shiny wet, gleaming red on the floor and rugs and furnishings. And the smell! From musty and dank, now evolved to acidic and burnt, tremendous wafts of scorched meat, unlike anything I'd ever put a nostril to, snaking their way up into my brain. Tracks, also. Of the kind sneakers might leave behind—Nike or Reebok—only these were tracks imprinted on the foyer's bone-white tile in bright crimson blood, and plenty of it. Smoke, too. Billows, floating in the air around me, I took note, as I trudged forward toward the living room where through sliding Pella doors I could see there was a private terrace beyond which a storm had begun to brew. And there were sounds as well. Very loud. Blaring, in fact. Could it be the movie *It's a Wonderful Life* echoing from the speakers of a second plasma tv in another room? Irony heaped upon irony, the sights, and smells, and sounds had me spinning in a vortex so that as I drew my Remington Colt and called out, *"Johnnie? Johnnie, are you here?"* I felt as if my brain had become a giant Cray computer barreling down some super-highway on my way to a smoking ditch of sensory overload.

George Bailey: What is it you want, Mary? You want the moon? Just say the word and I'll throw a lasso around it and pull it down. Hey. That's a pretty good idea. I'll give you the moon, Mary."

Mary: I'll take it. Then what?

George Bailey: Well, then you can swallow it, and it'll dissolve ... and the moon beams would shoot out of your fingers and your toes and the ends of your hair...

With no response, *no sound*, except the other-worldly voices of James Stewart and Donna Reed one room removed, I turned to my right toward the kitchen peering over the granite-topped island. I paused at the sound of faint gurgling noises equal to the babble of myriad infinitesimal creatures when suddenly I felt the vice-like clutch of a hand on my calf that turned my heart to a lead ball shot up into my throat until I was near gagging on it. Instinctively, my body swung around, my hand and the gun it held trained downward, when my eyes fell upon a naked woman crawling on her belly in a pool of blood, face and body charred to a crisp, throat slit ear-to-ear.

"Help me," she mouthed, sounds and not words passing from scorched lips. *"Please help me."*

So stunned I could not react with any emotion but shock, I lurched a half-step back before having the presence of mind to raise my gun toward the ceiling at the final moment before shooting, then knelt down beside her my pant legs soaking in blood.

"Amber, who did this to you? Who..." I could not finish the sentence but simply stared, eyes wide with horror, into hers.

"Help me," she repeated, then noticing the gun I wielded tried to reach for it, but sensing what she was up to I pulled away. *"Shoot me, Jack. Please shoot me,"* were the last words Amber Starr uttered before collapsing in a heap onto the floor.

Rising up from my knees, Amber's warm blood soaking through my Aididas and jeans to my feet, ankles, and calves, I leveled the Colt out in front of me and continued my gruesome march toward the voices blaring from the television set three rooms away. My senses were acute beyond anything I'd ever experienced—auditory, visual, and olfactory—I realized immediately as I plodded forward, the irony of the horrific murder scene not lost

on me as I sought to absorb every nuance—from blood,
to corpse, to the pungent smell of burnt flesh, now
overwhelming—all starkly juxtaposed to the Hollywood
dialogue coming at me like canon balls from out of
Havana's bedroom.

George Bailey: I know one way you can help me. You
don't happen to have 8,000 bucks on you?
Clarence: No, we don't use money in Heaven.
George Bailey: Well, it comes in real handy down here,
bud!

Step by cautious step, one foot in front of the other, I
told myself attempting to marshal the scattered troops of my
resolve into something that approximated courage. For all
I knew, Lights Out, scheduled to arrive hours before, had
met the same monstrous fate as Amber, "Johnnie! Johnnie,
you in there?" I shouted-out, but there was no response
just the disembodied voices spit out from the television:
actors playing-out some second-rate imitation of reality as
if to defile any semblance of meaning it might have held,
turning all that was sacred inside out, into evil, yes, but evil
trivialized, and human existence into a meandering farce.

"Johnnie!" I screamed-out again, tightening my grip on
the gun held out from braced arms, wondering if the killer
was still in Havana's bedroom lying in wait for me. Had I
surprised him? Had I caught him in the act and was he now
hiding behind the next door, gun drawn, or tucked away
behind a shower curtain in the master bedroom? Each of
these possibilities shot like tracers through my brain while,
alert as a terrier, I covered the twenty feet from kitchen to
the corridor leading to Havana's boudoir.

The Remington's blue-steel handle felt like it was

melting in my hands, sweat trickled down my sides and I had to sweep away a skein of perspiration cascading down my forehead and into my eyes when suddenly there came a crash of thunder equal to the explosion of a volcano blowing its caldera. The massive building shook at its foundation! I could feel its power through the soles of my shoes, but it was my eyes that reacted first because above me was a skylight through which the flash of lightning bolted causing me to jerk the gun upward so that I very nearly emptied all six rounds into it! But I didn't, and drawing deep from the foul air around me, continued to follow the swathes of blood left behind by Amber as she dragged herself from the room where she'd been slaughtered.

Beyond a walk-in closet, crammed with Cavalli coats and Gucci leather jackets, I crept; then on to a utility closet, untouched it seemed; and into the guest bedroom, where the over-sized bed was still made-up, all the while the voices, *those voices,* calling-out into the vacuum, their creepy dissonance jabbing at me like a sadistic kid poking a stick into the maw of a caged cougar.

George Bailey: {praying} Clarence! Help me, Clarence! Get me back, I don't care what happens to me! Get me back to my wife and kids! Help me Clarence, please! Please! I wanna live again. *Please, God, let me live again!*

Then finally, like a mountain climber planted at the edge of the universe, I stood at the doorway where the blood and voices had led me. My eyes traveled from the plasma television where Stewart, Reed and Barrymore acted-out their roles staring strangely at me from the screen, then on to the smoldering corpse that lay at the foot of Havana's bed. Once tall and strapping, the body was curled up into a black and oozing lump stark as the carcass of some species of sea creature drawn from its grotto now washed up onto the shore.

It was Reicher. Throat slit in the same surgical manner as Amber's, naked with severed penis and testicles crammed into his mouth, charred torso and limbs still steaming from the flames that had incinerated him, eyes wide open, not five feet from me, staring out in terror from what was left of his face.

I don't know how much time passed while I stood gazing piteously at Reicher's ravaged body. In truth, I'd never seen a man so thoroughly destroyed. This was not war, I was thinking. This was not the aftermath of an IED detonating amidst a crowd of civilians in Fallujah or a drone attack on an Al Qaeda stronghold in the mountains of Pakistan. No, *this* atrocity—a man and woman mutilated beyond recognition then set ablaze—had happened here, with me as its witness, in a New York City luxury high rise!

And it was with these thoughts swirling like eddies through my mind that the macabre spell the grisly murders had cast over me was broken by a rustling sound that came from the bathroom set back and to my right.

My eyes shifted immediately from Reicher's body as I turned, gun in hand, and began edging toward the unmistakable sound of someone stirring in the room adjacent. Could it be Johnnie Giambi, I wondered, too wooden to call out his name, too afraid that if it was Lights Out, he'd be in no better shape than Reicher or Amber, and that if it was the killer, any noise—even the sound of my breathing or rubber soles of my Aididas on the carpet—might give him warning enough to brandish a gun or knife and butcher me as he had the others!

It took me fewer than a dozen steps to find my way to the entrance of the super-sized bathroom where I stood eyes combing the elongated mirror set along the marble-top cabinet and double sink, then the walk-in shower, the toilet and bidet, and finally upward to the skylight through which I could see storm clouds scudding past overhead until, again, my concentration was shattered by a second trundling noise emanating from the cabinet beneath the sink, not three steps away.

I pointed the Colt .45 squarely at it and kicked the doors with my right foot, "Come out of there, *now!* I've got a gun!" I warned.

Then, I watched, finger twitching on the gun's blue-steel trigger, as the cabinet doors creaked open and the dark curly head of a young boy peeked out from inside.

"*Savito!*" I gasped, agog with amazement, as he crawled out from behind the nest of pipes and plumbing, then stood before me clutching an Apple iPad to his chest much as a young girl might hold onto a rag doll.

"*Savito, who did this? Who hurt these people?*" I pled, lowering the gun, moving closer to him.

"It was the police," he muttered looking down at his sneakers, body quaking, "the Special Police. They were looking for something. I think it was this," he said, eyes shifting to the iPad, "but I hid, and they did not find me."

I dropped to my knees to comfort him but such was the malevolence that permeated the place that even this simple act of kindness could not stand as I heard a voice call-out from the foyer, "Jack? Jackie, where are you?"

I looked to the boy—straight into his ardent brown

eyes to reassure him—but if they reciprocated at all, it was to tell me that he'd seen a lot in his nine years of existence and this was not over. 'What happened here is not the beginning of the end,' his eyes told me. 'What happened here is not even the end of the beginning!' Then, as I stood to make my way back to the penthouse entrance, Savito's brown eyes flashed amber, he pushed me aside, and sprinting fast as his legs would carry him, brushed past the man who stood at the doorway, and into the corridor.

"Savito, come back!" I shouted, lumbering after him until, stopped in my tracks, my eyes fell on Johnnie "Lights Out" Giambi standing in the foyer. "Johnnie! Thank God you're alive!" I roared rushing across the room to embrace him.

Nonplussed, the one-eyed, ex-MMA-contender surveyed the carnage, chin firmly planted on my shoulder, "Who was that kid? What the fuck happened here?" he asked, bewildered.

"Never mind that, you're alive, that's the main thing!" I gushed, staring into his face, grinning happily, as I held him at arm's length.

"Yeah me, but what about her? Jesus Christ, Jackie, this place looks like it was fucking napalmed!"

Lights Out broke away from me, then like a ghost amongst ghosts drifted into the living room and adjacent kitchen where Amber's corpse lay looking as grotesque as she was dead.

"My car broke down goin' over the bridge," he began rambling, and it was as if the murders had left a vibration in the air screaming out to be recognized and he was absorbing those messages through the pores of his skin.

"Ya know it's a clinker and I'm sorry I was fucking late but, Jackie, *this?*"

"Look," I said stepping forward and pinning him at the shoulders, "You were never here, you got that? I'm in the shit and will have to call the cops, but there's no reason for you to get involved. So go now, Johnnie! Get your ass out of here and pretend none of this ever happened, you got that?"

"What about you, Jackie? Ain't the cops gonna blame you for all a this?"

"No," I shot back, shaking my head with certainty. "I came here because Havana Spice called me! There'll be phone records. Besides, I've got Dougherty who'll corroborate the fact I was here on assignment. No, there's nothing here to connect me with this abomination, *or you,* at least not yet. So go on! Get the hell out of here now while I call NYPD Homicide!"

Chapter Nineteen

T he air in what the media would later christen the
"Chelsea Death House" felt scorched as I returned
to Havana's bedroom where Reicher's body lay
sprawled in a heap. The movie dialogue spewing from
the tv to drown the victim's anguished cries jarred me
back to myself long enough to recognize that this room
existed — *it actually existed!* I was not alone in some theater
of my mind, and in the next moment I was full of panic
and ready to flee; chilled in my mind, chilled in my heart.

I knew I had to call the police and since I was in the
NYPD's13th precinct immediately thought of "Big O"
Ewing who, believing I was CIA, would at least hear me out
before jumping to conclusions about my involvement with
the murders. *But not just yet,* I thought, noticing the tip
of Reicher's charred leather wallet protruding from what
was left of his back jeans' pocket. *No, whoever did this was
influential enough to have cleared the hotel, but that wouldn't
last forever so if I was going to do any investigating on my own,
it was now or never!*

I approached the melted mass of flesh and bone that
was once Ronnie Reicher, then reached for the wallet
lifting it from his pocket with a thumb and forefinger.
Odd, but while its exterior was eaten away at the edges,
the documents inside remained undamaged: a New York

drivers' license, credit cards, $300 in cash, and photo of Havana Spice. Understanding that time was scarce, I took a moment to study the photo all the same. If I had to guess it was taken recently and depicted Havana, not as her porn-freak fans would have her, but as I saw her. Dressed in a white peasant blouse with plain black skirt, flesh-color stockings and flats, Havana appeared more university student than porn star. 'Lovely beyond measure' was the phrase that passed through my mind then, noticing her perfect white teeth accentuated by tanned skin, shoulder-length black hair, dazzling eyes and smile, all of which meshed to give one the impression of, what was the word? The word was 'soul,' I decided. Havana possessed a *soulful* quality that travelled beyond a body that any man would agree was created for sultry summer nights languishing in all acts carnal. It was with that filament of desire ignited that I plunged an index finger into the wallet's inside pocket and fished-out a glassine envelope filled with the whitest powder I'd ever seen. *Heroin*, I recognized after sampling it, finger to tongue. *Pure*, I understood then, *extremely pure.*

I wiped the wallet clean of prints with my shirttail, returned it to Reicher's pocket, then made my way toward a solitary suitcase set beneath the tv, still belching its anthems, across the room from Havana's four-poster bed. It was unlocked and I opened it unsurprised to find what looked like a kilo of the same Afghan White Reicher carried on him. Significantly, the package was unstamped, signaling this was ultra high quality, yet to be cut, straight from an international broker.

I wiped the suitcase's surface clean and trundled to a nearby chiffonier where Havana kept clothes, then on to a zebrawood desk on top of which lay an assortment of bills—Geico to Verizon—along with five framed photographs: one of Havana as an adolescent after she'd arrived in the States dressed in Catholic school uniform; two publicity photos; and the final two of her parents, one as a couple, the last with Havana as a child in Cuba posing along with them. I took the photos in hand trying to assess what her background must have been like before immigrating to America coming to the conclusion that hers was a happy upbringing, both parents proud and stolid, with her beaming, pleased as a little princess on her birthday.

Shirttail in hand, I opened the top desk drawer. In it was jewelry ranging in quality from Bulgari to Soho storefront, writing paper and envelopes, but no electronics—not a laptop, iPad, or even a cell phone—causing me to wonder exactly what Savito had made off with while escaping the devastation now lain before me. Standing there, contemplating Havana's most personal belongings with Reicher's body not three feet from me, I felt not unlike an unemployed curator who twice a week stole away to visit the museum's private collection after hours: illicit, estranged, and terrifyingly alone. But it was what I discovered in a side drawer seconds later that changed all of that for me, both as an investigator and as a man destined, it seemed, to take an interest in Havana's life. *Letters!* A sheaf of them, handwritten, and bound together with a rubber band. A dozen or more. All personal. Three to her parents, unsent; six from her mother to her; the others to a woman named 'Rosa' who I imagined was her sister. With time running out, I stuffed them unceremoniously into the front of my Jockey's along with the glassine envelope before drifting back into the kitchen where Amber's corpse resided, her body transfixed in *rigor mortis* still staring up into the air pleadingly as if trying to escape the final moments of her hideous death.

Suddenly enervated, with perspiration soaking through my Hoya's sweatshirt, I plucked Ewing's card from my billfold and called him on his cell. For good or ill, the 'Big O' was alone in his car a few blocks away.

"O," I began explaining, ardent as I knew how, "there're two dead bodies here with me at the Eleven80 penthouse, neither in very good shape. Come alone, no siren, and I'll tell you everything I know, Uniforms to follow, you okay with that?"

"No," he grunted, "but I'll do what I can since with you guys involved I know this is already headed off-line."

"Thanks," I told him, but it was too late, he'd already cut the connection and was on his way.

I was sitting on Havana's Modani divan sipping Taliskers' neat from a snifter when Ewing showed up at the door. He reconnoitered the carnage and sniffed at the air, heavy with the stench of burnt flesh, like a terrier not yet engaged in the hunt.

"Nice work, Madson, you and what other psycho did this?" he inquired, eyes narrowing as he drew a Glock 17 from his shoulder holster and pointed it at me.

"I called you, Lieutenant, remember? Besides," I reasoned, taking a careful swallow from my glass, "Easy Pass records will show the time I left D.C. and when I arrived here which had to be a good thirty minutes after this bloodbath concluded. I'd suggest you check hotel cameras, but I'm betting the film's missing and the main recorder destroyed. These guys were pros sent by people accustomed to black ops, and 'wet jobs,' when they need them. No," I ventured, eyes fixed on the slaughter around me, "you won't find any evidence here, Lieutenant. Appearances to the contrary, this place has been sanitized."

Ewing scanned the penthouse suite, mind filing through what was to come: Uniforms sealing hotel entrances and exits, then canvassing the neighborhood for witnesses; homicide detectives interviewing hotel patrons, cab companies and 24 hour parking garages, then confiscating traffic cam and closed-circuit surveillance footage from within the hotel; crime scene technicians photographing bodies, lab personnel scraping beneath the victims' fingernails for skin and other DNA evidence left behind by the killer(s) during the struggle that may have ensued. But in the end, there'd be nothing. The bloody footprints in the foyer, they'd discover, were left by an unidentified boy's Nike sneakers, the traffic cams would show a black van with untraceable plates, the hotel recorder would be devoid of tape, and the DNA samples extracted would be those of the murder victims' exclusively.

Ewing's machinations came to a sudden halt. His head craned around to me and he looked vaguely defeated as if his soul had just suffered a penetration that released some not insignificant percentage of what was essential to his existence into the air. He lowered the Glock, his facial expression transformed during that instant from utter hopelessness to the fatalistic resolve of an overmatched athlete.

"All right, Madson, maybe you didn't do it. Maybe you're just some hard luck motherfucker stumbled into this nightmare, but whatever it is you have to say, say it now, before Homicide starts swarming every inch of this hell hole."

"It's this, Owen," I answered taking down the last of my Taliskers' and depositing the snifter on the coffee table in front of me, "Havana Spice called me in D.C. six hours ago. She claimed her life was in danger, begged me to come help her, said I was the only one she could trust."

"Trust with what?"

"I don't know now, but will soon. Havana fled the scene, Owen. I'll tell your people everything I saw here tonight, just don't lock me up now because if anyone can get to the bottom of this, it's a freelancer like me, not NYPD. See, in my opinion, it's a government agency that's behind this, but you know that, don't you? You've seen people eliminated, whether by gangs, or the mob, or even one of our own, haven't you, Owen?"

Ewing strode quietly toward Amber's body as I followed behind through the hallway and into Havana's bedroom. He studied Reicher's corpse sprawled on the floor, then stared out the patio window overlooking the Hudson River.

"I've been a homicide detective twelve years since retiring from professional football," he confessed. "During that time, I've seen people do things I never imagined one human being could do to another. Seen a man high on bath salts eat the face off his best friend; a guy so crazy-jealous he put his girlfriend in a room full of Dobermans, cut open her abdomen with a straight-razor, and let them tear her to pieces while he watch sipping latte in a lounge chair. But this?" He turned to me. "I saw the photos of that kid's head they found in your car last week: skinned, teeth pulled, nose, ears, lips and tongue cut out. Yeah, I've seen government work before, mob work, too, but this? Look at

my arm, man! See that gooseflesh?" he asked rolling the
sleeve of his white shirt. "Know why that is? It's this room,
Madson, and don't tell me you don't feel it, too."

"I know," I admitted tersely.

"I'm not ashamed about it, neither. Hell, I'm a football
player! Best running back Notre Dame's seen in the last
twenty years! And a family man! I've got a great wife and
two beautiful daughters! But one thing I'll tell you, Big
O, he's determined if he's anything, and I swear on my
Mamma's grave, I won't rest until I hunt down whatever
sick motherfucker's responsible for this, you believe that,
don't you, Madson?"

"Yes," I answered solemnly. "I'd expect nothing less
from a man like you, Owen."

The big man looked down at Reicher's body, nudging
it with the tip of his size 14 shoe, "Acetylene torch?" I
nodded. "Must have taken hours to do them like this," he
speculated, "so maybe it's like you say. Maybe you got here
from D.C. after all of this went down, snooped around
awhile, then got hold of me on my cell. If that's the way it
happened, we'll know soon enough," he said, eyes lifting
from Reicher's corpse and leveling with mine. "But before
all hell breaks loose, let me tell you something I think
you have a right to know. That kid's head they found in
your trunk? It wasn't the first. There've been others here
in New York, Connecticut, and Jersey, one far north as
Massachusetts, going back five years that we know of. It
may even be global, part of an international child porn
ring. That's why Woods from Homeland's involved; same
with your buddy Dougherty at the Agency."

"And the skulls, same MO, all of them?"

"That's what I hear. You were living in Oregon when

those homicides went down. That's why they released you. So whatever else you are, no one believes you're the killer. I thought you should know that."

Big O studied the expression on my face, the resonance of shock still vibrating within me, then chuckled sardonically, "It's a Wonderful Life, eh Madson?" he asked glancing up to the plasma tv, dialogue still blaring. "Well, better call Captain Davis, prep him on the shit storm to come," he sighed taking a Motorola handheld from his belt. "Connie, I've got a 512 here at the Eleven80. Send CSU and everyone available from DB. Also, a team of paramedics to make the pronouncement and a dozen Uniforms to seal the building, more if you have 'em. Might as well have the ME come along, too. Yeah, that's right, and ask Captian to give me a call on my cell before the media gets hold of this, over."

Big O took a step in my direction, his huge frame looming over me, "You packing, Madson?"

"Yeah," I answered.

"Let me have the gun before they find it and you have to call Assistant Director Dougherty again. I'll return it once you've been questioned and your statement's on record."

"Thanks, O," I said, staring into his fluid brown eyes, big as basketballs, as I turned my piece over to him. "Everyone always said you were a stand up guy."

"Yeah, right," he snorted. "Now get the hell out of here before the cops show up. I suppose I can trust you to drive that Porsche of yours five blocks without getting arrested?"

"Sure thing," I agreed, hustling passed him and out the door to Havana's penthouse, the sounds of oncoming sirens howling like the cries of mangled spirits cutting through the December night rain.

Chapter Twenty

After Ewing and the detectives at the 13th Precinct got what they wanted out of me, I made a B-line back to the Elysee where I peeled off my clothes and ran for the shower. Never had water cascading over my naked body felt so cathartic. It was like I was washing off every molecule of torched flesh that, from corpse to air, had settled onto me and the clothes I was wearing.

Afterward, I sat in a robe at my desk where like the Four Horsemen of the Apocalypse the death threat, Dougherty's cash, the glassine envelope, and Havana's letters, beckoned. Through the din of emotions my mind wandered—*rage*, at the torture-murders; *frustration*, at not being able to prevent them; and *paranoia*, about Havana's wellbeing—as I traced my current situation back to strategize a path forward.

THIS IS WHAT I KNEW: six mornings ago (was it six?) I awoke at the Georgetown Inn after having sex with a dancer named Amber Starr devoid of memory for the night before. Moments later, I stumbled out to my Mustang where in the trunk I discovered the decapitated head of what turned out to be an Asian boy shot full of embalming chemicals.

That evening I'm contacted by Tom Dougherty, former high school classmate, now Assistant Director FBI, who I hadn't heard from in a dozen years, asking me to help extricate him from a blackmail scenario initiated by an illicit affair he is having with Havana Spice. Spice, who's transformed herself from Catholic school girl to porn queen, moonlights as a sometimes call girl at the Casanova, an underground sex club in Manhattan, under the watchful eye of Hell's Angel, Ronnie Reicher. While at the Casanova, I encounter Amber, Reicher, and Havana engaged in a *manage a trios* after which I'm injected with enough heroin to OD an elephant, but survive to return to Georgetown where I receive a call from Spice begging me to return to New York to help save her from someone as yet unidentified.

Upon arrival at Havana's penthouse, I discover the mutilated bodies of Reicher and Starr, but in a fashion as staged as it was artificial: no security, not even a doorman; hotel cameras rendered inoperative; no evidence left behind, despite a plethora of blood and body parts; and no witnesses, except me, who discovers the bodies, a kilo of 100% pure Afghan White, and Havana's son Savito hiding from what he describes as the "Special Police," before fleeing the murder scene clutching an iPad to his chest!

LINKS! What were the common threads to be found amidst this swamp of sordid facts and information? I anguished, the bound sheaf of Havana's letters staring back at me like the ghost of Hamlet's father. *First,* Amber, Reicher, and Havana knew one another (intimately, as I discovered!) so my tryst with Amber that set-off the chain of events leading to my discovery of the boy's head seemed no small coincidence. *Second,* Dougherty's call, immediately following, and after years of absence from my life, may well have been connected to that grim find and, therefore, linked to both Amber and the head. *Third,* and most revealing: on the same night that Dougherty hired me to persuade Spice to back off blackmailing him, Special Agent Don Woods was in the midst of investigating him for reasons as yet unknown to me.

THE COMMON LINK was Tom Dougherty, I reasoned. *Dougherty* had a relationship with Havana and me; *Havana* had a relationship with Amber and Reicher; *I* had a relationship with Amber and Reicher: a tight little coterie of individuals bound together by sex, heroin, blackmail, and murder!

Still, hovering above it all was something larger than anything I could hope to fathom. Like bees in a hive, each of us was playing-out our roles in the pecking order, *but if we were the drones, who was the keeper of the hive?* I doubted it was Dougherty, racked with guilt and paranoid about losing his family, job, and status within the Catholic Church. Certainly, it wasn't Amber or Reicher, both dead. So, of the players visible to me, either Woods, Havana, or both, were more likely to have an understanding of the forces at work behind these murders than any theory I could possibly cobble together on my own.

Then, clinical as an entomologist, my eyes turned to each of the Four Horsemen lain before me skewering each like insects on a pin and holding them up for examination: the cash bulging from out of its envelope, the death threat silent as a tombstone, the heroin seductive as a naked woman spread-eagle before me, but it was the letters I took into my hands to study.

Fascinating beyond anything I'd imagined, even a cursory look told volumes about Havana Spice—who she was, who she pretended to be, and the grim travail that had become her life since arriving in the States. Understanding the fractured mirror that her existence had devolved into since then, I separated the letters into three categories: *Letters to her mother* based on the woman she pretended to be; *letters to Rosa,* her sister also living in Cuba, confessing the life she was, in fact, living; and *letters from her mother to her* that took me beyond the curtain to uncover Noemi Machado, the young woman hidden behind the story line of both.

What follows are excerpts from a "Category 1" letter, handwritten in Spanish on September 15th, beginning with the salutation *Mi Queridisma Madre,* "My Dearest Mommy":

My Dearest Mommy,

I know how sad you get since Popi died so I decided to write you a letter since soon it will be your Birthday. Also, you are always asking about Savito, so I am including photos of him. Oh dios mio!! How he is growing!! Every night I try to teach him Spanish, but he is as stubborn as he is handsome. All he wants to do is play computer games!! Still, I can't complain mi pequeno hombre is an excellent student, the brightest in his class!

Mommy, you will be happy to know how well my acting career in Hollywood USA is doing... Yesterday I had lunch with Mr. Brad Pitt, a famous movie star, and his wife Angelina Jolie, who keeps her last name for show business reasons. B.P. is as handsome in person as he is in the movies, but his wife is all skin and bones! My agent arranged this lunch so that photographs could be taken of me with a 'cieton alguien' for People, a magazine sold in practically every grocery store ... But what makes me most happy is the man who accompanied me to that lunch. His name is Ramon and, Mommy, I think I may be falling in love with him!

Ramon is an important business executive who I think shares the same feelings for me, so that perhaps one day he will ask 'la pregunta grande' to which I will answer "Si!! Si!!" Would you someday like little ones running around your house again?? Can you picture me surrounded by screaming muchachos, bent over a hot stove cooking arroz con pollo? Now, I know you are laughing—Ha! Ha!!—but who knows since love is love and, Dios quiere, anything is possible in the USA!!

I love you, Mommy, and miss you soooo much!! Please have the happiest Birthday ever, mi amora, and just to be sure I have wired $1000 through Western Union to help make it so!!

Tu hija amorosa,

Noemi

I stared long and hard at those letters, each stacked atop the other, thinking that it wasn't paper I was looking at but a pile of broken dreams. There was something sad about the fact that Havana wanted so desperately to be someone important, a woman others looked up to, and that somehow she had failed so miserably.

But if I wanted answers to how the hopes and dreams of Noemi Machado had degenerated into the tawdry reality of Havana Spice, I had only to read the letters she'd written to 'Rosa' about her nightmare existence since coming to live with her Uncle Marco in Union City, New Jersey as a child of fourteen.

What follows are excerpts taken from a "Category 2" letter written October 16th by Havana to her sister beginning with the salutation *Queridos, Rosa, mi unica verdadera amiga*, "Dear Rosa, my one true friend."

Dear Rosa, my one true friend,

What I write to you alone about, is the blackest of true things, this life I am living! Each night I pray to escape the giant hands that grab me as if from out of a nightmare, but it is no use! I am ruined forever!! These bastardos that keep me like a prisoner will never let me escape and, if I try, swear vengeance on Savito with acts of violence worse than what they have done to me!! Gang rapes and forced heroin injections were my steady diet from the day I was sold into slavery by that dog, Marcos, and now that I have proven my worth as an 'earner' in pornographic films, it is too late!! My soul is polluted and I despise all that I have become!!

I pray, dearest Rosa, that you will keep my darkest secret from Mommy. No doubt, it would kill her to know the truth and so I am asking you to protect her from all that has happened to her daughter!! Each night when I go to sleep, I pray for God's help that He will forgive me for the sins I have committed. I know that He hears me and would never turn His back on even His most wretched creature but sometimes, Rosa, I wonder if my faith is strong enough to go on!

Most recently, I have sensed a change in my world that would leave my heart frozen with fear if I had any feeling left inside me at all! Il Gigante has been acting strangely and there are odd twists in the things he has requested of me and of Amber, all of it connected to a man I have been having sex with named Dougherty. Since then, it is as if Reicher is being used by this society of 'Special Gentlemen' that I have uncovered, but I don't know what to do about it. Suddenly he, too, is afraid for his life and no better off than me!

And so, dearest Rosa, I confide to you my most guarded secret. To protect myself, I have secured certain information so dangerous that even after I am dead, should they choose to kill me, the entire

world would be shaken by what is revealed. SHHH!! This is my
salvation!! Perhaps I have begun to understand that the path to a
horrible death may also be the way out of Hell for me and my son!!

Vuestra confianza correspondial,

Noemi

So that explained it! Havana, then the Catholic school
girl Noemi, had been abducted by her uncle and sold into
the sex slave market! But could it be? Was there, churning
beneath the Cuban sub-culture of Union City, New
Jersey a human trafficking industry unsuspecting young
immigrants *could* be sold into? Did it exist? Like most, I
had seen documentaries about the global sex trade aired
on programs like *60 Minutes,* but here it was staring me
in the face, its poster child, Noemi Machado, drugged,
serial-raped, terrorized and transformed into porn star-
sometimes call girl, Havana Spice!

And what of her closing remarks, so riddled with
desperation. She'd made reference to a "society", one that
sent a quiver of terror down the spines of even Reicher
and his gang of crank-head bikers. Could it be this society,
whose existence she'd confided to Rosa, loomed over all of
what had happened since I awoke that fateful December
morning with Amber Starr's voluptuous lips caressing my
cock?

So far as I could tell, I speculated, turning my attention
to the last stack of letters, the only two people who could
answer that question were Woods, headlong into his
investigation of Dougherty, and Havana, herself!

I quote now from a "Category 3" letter penned on
November 6th by Havana's mother, Esperanza, to her

daughter, which begins with the salutation, *Mi Angel de Amor, Noemi,* "My Loving Angel, Noemi":

My Loving Angel, Noemi,

My heart flutters like a leaf in the wind each time I see a photograph of "my little man," Savito. He is so handsome and from early photographs of your father I can tell you he looks like Popi's brother or his son! Of course, it is good that Savito enjoys arithmetic, but there are two lessons he must never neglect, his study of the Bible, and his study of what it means to be a Cuban man! Also, you should try harder to teach him Spanish, which is the language of both great men and lovers!

I try not to boast, Noemi, but you must understand how little new there is to talk about here and so I'm afraid I brag too much about your successes in America. I am certain the other women are tired of hearing about you, but in the end we are old and the eyes of even the least interested glimmer with eagerness to hear about Hollywood and your movie star boyfriends! Oh, mi amor, we are all so proud of you and thankful for the money you send across the ocean to us! I know you are a grown woman now with a son and wonderful life of your own, but I tell you that when I close my eyes and think of you I see my little daughter, tall and skinny with the eyes of an Angel, dressed in a white jumper with no shoes on her feet!

Again, I thank you for the news and photographs. They made my birthday a most joyous one.

Yo teamo mas que amor propio!

Mommy

I returned Havana's letters back onto the desktop and poured three fingers of Glenlivet into a Styrofoam cup mulling them over along with the implications of all that had happened during the past week. If indeed I'd been cast into a maelstrom of shit which was neither comprehensible nor actionable, I reasoned, I could either drop the case altogether, or dive deeper hoping to uncover the truth behind the torture-killings at Eleven80, what the media was calling the "Headless Horseman" murder at Georgetown, and the enigma of Havana Spice.

Stumped intellectually, I downed my scotch and poured another staring at the blank wall in front of me with intensity enough to burn a hole through it, then asked the most profound question I knew: *what would Jack Madson do? In your heart of hearts, with the chips down, once the fears and doubts were stripped to the bone, what was left?* I pressed. *Who was Jack Madson and what would he do??* Then, smooth as a six-shooter drawn from a gunslinger's holster, the answer came to me: *Jack Madson would not look on supinely. Jack Madson would not run. Jack Madson would stride down the fucking main street of Dodge, gun in hand—blazing, if need be—find Havana, confront the bad guys, and bring the motherfuckers to justice!*

I took down the second three-fingers of scotch in a gulp, spilled five tabs of Benzedrine into my palm from a script container in the top desk drawer, and downed them with another drink. Three people were already dead, I calculated. As things stood, Havana may have escaped, may have been captured, or murdered like the others—there was no way of knowing. Beyond that there was still my own situation to consider, I ruminated, eyes falling like those of a vulture on the death threat that lay not six inches from my right hand. Who was to say that whatever hit team had taken out the Asian kid, Reicher, and Amber weren't coming after me next? *No,* I decided with the kind of resolve that had launched both the best and worst of my life's endeavors, *if there was anything I'd learned as a fighter, cop, and Wall Street exec, it was that failure to take the initiative put a man on the defensive leaving him dead meat for a strategic opponent. To the contrary, one of the keys to warfare—Sun Tzu to Roberto Duran—was to proactively seize the initial advantage then use it to destroy one's enemy.*

How did this apply to me? From that moment on, I was determined to search-out Havana Spice and bring to justice those responsible for this rash of brutal murders, starting with the last place I'd seen her alive, eight stories below the city streets, at the Casanova Club, in underground New York!

Chapter Twenty-One

D ressed and ready for battle in black shirt and pants, military jacket and boots, I was in no mood to suffer fools lightly. The questioning at 13th Precinct headquarters had left a foul taste in my mouth as I left the Elysée Hotel for Chinatown. And, given the evening's outcome, I can tell you that jagged edge of anger, coupled with the nagging memory of Amber left for dead, made for a combination not unlike *nitro* and *glycerin*.

The arrogance of the cops, disrespectful as street thugs, trying to connect the "Headless Horseman" murder to the killings at Eleven80 was a test of patience Mother Theresa could not have survived, I seethed, taking the Porsche up 34th to Canal Street, but beating the homicidal maniacs responsible for those atrocities to the punch? That was a feeling I could learn to savor, I thought, the metallic piquancy of adrenalin, nerves and balls-out revenge hanging on my tongue with a taste not unlike copper. I was on the prowl, inner demons unleashed, rage given vent in what at moments like this I could nearly believe I valued more than life, itself. Tonight I was going to locate Havana Spice, a woman I'd come to understand had been used as a tool to blackmail and later coerce my long-time pal, Tom Dougherty. In the bump and stir of this Alice-in-Wonderland society of ours, I'd stepped through the looking glass to find blackmail turned to murder and murder turned to depravity, and whether it was self-preservation, or balls-to-the-wall fury that motivated me, I'd made up my mind, *this would not stand!* It was in this state of mind, with a drug store's worth of amphetamines coursing through me, that I parked the Porsche one-half block from the acupuncture clinic that served as a front for the Casanova. Of course, I was packing. Who wouldn't stash a weapon knowing that the Asian beauty, Chok Por, would have her Flying Dragon boyfriend, Jin Lee, standing guard with a small army of security to back him?

A man on a mission, I stomped down Mott Street, then entered the clinic, knowing where each was positioned in advance, fully expecting to get the answers I'd come for. It was Chok Por, decked-out in the same emerald green dress, who first saw me, screaming at decibels usually reserved for Italian operas.

"Get out! Get out! You no welcome here!"

"Shut up, I need to talk to you," I growled, eyes riveted on both her and the Dragon stationed not five feet away.

My eyes and Por's locked momentarily, her furtive glance shifting to Lee, then to a spot midway down the counter invisible to me. In less time than it took her to lift a hand to it, I pulled the Remington and trained it on her.

"Get away from that alarm! Now!" I threatened, edging forward, eyes alternating back-and-forth between her and her punk boyfriend. "I'm not here to hurt anyone. You answer one question and I'll leave like none of this ever happened, *where is Havana Spice?*"

"Look up above you, asshole, security cameras," Lee smirked, toothpick dangling from the corner of his mouth as he began circling around me. "Sixty second from now you be wishing you were never born."

"Yeah, and you'll be dead if you take another step in that direction," I promised, keeping the gun on him as I spoke to Chok Por. "Someone comes from behind that mirrored wall and I blow his fucking brains out, you got that? Now step away from that counter and answer the question, *where is Havana?*"

Jin Lee stood, still smirking. His jet black hair glistened in the glow of the room's fluorescent light, eyes honed on me as Chok Por stepped away from the counter in his direction.

"I don't know where is Havana Spice," she spat back. "She no come work three days now, not since you here last time."

With those words I noticed the sudden flash of a long-blade straight razor as it sprung open, visible in the mirror behind her, and watched Lee take three lightning quick steps toward me. There was no specific thought that crossed my mind but at that moment, with senses acute and muscles taut as piano wire, I felt a kind of snapping sensation. It was the sound of reason giving way to survival instinct, I understood then, pivoting sideways in time to deliver a tremendous kick to the boy's groin before he could slash me! Lee's legs buckled on impact. The straight razor skidded across the floor. Bent over in agony, the kid was an easy mark and with both hands rolled together in a ball I drove my closed fists down onto the back of his head. Down he went, face forward, collapsed but still conscious, writhing in pain as Chok Por made a run for the alarm, a gun she had hidden behind the counter, or both.

"I wouldn't do that if I were you," I cautioned, the rage at everything sordid and corrupt in this fucked up world as evident in the glower in my eye and power of my cadence as the hank of shining black hair I clutched in my fist. Chok Por froze in her tracks. *"Now you're going to tell me what I want to know or I'm going to break a bone for every second you keep me waiting!"*

I threw Lee, head-first, down onto the floor and, as he lay sprawling, stomped down with all 190 pounds of my bulk, mid-leg, shattering his knee cap, and that set him howling.

"Like that?" I baited, watching as her frantic eyes, wide with adrenalin, flew up to the security cameras. "Cameras?" I shot three slugs rapid-fire into their lens blowing them off and into the air like fragments of a plaything, then stomped my right boot down full force onto Lee's face turning his nose, mouth, and forehead into a gushing fountain of crushed tissue, bone, and cartilage. The howling stopped. Jin Lee was unconscious. I dropped to one knee, then with the icy resolve of a clinician opened his mouth and plunged the blue-steel barrel of my Remington .45 into it.

"I just left Havana's apartment. Amber Starr and Ronnie Reicher, both dead. I'm not going to let that happen to her, and will leave your boyfriend's brains splattered on the floor to prove it," I swore, chest heaving, feverish with a flood of onrushing images of Amber's body scorched and blistered, begging for a bullet through the head, and Reicher's smoldering corpse, face burnt beyond recognition, sweeping through my brain like raging waters burst beyond a collapsing dam! I cocked the gun, desperate as I battled the pictures in my head back, deep into the abyss from where they emanated, breaking teeth as I shoved the weapon down Lee's throat. And it was with the 'click' of my gun cocking and the force of its barrel plunged beyond his esophagus that he returned to consciousness, eyes bulging as he stared, panicked, into the face of Death, itself. But like a tsunami's implacable surge, the images raged! Visions like flash bulbs popping of the Asian boy's head, raw and oozing, my Dad lying in his bed, skull blown-off with a shotgun; my father-in-law, Barton Crowley, taunting as he smiled, stark as Satan, himself! And at that moment I knew there was a time bomb ticking inside my head with no more than a fraction of a second before it triggered!

Slowly my eyes rose from the bloody mess that was Lee, met with Chok Por's and stayed there. A feeling of joy rose up in me the way the lyric of a song might remind a man on the edge of insanity that soon he will be insane again but that out there was a world more interesting than his own.

"Okay, okay!! Havana no here!!" Chok Por screamed, terrified now that someone would burst into the room, knowing that I'd kill her, Lee, and anyone else who tried to stop me. "No one know where she go, they take her! They want kill her!! Try Ram Rod near docks where Reicher work as bouncer. Bikers there!! Maybe Havana there, too!!" she cried-out, unable to contain the rush of anxiety that infused her, scrambling toward her teenage boyfriend as I withdrew the gun from his mouth and stood watching her cradle his head in her lap as she whimpered and sobbed, not so tough anymore.

"Is what you told me true?"

"Yes," she moaned, "true, yes, true."

I raised my combat boot menacingly above the fallen Dragon's crotch prepared to stomp his testicles into the concrete as he laid sprawled semi-conscious before me. "You know I'll be back if you're lying," I vowed, a fiendish grin spreading across my face.

"*It true!! You find answers at Ram Rod, I swear Christ!!*" she screeched miserably. "*Now you go!! Go now before cops come and there be more trouble for everyone!!*"

"When they ask, tell them it was Jack Madson, did this, you got that?" I prodded, returning the heel of my boot from Jen Lee's privates back onto the floor.

"*Yes, yes, I tell. Just like you say!!*"

I flipped a business card at Lee's protracted body lying in a pool of blood at my feet, "Here you go, *asshole*," I muttered, knowing full well the Casanova didn't need cops to settle their scores. Places like the Casanova Club had their own "Special Police."

Chapter Twenty-Two

I don't know why I didn't head-out from Chinatown directly to the Ram Rod that night. Maybe I knew there was a 100% chance that a cadre of Special Ops-types were waiting for me and came to the conclusion that I wasn't bullet-proof after all. More likely, the reason was that once I hit Mott Street on my way back to the Porsche, I felt overcome by fatigue. With the effects of the Benzedrine wearing thin, my body began to function the way an old-fashioned clock winds down, so by the time I made it back to my room at the Elysée it was 3 a.m. and I was very near the point of collapse.

With head spinning and a monster migraine on the horizon, I tossed the empty bottle of Glenlivet into the trash, forced to settle for three 4 ounce bottles of Smirnoff gathered from the mini-bar. I took them down in three separate gulps along with two Ambien and had stripped to my Jockeys before noticing the red light on the hotel phone flashing. The message was from Dougherty.

"Hiya, Jack," it went upbeat enough for me to know he was calling from home with Annie within earshot, "I heard you were in town and thought you might like to come out our way for dinner tomorrow night. I've told Annie all about you, kids, too. So how 'bout I send Douglas, our driver, to the hotel to fetch you at, say, six? And, Jack, don't even think about bringing wine or anything like that. Just yourself, Jack. Annie and the kids are keen to meet the old high school chum they've heard so much about!"

I couldn't help but chuckle as I hung up the phone, mind, body, and soul drifting high up into Cloud Ambien trying to remember if Dougherty and I were ever really as close as he seemed to remember. As broke as he was rich, the two of us had masterminded what came to be known as the "ring of thieves" amongst the student body at St. Damian's, him for fun and me for money. During that time, I remembered, a small band of us would pilfer cologne, CDs, cigarettes, and liquor from department stores like Klein's and Bamberger's, and sell them from out of our lockers.

Then, one time after Tom had somehow gotten his hands on a cache of fireworks he asked me to store, someone blew up a toilet bowl in the boys' room causing a flood that set every monk—Headmaster to Dean of Discipline—off like the Hounds of Hell to find the culprit. Now, it wasn't me, that much I knew, but when that night every locker was searched and they found a case of M50s in mine, they had little appetite for explanations and off I went, expelled, no questions asked.

Five days later, after marathon meetings held between Father Mark, the school's Headmaster and my dad, I was allowed to return but not without consequence. For me at home, it was the ass-whipping of my life carried out with a razor strap handed down from my father's father for such occasions; for me at school, it was suspension from all clubs and athletic programs for two years, a punishment that sent me flying into the arms of Golden Gloves boxing.

But to this day, I always wondered who blew up that

toilet bowl in the boys' room at St. Damian's so many years ago. Could it have been Dougherty? I asked myself. This, the last fragment of a thought to cross my mind before I settled onto a cloud high in the sky where I sat on a throne assuming my rightful position in the Kingdom of Oblivion.

The next morning, after a phone call from Tom confirming my visit to his 'European style estate,' I cleaned up best I could foregoing my usual work shirt, jeans, and Adidas for what was left of my Wall Street wardrobe: charcoal gray Cardin slacks, Burberry blazer, and Johnson Murphy loafers. All sickeningly preppie, I conceded, catching a glimpse of myself in the mirror, and emblematic of exactly how far the hands on the clock had moved since my corporate raider days at NuGen. Still, if I was going to be driven in a limo by Douglas, their chauffeur to pay a call on Mr. & Mrs. Thomas W. Dougherty's New Jersey enclave, the least I could do was dress for the occasion!

Yeah, I had the right clothes, I ventured then, but the guy wearing them might need some prep-work, I projected, studying the image of the haggard-looking man before me, wondering how long I could go on like this. Then suddenly, painfully, I was awash in feelings of inadequacy. I felt dirty, tainted by the beating I'd given Jin Lee, the terror I'd inspired in Chok Por, the places I frequented and the man, who like a straight jacket, had somehow fit himself over the person I wanted to be. Now, here I was, on my way to seeing Dougherty with his perky, intelligent wife; and their three kids, bright with faces scrubbed, on their way to success and social prominence. *Jesus Christ! How the fuck had I gotten myself into a predicament like this?* I asked myself, falling back on 'old reliable' when it came to priming for social occasions—and most others—tossing down three Medidate with a shot of Jameson's before taking the hotel elevator down to the lobby where Good Ol' Dougie patiently waited.

Still, it was only on the drive through the Lincoln Tunnel and on into the Morris county countryside that I came to fully appreciate exactly how far up the food chain Dougherty had gravitated since our high school days. Once graduated, I'd gone to Georgetown, never completing my degree, and Tom off to Harvard, then Stanford, where he'd earned his MBA. All of this I knew, but it was while in the limo checking directions to his place on my IPhone that the true meaning of the phrase "European style estate" hit me like a wrecking ball: Tom Dougherty wasn't just successful, *Tom Dougherty and his wife, Annie, were lousy rich.*

If that wasn't apparent from his position at the Agency, it became abundantly clear while browsing the internet where an ad for the estate they'd bought six years earlier from Sotheby's was still posted along with a more recent article in *Architectural Digest* featuring their "ultra-chic" Mendham township mansion.

So, here was a question, I postulated, sitting back in the limo's plush leather seat, how did a guy like Tom Dougherty come to acquire that kind of money? Clearly, it wasn't working at the Agency, notorious for its low pay regardless how high up you'd climbed. Even as kids, though his father was a successful attorney, his family sure as hell wasn't the one-hundred million dollar kind of rich! *So, where did it come from?* The answer came from, of all places, *Architectural Digest* which, true, featured the former Steven's estate they'd purchased, but also Annie Torsten

Dougherty, heiress to the multi-billion-dollar Bradley Torsten publishing empire, along with it.

I closed-out the Sotheby's webpage and looked up from my IPhone as the limo made a wide right turn into a long pebbled drive with entrance marked by a pair of stone lions. Beyond the stone walls, set on the crest of a hill, stood the Stevens' estate about as inconspicuous as a tarantula on a slice of angel food cake.

Chapter
Twenty-Three

Once the limo pulled up the circular driveway and parked in front of Dougherty's mansion, the front door opened and it was like looking at a photograph from Mitt Romney's family album. Two German Shepherds raced out the door, jumping at the backseat window from where I stared out at the Dougherty's: Tom, with his arm around Annie, framed by Matt, on break from Princeton, Elise, their Morristown-Beard high schooler, with Danny, their nine year-old, firmly ensconced in the bosom of Catholicism at St. Joe's, looking playful as an otter.

"Blondi! Prinz!" Tom called-out, "Get over here!" he commanded as, still barking, the Shepherds returned to his side, then sat there tame as the stone lions that marked the entrance to the estate.

By then, Douglas had come around to open the back door and I exited, the family album photo disintegrating as both Tom and Annie made their way toward me.

Annie was pretty, blonde, and perky in that Katie Couric kind of way that left you feeling she could grin her way through a leper colony. Dressed less formally than I'd imagined, and despite the sixty degree weather, she wore a short white skirt, bright blue cotton shirt, sockless, with Reeboks, and seemed more likely on her way to a tennis match than dinner with me.

Tom, for his part, wore a pair of gray slacks, firm at the waist, with a black button-down shirt, as he extended his hand to me, oh-so-Ivy League, "Jack," he greeted in a firm voice, "so glad you could make it," then releasing my hand, turned to Annie, "Jack, this is Annie. Annie, this is Jack," he boomed as she extended her hand breaking into a grin fabulous as a Gold Medal swimmer emerging poolside at the Olympics.

"So, you're the infamous Jack Madson," she proclaimed. "I don't think a day goes by that Tom doesn't have a story to tell about your high school hijinks together!"

"I'm sure those stories have been well-burnished over the years, but it was all fun, and shaped the lives we lead today, I suppose."

"Indeed they did!" she agreed, a burst of energy emanating from her eyes and from that smile, so winning. "Now, come along with me, Mr. Madson," she offered clasping my hand like a school girl as we entered through the front door, already adorned by a huge Christmas wreath with gold crucifix at its center.

"Lovely place," I commented, entering a high-ceiling foyer large enough to produce echoes. "I saw an article about it in *Architectural Digest*. It said you were A-List when it comes to gardening, is it true?"

"Oh, *that!* Yes, we enjoy our gardening, don't we, Tom?" she asked, sidling up to her husband. "But for us it's a metaphor. As *Opus Dei* prelates, the real garden is the world we live in. For Tom and I, the beauty of life is tending to the needs of others in this world which is God's garden here on earth."

I guess I was rendered speechless if not by the candor of the remark, then by the absolute conviction with which she said it, but more by the circular pattern of open wounds I noticed peeking out from above the fringe of her skirt on both thighs.

"You're staring at my legs, Jack, not because you like them but because you see my piercings. You're Catholic, but you've probably never heard of a cilice, this spiked chain I wear around my thighs as mortification; atonement for the sins I've committed, and those I've yet to commit. St. Paul wrote, 'For if you live according to the flesh you will die, but if by the Spirit you put to death the deeds of the body, you will live.' *Opus Dei* Catholics are the real thing, Jack, we live our faith every moment of every day."

Again the silence, a vacuum that Tom surely felt the need to fill, "You'll have to excuse Annie," he explained, flashing a grin, then looking to his wife fondly, "sometimes she forgets that not everyone is a practicing Catholic, even those who've been immersed in the Church's teachings for the better part of their lives."

"Heathens like me, you mean?" I asked, semi-joking. "Well, not to worry, the Sisters of Charity made sure I knew enough Catechism to give the Pope lessons on Catholic doctrine!" I quipped, noticing now that like mendicants gravitating toward an altar, the family photograph had re-configured with Matt and Elise at their side, and Danny in front, giggly, with braces on his teeth, blue eyes mischievous as ever.

"So here's the gang!" Tom announced proudly. "I suppose by now you know them well as anyone!"

"Nice to meet you," I volunteered, shaking hands, stiff and formal, with each as they stepped forward.

Afterward, Tom whisked me down a corridor to a large, wood-paneled room he called his "gentleman's study," complete with wet bar and billiard tables while Annie put the finishing touches on dinner.

We sat across from one another smoking Caribe cigars and sipping fifty-year-old brandy from snifters. Then, he got serious.

"I guess it's easy to understand why I pulled you into this mess I've been living with over the past months. As you can see," he said, spreading his arms expansively, "I've lived a charmed life for all of these years: money, great house, wonderful family. Can you blame me for not wanting to lose it?"

"Tell you the truth, I've never been inside a house like this, or seen a better looking family, but this hasn't been simple as you first made out, friend. People have died."

"And Havana Spice," he asked, taking a puff from his cigar. "Do you know where she is?"

"When I got to her place, she was nowhere to be found. What I did find was two dead bodies. Mutilated beyond recognition, then set on fire. Havana's kid was there, too, but he ran away before I could find out anything from him."

"What about the penthouse? You searched it, I suppose?"

"Yeah, I did. Found a kilo of heroin and some of Havana's letters. An interesting woman, to be sure."

Dougherty took another puff from his cigar. With white hair and amber eyes piercing through the smoke around him, he could have been a Celtic shaman as he stared straight ahead assessing me, gauging, I guessed then, what I did or did not know about Havana and him.

"You took the letters with you?"

"I did."

"Evidence from a crime scene," he noted, clicking his tongue in disapproval. "And you read them?"

"Yes."

"What did they tell you? About Havana? About her relationship with me?"

I took a sip of brandy, then decided to polish off the entire snifter. Tom didn't know what I knew and to an FBI man that gap between must have been torture, so I waited him out: his presence against mine, two sea creatures buried deep in the ocean silt, exuding the repellant communications of exotic life forms one to the other.

"They didn't tell me anything I didn't already know," I said begrudgingly. "Just that she isn't the monster I'd first imagined and that she was probably being held captive by Reicher and his Angel buddies. Could be it wasn't her, but him that was blackmailing you and now he's dead."

"Nothing more?"

"No," I lied.

"So it could be our problems are over."

"Possibly."

"But Havana? You don't think she's dead, do you?"

"There's no evidence to support it. My guess is she either got away or the killers took her with them. It's hard to say which, but I'm looking into it."

Dougherty's eyes turned keen, "And you're sure there

was nothing in those letters that would help to identify the killers or where they may have taken her?"

I shook my head. "You seem to have an unhealthy interest in the answer to that question," I postulated.

Dougherty laughed. He downed the last of his brandy, eyes twinkling, with a good Irish smile, "How the hell do I know what a girl like that writes to her mother in letters!" he roared, clapping his arm around me. "So, all right, you keep 'looking into it,' until you find Havana Spice, dead or alive, and I'll keep paying you. But for Christ's sake, Old Boy, let's forget about all that for now and have some dinner!"

We left the gentleman's study for the dining room, Tom's arm still draped over my shoulder as we trudged through an elongated hallway. Odd, but despite his wealth and position at the Bureau, Dougherty hadn't changed after all of these years in at least one respect: his incredible ability to change from one persona to another in the blink of an eye! At one moment, he was "serious Tom," with eyes intense as a panther's, then, before your mind could register the change, he was "Tom, the back-slapping Irishman," or "Tom, the guilt-ridden *Opus Dei* Catholic." And for me knowing him now and knowing him then was like a roller coaster ride through a House of Mirrors. Which Tom would it be once we sat down to dinner with his wife and kids? I wondered, numbed by the grandiosity of each of the rooms we passed through along the way.

Once arrived, I saw Dougherty's kids patiently seated on skirted chairs surrounding a French walnut table with a giant crystal chandelier overhanging it while Annie tended to the details of the table settings sans maid or butler.

"Yes, it's just me!" she declared as Tom and I assumed

our places. "The maid and chef are off tonight so I thought I'd cook something simple and hardy, prime rib and new potatoes. I hope you enjoyed the tour Tom gave you?"

"Frankly, I didn't know what to expect. I've never been inside a house like this before. It's much brighter than I'd imagined."

"Thanks," she answered, looking to Elise who began serving. "We've renovated the entire place to give it an open-air feeling. It's neoclassical. At least that's what they tell me."

"Even the paintings…"

"That's right," Tom chimed-in, "the one above the sideboard is a watercolor by Echo Eggsbrecht. Annie discovered her at Gallery Sixtyseven two years ago. It's called 'Building a Desert,' though I can't imagine why since those yellow flowers are some of the brightest colors in the house."

"Roberts Smith wrote about it in the *Times*, Mr. Madson," Matt lectured in a pinched, nasal voice. "'Eggsbrecht distinguishes herself with empty landscapes whose roiled grass is meticulously revealed with wry contradictions and bits of Americana.' What he means is, she uses bright colors to cover up the darkness beneath. It's satire, cynicism disguised as joy."

"Looks like scrambled eggs dumped on a rug," Elise commented, "and not worth the $250,000 Mom paid for it."

"Looks like puke on a pile of crap to me!" Danny bested in a low rumble, looking up from his dinner plate, then smiling at his older sister.

"That will be enough of that, young man!" Annie fired back, nothing if not the control freak she'd admitted to being in the *Digest* article. "Now you're going to stop this nonsense and settle down while your father gives thanks to our Lord for the food we're about to eat. Tom, will you lead us in prayer?"

Dougherty nodded as like clockwork each head at the table bowed, eyes clenched shut.

"Thank you for the food we eat and the blessings you have bestowed on us, O Lord. Direct Thee, our actions by Thy holy inspirations, and carry them by Thy gracious assistance, so that every word may be brought to its fruition through Christ our Lord, Amen."

Truth be told, it was near impossible to screw up a prime rib of the quality Annie served that night and I cleaned the dog dish with relish, regaled in the current status of each of their children's lives. Matt, an academic genius caught between avocations involving the "quixotic mix of law, theology, and philosophy;" Elise, a straight A student, pursuing her passion for modern dance at the 92nd Street Y in Manhattan; and Danny, the happy-go-lucky jokester, eking his way through St. Joe's detention-to-detention, trying to get his share of attention in what appeared—purposefully—a highly competitive family mix.

After dinner, each excused themselves, Elise and Danny to do homework, and Matt to visit his sweetheart, a pre-med student at NYU, which left Tom, Annie, and me alone, sipping freshly brewed Columbian coffee.

"You know, it's amusing, Jack. A man like you must come here and see our big house and loving children and say 'Wow! What lucky people! They never had to work for any of it!' but it isn't that way. It's FBI policy to move families so agents don't spend their careers enjoying places like New York. There are twelve major cities, and we spent time in six of them, no questions asked. Not an easy path for a family, or a marriage."

"Trust me, that's not what I'm thinking," I begged off. "What was it Dostoyevsky wrote, 'Another man's soul is darkness'?"

"Well, that's a start," Annie gibed with a wry smile. "Tom tells me you're a private investigator?"

"That's right, I've been between careers since leaving NuGen, an acquisition house in the city. Tom's been giving me a hand getting a license and, yeah, I hope to make a career of it."

"I didn't know they still existed except in those paperback books you see in drug stores. Is that really what you want?"

"He enjoys the work because he's good at it, Dear, that's the point. Jack understands the mechanics of white collar crime which in my opinion brought the financial world to the brink back in '09! No, I tell you, he's among the best I've seen, and I've seen plenty."

"I certainly didn't mean to demean the profession, you understand that, don't you, Jack?" she asked, radiating good will with that smile of hers.

"No harm, no foul, but one question, was it religion or something else that got you through those years carting your family from city to city with the FBI?"

I'd directed the question to Annie, but it was Tom who answered.

"It was our faith! Annie was my rock, but I was drinking heavily in those days. Lost. Marriage falling apart. Family in disarray. But I promise, there's nothing more powerful than a woman who's decided to devote her life to God and Annie led me through it."

"*Opus Dei* was like food for us," Annie hastened to explain. "After Tom underwent *spontaneous conversion* it was as if a special place in his soul suddenly came to life again."

"Spontaneous conversion?"

"It happened at the Vatican six years ago," she continued. "My father arranged a private audience with Pope Francis. That was spectacular enough, but it was while touring the catacombs beneath St. Peter's Basilica while viewing the Incorruptibles that like a lightning bolt, God pierced Tom's heart and the Spirit engulfed him! I promise I'm not exaggerating when I tell you the power of it knocked him physically to the ground!"

"Incorruptibles, the bodies of saints that don't decompose after death," I remembered.

"That's it exactly!" Tom interjected. "I could start with Pope Innocent XI, who died more than three hundred years ago, or Pope John XXIII, who passed in 1963, but there are dozens of others, preserved as if they'd simply gone to sleep. It's a miracle you have to see to believe, some of them recently passed like San Padre Pio, who died in 1968, others much older like St. Bernadette Soubirous, who witnessed the vision of the Virgin Mary at Lourdes, who passed in 1253. Each of them miraculously preserved by God to prove His existence, and to touch the heart of men like me, Jack. That experience, seeing His work firsthand, was the greatest single moment of my life!"

"All because of that phenomenon?"

"For months afterward I tried to explain it from a forensic point of view. Alkalinity in the burial soil, the ground temperature in the places they'd been interred, humectants administered by Vatican morticians, but none of those covered it. There was no label that would fit except one: these miracles were incontestable proof that the hand of God had intervened in the mortal lives of men!"

I stared hard across the table at Tom, studying his face and the glint in his eyes once he'd finished. Despite his prematurely white hair, he suddenly looked no more than thirty years old. His wan complexion was ruddy; his chiseled lips and chin rigorous, but it was his amber eyes, now fiery, that were strikingly different. The left was aloof; the right eye belonged to a fanatic.

"So, you see, I'm not the only one who's visited by the Holy Spirit," Annie observed, a self-satisfied simper curling her lips, "but there's an article I'd like you to read. It's not about tangible miracles like the Incorruptibles, but subtle ones like Christ's triumph when the prodigal son returns to His church. It was written by Reverend Michael Greer Geisler, an *Opus Dei* prelature, and deals with salvation. You see, whether you know it or not, you are a virtuous man, Mr. Madson. I can see that by the way you carry yourself, but you're blind to it. Perhaps Reverend Geisler's article will be like a pair of glasses that will allow you to see yourself and who you really are."

Tom appeared as hopeful as his wife, literally beaming, as they awaited my response which must have been a disappointment.

"I appreciate the sentiment, Annie, but maybe religion needs to hit a guy like me the way it did Tom, right between the eyes. Keep your article. If ever there's a time when I find the truth that you have we'll try again but, believe me, it would take a miracle to change my life."

"God makes miracles," she countered. "He does it to show that nothing is impossible."

"I think miracles happen on a small scale, Annie. A life is saved, a baby is born. That's enough for me."

"Your life is like Augustine's prayer: 'God make me good—but not yet!'" Her eyes, bemused now, shifted to her husband. "Okay, Tom, I'll leave you two to discuss crime fighting and politics, but for me it's late and there's a steeple chase in Bernardsville we're hosting first thing tomorrow. Good night, Jack Madson, I will pray for you."

So the empty hours of the night came down upon Tom and I as we took a final snifter of Courvoisier ("Good for the digestion, Old Boy!" he roared) and just before I left, already into his cups, he passed along an envelope filled with cash.

"You know we're friends, Jack, fabulous friends, and I suppose you know by now I have enemies. More enemies than friends, that's why I value our friendship so much. It's rare to stay as close as we are after all these years," he blathered, draping his arm around me again.

"I know, Tom, I know. Now you go to bed and don't worry. You'll see, this will all straighten itself out before long."

"Thank you, Jack. Thank you so much," he said as I turned and got into the waiting limo.

We never did return to the subject of Havana Spice, the murders of Amber and Reicher, or even the "miracle" of Incorruptible Corpses after Annie retired. We didn't need to, I already had plenty to consider on my ride back to the Elyse.

For example, I'd withheld Havana's comments in letters to Rosa about the "Society", but Dougherty was certainly digging for something once her name was mentioned. For that matter, how did he know that most were to her mother? I never told him that, and though it was possible she had, it seemed odd that he made reference to "letters to her mother." Was it a slip up on his part? Had he known or suspected what was in them all along? Was there something in them, or something he thought might be there, that he was afraid I'd uncovered?

Finally, and most disturbing, was Tom's obsession with *Opus Dei*, the so-called Incorruptibles, and Annie's cultish belief in the all but forgotten practice of mortification. While I admired the *Opus Dei's* sense of purpose, in practice the idea of cilices, and hair shirts, and lay celibacy, to me bordered on the bizarre.

These observations, contradictions, and incongruencies tumbled dense as steel bolts in my mind that night from the moment I stepped into the limo until I stepped out, entered the hotel lobby, and took the elevator up to the fourteenth floor.

There in the hallway, I inserted the card key into the lock, opened the door, and switched on the light to my room. If I did not believe in miracles five seconds before, I most certainly did after that because waiting there for me, dressed in a snow white, lace-up bustier with garter belt and spike heels, stood Havana Spice.

"Anything you want," she said in a clear, husky voice, eyes blazing.

Chapter
Twenty-Four

I stood in the doorway held in the grips of a force that like a ghostly cloud swirled up from my shoes, and at that moment I felt vertiginous, as if I was standing on the ledge of a tall building with winding ribbons of miniature cars and people streaming on the street below. *Was this a dream?* I wondered, tempted to reach out and touch her. But, instead, I took her in, every part of Havana Spice.

Her eyes, black and dazzling, reached out to me with a level of sexual energy so savage I thought I would melt. *"Yes, I want you,"* those eyes commanded, *"I want you in every way that a woman can have a man and a man can have a woman!"*

And I believed her like a prayer as my own eyes devoured every inch of the woman who stood before me. Her mouth was strong and inviting. Her lips were parted ever so slightly to expose her perfect white teeth so that she seemed as ready to take a lover's kiss as to give one. But it was her jaw, set square and strong, that signaled the level of resolve she held when it came to quenching the fire within her, a lust that I imagined had smoldered as she lay near naked on my bed waiting for the door to open.

To me this was a revelation. How many men had she been with? How many women? I dared not guess, but these thoughts were as remote to me as a calculation of the land mass of Asia. Tonight, Havana Spice was with me in my hotel room, I was finally beginning to comprehend, and truth be told, *I could not take my eyes off her breasts*. Large and well-shaped, they were the color of *café con leche*, barely covered by the bustier from out of which peeked, the eminently darker flesh surrounding her nipples, hidden but obviously aroused as they heaved beneath the bulging cups that sought to contain them.

Havana was hot all right and as my eyes traveled down to her bare mid-rift and on to her pussy, I was stunned to watch her as she watched me. Truly, she seemed prisoner to her own self-discipline (was it the Sisters of Charity?) because with eyes feverish, Havana stood up straight as a soldier in her spike heels, heroic to the last, until finally she extended a glass of Dom Perignon, "So what will it be, Senor Jack?" she asked leading me to the bed.

But I did not answer readily. No, instead, I watched her walk in front of me as I sipped my champagne. And if my first impression was that she was a 21st century sex goddess, my second was that Havana walked like no other woman. Her long legs were taut and shapely, her tanned thighs firm, but for all of what I had lusted over, Havana's ass was surely the prize. The very notion of that carmel circle of pleasure, opened up pink like the entrance to a second universe, awakened my dormant libido from the depths of its slumber.

Then, she turned toward me. At first her large, soft eyes appeared questioning, but recognizing the glimmer of desire in mine transformed in an instant from solicitous courtesan to blazing hot lover as the spark between us jumped from eye to brain to crotch. Blood! My member was full of it, engorged, with balls churning like the hammers of an industrial engine. And now the giant had come to life, rock hard and ravenous, *"I want you,"* I growled, a monster on the prowl within me. *"I want to devour you. I want to fuck every hole in your body!"*

Havana smiled and pulled me down onto the bed beside her. Her hand reached for my cock and began stroking it. She kissed me gently on the lips and slowly slid down, pushing away the fabric of my shirt, to suck my nipples as her face glided implacably toward my erection set free from its prison, and let me say now freeing my member was tantamount to releasing a lunatic from out of his cell back out onto the streets. *"He liberado a un hombre salvaje. Ahora debo domarlo,"* she said just before taking the head of my cock into her mouth.

"No!" I protested. "I want to make love to you!"

Reluctantly she removed those tender lips from me and whispered, "This is hole number one. Before this night is over, I will give you all three of my holes," she pledged solemnly and then continued doing things with her mouth, tongue, and teeth that had me clutching the bed sheets, clenching my fists and toes until finally—with teeth gritted and loins aching—I was sent hurtling over oceans and out into space, then into deep caverns strewn with stalagmites and stalactites, into a desert grotto where clearing the hurdle from life to death and back again, I finally climaxed.

"You're amazing," I whispered.

She lapped at the head of my cock making a point afterward to lick her fingers, "I like the way you look. I like the way you *taste*," she said.

I reached for her then and she climbed back on top of me so that we lay face-to-face with her on top.

"Now it's my turn," I promised, but it was too late because eager as a school girl, she'd already wriggled my cock inside her and begun swaying her hips, maddeningly slow at first, then deeper, and deeper still.

Her pussy was wet, drenched in fact, but tight as it was I slid in-and-out easily before grinding up into her and soon our bodies began to obey a master rhythm that from far away as the drumbeat of an unseen army sounded. Faster and harder, we labored closer to animals in the frenzy of combat than lovers: biting, clawing, grabbing hair as we stole handfuls of each other en route to orgasm and then—*nothing*—spinning in suspended animation, a kind of mini-death where all pain and worry, fear and anxiety, simply vanished into a black hole of ecstasy!

Afterward, with head propped in hand and elbow staked into the mattress, she stared at me dreamy-eyed and said, "I've never been able to come with a man before. Not that way."

"Is that a prop?"

"It's my way of saying, I like you. I like what you do to me, Senor Jack."

I edged over and kissed her on the lips. Satisfied and drained of tension, she had never appeared more beautiful, "Maybe we're not so unalike. Both damaged goods, but I'm starting to think you're a special lady. A good woman found herself in a bad place. I believe that, or at least I want to."

"And you are a gentle man. That's different from a gentleman. I've been with lots of men who call themselves 'gentlemen.'" She smiled brightly, "You saved my son's life."

"Kid saved himself. When I got to your apartment, I found him hiding in a cabinet beneath the sink. He's a bright boy," I laughed, "got the hell out of there and never looked back!"

"And you came when I called," she added happily. "Why, Jack? Why did you come? Was it to help me or talk about your friend Tom Dougherty?"

I rubbed a hand across my beard-stubbled face understanding that when a woman asked a question like that there was no 'right' answer. But in my room that night it was like I had come into a place I'd been expecting to enter all my life. There seemed nothing I couldn't tell her.

"I wasn't about to let you get hurt and do nothing about it," I confessed, "but I also wanted to help Dougherty, though I find that ambition diminishing by the day."

"Liar!" she blustered. "You came to help me and you came for a reason," she concluded, black eyes dancing. "It's because you have feelings for me, Jack. You like me and didn't want to see me get hurt!"

"Look, what I said before, that we 'weren't so unalike,' I meant it. You and me, we share a passion for life. Those feelings are buried deep inside us both and covered by scar tissue, but they do exist. I know that about you. I could feel it in the way we made love tonight. My father used to tell me, 'Son, this is not Heaven,' and he sure as hell did his best to keep it that way, but I know that you care deeply about your family and your son Savito. I want to help you get out of the life you're living, Havana, but you need to tell me what this is really about. Who killed Amber Starr and Reicher, why are you blackmailing Dougherty, and why this relationship with the Angels, and the porno circuit they've got you working. Is that who you are, or is the real you here in bed with me, *so fucking lovable?* I need to know the answer to those questions, can you understand that?"

"When I was a little girl in Cuba, my father would tell my sister and me stories about the United States. 'This is a land of freedom!' he would declare. 'A place where no child goes to bed hungry, where God still watches over his people. But in Cuba, the Communists have insulted God and He has turned His back on our Island!' After my father died, of course I remembered his words and when the opportunity came to leave Havana with my mother's sister, I left never stopping to consider what living there would be like after leaving them behind. I think you know the rest. If you read my letters, then you know what happened after that," she admitted, shuddering at the horror of it all as I gathered her in my arms.

"I know about your uncle and what happened once he took you in," I told her, my cheek pressed hard against hers, "but you've got to tell me what it is that keeps you trapped in the life you're living. Is it Savito? Have the Angels or this 'Gentlemen's Society' you wrote about, threatened to harm him if you try to leave because…"

Havana covered my lips with her fingertips, "No! You cannot talk like that, Senor Jack. Not here, not anywhere! They may be with us now," she cautioned. "They could be here in this room and we would never know it!"

"There's no one in this room, Havana. The shades are drawn and the door is locked. It's just the two of us, Baby."

"You don't understand! They may be listening. They may be watching with some hidden camera smaller than a grain of rice. That's what they do, Jack! That's the kind of power they possess and there's nothing you can do except pretend that everything is normal. If you leave them alone, they may not bother you even now that they know who you are, but that is your only hope of surviving."

I stared deep into her ebony eyes, sparkling now with concern for me, "Oh, my poor Baby, what have they done to you? Was it Reicher convinced you of all this because Reicher is dead and you're with me now, Havana, and don't have to fear that man ever again!"

"Don't you see? They want you, Jack! I don't know why, maybe it's Dougherty, or something you uncovered during your investigation, but I don't think that even dropping this case will free you from them now. You see, the world I live in, and now you, has been turned inside out so that nothing is real anymore. In Cuba, everyone was forced to live two lives. The first was the 'actor's life.' The person you pretended to be in order to survive each day. The second was the secret life, the life of the *real* you, which you were forced to hide but knew existed beneath the surface. But now," she said, eyes lit with irony, "God has played the cruelest of jokes on me because He has reversed them. Today I remain two women, but I live in an altered world where life has become the rehearsal and the actor has become real. So we must laugh," she proclaimed, giggling with sudden abandon as she poured two more glasses of Dom Perignon, "if not at the way we live, then at the magnificent joke God has played on us because all we have now is each other, Senor Jack. And that may be all we ever have again!"

We downed our drinks in a gulp, Havana suddenly animated as I sank into the shadows of fatigue.

"You still haven't answered my questions, not one of them, My Dear," I noted as she threw a long tanned leg over my pelvis and climbed on top of me.

"Estas un poco cansado, si, Bebe?" Havana asked gently.

Giving way to the shadows, inexorable now after a week straight of cops and accusations, high-tone criminals and brutal murders, indeed even I had to admit the curtain was coming down on anything that resembled vigilance.

"The answers to my questions," I reminded in a far off voice as she began rubbing my back with the palms of her cool hands and stroking me with her long fingernails.

"The truth is that I don't know who killed Amber or Reicher, Senor Jack, because I fled the apartment before they came, before even Amber and Reicher arrived with Savito. The truth is that I never blackmailed your friend. In fact, it is he who has been blackmailing me," she whispered with a wan grin, beginning now to punctuate my massage with the dip of her head to lap at an earlobe, stick her pink tongue into my ear, or caress the nape of my neck.

"Dougherty blackmailing you?"

I craned my head around to question her further but was met flush with an open-mouthed kiss dizzying in its ardor.

"*Shut up and kiss me, Jack,*" Havana seethed, turning me on my back again with a rising passion that I could feel hot as a blacksmith's irons in the thighs that straddled me.

Need I tell you that it wasn't the massage I recollected the next morning when I awoke to find Havana gone leaving me with not so much as an empty tube of lipstick to remember her by? Or, that despite my best intentions, not one of the questions that so plagued me had been satisfactorily answered?

No, those were not the thoughts set tumbling in my addled brain that morning as I took the pillow where

Havana had lain her head into my hands and breathed in the scent of her perfume. It was, rather, the fact that—insignificant as it might appear to someone other than myself—Noemi Machado had lived up to her pledge and willingly offered the last of the carnal pleasures she had to give a man; the final gift that Dougherty noted she'd held back from all others as perhaps the last vestige of her second, *real* self, which had all but disappeared.

Chapter
Twenty-Five

Late that morning I packed my gym bag and left the
Elysée for Brooklyn, but it wasn't Lights Out I was
going to see, it was a chance to bang on a heavy bag
at Gleason's gym on Front Street. There I could think,
sweat, and pound-out my frustrations on a speed bag or
some unsuspecting sparring partner mistaking me for an
easy mark.

Just stepping into Gleason's was like being baptized
such was the level of integrity one felt upon entering
the place: the smell of sweat and leather infused the air,
the ratta-tat-tat rhythm of speed bags cracking as boxers
delivered blows to heavy bags dangling from the ceiling
while others sparred in the three 10'X12' rings positioned
at its center. My eyes combed the fight posters—Dempsey,
Ali, Robinson, Duran—that plastered the walls.

Iran Barkley an ex-light heavyweight champ from the
1980s nodded a stoic greeting, collected my ten bucks and
put it in a cigar box along with half-a-dozen others. Above
him hung a wooden plaque bearing a quote from the poet
Virgil, "Now whosoever has courage, and a strong spirit in
his breast, let him come forth, and put up his hands."

Five minutes later, I was working a heavy bag, wearing a Wrigley Field sweatshirt, black trunks, and black Aididas with leg weights. And pound the bag I did, contemplating with every left and right the pieces of the mosaic that I was convinced was assembling before my eyes. Was I standing too near? Too far? Did I need to squint or look askance to see what those pieces were showing me?

I shot a quick glance to the wall clock, then launched two jabs and a quick right over the top thinking about Havana and what she'd told me. She didn't know who killed Amber or Reicher, she swore, and I believed her. Or, at least, I believed she didn't know the specific individuals who'd murdered them. But the ones behind those atrocities and the others I'd heard about? I was certain it was 'they,' whoever 'they' meant to her. Havana also told me that "I never blackmailed your friend. In fact, it is he who has been blackmailing me." Now there was a supposition harder to swallow, I reasoned. Why would Dougherty, arguably the most powerful law man on the Eastern seaboard, want to blackmail a woman like Havana?

The bell marking the end of the first round sounded. I wiped a skein of sweat from my face with a towel. No, Dougherty blackmailing Havana made no sense, I concluded, though the better part of me was tempted to believe the truth behind even that. Perhaps what Havana said and what Havana was trying to communicate were two different truths, one technically accurate, the other not to be taken literally. So what was she *trying* to tell me? I wondered as the bell signaling round two sounded.

I moved toward the bag then pounded it once, twice, three times with powerful body blows coming up to crack two short left hooks followed by a right cross. Her message,

I thought then, was simple. She wasn't blackmailing Dougherty. Reicher and his Angel pals were doing that using her as bait. More, there was no way Havana was strong-arming Dougherty, a man who had all the power and money his position could command. In that sense, then, Havana's explanation may not have been as literal as it was truthful. She was being used by both sides and it was Dougherty who had turned the tables on Reicher and the Angels! Or was it? I kept asking myself. Or was there something deeper to what she'd confided, to what each of the scattered pieces of the mosaic I was trying to assemble seemed to be screaming out at me?

The bell rang-out ending rounds two, three and four with that question and others still dogging me like hooded strangers. I finished my fifth and final round with a five punch combination, crisp and deadly.

Once back at the hotel, I decided to give Vicky Benson a call since it had been a while and she was probably searching the OBITS daily trying to get a line on me. I decided our discussion would go easier over a drink so I poured myself a Glenlivet neat and was quietly sipping from my glass as we spoke.

"Where are you, Jack?" she asked like the worried older sister I never had.

"Still in New York at the Elysée, why do you ask?" I baited, knowing full well the rise it would get out of her.

"'Why?' Is it that what you just asked me sitting here in Georgetown with Harris and Woods practically breaking down the door to my office? Two more murders since you left DC—Reicher and Amber Starr—both killed then set on fire practically the minute you set foot in New York!"

"Easy now, Vicky," I assuaged, pouring myself another

scotch as I wedged the receiver between my neck and shoulder. "You know I had nothing to do with any of that, now here's the good news..."

"Yes, please, Jack, tell me the good news."

"It was me who called the cops, Owen Ewing to be specific, and guess what he told me on the QT?"

"Surprise me," she said miserably.

"That Asian kid's head they found in my car? It wasn't the only one. There've been at least half-a-dozen cases just like it spread across the east coast going back two years or more," I explained. "Two years, Vicky. I was on the other side of the country then so they knew it wasn't me that did it, *understand?* This isn't about me, it's about Dougherty."

"Dougherty? I don't get it."

"Maybe it's political. You know how these agencies dick around with each other. Or maybe Tom's guys have uncovered something that threatens Woods over at Homeland. Could be any one of a dozen explanations, but one thing sure, Woods is using me to get to him and I'm certain now it has something to do with these murders."

"Jesus, Jack, how do you get yourself into these situations? You know I know about your 'altercation' with Jin Lee, don't you? Anyway," she moaned, "for God's sake, just take care of yourself, will you? I don't feel like attending your funeral like some heartbroken former lover. Are you hearing me, Jack? I worry about you being 'iced' or 'smoked' or whatever it is they're calling it these days. Is there anything I can do to help?"

"Just one thing. I'm going to FedEx you that death threat I found in my jacket pocket. The one from the Casanova Club?"

"Okay," she said listening carefully.

"I need you to have it analyzed. I doubt there are any prints or DNA, but the paper is unique: custom-designed with the watermark of an image I can't make out running through it."

"I know just the man," Vicky retorted. "An epigraphist from the Smithsonian who spends his life studying ancient scrolls and inscriptions. If he can't identify it, no one can."

"I'll have it to you by tomorrow morning. In the meantime, I'll be over at the Chelsea docks trying to track down Havana. Near as I can tell, along with Dougherty, she's the focal point of all this and her life is in danger. Logic goes, if I find what's driving Havana, I've found who's behind these three murders and the others Ewing told me about."

"So Havana Spice has gone missing?"

"Yes."

"And you're worried about her?"

"Yeah, I am. Is there a problem with that?"

"No," Vicky hesitated, "it's just that…"

"Yeah, what is it?"

"Jack?" she asked in a voice as sober as it was sobering, "you're not falling in love with a porn star, are you?"

After I hung up the phone, I downed a handful of Percocet with a swig of scotch, straight from the bottle. This was a "sloth" day, I told myself, time to kick back alone with my thoughts about the Dougherty case, which seemed all-consuming these days, and, yeah, thoughts about Havana's well-being. More recurrent than any of those, however, was the memory of my mangled relationship with Tiffany that, like the raw nerve of an exposed tooth, had lately deteriorated into obsession.

My mind numbing now, and with an electric tingle

running from my arm to my fingertips, I took a last gulp from the bottle and slammed it down as I prepared to write. An e-mail would not carry the weight of the emotions I needed to convey, I decided, so I pushed aside the laptop opting for a Uni-Ball pen and a sheet of hotel stationery, hands trembling not from the booze and oxycodone but from the likely prospect that I'd be spending the rest of my life estranged from my daughter.

December 18th

My dearest Tiffany,

Please do not hate me. I know you feel that way now, but maybe some day I can prove that I am not a man to be hated. I love you so much, Tiffany, and miss you every second of every day. You may not believe that, but it is the only thing in my life that I know to be true.

When I left you and your mother, I was sick and confused. I never wanted to hurt anyone, most of all you, but I know that I did and for that I am so sorry! Can you find it in your heart to let me make it up to you?

There is a song by Hank Williams. It's a love song called "I'm So Lonesome I Could Cry," and it's about sadness, I guess you could say.

> *"Did you ever see a robin weep*
> *when leaves begin to die,*
> *Like me he's lost the will to live*
> *I'm so lonesome I could cry."*

I know how Hank Williams felt when he wrote that lyric because since you cut me out of your life I feel like I am living on a deserted planet even when I am surrounded by hundreds of

*people. I feel like someone has cut off my arm, Tiffany, and I'm
standing invisible in this large crowd bleeding to death.*

*What I'm trying to say is that I understand that it's late to
start now, but I know I can be a good father to you so please don't
cut me off! Please let me try again. I have so much love to give you.
So many things to share... please, please...*

Then I stopped writing because between the Percocet
and fifth of scotch, the dam had burst and tears were
streaming down my face. *Some tough guy! Some detective!* I
thought, eyes scanning what I'd written before rolling it
up into a ball and tossing it into the trash basket.

I stared at it lying atop empty beer cans, discarded
candy wrappers, and old newspapers until my head
dropped down onto the desktop, the words and melody
of Hank Williams' song echoing like poetry through the
canyons of my mind.

Chapter Twenty-Six

I guess you could call the next day a slow-starter. Unconscious from the combination of Ambien and scotch for three hours, I awoke marooned in a neon desert of night—sober, cold, and wholly electrified with premonitions concerning what new calamities awaited me. As it turned out, the next morning was no concern since I didn't get out of bed until 2 pm and spent the next several hours trying to prep myself for that night when I'd be headed to the Ram Rod trying to find answers to questions like who killed Ronnie Reicher and Amber Starr? More, who was behind those murders, and the ones Ewing had clued me into, convinced as I was that Havana Spice wasn't telling me near all of what she knew.

Feeling lazy as a house dog, I called room service to bring up a club sandwich and bottle of Sam Adams, then luxuriated in a hot shower meant to rouse me from my funk. *Well, that didn't work*, I was thinking as I wrapped a towel around me, *best to rely on Old Faithful.* "Old Faithful" for me was what I did every morning upon waking. That is, pull a pint of scotch and half-dozen amphetamine containers filled with Adderal, Focalin, and Benzedrine from out of my sock drawer, chew a handful, and wash them down with the better part of the bottle. *Breakfast of Champions!* I marveled, standing before the bathroom mirror still dripping wet, the electric eels of amphetamine already slithering their way through nerve and synapse igniting them like the lights on a Christmas tree each along the way. Body warming, beard-stubble jaw thrust forward and my laser-like eyes their old selves again, I slapped my face hard, then glowered, *"This is it, my friend!"* I challenged. *"Get ready to rock n' roll 'cause tonight you're fighting for the fucking heavyweight championship of the world!"*

It was a short drive across town to the Ram Rod on West Street, a BDSM bar, just re-opened after a homophobic psycho named Raymond Crowley opened fire with an Uzi killing four and wounding twelve others a decade earlier. Why did he do it? "Gays are agents of the devil," he told the platoon of cops who finally managed to wrest the weapon from him. "They were stalking me, trying to steal my soul just by looking at me!" So much for the theology of the insane, I concluded, as I pulled my Porsche 911 past the fleet of Harleys parked in front of the bar grabbing an open spot near the Hudson Piers.

Back in the day, "leatherman" clubs like Ty's, Spike, and Badlands flourished, but with the onset of AIDS and violent incidents like the one at Ram Rod, most had been shuttered by the NYPD "morals squad," or gone underground catering to a narrower, more sophisticated clientele. The Ram Rod seemed the exception, I couldn't help but notice as I navigated the clusters of patrons standing outside its entrance, some wearing chaps and cowboy hats, heavy steel chains dangling from their necks onto their bared chests, others' fists covered by black leather gloves with stainless steel knife blades attached, a tribute, I supposed, to Freddie Kruger. No, there was nothing terribly sophisticated about this crew or their Hell's Angel protectors who clustered around their Harleys smoking cigarettes, tats running up and down their arms, dressed in jeans, riding boots and biker vests, sleeves cut, with the infamous laughing "Death Head" sewn onto the back.

I approached the doorman, who along with three massively large Angels, appraised me. *What were they thinking?* I wondered, eyes rising slowly to meet their gaze. *Had Casanova Club security forwarded them an on-line photo that they were trying to estimate against the man standing in front of them?* The doorman, a scrawny skin head, half-dressed in a Nazi officers' uniform, looked to the roughest-looking of the three bouncers, a bearded man, built like an ice cream truck.

"He's okay," he pronounced after frisking me shoulder-to-ankles.

The doorman nodded, "Twenty bucks cover," he told me.

I handed him a twenty. He stamped the back of my hand with a red "Double R" logo. The Angels moved aside as I passed beyond a black velvet curtain and stepped into the cellar where men in every kind of costume were walking around: some faux cowboys, bare-chested and pantless, in leather chaps and jock straps with cowboy hats; some faux bikers with black leather caps, pants, riding boots and patches that designated no more than the fact that they were patrons of the Ram Rod with a preference for S&M, electro sex, or down-and-dirty B&D. Beyond the polished bar that extended one-half the club's diameter was a stage where go-go boys danced, twenty dollar bills crammed down the front of their G-strings, tokens of appreciation from adoring middle-aged men, who enamored as star-struck teenagers hung over the bar to touch a thigh or steal a glance at the not unsubstantial genitalia that peeked above or below its scanty black sheath.

I didn't bother to loiter amongst the cock hounds cruising around me like gnats but gravitated toward the harder stuff that went on a floor below, its entrance denoted by a neon sign that blinked "THE CELLAR DOOR" above the spiral staircase. Now I'm no poet, but even I understood the metaphor as I took my first step downward, the words "Get set," passing my lips as I descended.

The first sensation I experienced was the smell of ammonia as if I was entering a city morgue or malaria ward of a Third World hospital: harsh and acrid, the odor was fierce and, upon first exposure, I swore it was disinfectant, was it Lysol? But I was wrong, I discovered once I got to the foot of the stairs and my eyes combed the dozen or so tables randomly assorted in front of what looked like an elongated latrine set against the far wall of a concrete bunker.

If the Ram Rod's upstairs was for dilettantes, the Cellar Door was for aficionados who'd ridden the dragon of their perversions far beyond the point of caring about who they were or where they were headed. Here a smattering of men, their hands and faces pale and white in contrast to their shiny black leather outfits, sucked down martinis or guzzled large mugs of beer as two blonde men, stripped naked and pinioned to the wall, were alternately whipped or electro-shocked by a stout man dressed in the remnants of a Nazi officers' uniform who held a cattle prod in his left hand and a black-studded whip in his right. *Crack!*

Prod! Crack! Prod! he proceeded, stopping occasionally to swill down a draught of beer or take tiny bows to the audience before turning his attention back to his subjects. *"Stille! Verschlossen, sie Scheibe-Essen wurden als Flittchen benzeichnet!!"* he screamed beginning his regimen again, whipping legs and buttocks, electro-prodding genitals to the audience's delight, while not ten feet from him patrons lined-up behind a second performer, semi-clad in Nazi paraphenalia, who was urinating over the face and body of a third subject, this one middle-aged and balding, bound hand-and-foot to a wooden rack with head cocked upward. *"Trinken! Trinken, du Schwein! Sie wissen, dass Sie en lieben Hure!!"* he taunted, luxuriating as he spread a steady golden stream over him.

It was then that I realized it was not disinfectant but urine I was smelling, puddles of it, and I was in fact standing square in the middle of one! For me, there was no amusement in what I saw, more like panic as I felt the sudden urge to run up those concrete stairs, out of the bar, and back onto the street where I could breathe fresh air again! But just as I was weighing options whether to stay to get the information I'd come for or flee in what seemed an act of survival, I felt a tap on my shoulder and turned to see one of the scariest men I'd ever laid eyes on.

"My name is Chemo," he rumbled dully, extending his hand to me. "I don't know you."

I accepted his hand, "Name's Jack," I answered, gathering myself again for the shock of his first impression. "I'm a friend of Ronnie Reicher's."

Chemo, who stood just five-eleven but weighed about three hundred pounds without an ounce of fat on him, was apparently well-named since he looked very much like a man who'd undergone extensive chemotherapy, years of it, if not a decade's worth. In truth, he looked like a mummy: Boris Karloff, Lon Chaney, Jr., Jason, from the slasher movies without the mask! His black hair hung like long greasy strings from his blue-veined scalp. His red-rimmed eyes beamed psychosis, but it was his skin, discolored and caked, that took one's breath away. Skin like he'd been wearing a rubber mask that had desiccated after years of exposure to the desert sun and could now be scraped away layer-by-layer with the blade of a Swiss army knife or a woman's long, paste-on fingernails.

"That's funny, 'cause you don't look like no friend of Ronnie's. 'Sides, nobody much liked him anyways, and now he's dead."

"Yeah, I know," I said, "and I'm trying to find his killer, that cut me any slack?"

"Not really. Reicher was a douche bag far as we was concerned, hangin' out with that Puerto Rican whore like some kinda lap dog, but I don't guess that's a problem no more."

"How's that?"

"She's dead, man. Shot in the face with a twelve-guage by a psycho John she picked up, body set on fire for good measure." Chemo looked at me squarely, "Hey, you ain't no cop, are you? 'Cause you sure look like one."

"You know, we just met, Chemo, so let me set things straight early. I hate cops; hate the way they look, hate the way they talk, hell, I hate the way they smell, you got that?"

The big man chortled, his wary eyes still on me, "So I guess you're okay then, ain't you, Mr. Tough Guy? Well, like I said, nobody's sheddin' no tears over Reicher or Havana Spice."

"Can I tell you something personal, Chemo? What you said really shocks me because I spent the better part of a night laying the wood to her day before yesterday. You sure she's dead?"

"Happened last night, brother Angel saw the body. Ain't nothin' left but a pile of bones and some fillings."

I watched Chemo's eyes shift over my right shoulder to a table where three Angels sat talking, the one in the middle holding a Marlboro Red between his thumb and forefinger as he blew smoke rings observing us as we spoke.

"Uh-oh," Chemo uttered instinctively.

"Who's that?" I asked turning my attention back to him.

"That is God. Sonny "P4" Coulter, boss of HA's New York chapter. Gotta go now, Jack," he bade pushing his square frame forward like a battleship called into action.

My eyes jumped beyond Chemo's lumbering physique to Coulter, who looked to be about fifty years of age with salt and pepper goatee, high-cheek-boned face, and wizened black eyes of a man who'd seen a lot of bad in his life. He smiled, snubbed-out his Marlboro on the tabletop, and raised his forefinger in my direction like a gun. He cocked his thumb back, and pulled the trigger.

I nodded to acknowledge what seemed to me a downright inhospitable gesture, knowing all along that in Coulter's world this was a "mud" test; an Angel's version of 'show me your *bona fides*.' I had no choice but to oblige. If I left immediately, I was a coward, and if I stayed and ignored him, I was dead meat, leaving me with just one option which was to follow behind Chemo and confront him.

By the time I arrived, Chemo was hovering solicitously over the chapter's godfather and the two troglodytes that flanked him, New York Hells Angels patches prominent on their cuts.

"Hey! What are you doin' here?" Chemo asked, turning first to me, then to Coulter who waved him off as one might a mosquito.

"My name is Jack Madson," I said, extending my hand across the table. "It's an honor to meet you."

Coulter stared at the appendage like it was the last dangling girder on a bridge to nowhere.

"I know who you are and if I were you, I'd hop into my Porsche 911, head back to the Eel-ee-say hotel, pack my bags, and get the fuck out of New York. You know why that is, Jack Madson? It's because if I was you, I'd be smart enough to have a future, any future, which is what you won't have if you stay."

"With all due respect, I can't do that, Sonny," I said withdrawing my hand. "I'm on assignment. That's what I get paid for. It's how I make a living."

He nodded, that same supercilious grin still stamped over his countenance, "Your decision, Jack. But now you've been warned, by me, in person."

"Thanks, Sonny, I appreciate your honesty. Now I'm going to leave, but it isn't because I'm not enjoying our time together. It's because I just got word a friend of mine had her face blown off with a shotgun last night. Havana Spice didn't deserve to be murdered."

Sonny Coulter shrugged, cool and non-committal, "All God's children got to go some time, Jack. There ain't no exception to that rule, just where, when, and how ugly."

I turned to leave, Coulter's glare drilling through my back like the eyes of one hundred men as I stomped across the room then climbed the staircase back up to the first floor. By then, the upstairs had turned as raucous as the downstairs was sodden. The go-go's, totally naked except for cowboy boots, were stomping upon the bar top where they danced coyote ugly, beaming, to the thwomping blast of Credence Clearwater's "Run through the Jungle." The Angels, who were supposed to act as "security," cranked up on vodka shooters and meth, were as into the moment as the leatherman pervs who surged in waves toward the bar reaching out for their fantasy lovers always, it seemed, just a finger's length away.

Thought it was a nightmare,
low, it's all so true,
They told me don't go walkin slow,
the devil's on the loose,

John Fogerty wailed over JBL speakers set kati-corner above the room.

The Ram Rod's entire ground floor had become a giant mosh pit. The lid was off. Something wanton and hysterical had been unleashed and was swirling around the room like phantasms and I did not want to know where it led, I thought, pulling myself from its magnetism just as the long-bearded bouncer who'd frisked me staggered by, a can of butane in his hands. I watched him douse the bar from one end to the other, let loose a rebel war cry, then set it ablaze, engulfing the bar in flames, dancers still dancing, Angels set howling to the rafters with delight.

Better run through the jungle,
Better run through the jungle,
Better run through the jungle, and don't look back,

Fogarty's words faded into the night as the door shut

behind me and I walked fast as my legs would take me across West Street back toward the docks where, with Porsche in sight, I pressed the "unlock" icon on my electronic key.

I remember shivering from the freezing night air coming off the Hudson and hearing the click of the car doors unlocking. Then there was a second sound like the low pitch rumble just before a large clap of thunder, a flash, and the sight of the car as if in slow motion coming apart, literally blowing into pieces before my eyes. It was only then that I heard the powerful roaring sound that caused the ground to quake beneath my feet, and saw the gray cloud rushing toward me, knocking me to the ground before I could imagine what had happened.

When I looked up, the Porsche's frame and engine were in flames with doors, wheels, and engine parts scattered and still smoking, some hundreds of feet away. Then, there was total silence. I remember trying to stand and I did. This pleased me. *I can stand. I still have legs and arms,* I remember thinking, alarmed to find blood oozing through the fabric of my shirt, following it upward from my right arm, to my shoulder, and finally, to my neck. I raised my left hand and touched my forehead where I plucked a shard of glass from out of the wound that was bleeding. I held it in the palm of my hand and stared at it like a talisman, my nostrils filled with the smell of burning rubber, eyes falling once more to the car as it burned.

Jesus Christ, I better get the fuck out of here, I remember thinking during the instant of realization that followed, *somebody's trying to kill me!*

Chapter Twenty-Seven

When I first started this confession, or deposition, or whatever you attorneys call it, I told you I wasn't going to sugar-coat the events that led up to me being incarcerated here at MCC—not the murder, not my so-called acts of terror, not any of it—and so far I believe I've lived up to that promise. So I guess it won't disappoint the infamous Jimmy Bryant, "attorney to the stars," if I leave out the details about my trek from the Hudson docks back to the hotel that night after the explosion. Plain and simple, there's not much to tell except that I hopped the first cab I could find and remember almost nothing of the trip back, the elevator ride to my room, or what I dreamt about after crashing fully clothed on my bed.

Fact is, I was in a state of shock with hands trembling and body quaking, more than a little concerned about what the bastards trying to smoke me had in mind for an encore. I didn't need a CPA to calculate that between the Asian kid, Reicher, Amber, and now Havana Spice, there were more bodies lying around the east coast than on a theater stage after the final act of Hamlet. A fact that left me harboring no small degree of anxiety when it came to my odds of surviving now that I'd told Sonny Coulter, and therefore every Hells Angel coast-to-coast, I wasn't backing off the case.

So it was actually comforting when after waking the next morning, and swabbing the nick on my forehead with alcohol, I received a call from Lt. Owen Ewing, NYPD, who was waiting in the hotel lobby.

"Give me five," I muttered into the receiver, applying a Band Aid strip over the 1" long cut over my right eye. I switched off the mobile, eyes riveted to the bathroom mirror thinking *Hey, fellow, that shard of glass could have put your eye out!* But it hadn't and deep into the shit as I was, I could always point to the fact that I was still in one piece, living large in a first rate Manhattan hotel, feeling like I'd finally sunk my teeth deep into something major. I shook three tabs of Benzedrine into my palm and took them down dry. Just what that *something* was had eluded me so far, I admitted, staring at the man in the mirror, but morning shakes aside I knew I was closing in on it; otherwise, *why would they want me dead?*

Once I got off the elevator, I scanned the lobby for Ewing, not hard to find standing 6' 3" and 240, but I guessed he got tired of waiting and meandered into the Monkey Bar. Sure thing, he was sitting at the bar dressed in an off-the-rack gray suit, nursing a Heineken draft. Big O smiled despite himself when he saw me poke my head into the entrance and waved me over. The gesture, coupled with that spontaneous grin which vanished once I engaged it, made me hopeful this wasn't going to turn-out like our previous 'do you have any idea how fucked up you are?' conversations.

"How's it hangin', O?" I asked extending my hand which he accepted with a back-to-business grunt.

"Let's grab a corner booth," he suggested, rising.

I followed him and we sat. "Yeah," I told the waiter who tagged along behind us, "give me what he's drinking," causing him to disappear while O settled into his seat, folded his large hands on the tabletop, and stared at me.

"You know why I'm here, don't you?"

"Does it involve a car?"

"You're damned straight it involves a car. A Porsche 911, rented from Elite Motors, and blown to hell last night over at the docks!" Ewing shook his head and I could almost see him acting-out the same 'your Dad's pissed-off' routine for one of his two young daughters, Julia and Elise, when they came home with a less than perfect report card. "Madson, I swear, I worry about you. You're screwin' around with Sonny Coulter now, that it? You know why they call that crazy bastard 'P4'? It's because he plays with explosives, man! He not only plays with that shit, he kills people with it. San Francisco, three years ago, he blew up an entire city block just to get revenge on a rival gang member." O took a long sip from his draft beer. "Leveled four houses and killed seven innocent civilians, two of 'em kids, girl age seven, and a six-month-old baby boy!"

"But you couldn't prove he did it."

"That's right," he retorted, slamming his mug back onto the table, "but we knew it was him and the Angels. FBI made the locals back off. Claimed they were going for something bigger. RICO conspiracy or some such crap!"

"And you never bought it."

The Big O sat back in his seat, massive arms extended over the back of the booth, "You know how it is with those guys. FBI, CIA-types like you. It's never black or white. Always shades of gray, isn't that the way you guys spin it?"

"You know, O, I'd say you're not having such a wonderful day, am I right?"

"You could say that. Maybe not such a wonderful life, either. Homicide! Who in their right mind would want to do this for a living 'cept it pays the bills for the wife and two daughters? A lot of sick bastards out there, Madson. Psychos who cut kids' heads off, shoot 'em full of chemicals — *sick* — but none more dangerous than Sonny Coulter and his compadres. That's what I dropped by to tell you: stay away from that guy, Madson, he's bad news."

"And not a word about the car? I'm disappointed."

O threw a giant hand out in my direction, "What the hell do I care about a blown up car when it's owned by Elite. Those guys are all mafia. For all I know it was them that blew it up in the first place."

"You don't really believe that?"

"Nah, it was Sonny, Jack. It was Coulter telling you to back off his turf, whatever turf that happens to be. What you received today was a warning. A priority e-mail telling you to get the hell out of New York, if you know what's good for you."

"Sonny's into explosives, but he and his boys are also into drug distribution. All of those HA chapters here and in Europe. What is it, crystal meth?"

He took a long look at me, then gulped from his beer mug, "It's heroin," he volunteered, tossing the information out onto the table like a poker chip. "All the rage again. Shoot it, smoke it, mix it with your Red Bull. The junk they're hawking is 100% pure, straight from Afghanistan. Some say they ship it in GI coffins from Kabul, but that's just what I hear."

"Angels in Afghanistan?"

"Not a chance. Like you say, they got clubs, the channel, to distribute. Who brokers it into the U.S., I couldn't say, thought it was hotshots like you over at the Company."

This time it was me who shook my head laughing, "Not me. I'm just the friend of a guy who runs the FBI up and down the east coast. We went to high school together."

"Yeah, that's right, Dougherty. Another covert bad-ass…"

"If that's true, don't tell his wife or pastor, they're liable to excommunicate you! Dougherty's straight as an arrow. A lifetime of bureaucracy's the worst crime he's ever committed."

Ewing didn't respond, just stared at me while I took a long drink of beer. The prosaic nature of that look was enough to have me change the subject, which I did, gesturing toward the painted murals of Tennessee Williams, Benny Goodman, Ellington, Hemingway and Fitzgerald on the walls that surrounded us.

"Ever wonder if these guys from the forties and fifties had to put up with the shit we do?" I asked innocuously.

"Same old, same old," O answered, swigging down the last of his Heineken. "I doubt life was any better back then."

"Wait a second," I interjected, taking hold of his forearm as he got up to leave, "I wanted to ask you something…"

Ewing's eyes flew to my hand on his arm and then to me, "Yeah, what's that?" he asked, not entirely certain what could have inspired me to reach out for him as I did.

"It's about a woman. She used to hang out with a biker named Reicher who bounced at Ram Rod. Her name is Noemi Machado, but if you know her, it's probably by her stage name, Havana Spice."

"Spanish broad, big into porn?"

"That's her. Angel named Chemo told me she was murdered night before last. Said a John took her home, shot her dead, somewhere in the Poconos."

The Big O may have started out as a tight end receiver at Notre Dame back in the day, but he was pure detective when he looked into my face to see the pain and sorrow, "Man, you got it bad, don't you, Madson?" He sniggered. "Well, I wish I could tell you otherwise, my friend, but what that piece of shit Chemo told you is true. Police report came in over the wire this morning. Havana's dead all right and, if you ask me, the world's a better place for it."

Ewing left the Monkey Bar, but I stayed on for a Scotch (or was it two?), then went back to my room where I decided to call Dougherty and put him out of his misery. His nemesis Havana Spice was dead. Surely that called for celebration, and maybe a bonus given my old pal's generosity, but I was in nothing like a celebratory mood. To the contrary, the thought of Havana murdered had turned my world into a vortex of mixed emotions. Sure, she'd lured Dougherty into a sexual liaison, but it was Riecher and, no doubt, Sonny Coulter who forced her to do it for the one hundred thou payoff, but more important, I suspected, to have him turn a blind eye to their heroin ring with claims of an imaginary RICO case against the Angels down the line. Yeah, it all made sense but what I couldn't reconcile was Havana dying so cruelly and in such an ignominious way. What was it that she ever wanted out of life, anyway? The love of a father? A decent life for her kid and a man to settle down with?

I dialed Dougherty's private number intent on delivering the 'good' news dry as the man on the Six O'clock News.

"Hey, Tom, this is Jack. Looks like your problems are over."

"Beg pardon?"

"I got news last night and confirmed it with Homicide: Havana Spice is dead, murdered, two nights ago in Pennsylvania. With Reicher gone, it's safe to say that's the end of it."

"Why, that's terrible," Dougherty stammered. "I mean, she was so young. She had a son…"

"Yeah, well, that's not your problem or mine, either. I thought you'd want to know before I head back to D.C."

"You're leaving?"

"I live in Washington, remember? This assignment's history, 'course if you want to give me a little something extra…"

"Yes, of course, let's say, ten thousand dollars … as a bonus for your efforts. But that's not why I'm hesitating, Jack."

"Oh?"

"There was an IPad Havana talked about. A diary, I guess you could call it, that I have good reason to believe exists. In it was a list of her clients. There weren't many, but I'm sure I'm on it, along with the details of our encounters. I need that diary, Jack. I need you to recover it and bring it to me so it can be destroyed. Can you understand why? Can you see why I can't let that information fall into the wrong hands?"

"Yeah, I can, Tom, but why didn't you tell me this before?"

"Of course, you'll need a car," Dougherty hastened to add. "I know what happened last night and you'll need something to get around in, so let me have a replacement sent to your hotel…"

"No, Tom, I asked 'why didn't you tell me about it before?' The diary, why are you only telling me about it now?"

"Because I was concerned! Afraid that if I made this imbroglio too complicated, you'd turn me down and not handle the case! We've come so far, Jack. So close to erasing this horrible mistake from my life and now we're almost there. Can I ask you, please, as a friend, to bear with me just this short while longer?"

"I'll think about it," I said, making no attempt to hide my annoyance. "Bring the car, bring the money, and I'll get back to you in a day or two. I'm not the kind of guy to keep a client waiting, that much you can count on."

"*God bless you, Jack,*" were the last words I heard trailing off before I jabbed my forefinger into the red patch on the screen of my IPhone to end the call.

Chapter
Twenty-Eight

"*G*oddamned *Dougherty!*" were the first words that crossed my lips after ending our call. *So now it's the diary, what's next sex tapes on the internet? A network interview with Oprah?* Truthfully, I could not explain the degree of resentment I was feeling toward him in any rational way. *Was it the fiasco with the demolished Porsche, the Angels at Ram Rod, or Dougherty, himself, and his never ending story of church and family, position atop the FBI hierarchy, and blackmail case whose roots I felt I'd been following from New York to Beijing and back!*

I plucked a fresh bottle of Jameson's from the side drawer of my desk, opened it with the urgency of a man with a Black Belt in alcoholism and took a long pull. *Fuck it! I'm out of here!!* I thought then. *No more Tom, no more case, just the car and the ten grand in bonus I planned on receiving before telling him that for me this assignment was history!*

I took a second pull from the bottle and along with the warmth the whiskey provided came the lingering sound of her name drifting into my mind with the lusty froth of a summer breeze. It was only then that I understood the root of my anger. It wasn't Coulter, the car, the fact that serious men seriously wanted to kill me, or even Dougherty, self-absorbed and feckless as he seemed to me then. No, it was the murder of Havana Spice that had rattled my cage so that I couldn't concentrate or hold a thought in my head anymore.

Havana Spice, Christ, how I already missed her! No sooner would her name pass my lips than my mind would wander over every aspect of her carnal virtues. Havana was brilliant! Havana was delicate! Havana was greedy and generous, deep and fierce, with a heart that stirred my soul and a libido that ignited passions I never imagined existed within me. *"Fuck!"* I swore aloud, tortured by the knowledge that I'd never spend another night with her, or feel the warmth of her flesh, or the thrill of her kisses.

No, it was no use! I couldn't be alone with my thoughts in this hotel room, I decided. The memories were too powerful, the paranoia inspired by the certainty that powerful men wanted me dead had crystallized into a knot of fear that like a bright and shiny piece of nuclear waste was burning a hole in my mind. *"Giambi,"* I whispered solemnly, *"if anyone can help me sort through this nightmare, it's Lights Out, who knows me better than anyone!"*

My first inclination was to take the F train to Delancy Street and meet Johnnie at Mehanata, one of the few places where his reputation as a fighter still warranted free drinks, but Dougherty made good on his promise, and by the time I'd made arrangements with Lights Out, I got a call informing me that a Porsche was waiting outside the hotel along with a sealed envelope at the front desk. Well, let it never be said that "Gentleman" Jack Madson is an ungracious man! Without equivocation, I took a final swig of Jameson's, stashed the half-empty bottle in a gym bag atop my boxing gear, then headed downstairs to collect my bonus and freshly-leased convertible, courtesy of Thomas H. Dougherty, Assistant Director Federal Bureau of Investigation.

Vitali "Ruby" Rubinoff, the owner of Mehanata's, must have lived in the place. Every time I'd been there, the rolly-polly Russian with the shock of combed-back black hair was there to greet patrons, and if his booming voice and bear hugs he administered didn't provide enough local color, the three floors of his Moscow-themed night club certainly did.

An MMA fanatic, multiple big-screen tv's lined the walls of each of the three floors, accessed by long staircases at the end of which stood mahogany bars crowned by a glass cubicle he called the "ice room." There, to the blaring sound of Russian disco, patrons isolated themselves in sub-freezing temperatures drinking all the on-the-house vodka they could handle during five minute intervals until they staggered, dazed and smiling, out of the ice box where they collapsed into their friends' arms.

"Jack! Jack!" Rubinoff boomed. "Welcome!" he greeted, pulling me into one of his famed bear hugs. "Johnnie at end of bar, watching his fight with X-Man, *that son of a bitch!*" he cursed, spitting on the floor. I nodded. "Remember, his money no good here!" the heavy-set Russian called out after me and soon I was seated on a bar stool beside Lights Out, bobbing and weaving along with the images of X-Man and himself as they battled on the screen.

"What'll it be, Jack?" the bartender asked as I took a seat beside him.

"Sam Adams, draft."

He drew a beer from the tap, and set it in front of me. I had to nudge Lights Out so engrossed was he in the replay of the fight.

"Hey, Jackie, good to see ya," he said, turning his good eye to me.

"Same," I told him, taking a gulp of beer, "maybe you're busy, but I was hoping to run a situation by you for a sanity check."

"Never too busy for you, Jack," he answered, turning his back to the tv and the image of himself now on his back taking the 'ground- and-pound' beating of his life. "I hate watchin' this fight, anyways. Makes me feel like drivin' to Philly and ripping X-Man and his manager's heads off. What is it work?"

"Call it that. You know this Dougherty case I've been on. Turns out Havana got her head blown off with a shotgun couple of nights ago in Pennsylvania."

Lights Out blinked his one eye, then lowered his head, "Yeah, I heard. Sorry, I know you had a thing for her."

"Maybe I did, but here's the twist. Havana kept a diary with some embarrassing information Dougherty needs to recover. He's willing to pay top dollar for it."

"Yeah?" he asked glancing up at the bandage on my forehead. "What'd he pay you for nearly gettin' blown to hell along with that Porsche of yours last night?"

"Ten grand and a promise to get me my PI license once things are settled."

"FBI guy a good payer? Don't make no sense," Lights Out observed taking a sip of beer. "Cheapest bastards in the world work for the Bureau, ask anybody ever dealt with 'em, cops, informants, they don't pay shit, Jackie, never did, never will."

I shrugged, "This one's an Obama one-percenter, married the queen of the prom, father-in-law practically invented the New York publishing industry. Trust me, coin is not his problem."

"What is?"

"That's where I draw a blank, John. Guy's more Catholic than the Pope, got three Ivy League-type kids, an estate in Mendham, and a wife looks like Charlise Theron on her way to the polo matches, but I know there's more to it than that."

Johnnie Boy downed the full measure of his beer, then tapped the rim of his mug for another, "Let's see, you got Havana Spice, heavy into porn, who's hookin' on the side; you got Ronnie Reicher, her Angel boyfriend, runnin' scag; you got a mountain of Afghan white you come across in Havana's apartment along with Reicher's body and the torched remains of Amber Starr, a stripper who's also hookin' on the side; you got your pal, the FBI boy wonder, who put you in the middle of this shit storm; and now you got Sonny Coulter who runs the Angel's smack operation up your ass 'cause he thinks you're on to him and probably workin' for Dougherty, that about right?"

"In a nutshell, yeah, I guess so, what of it?"

"You see Ruby over there?" Lights Out said motioning toward the club's entrance. "One time he told me somethin' I won't never forget, 'if you're in a situation and what's happening don't make sense,' he told me, 'it's either about a woman, money, or both.' What you got here, Jackie, is a 'woman' and 'money' situation goes back to the days right after Prohibition. The 'woman' is the porn business and—no offense—Havana and broads like her. The 'money' is drugs—heroin, from you tell me where..."

"*Afghanistan,*" I whispered.

"Bingo, my brother! You know, I hang out with cops 'cause they buy me drinks and shoot the shit about back in the day when I was a fighter. Well, I hear those guys talkin' and sometimes I learn about stuff. One thing I learned is how the mob got started here in New York and I'll tell you it was Lucky Lucciano, who was a fucking criminal genius. You know why he was a genius, Jackie?"

"No, why?"

"Because after Prohibition, when sellin' booze was legal and the mob needed somethin' new to cash in on, it was Charlie Lucky who had the idea to put trim and scag together for the first time, like in a business. Heroin was cheap, people wanted it, and they'd pay good money for it. Prostitution, same thing: illegal, lots a women around, and guys'd pay top dollar for a good piece of ass. Now here's the thing," Lights Out confided looking up at me sly as a miser, "what Luciano figured out was that if you turned these broads into junkies, they'd work for their daily fix, not money, and never leave because once they got hooked, where the fuck they goin' anyway?" He slapped my shoulder with the back of his hand, "See what I'm sayin'? What you got here ain't nothin' different. You got the Angels with their scag. You got the women with their porn. A fucking marriage made in Heaven, am I right, or am I right?"

"Okay," I said, tracking his logic point-by-point, about to be impressed, "but where does it lead? I mean, what does all of this do for my case, if what you're saying is true?"

Johnnie Boy was already laughing as he guzzled what I feared was his umpteenth beer, "That's what I'm workin' on, my brother," he said, cuffing me around the neck and pulling me toward him. "Where it leads is this: if what I'm tellin' you is right and Havana is the 'woman' and Afghan White is the 'money,' then who's the fucking brains behind it, Jack? *Who's the Charlie Lucky in this situation who put those two things together?*"

I considered what he was telling me. Havana, Reicher, Amber, and the Hells Angels operating individually were four distinct entities. It was the coordination of what each brought to the table that made the sum worth more than the individual parts, the result of which transformed four societal misfits into something that was beginning to resemble a global criminal organization patterned after Lucciano's brain child, America's version of the Sicilian mafia.

"You know, Johnnie, you may be the only fucking genius I know," I marveled, wondering who my 'Charlie Lucky' could be, if we'd ever crossed paths, and if the epicenter of his operation was in New York, or the United States, for that matter.

Johnnie stabbed a forefinger to his temple and began tapping the side of his head, grinning broadly, breath heavy as kerosene, "I'm workin' on it, my brother," he roared, laughing. "I'm workin' on it!" he repeated, then, realizing his mug was empty, craned his head around to Rubinoff, who stood at the end of the bar, and shouted, "Hey, Ruby, bring us two shots a Jameson's! And, for Christ's sake," he protested, motioning toward the screen across from us, "if you're gonna play my MMA tapes, at least show a fight that I fucking won, will ya?"

Once back at the hotel, I took a nightcap at the Monkey Bar and brought a second Glenlivet-rocks back up to the room. Sitting at my desk sipping scotch alone in the dark that night, I felt like the lone survivor of an apocalyptic episode as thoughts of Havana and Tiffany raged like the voices of wounded souls from out of the void. *What had I done? What didn't I do? Was there something I could have changed that would have saved Havana or breathed life into the moribund relationship now all but ended with my daughter?* And sitting there in the dark that night, it was as if my failures like jackals had begun gathering in a pack around me as Havana's voice was joined by Tiffany's, and Tiffany's by that of my ex-wife, then by my father's bitter recriminations, until I could not give names to all the pairs of eyes that tightened in that circle around me.

Enough! I felt like screaming back at the cacophony that like daggers were coming at me from out of that circle, and like daggers each voice registered deep into what was left of my ravaged psyche. *Yes, I loved Havana!* I spat-out taking the first of them. *Yes, I'd give all that I possess to re-connect with Tiffany!* I anguished absorbing a second and third. *No, I was not a faithful husband to you, Jennifer!* I bellowed attempting to extract a fourth and fifth dagger. *Yes, I plead guilty to wholesale transgressions against anyone who ever tried to love me!* I shrieked, as the sixth and seventh tore into me, *just stop this torture and leave me in peace!!*

Then, they did. And like a curtain falling, there followed a profound silence ended by the ringing of the telephone. It was Vicky Benson my ex-girlfriend and attorney.

"Hello, Jack?" the voice at the other end of the mobile inquired. *"Jack, are you there?"*

I swallowed hard, wiping the sweat from my forehead, "Yeah, it's me, baby," I stumbled, trying to orient myself.

"Jesus, you okay, you sound awful?"

I grabbed my glass and took down the last dilutions of scotch and ice, "Sure, I was asleep, dreaming, that's all…"

"Well, sorry to wake you, but I've been trying to make contact for two days now. I wanted to know what happened with Havana and your biker friends."

"Havana's dead," I answered bluntly, "murdered by some maniac in the Poconos mountains. Details are still sketchy. So far as the Angels, it seems guys like that will always be around to exploit Havana or women like her."

"You must be devastated!"

"A little tired, a little angry, that much I'll give you."

"Come home, baby. There's nothing left for you in New York," she cajoled in a soft, urgent voice. "The work Dougherty hired you to do is over. You've done all you can. He has nothing to be concerned about anymore and neither do you."

"She had a diary."

"What?"

"Havana kept an electronic diary with a list of clients. Dougherty needs me to locate it for him."

"*Don't!*" she snapped back instinctively. "*You did what you promised! It's not right for him to ask more of you now!*"

"I'm not a guy does things by halves," I reminded her, a timbre of resolve creeping into my voice. "Tom likes to play the role of a victim, always has, and he's paid damned well to have me think of him that way. He'll come out of it on top, guys like him always do, but I have a feeling he may need someone in his corner this time."

"Yeah, sure," she answered, resigned to the fact that I

was not about to leave a friend hanging, "but since I know how stubborn you can be and that in the end you're going to stay anyway, you should know that I got the analysis back on that death threat you sent me."

"Yeah?"

"Doctor Heitbaum, the professor I told you about at the Smithsonian? He analyzed the stationery and identified the image that runs through that watermark you were wondering about. It's a cockroach, Jack, a common *blattaria*, does that mean anything to you? Because even Heitbaum admitted he hasn't a clue."

"A cockroach?" I repeated, mind set scrambling like an intruder ripping open doors to the rooms of a deserted mansion in search of a connection, *any connection*, with Reicher or Havana, Woods or Ewing, the Ram Rod or Casanova Club. "No, I can't imagine what the image of cockroach has to do with me or anything related to the Dougherty case."

Chapter
Twenty-Nine

That night I lay awake for a long time watching the random play of city lights across my ceiling. The battle had been waged between the necessity of sleep and the stark truth that I did not want to close my eyes for fear of dreaming. Do I splurge for a few more Sucinol and get a couple hours sleep or pass into morning without it and try to make it through the day on stimulants?

It was the Succinol that won out. Who could get through the eighteen hours I saw in front of me without a decent night's sleep? Not me, the voice of surrender conceded before walking into the bathroom and seizing two script containers, one for Succs, the other my old standby, Ambien. ***DO NOT CHEW OR CRUSH!!*** the warning label cautioned. "Thanks for the advice," I murmured, splitting open the capsules—two Succinol, then two Ambien—pouring the multi-colored beads into my mouth, then taking them down with a pull of Jameson's.

Yet, I did not fall asleep for over an hour, every nerve of my body protesting against the long day that had just ended as scenes from my conversation with Lights Out played back in my head. Could it be that Giambi had discerned the single element that tied the multiple coincidences that plagued me about the Dougherty case together? Perhaps there was a 'Charlie Lucky' who presided over an underground empire with tentacles that extended far beyond New York or even the United States into Russia, Europe, and China. Or maybe it was me who had become like the gambler who puts all he owns on a single bet so desperate to win that he comes to believe the longer the odds, the better his chances.

No matter, once the flag of surrender was hoisted and my eyes closed, the pandemonium I'd feared was let loose from the bleakest corners of my subconscious and I was alone fighting one of those one-man wars that leave not a single corpse in the morning. It began with the usual streams in my head of grainy, out-of-synch newsreel footage involving my father's suicide, but soon graduated to include more recent entries into my repertoire of nighttime terrors involving Tiffany, spinning away from me into the frozen desolation of deep space; Havana, naked and trembling as she floated atop a ramshackle raft on a winding river of acid; waves of cockroaches, black shells iridescent, a buzz coming off them one thousand times multiplied, devouring the core of a globe that mapped the geographies of the civilized world. Then, finally—just as I felt my heart would burst like a trapped falcon from out of my chest—I leapt up in a cold sweat to see the image, half-realized, of Salvatore "Bill" Bonanno floating, upside-down, near the foot of my bed.

There he floated, a full three feet above the carpet, black cowboy boots greeting me at eye level, head set just above the mattress, a resigned expression on his face.

I rubbed my eyes and took a second look, "Bill?" I

asked, surprised at his most recent incarnation, if not by the visit, itself.

Making one's way through eternity must not be so easy, I realized then, as the upside-down Godfather's voice cracked-up as with a defective satellite connection, "Ironic, ain't it?" he observed, a lone voice calling out to me from the busiest intersection of seven thousand universes. "Your prayers were answered and I ain't in Hell," he said, waving a hand around him to emphasize his condition, "*but this?*"

I nodded, "It's a bitch being dead, I suppose, but I'm glad you're here, Bill. I need your help bad."

"It's about that case you been workin', am I right?"

Again, I nodded, "I'm at a crossroad and I don't know which way to go. I need a clue, Bill. I need something to go on!"

To him, through the electric mist of an undiscovered time and space dimension, my supplications must have seemed whiny as an adolescent pouting over a parental curfew because Bonanno's body, his entire frame began bobbing like a giant cork on a turbulent sea. His expression was vexed.

"Revir," he stated off-handedly, then more emphatically, "Revir!" he repeated. "Revir!" Then, like a sunspot had suddenly come and left again, the transmission cleared, "*The river, the river,*" he was saying.

"I don't know what you're talking about!" I protested, starting to feel ridiculous talking to the upside-down man hovering three feet above my bedroom carpet.

"*Blood, lots of it ... Cut up into pieces ... Like DeMeo ... Roy Demeo ... fucking monster!*"

"*Who, Bill? Who's a monster?*"

"*Akfak*," he answered as if passing a solemn truth along to me. "*S'it ruoy eulc. Eht ylno eno I nac eivg uoy!*"

"*What? What are you saying? What are you trying to tell me! Is it Latin? Greek??*"

At that moment, amid the static of something that felt like intense electrical energy, Bonanno's entire frame suddenly uprighted itself and he loomed over me. Bill was urgently trying to tell me something, I realized, but his words were fragmented, when with a popping noise not unlike the sound of a television switching off, he was simply gone, vanished from my room and from my life, I thought!

"Bill?" I asked, eyes combing the room, but there was no sign of him.

I shook my head clear, even pinched myself to see if I felt the expected twinge of pain before rising up from the tussled white sheets and walking to the bathroom.

Neither Bill Bonanno nor anyone else was there to greet me once I flicked on the lights, and I remember the tile floor was cold on the soles of my feet. "*Must be the Succinol ... Must be the Ambien and whiskey,*" I whispered, approaching the sink where I switched on the faucet and threw cold water onto my face. I pulled a towel from its rack, dried my face then looked up into the medicine cabinet mirror and was jolted back to see, not my face, but Bonanno's face staring back at me touching the opposite side of the mirror with his fingertips as though trapped behind the glass!

"*Bill!*" I gasped, but there was no response, just this odd, disoriented expression that began to settle as I stood watching, into one that seemed far more focused, eyes wide with alarm.

During that terrifying instant, I noticed again that he seemed more shadow than substance, *there* but not totally *actualized*, and that a kind of mist hung around him that finally began to haze the mirror itself so that when he took his right index finger and began moving it across the mirror's opposite side, letters began to appear.

The first was what looked like a backward 'L'. The second was an 'I'. The third was a 'V'. The fourth, and final letter, crudely written and in block as a child might write it, was a backward 'E'. Though distanced from one another—one letter dropped down, the next veering up—I could nevertheless make out the word he had drawn. The letters spelled the word 'L-I-V-E'. Then, the ghost of Bill Bonanno looked one last time into my eyes to check for understanding and, seeing it, disappeared with the same breathtaking suddenness that he'd come!

There I stood, staring into the mirror, paralyzed by, what was it, fear? Disbelief? Whatever emotions rose up within me, one thing was certain, the impact of the experience left me quaking as I stared at the letters, imprinted over the image of my own face now, watching them fade until nothing—not the letters nor the word nor any fragment of them—remained.

Afterwards, I walked to my desk and scrawled the message Bill had left for me onto the blank page of a legal pad in large block letters, careful to duplicate its style and idiosyncrasies. I studied it, wondering what reason he'd have for wanting so desperately to communicate a word so insignificant. For a good time after that and even once I'd settled back under the sheets, the impact of what had happened reverberated like the aftermath of a shotgun blast around me; asleep, and yet not asleep, the numbness of booze and drugs ebbing and receding in my head like a nocturnal tide. "*DeMeo, Roy DeMeo,*" my mind played and re-played. *I knew that name!* I'd heard Bill mention it not once but twice over a dinner at Patsy's in Manhattan with my father-in-law Barton Crowley, *but who was he?* What connection could he, or the final message he'd chosen to leave behind possibly have to the Dougherty case? I struggled to fathom through most of the night.

It was only after the sound of three pounding raps on the door to my hotel room that I stirred from my drug-induced slumber. "*Shit!*" I cursed, forced to desert the warmth of my bed to trundle to the foyer where I opened the door, startled to find Ruby Rubinoff standing in the hallway waiting.

It didn't take Sherlock Holmes to see that the Russian, normally so jovial, wasn't there to tell my 'dollar and a dream' had just won the New York lottery! Rubinoff's head was hanging like a hound dog's as he shuffled from side-to-side, a copy of the *NY Post* in his right hand, a bottle of Jack Daniels in his left. His eyes were rimmed red and it looked like he may have been crying.

"Jesus, Ruby, what's wrong? Klitchkos lose their titles to a Chinaman?"

"Not here for funny time, Jack Madson," he finally brought himself to say, making eye contact for the first time. "I come to tell you before you see News," he said, jabbing the *Post's* afternoon edition out at me like it'd been soaked in anthrax.

I took the paper and began paging through it, but realized I need go no farther than the front-page photo of a battered Ford Pinto being lifted by crane from out of the Hudson, the oversized type leaping from the page like a siren from Hell. "**I COULDA BEEN A CONTENDA**," the headline read, and that was all I needed to know that Johnnie Giambi was dead.

"Come in," I uttered, moving to the side as Rubinoff entered the foyer.

"You want drink?" he asked holding up the bottle.

I nodded.

He moved into the office area of my suite and took two glasses from off the counter near my desk.

"When did it happen?" I asked.

"They find body in river yesterday morning."

I approached him. He handed me a glass half-filled with no ice.

"That makes no sense, I was with him last night, so were you!"

The heavy-set Russian took a gulp from his glass. He swallowed, lids at half-mast as his eyes lifted to meet mine, "We see Johnnie two nights ago, Jackie, what day you think is?"

"It's Wedneday," I said.

"You crazy with booze!" he rumbled. "Today Thursday, my friend, *Thursday!*" he repeated, then offered a half-hearted toast, "Better drink whiskey."

My eyes flew to the digital clock on my console. Yeah, it was 9 am, but 9 am Thursday, *not Wednesday!* I had apparently slept for a day and a half, nearly twenty hours, without waking, I realized, making no pretense of my amazement to Ruby whose tubercular hack ceased as he reverted to the business at hand.

"You good friends with Johnnie?"

"Twenty years."

Rubinoff nodded, then with a sizable effort reached

around to his back pocket to retrieve a paperback book. "I go Lights Out apartment yesterday with Bronco, after we hear he dead to get personal effects. Not much to talk about, twelve hundred dollar, not enough even for funeral, but he leave this for you," he said, handing me a worn paperback edition of *Metamorphosis*, by Franz Kafka.

"Johnnie left this for me?" I asked, eyes honing immediately onto its cover design which depicted an enormous cockroach bearing the head and face of a man.

"Look, see note from Johnnie," he suggested, touching the slip of paper peeking from out of its worn pages as he stepped toward me.

It was a handwritten note and classic Johnnie Giambi, I thought as I read it:

Jack,

Here's a book has to do with Dougherty. Don't know how, but I'm workin on it. If I don't make it through tonight, you need to find out yourself. Cockroaches! What a crazy bastard this guy Kafka musta been!!

Take care to take care,

Lights Out.

"How'd he die?" I asked.

"Not good subject," Ruby blustered shaking his head clear of what I imaged must have been a horrid death for Johnnie. "He die bad, Jack. No good for him. Too nice man for killed like that!"

"Johnnie was murdered?"

Rubinoff poured another drink for us both, "Cut up like animal in butcher shop. In river just two hours.

Dead before he hit Hudson. Body chopped in pieces like chicken." Ruby had to stop then, trying to hold back a sob that would not be suppressed. He downed his drink then put his arms around me, holding me close to him. "This no good, Jack. Police worth shit. Say they get killers but I don't believe. Someone do something, but who, not us? Not us!!" he bemoaned sobbing once more into my chest as I held him.

"Funeral?" I asked, still reeling from the news and from fucking life, in general.

"Tomorrow. Saint John's, West Side, 10 o'clock morning. Bronco pay for priest. I pay for grave stone. Johnnie have not many friends? I don't know, but you be there?"

"Yeah, I'll be there," I promised, watching Rubinoff pull away from me toward the door like an ocean freighter drifting into midnight, eyes still locked with mine. "You going to be all right?" I asked him.

"Fine, yes, fine," he whimpered. "Here," he said passing along the bottle of Jack Daniels, "you keep bottle. I go back bar, get drunk watch Johnnie fight film."

I accepted the bottle without protest. He was right to leave it, I needed a drink in the worst fucking way, I was thinking as I re-filled my glass then drifted, as in an opium dream to the refrigerator for some ice.

Johnnie was dead, murdered, I pondered, opening the refrigerator door, and something just short of two days had passed without me knowing it. *"Shit-fuck!"* I muttered, realizing I was setting new records even for myself in the area of blackouts and addiction, but before I could complete my reverie, my body and mind froze so that the thought hung in mid-air, skewered by the sheer force of the abomination set before me like a chunk of Hell, itself, risen up from the netherworld to greet me.

I reached into the mini-fridge, took it into the palm of my hand, and stared at it for an instant that seemed more like hours, my entire being numbed with shock, before a howl of despair tore loose from the corners of my soul, loud enough to shatter crystal, anguished enough to make strangers on the street weep for humankind with the sheer force of its depravity.

It was the head of Johnnie Giambi! Eyes plucked from their sockets, lips removed, nose and ears severed, face skinned to the skull! Then I stood, still holding Johnnie's head in my hands, and ran across the room to my desk where I suddenly remembered that Roy DeMeo was the mass murderer-hit man who'd dismembered his victims appendage by appendage, organ by organ, *hundreds of them*, in the blood-laden bathtub of his Brooklyn tenement while working for the mob; and my eyes flew to the mirror above the desk to see the reflection of the word I had scrawled onto the legal pad, now re-configured, the voices, thousands of them, screaming at me, chiding, berating, laughing hysterically from out of the void.

E-V-I-L was the word that Bill Bonanno had scrawled with his fingertip onto the mirror's opposite side, not *L-I-V-E*. His message was—*EVIL, EVIL, EVIL!!*—but it was only now that I understood what he was trying to tell me!

Chapter Thirty

Need I describe to you the horror I felt that
morning, and the one beyond that, sleepwalking
like the *undead* through introductions to strangers,
embraces by friends and yes, tears, many of them shed
for Johnnie and the unimaginable indignities he must
have suffered while dying? The funeral at St. John's and
burial at Sacred Valley were like a carnival complete with
strong men, midgets, and circus barkers. Johnnie's fellow
combatants, trainers, promoters, and East Coast Mafia
backers were out in force along with their women and,
my god, it was like the Vegas strip at midnight replete
with every hooker Los Angeles to Beantown phaser gun-
transported to Hell's Kitchen in New York.

Odd, but aside from Ruby Rubinoff, Vicky Benson, and
Eddie Lawler, in from D.C., there were just two others that
didn't fit snugly into the surreal world of Johnnie "Lights
Out" Giambi, and that was Tom and Ann Dougherty. Both
sat solemnly to the back of St. John's Catholic church:
Tom dressed in a dark three-piece business suit and Annie
in a black Kenzo dress, eyes clenched shut as they knelt
praying the rosary. Then, at Sacred Valley cemetery, with
the number of mourners cut by half, they stood holding
hands at the grave's perimeter to watch as Johnnie's casket
was lowered into the ground repeating the words along with

the priest, *'ashes to ashes, dust to dust'* and then it was over. Handshakes, embraces, a last drink with Vicky and Eddie Lawler at Ruby's place before they headed back to D.C., but it was Tom's parting words at Johnnie's grave that sticks with me even today. "Sorry for your loss. I know you cared about him, Jack," he told me, "but he's in a better place. Johnnie's happy now that his time here has ended." He stepped to the side after that, watched Annie give me a hug, then they left, just sauntered away, dry-eyed and self-satisfied, back to the limo waiting curbside and their multi-million dollar estate. 'Johnnie's happy now,' he'd advised and I guess that was supposed to make me forget the fact that my friend had been murdered, body ripped apart and dissected like a laboratory specimen by a psychopathic serial killer. 'Johnnie's in a better place ... Johnnie's happy now ...' *Yeah, right,* I was thinking, eyes lit with fury as they prowled the empty graveyard. *Fuck you, Tom, you condescending hypocrite! What do you know about Johnnie Giambi? Or Havana Spice? Or me? Or any-fucking-body??*

So what was my disposition later that afternoon while sitting at the desk in my hotel room in front of my Dell XPS laptop? Already passed through the multiple stages of grief like lava spewed from a volcano the molten rage that possessed me had transformed to an unshakable resolve. At first, I saw solving the Dougherty case as a path back into the mainstream, a man with a modicum of talent when it came to criminal investigation walking through the last door of opportunity still open to him, but now all of that had changed. No longer playing *not to lose*, I was playing a 'winner take all' hand in a life or death poker game and didn't give a damn which it was going to be, *I simply wanted to win.* And what was the 'win' for me? It was stabbing, or shooting, or blowing to pieces, or strangling to death with my bare hands, Johnnie Giambi's killer and maybe more than that, *but not one fucking iota less!*

I paged through the book Rubinoff had passed along, *Metamorphosis* by Kafka, the final communication Johnnie left me prior to his murder. The paperback's cover was nothing short of grotesque: a cockroach, dark shell glittering, with the face of a man, antennae sprouting out of his head, staring out at its audience, remote and unabashed. On the back cover was a promotional tagline: "Franz Kafka's *Metamorphosis* is one of the great novellas of the 20th century and is widely studied in colleges and universities across the western world," followed by a brief description of the work, "This story begins with a traveling salesman, Gregor Samsa, waking up to find himself transformed into a monstrous insect-like creature."

My wary eyes returned to the macabre cover design as I closed the book and switched on my laptop. Kafka's story of man-become-insect obviously meant something to Johnnie, and me, given Vicky's revelation that a cockroach watermark had been stamped on the stationery of my death threat. I opened a 'search' for *Metamorphosis* settling on a *N Y Times* article, "What is the Essence of *Kafkaesque?*" written by NYU professor Karl Fredrick. "*Kafkaesque* is when you enter a surreal world in which all you control begins to fall to pieces and you find yourself battling a force that does not lend itself to the way you perceive the world. You don't give up, you don't lay down and die. What you do is struggle with whatever strength you possess. But, of course, you don't stand a chance. That's *Kafkaesque,* and one's resignation to that reality, forms the basis of *existentialism.*"

So, the cockroach man, along with Sartre, Kierkegaard, and others, were existentialist apologists who believed that since life was 'absurd,' and beyond human comprehension, no one has a lock on the truth. Okay, fair enough, I supposed, launching another 'search,' this time for *existentialism*, coming upon the translation of a definition written by Pierre Mainguy, professor of philosophy at the University of Paris. "A central proposition of existentialism is that the most important consideration for a human being is the fact that he or she is an individual rather than what roles or preconceived societal categories the individual fits. Thus, human beings, through their own *consciousness*, create their own values which gives meaning to their life irrespective of societal norms or traditional outcomes."

Now here was a jump in logic worthy of an author who writes about men transformed into cockroaches! Fredrick, in his definition of *Kafkaesque* had laid the foundation for a leap by Mainguy in his definition of *existentialism* equivalent to that of a man hurtling from one bank of the Grand Canyon to the other! **Fredrick**: *life is incomprehensible, therefore, one man's truth is as meaningless as another's.* **Mainguy**: *life is indeed incomprehensible, therefore, society's truth is without meaning leaving one free to replace society's strictures with his or her own.* Implicit in all of this, then, was the belief that an individual's perceptions of what is good or evil, normal or deviant, trumped any laws or conventional morality put forward by society. Existentialists, then, *true existentialists*, were a society unto themselves whose only rule was that, for them, there existed no rules.

I stared at the screen attempting to digest the implications of what Kafka and existentialists, in general, put forward vis a vis the kaleidoscope of moving parts

I'd uncovered during the Dougherty investigation. What did it all mean? What could it mean once each piece was assembled in the proper configuration?

The first tie was the stationery's watermark, a cockroach according to Heitbaum, linked to Kafka's existentialist novella left behind by Johnnie. Another was the name dropped by Bonanno when he uttered the name 'Roy DeMeo.' Murdered himself in a mob rub-out, the infamous hit man didn't kill his victims, he gleefully beheaded them, ripping their bodies apart not unlike the wanton killer who'd beheaded the Asian boy, Johnnie, and perhaps a dozen others, according to Ewing.

But there was more, I speculated, attempting to pull the connections back into focus. Yet, what I recalled wasn't the memory of a conversation or event but a sensory experience, the sickeningly sweet smell that roiled from out of the sack that held the head of that Asian kid, setting my head whirling freefall to the brink of unconsciousness. The same odor I'd experienced in my hotel room when I opened the refrigerator to discover Johnnie's head, mangled by identical slashes and incisions. It was clear to me that both atrocities had been committed by the same killer and in the identical way, but it was the smell that intrigued me. Formalin was the chemical agent Forensics had identified, Woods told Vicky and me while at the Tombs in Georgetown: *formalin, phenols, methanol, and quaternary ammonium,* all "fixatives" used by morticians to give the mortal remains of their clients the appearance of one who was sleeping rather than dead. *'Dust to dust, ashes to ashes,'* the priest had proclaimed at the foot of Johnnie's grave, but the chemical concoction identified by Wood's team and injected into the Asian boy's cranium, and Johnnie's as well, seemed the madman's attempt at circumventing the fate of all things mortal, elevating his victim in some bizarre way to the realm of ... *incorruptible.*

The thread of coincidences seemed to finally be pulling together when I heard a rustling sound emanating from the adjoining room. Flashes like chain lightning lit the darkest recesses of my mind where the devil swaggered over images of severed heads and body parts strewn about neat in piles. If it was an assassin sent to kill me, I wasn't going to make it easy, I vowed, lifting my Remington Colt from the side desk drawer, flipping the cylinder open to make certain it was loaded, and gravitating like a ghost from out of my chair.

Stealthily, I strode toward the bedroom, its door half-open, as I came upon its entrance, back pressed against the outside wall. Then, filling my lungs with a gulp of air, I braced myself for what was to come and burst into the room, weapon held at eye level and gripped tight in both hands, as I scanned the room's contents corner-to-corner: closet to chiffonier, vanity mirror to bathroom entrance my eyes, narrowed to needle points, finally settling on the bed at room's center where like an eyeball spiked to a wall my focus froze and locked.

It was Havana's son, Savito, Nike sneakers dangling off the side of the bed where he sat playing *Zombie Geek Mercenaries* on his IPad.

"She's not dead," he said, looking up to me, unfazed by the gun I had trained on him.

"Who?" I asked, lowering my weapon. "Who's not dead?"

"My Mom, Havana Spice. She's not dead."

"How did you get in my room?"

The boy closed the app. "The maid let me in last night when you were out. I slept in the closet," he added as the zombie mercenaries vanished off-screen, replaced by what I imagined an army of powerful men across the East Coast had been scrambling to recover. It was Havana's electronic diary. The one she'd told me about with the names of 'Society' members; the one Dougherty anguished would find its way into the hands of his enemies.

"See here," Savito said, pointing to her final entry, dated December 17th, 2:30 am, four hours after the estimated time of her murder. "It wasn't her they killed. It was another lady who they used for movies that only *looked* like her."

I shoved the Remington inside my belt and took the IPad into my hands, studying the unlikely catalogue of events that was the life of Noemi Machado:

2:30 am

Desperate now waiting for rescue at Beethoven Café in SoHo. Scared for Savito, but Sonny promise he is safe. Now I must trust him. Terrible! Horrible! Lucy Sanchez murdered! Shot in head because Sonny tells killer she is me. $10,000 is what this man pays to leave Casanova Club with Lucy that night. $10,000 for her life! SUV speeding down street. Sonny and others here now. Please God let Savito be safe! Bikers with him all carrying automatic weapons. Surround entrance to café. Sonny in charge, coming to take me to safe house. I see Savito's face in back window of SUV. He see me. Savito is smiling and I'm thinking now I want to hold him in my arms forever!

"The safe house, Savito, where is it?"

"In Queens on the 'Ave.' It used to be an apartment

building but no one lives there anymore. Just Sonny and El Gigante when he was alive. El Gigante told us to go there if we were ever in trouble and had nowhere else to go. We're like that now, Mr. Madson."

"El Gigante? Was it Reicher who told you this?"

"Yes. It used to be called the New Canaan projects, that's what Sonny said, but now they don't call it anything, just the 'safe house.' That's where my Mom is hiding since the man who thought Lucy Sanchez was Havana Spice shot and killed her 'body double.'"

Chapter Thirty-One

I t was late afternoon by the time I got the full story out of Savito, so battle scarred that even the lurid details of the way Lucy Sanchez was murdered found him calm and logical if not more than a little concerned about his Mom's ultimate fate. Savito's entire mentality seemed to have evolved to survive in the house of mirrors that was Havana's existence and it reminded me of the quote from Dostoyevsky's *The Brothers Karamazov*, "You have become her sadness and live in a different state of mind."

And so it was, as the two of us stood outside the Elysée Hotel waiting for my car to arrive, Savito burrowed deep into the techno world of "Boot Camp Zombie Surfers", perhaps his only escape from the trials of this 'real' world the rest of us begrudgingly embraced. But before my Porsche arrived, a shiny black Lincoln Continental glided up to the hotel portico with a driver and two passengers in the back seat. The economy of its coming and the practiced exit of the two men in the back set a spark flying out from the primordial pocket of nerve ends guys like me have had planted in their brain, but efficiency trumped instinct as I swung around to Savito who was standing beside the doorman, *"Go now!"* I urged. *"Go to your Mom and take the IPad with you!"*

Street-wise as he was, the kid was on his way to the 54th

Street subway by the time the men took positions on either side of me. Both were well-dressed and could have been twins, one wearing a pearl-gray fedora, dark blue suit, and black overcoat, the other one hatless.

"Who was that boy you were with?" the tall, rangy one to my right demanded.

"Oh, him? That was my love child. Product of a Miley Cyrus concert back in '08," I beamed as Savito disappeared into the underground.

"See what I told ya?" Twin #2 crowed twisting my left, then my right, arm behind my back and cuffing me. "A real wise-ass! Now wipe that smile off your face before I wipe it off for you. You're coming with us, asshole."

And I must admit, if neither was a candidate for *Time* magazine's "Man of The Year," the least you could say was they knew how to strong-arm a man, and before I could raise a hand against them, I was shoved into the back seat of the Lincoln, door slammed behind me.

"Where are you taking me?" I asked, trying to adjust position for the pain of the cuffs clamped behind my back.

"Shut up," answered the nastier of the two.

"No, he deserves an answer," the second objected. "Besides, it's not like he's blindfolded. We're taking you to the U.S. Mission on 1st Avenue. Our boss wants to talk to you. He thinks you can help us and maybe he can help you."

"Charming, fellas, but there's nothing very diplomatic about any of this. So far as I can tell, I've just been kidnapped."

"See what I mean?" the other man upbraided. "I studied the profile. This guy's a piece of shit."

"Yeah, maybe," Twin #1 concluded, "but he's *our* piece of shit and the SAC wants to talk to him."

And that was it. Sure, I tried the obvious, a heated protest, a piss-warm threat of legal action but handcuffed as I was with two trained operatives on either side of me I wasn't feeling much like Daniel Craig ready to push a backseat ejection button that afternoon. No, I was stuck, mouth shut, pondering the first class talent I had for leaping headlong into every shit storm I happened by from that moment to the time we approached United Nations Plaza and entrance to the 26-story U.S. Mission where the Lincoln disappeared into the compound's underground lot.

Still, once my handcuffs were removed and the three of us marched to the private elevator headed for the third of four floors below street level, I knew at least one truth about my abductors. Twin #1 had used the term SAC, Special Agent in Charge. These were government agents, probably Special Ops, and I was on my way to meeting the head of their operation.

Down a labyrinth of empty corridors I trudged feeling like a prisoner on his way to a gulag before we came to an office marked 'secure' where, when the door was finally pushed open, I could only nod, sneering.

"Woods," I said sourly, "I might have known you, or someone like you, was behind this. So what's your cover this time, a diplomat serving at the U.N.?"

The compact, middle-aged SAC with clear blue eyes cold as December rose from his desk and approached, his two flunkies falling away like a snake's old skin. Knowing I'd refuse to shake his hand, he withheld the gesture and answered my question.

"We moved here after World Trade Tower #2 came down. It was supposed to be temporary, but some of us liked it and it became home to Group 41 charged with the investigation of U.S. intelligence agencies A to Z. We 'police the police' you might say. Not so well liked, as you can imagine, but with NYPD everywhere, K9 units, and the building, itself, built to withstand terrorist car bomb attacks, the place begins to grow on you."

"It looks like a fucking prison," I observed.

"Yeah," Woods agreed, voice trailing off as if to concede we had little to discuss outside of the obvious topic that so obsessed him. "I suppose I should apologize for the way you were brought here, but your track record for cooperation hasn't been so stellar."

"It's true you and me don't hit the sweetest notes, but kidnapping? I ought to sue you and whatever goddamned agency you're working for."

"Maybe you've never heard of the Patriot Act?"

"Maybe you've never heard of the Constitution!"

"All right, nobody says we've got to be asshole buddies, but when you see what I have to show you it may change your mind about me, and the people you work for."

"Dougherty again, huh? Don't you think you've trotted that pony out once too often?"

Woods nodded to the twins who started toward a second closed door behind him, "No, I'm afraid I can't agree, Madson," he muttered gloomily.

"You realize that while this Group 41 of yours is busy trying to frame Dougherty, a serial killer is loose! Ever thought about that, or the victims of this maniac like my friend Johnnie Giambi?"

Woods took my rant in stride, and it felt like I was shooting bullets into a corpse so profoundly pitiful did he appear as he turned toward the door, now open, and entered the back room, walls plastered with surveillance photos, nearly all, it seemed, of Dougherty: *Tom walking into St. Patrick's cathedral in New York with Gambino crime family boss,* **Anthony "The Pimp" Coscarelli**; *Tom meeting with* **Senator Jacob Mathias**, *Chairman of the Defense and Finance Committees*; *Tom shaking hands with Russian mobster* **Alexi Petrovitch** *in Moscow*; *Tom sitting at a conference table at an unidentified location surrounded by Columbian drug lord* **Carlos Padilla**; **Mohammad Tasserbehji, the "Butcher of Kabul," Senator Jacob Mathias,** *again, and* **Xui Li Zhou,** *identified by INTERPOL as the most notorious human trafficker alive.*

"Okay, you've got pictures of Dougherty with some global bad asses. It's his job to track down guys like that and infiltrate their organizations, so what?"

"During the Gulf War, General Schwarzkopf hung a photo of the Republican Guard leader, Qusay Hussein, on the wall opposite his desk," he responded, opting to ignore my question. "Claimed he got to know him that way; the way I'm beginning to comprehend Dougherty. We think we can lure him out of his rat hole with your help."

"My help? I'd rather move back to Oregon!"

"Too late for that, Madson. Like it or not, you're either with us or him now."

"You've got a dozen agents in this building could take him down easier than me! That's what this is all about, isn't it? To take Tom down and the FBI hierarchy along with him?"

"It's a question of access," Woods explained, blue eyes locking steady with mine. "Dougherty has top security clearance. That means what we see on NADDIS, PATHFINDER, EPIC—the tools we use to track global criminals—he sees, too. Your high school chum's obsessed by the possibility of infiltration so it has to be a man of his choosing, someone close to him who he feels the need to include in the warped world he's created. We could work for a decade and never achieve something like that. He knows you're a straight shooter, Madson. He trusts you. There is no one else. But here," he said motioning the lights to be dimmed as we sat down at an oblong table facing a video monitor, "maybe this will change your mind about cooperating."

Then, I watched. And, yeah, what Woods showed me was shocking to the core: secretly recorded tape of sex slaves, ages four to fifteen, Beta programmed by their "handlers," giggling as they injected themselves with their daily fix of heroin; young boys bound and whipped by hooded men in combat fatigues, performing fellatio for their amusement, others chained to walls and tortured with electrodes attached to various body parts; young girls handcuffed and sodomized by anonymous men, some engaged in cunnilingus, others dressed for sexual role play in the costumes of nurses, French maids, and school girls, then gang raped en masse; all of them starved half to death by day and left to sleep in dresser drawers, dog crates, and bamboo cages by night.

"Not so pretty, eh Jack?"

I shook my head numbly, mind flying like a kite in a hurricane to thoughts of Noemi Machado and her tortured youth, and there the image of her hung, battered and torn to shreds by the storm's sullen violence. "Sickening!" I rumbled, still reeling from the travesties I'd witnessed, still contemplating Havana and my high school companion, Tom Dougherty. "People in Tom's position are framed sometimes, Woods, by police or competing agencies," I argued, pointlessly. "Tom's got a beautiful family; a home in Mendham. He and his wife, Annie are *Opus Dei* Catholics. What reason would he have to do something like this?"

Woods advanced the disk another track, blue eyes focused, along with mine, on a mix of evidentiary tape, camera honed this time on a solitary man, hood removed, participating in the mayhem of group sex, Beta programming of recently abducted newcomers, and sexual torture of children and, as I watched, bits and pieces of information that should have been clues all along swept through my mind with the ferocity of an avalanche, *"It's Kafkaesque, this society of ours. Like Joseph K in The Trial or Gregor Sansa in Metamorphosis,"* Dougherty had *said during our meeting at his estate in Mendham. "It's a Society of 'special gentlemen,'"* Havana had *written in the letters to her sister; The cockroach watermark on the death threat; Tom and Annie's conversion to Catholicism after witnessing the miracle of incorruptible corpses at the Vatican,* these recollections left me quaking with horror!

"Like you, we were fooled. Sure, we saw the numbers soaring when it came to heroin pouring into New York, and got our first clues about human trafficking here in the city, but no one suspected Dougherty, not even me. Then, we get a report from NYPD Vice about a twelve year old girl, third degrees burns covering 90% of her body, found in a garbage bin in Chelsea. Doctors say she won't survive the night, but she holds on long enough to tell us she'd been abducted from the driveway of her home in Ann Arbor, Michigan five years earlier and sold as a slave. She talks about an "underground circus" and how she was forced to have sex in rooms with strange men and most of us assume it's the trauma talking, but I figure 'here she is lying in a hospital bed, burned half to death,' so there must be something to it. Then she tells us about her "boyfriend" who sold her to a man who had this fantasy about tying a young girl to a bedpost and setting her on fire. So the boyfriend sells her and, yeah, this sick bastard does what he set out to do. Ties her to a bedpost, douses her with butane, lights her on fire. She doesn't remember anything after that. A city worker finds her and that's where it all ends, but I get to thinking, maybe there could be a "circus" like that underneath the streets of Manhattan, and maybe we should start looking."

Woods stopped talking then, perhaps to assess the emotions I was feeling, but I knew there wasn't much to see. Truth be told, I was angry, dumbfounded, and embarrassed. "You wouldn't have some whiskey around here, would you?" I asked.

He leveled a stare at Twin #2, "Bottom drawer of my desk," then looked back at me.

"Tell the truth, Woods, I feel like I'm in the middle of a bad dream! If what you're saying's true, Dougherty would have to be crazy, *insane*, and I just can't get my head around that. Tom and I go back a long way. Shit, we had our first drink together!"

"People change."

"Or not," I shot back bitterly, taking the glass of whiskey, downing it, and holding my glass out for another. "Maybe that part of Tom was always there, but latent or worse *hiding*! What kind of man could live with himself after doing these things?"

"They call it the Kafka Society," he elaborated,

forwarding the disk to a track containing physical evidence linking Dougherty to the Society: a thread of clothing, DNA graphs of matching blood samples, a "Burn After Perusal" copy of off-shore bank accounts through which millions had been laundered. "It was Dougherty's invention based a philosophy put forward by European writers like Kafka and Sartre popular in the 1960s. Those surveillance photos I showed you, of Dougherty with Zhou and the others, represent the Society's governing board. Of course it's highly lucrative, but these men are in it for fun. The Kafka Society and their existentialist beliefs are a way these monsters can justify what they do, carrying out whatever twisted fantasies they can conjure, doing anything, literally, that earns money or gives them pleasure."

"The Cassanova Club, that's their headquarters, isn't it?" I asked.

"Yeah, that's right. The old Lehigh Valley freight terminal. They use the city's abandoned underground railway system that runs from there to the old Central Stores warehouse ten blocks away. Five miles of connecting tunnels constructed back in the 1930s where uptown trains were driven directly into terminals, loaded with coal or iron ore, and sent back above ground to major cities along the east coast. Only now it's children and heroin"

I held my glass out for a refill, Twin #2 seemed amused as he poured me a third, and for a wad of spit and a piece of chewing gum I'd have knocked him through the fucking wall, but turned back to Woods instead, "What about the heads?"

"Heads?"

"Yeah," I answered, suddenly agitated. "The human head I found in the trunk of my car, the ones Ewing from

NYPD told me about, and Johnnie Giambi's? How are they connected, and please don't tell me they're not because I won't believe that for a second!"

"Fact is, we don't know how they're connected, not yet anyway, but the human remains," he began, advancing the disk again, "with the exception of Giambi's, are all those of children between the ages of..."

"No," I said, waving him off, "no more! I don't need to see any more of your evidence or those ... *tapes*. I'm convinced Dougherty is everything you say, I just don't know what you think I can do about it. I'm no cop, or secret agent. Shit, I don't even have a PI license!"

"Meet with him, Jack," he implored. "We have reason to believe he'll approach you about working with him. We know him intimately now, *how he thinks, how his mind works,* and we believe we have a fair insight into you, too. We know you're not like him, but he believes you are. He needs to believe that you're cut from the same cloth and that's the opening we've been waiting for to entice him out into the open, give us the primary witness we need to take him down, and destroy the Kafka Society forever."

"A wire?"

"No, he's too smart for that. Just meet with him. Be yourself but act as though you're open to the idea of joining. If our people are right, he'll take it from there. All you have to do is keep your eyes open and let him walk you through his operation: the drugs, the pornography, the human trafficking. You don't want to see the evidence of what these sick bastards are doing to innocent children, Jack, but closing your eyes doesn't make it go away."

I grabbed the bottle of Jamesons from out of Twin #2's

hand and poured myself another drink, "How bad do you want him?"

"Name it," he retorted.

"You get Abbott and Costello out of here and we'll talk, man to man," I said glancing over at the twins. "I don't like being played for a sucker, and I like men who make their living on the misery of children less than that."

Chapter Thirty-Two

The next morning I awoke minus the kid and Havana's diary, but not without a hangover worthy of the occasion. Yeah, sure, I'd agreed to find out what I could about the goings on at the Casanova Club and get back to Woods with it, but there was more to it than that from my side. Today I was going to see Dougherty and he was going to tell me every fetid detail about the so-called Kafka Society and the savage murders so intricately interwoven into the fabric of the double life he'd been living, consequences be damned!

Still wearing the Hoya sweats that substituted for pajamas, and with what felt like African war drums beating in my head, I chewed two Adderall and an extra strength Excedrin, washed it down with a cup of day-old coffee, and dialed Dougherty's private number.

"Hiya, Jack," Dougherty answered sprightly.

"We've got to talk *now*," I demanded.

"You've located Havana's diary."

"Yeah, read all about you and that private club of yours; not affiliated with *Opus Dei*, I'm guessing."

A significant pause followed during which I envisioned Tom's toothsome grin as he savored my meaning.

"I was expecting this call, but much sooner. You know, Jack, you're the best friend I have, but not much of a detective. Come to my office, 601 W. 26th Street, 29th floor. I think you know the neighborhood," he added, "just a stone's throw from the Casanova Club."

It took me less than twenty minutes to throw on a pair of jeans, sweatshirt, Yankee warm up jacket, and Adidas, before I was out front of the hotel hailing a cab. *So where in Christ's name was all of this headed?* I struggled to fathom and, in truth, my mind was at war with itself when it came to the subject of Dougherty, one camp still in denial, the opposing camp hell bent on revenge. And if that outcome had yet to be settled, a second deeper fissure tore at the bedrock of my embattled psyche: the overwhelming sense of relief I'd felt knowing that Havana Spice and Savito were safe pitted against the bitter enmity that rose like bile from my gut understanding how artfully Dougherty had played me.

I paid the twelve dollar fare and exited the cab, a sense of foreboding mounting at the fringes of my consciousness as I reconnoitered the block-long building that towered above me. Massive as it was, I'd never paid much attention to the Starrett Building but had taken a moment to 'google' the address before leaving the hotel. As Dougherty promised, it was a few blocks from the above ground entrance to the Casanova Club and filled the neighborhood between 11th and 12th Avenues and 26th and 27th streets standing just two blocks north of the Chelsea Pier.

Built 1930-31 and encompassing more square footage than the Empire State Building, it was constructed in an art deco motif boasting eight miles of ribbon windows stamped into stolid red brick with green frame windows that "gleamed like sapphires when struck by the sun" architectural critic Lewis Mumford observed. Even for its time, the Lehigh Valley Freight Terminal, as it was known then, was deemed "oddly constructed," but that surprised no one since the designers had built it directly atop the railroad's underground freight yard and a network of tunnels running from the Westside Pier into terminal stations where freight cars once unloaded half a million tons of industrial materials each day.

Still, if the building's exterior seemed like something from out of *The Wizard of Oz*, its lobby must surely have been wrested from the pages of Sartre's existential novel *Nausea*, I was thinking as I entered. Designed in an "industrial expressionist" motif, the Starrett Building's lobby seemed a tribute to the macabre: murals depicting steelworkers hoisting ladles filled with molten iron into open-hearth furnaces; clocks, large and small, hands frozen in time; abstract geometric shapes cut from stainless steel with mounted flood lights positioned above and below. "What we have created here is radical aesthetics ... a look that surpasses actuality!" boasted German architect Eric Mendelsohn at the building's opening ceremony.

I walked to the elevator and pressed the 'up' button, my eyes catching those of an Otis elevator repairman working on an open car opposite me, then the janitor sweeping the floor, and the female exec reading a copy of the *Wall Street Journal*. My mind flashed back to the moment I first exited the cab and the derelict I caught sight of drinking wine from a bottle in a brown paper bag, and the cop on the beat smoking a cigarette, and the guy with the beard handing out flyers for The Gym, a nearby gay bar. *Cops! All of them, undercover cops!!*

"Jack! Over here!" I heard Dougherty call out to me.

I turned toward him, standing at the other end of the elevator bank near a black, unmarked door, "You'll never get where you're going on one of those," he sang-out, flashing an amiable grin.

I walked toward him, wary as he was convivial, while he stared into an iris scanner placing the five fingers of his right hand onto a security identification pad, then opened the door which led to a private elevator, floors 19 through 29.

"Glad you decided to meet me, Jack," he said, slapping me on the back. "For a moment there, I thought you might report me to the police," he added, eyes twinkling.

I realized then that carrying on a conversation with Dougherty was like taking dinner in a room where the light bulbs kept blinking on and off; he never gave you a chance to get comfortable, "What is this place?" I managed to ask.

"Floors one through nineteen house the businesses of fashion designers like Tommy Hilfiger and Hugo Boss, and that's no accident," he explained comfortable as the guide on a Disney tour, "but the ten stories above are *verboten* to the public. That's where JTTF, the Joint Terrorism Task Force, a coalition of intel agencies FBI to ATF, work counter-insurgency identifying, tracking, and bringing to justice drug lords, international terrorists, you name it."

The elevator doors opened at the 29th floor. We exited, passed through a set of double doors, and entered a gymnasium-sized room abuzz with activity.

"Each of these six rows of cubicles are manned with agents working the globe for a specific agency," he announced making his way toward the front of the oblong room. "ATF works the firearms and explosives side of the street. The second and third aisles, CIA and ICE, track bad actors through computer data banks that link with State and NSA so we know what countries they've entered or left, even where they're headed, most of the time. The fourth row is FBI. We run the Terrorist Financing Operations Unit and because the others lack authority to make arrests on domestic soil, we represent the enforcement arm. The most interesting of the bunch," he said with a wink. "The fifth aisle is DEA, tasked with coordinating U.S. drug investigations here and abroad; the sixth is Homeland Security, whose job it is to monitor electronic communications and federal transportation systems."

Dougherty swaggered to a door bearing his name and title, set beyond the six SAC desks lined up horizontally in front of the JTTF brain trust and we entered his office. Elaborately decorated, it was more like Tom Dougherty, the multi-millionaire, presided here than Dougherty, Assistant Director of the FBI. Copies of *The Trial, No Exit, The Penal Colony,* and *Metamorphosis* adorned his bookshelves along with inscribed photographs of him with American presidents Clinton to Obama; Secretary of State Colin Powell; Russian President Vladimir Putin; China's Premier Wen Jiaboa; and Popes Paul VI through Francis. Most notable were the etymological drawings hanging on the walls, many of them depicting cock roaches, American, Asian, Tropical, even those long extinct such as *Carboniferous Archimylacris* and *Apthoroblattina.*

"How much of this do you control?" I asked as Dougherty made his way to a globe of the world that opened to reveal a bar.

"Most of it; no, all of it," he corrected, dropping an ice cube into his glass. "Care for a scotch? Neat, isn't that the way you take it?"

I nodded.

"Fact is, the Bush administration Higher Ups were crazy with panic after the 9/11 attacks, Powell, Chaney, Condi Rice; all understood that the Agencies weren't worth a tinker's fuck when it came to preempting domestic terrorist attacks. So, by virtue of presidential decree JTTF was created. Bureaucrats that they were, they hadn't a clue how to do it, so it fell to me and a handful of others for whom their concept meshed perfectly with what we'd set out to accomplish."

"And what was that?" I inquired, accepting the drink he handed over. "Anything to do with the serial killer whose's been severing the heads of fourteen-year old children?"

Dougherty brought the glass to his lips, and as it came down I noticed the most peculiar smile, evil, I thought, yet he had never appeared so young.

"The administration," he continued in an insistent voice, "wanted a Joint Terrorism Task Force and I found them the ideal location, here, in a building that's indistinguishable from the day-to-day goings on in the city, but centrally located, and secured. If ever there was a terrorist car bomb, even a jet crashing into the building, we had five miles of underground tunnels to weather the storm or escape if we so chose, who could do better than that?"

"And the Casanova Club? I'm imagining it lends itself to those same parameters?"

"Why not? They're bureaucrats! What was it Reagan said, 'governments come and go, but bureaucracies live forever,' well, that's the way it was. From Bush to Obama no one remembered what the point of JTTF was anymore, and despite the lavish arrangement you see out there, nothing's changed. We're still the myopic cyclops taking swipes at shadows in the night, but not us, not the Kafka Society. '"Where do you hide a leaf?" the professor asked. *"You hide it in a forest!"* the gifted student answered.' So, yes, we set up our headquarters alongside one of the United States' most elite anti-terrorist units. Clever, wouldn't you agree?" he asked, eyes alight as he sipped again from his glass. "God, I'm glad you've come to me, Jack, instead of the police."

"Don't be so sure. Woods and his internal affairs boys have already been in touch."

"What did he tell you?"

"He thinks he's got you dead to rights."

"Ridiculous! He's got nothing on me. What? Those family photos of runaway kids he trots out to show anyone who'll look at them? Some grainy video taken of someone he claims is me? Woods is a zealot, Jack. It's true we have an organization. It's also true that our mores venture far afield from most, but not like that, not like he tells it."

My eyes lifted to the bookshelves and the etymological drawings on the walls as he plucked two Cohibas from the inside jacket pocket of his D'Or suit.

"Kafka, is it?" I asked. "You know, since my conversation with Woods I've been wondering, how does a man like you become a man like you, Tom?"

He offered me a cigar which I declined, and lit his smiling, "I remember back in high school you used to write stories," he said, exhaling a stream of smoke that made him all but disappear. "Do you remember the one, Jack, a Western about a cowboy in Dodge City?" he asked from behind his cloud of smoke. "How your main character—was it a man named Ford?—took on the gun for hire paid for by the town's corrupt bankers, and how he finally died in the end. 'I'm dying, but I've never felt so alive!' isn't that what he told the girl that loved him, lying in the dust on the main street before the sun went down and the curtain fell? We aren't heroes, you and me, Jack. The world doesn't make heroes outside the short stories young boys like you write in high school, but you never understood that, did you?"

"I'd like to knock you through that fucking window," I said, looking past him and his desk to the 29th floor's plate glass window. "That's what my hero would have done."

"Violence," he observed puffing again on his Cohiba, "it was always part of your character, but you still don't understand the full measure of your rage, or what put it there to begin with. Was it finding your father after he'd blown his head off, or your inability to finish just about anything you ever started, your studies at Georgetown, your career, your marriage, for that matter? And that's the difference between you and me, Jack. We share our rage in equal measure, but I've channeled mine, have since before we met at St. Damian's. An Italian movie called *Investigation of a Citizen Above Suspicion*, ever hear of it? Goddamned film changed my life! A homicide detective kills his mistress; the trail of clues leads back to him, yet such is his status that the police are incapable of finding him guilty. Who would question the most diligent amongst the diligent, the most patriotic amongst the patriots? But, all of this must be obvious now, even to you. I invented the persona of Thomas H. Dougherty so the real Thomas H. Dougherty could exist, so that I — this Tom Dougherty that stands before you today — could walk amongst members of 'civilized' society invisible to them! You see, this world,

the one you purport to live in? It doesn't exist to men like
me. We refuse to acknowledge its existence so we needn't
follow its rules. Right-wrong, legal-illegal, moral-immoral,
to us these concepts are irrelevant, can you understand
how liberating that is?"

"Ever see your victims, Tom?"

"Anytime I want, which is to say, often. I like the way
I earn my daily bread, Jack. What I do and what I believe
are one and the same. Even you have to admit there's
something to be admired in that. Not like these others:
the Born Agains, the Politicians, the New York City
bloodsuckers disguised as bankers, attorneys, CEOs, our
'leaders.' Wars, Jack, *over religion*," he laughed. "The sewers
run thick with the blood of those quietly suffering citizen-
sheep raped and pillaged in the name of 'society'."

"No hair shirts, for you, I'm imagining."

"No," he said, smiling slyly, "no hair shirts or cilices.
Just money and pleasure! All we can take for as long as
we can take it! And, then, guess what? We start all over
again!" Dougherty walked over to the plate glass window
looking very much in his element. "Look here, Jack," he
proclaimed looking down at the streets below. "Nobody
thinks in terms of human beings anymore. They're
a commodity like rice, or wheat, or pork bellies," he
chuckled. "Governments don't, political systems don't,
even religious institutions are more interested in picking
the next president than people!"

"You were religious once," I observed.

"Oh, I still believe, Jack, in God and Grace and all that.
But most people are happier dead. See them down there
scampering around like insects? They don't miss much
once they leave here, so occasionally I pluck one or two,

or five, or one hundred, from out of one labyrinth and put them into another. No better, no worse for them, and as much as a hundred thousand dollars apiece for me. Even you can see the practicality in a proposition like that, can't you, Jack? No different than the world around us except that I'm not nearly so hypocritical. Governments, banks, churches; they all have their Five Year Plans, and so do I!"

"The Kafka Society?"

"That's right," he agreed, pointing his Cohiba at me like a scabbard. "Why do you think Kafka turned Gregor Sansa into a cockroach? It's because people judge others by appearance not reality. The *real* Gregor Sansa hadn't altered one iota but his *appearance* had, so he became repulsive to conventional society who suddenly looked at him the way you're looking at me right now. We know who we are: the best criminal minds in the world come together globally!"

Dougherty stopped momentarily to appraise me from behind his cloud of smoke as looking down onto the streets of Manhattan he clapped his hand over my shoulder, "Oh, come on, no need to be so glum. It was going to happen anyway. If not here in New York with me, then with some Chink in Hong Kong, or former KGB thug from Russia or the Ukraine. My God, Jack, it's only business!"

"You're a sick man, Tom..."

"I'd like to cut you in, you know," he said, puffing his cigar in assessment. "We used to do things together, Jack, can you remember those days in high school? The phony ID business? We had all our friends drinking in bars, picking up nigger girls in Central Ward nightclubs, fifteen and older!"

"I remember I got suspended," I countered, "and you walked away from it."

"No worse for the experience, Jack. No worse for what happened because they all loved you, whether you knew it or not. Oh, yeah, Jack *this* and Madson *that*! The Monks, lay teachers, your fellow students! Well, I have no real friends like that now, not in the Society. Besides, who could trust them? A Romanian flesh peddler here, a Bangkok heroin dealer there, hell, the president of Afghanistan has been shipping us two tons of morphine per year in the caskets of dead GIs for over a decade now! Our human cargo is shipped from right here in Chelsea with all the right people cut in! But these men we're discussing? They're not stand up guys like you and me, Jack. Believe me, I could use someone around here that I could really trust!" he said, moving to his right, where the bookcase hugging the west wall to his office opened up to a hidden corridor. "Here, come along with me, I've got something to show you."

Myriad emotions wormed through me like the tendrils of some species of small but deadly parasite as I followed Dougherty to a private elevator then down thirty-seven floors, eighty feet below the streets of New York: *fear, indignation, anger,* all part of the mix which ultimately produced the effect of sedation. Yes, I felt vaguely sedated, perhaps suffering from mild shock, and I knew I was approaching the end of a very long road when it came to Dougherty; a road I was convinced would leave one or the other of us dead.

From there he took me through a narrow corridor leading to a miniature subway station, neon lights streaming across its ceiling like electric eels. I watched along with him in awe of its sophistication as a train of five open-air cars approached, driverless, and took my place on the cushioned seat alongside him. It occurred to me then that those underground trains must connect the Starrett Building with the freight terminal he'd described and the Casanova Club not unlike the subways running between the Capitol Building and Congressional offices in Washington, D.C. I'd read about, complete with tv monitors and closed-circuit cameras.

Certainly, Dougherty could have started there, but perhaps it seemed banal to him and so he began with an epistle as subtle in its nadir as the gas chambers at Buchenwald. No matter, given the nature of my journey into the bowels of Hell that morning, what Dougherty railed about was of little consequence. I was numbed, yes, paralyzed by the spectacle as the five car subway dipped one level lower into what must have been the sewer system of old New York at the turn of the 19th century, a river, like a slipstream diverted one century past, running parallel to us as we approached the gallery of horrors beyond its western-most bank: children, boys and girls, some no more than five years of age, shackled in bamboo cages, screaming out to us for food, or medicine, or freedom, the recollection of my dreams and Bill Bonanno's words rising up like succubi from the deepest recesses of my mind. *'Revir,'* he had said, *'the river'*, and now I understood what he was trying to tell me; I understood everything; I understood it all!

"Human trafficking has replaced manufacturing in this country," Dougherty declared, talking over the electric hum of the subway and roar of moving water that cut through his Empire. "It's cheaper, free, in fact. We sell them as they are, often for films or personal amusement, sometimes for body parts, black market medical. Do you know the profit margins in that? Like waking up and winning the lottery every morning. And here's the best part, Jack, no taxes—did I mention that?—city, state, or federal!"

I stared into Dougherty's face, cast a furtive glance at the scores of cages listening to the cries of the motherless souls stranded beyond the river of sewage, then turned back to him. Beyond Dougherty's snow-white hair, plastic-surgeried face, and bleached-white teeth were Shakespearean closets of evil ready to be set forth, and I was convinced then that the Devil perpetrated none of it Himself, he didn't have to. The Devil's genius lay in his ability to shield men like Dougherty from God's grace and let human nature take over from there!

"Why are you showing me all of this?" I asked. "Planning on putting me in a cage, too?"

"You know, Jack, I'm beginning to think the world is filled with geniuses but only a few survive because the rest perish from having to repeat themselves! We're best friends, have been since we were kids! That's why I'm showing you this and talking to you, realistically, about that diary, the one you got from Havana," he added, a covey of armed guards saluting as the train slid by the entrance to the Casanova Club. "You know she's a clever one, *bitch that she is!* She and that son of hers managed to hack into one of our data banks and get a list, a very confidential list, of Society members and let me tell you up front, it is an impressive one," he stated as the train looped up a level on its way back to the Starrett Building. "I notice you didn't bring that diary along with you, or am I mistaken?"

"I've got it. Just not with me."

"I figured as much. The ever-clever Jack Madson!" he laughed. "Well, take a look at the monitor in front of you.

What you see might make you think twice about holding out on me."

My eyes lifted to the closed-circuit television anchored into the car's upper console, the impact of what greeted me equal to that of a blinding flash, brighter and hotter than the implosion of the sulphurous rock that boils at the center of the sun. I blinked once, and once again, in disbelief at the image of my daughter's tortured expression, pinioned hand and foot to a concrete wall, writhing in pain.

"They're going to kill me, Daddy, and I know they mean it," she shrieked, crying hysterically into the camera lens. *"They're going to kill me if you don't give them what they want! So, Daddy, Daddy..."* she'd begun pleading when, with a sound as subtle as a 'click', the screen went dark.

"Tiffany, baby. *Tiffany!*" I repeated, prepared to leap body and soul into the monitor's void to be carried along with the streaming electrons back to their source, a bunker somewhere in the Starrett Building, I would swear, where Tiffany was held captive.

"Lovely girl, Jack," Dougherty observed as the car came to a stop. "Maybe you noticed the device above her? A chemical agent whose advantage I'm only now beginning to fully appreciate. I was introduced to it by Dimitri Salita, a Russian gangster you may have read about in the papers. Hydrofluoric acid, heated, then vaporized through a fogging gun. The wonder drug of modern torture! So powerful its fumes alone dissolve the calcium in a man's body. But expose an organ to it directly, say, the eyes or lungs? Well, it doesn't burn the tissue like normal acid, no, it penetrates into the bone, *the bones,* Jack! The most excruciating pain I've ever come across and, trust me, I'm a student of human misery."

"I'd like to choke the life out of you with my bare hands right now if I could, Tom, you know that don't you?"

"Yes, but you won't," he answered, "or you know you'll never see Tiffany again. At least not the way you remember."

"That easy for you to kill a human being, is it? Amber, Reicher, Johnnie Gambi, now my daughter?"

"You're finally starting to grasp what we're all about, aren't you, Buddy? That's right, and soon your eyes will be opened and you'll come to the realization that you've been brainwashed by convention. Exquisite this philosophy of ours: beautiful, and exquisite, and sublimely effective! So, let me propose two simple alternatives," he offered, tossing his cigar into a pool of water near the tracks. It made a hissing sound then floated like flotsam down river as we made our way back to the Starrett Building. "Alternative One: turn the diary over to me and I return your daughter, not a hair out of place, along with the chance for you to finally be on the right side of history. Alternative Two: you keep the diary and turn it over to whomever you wish, and you'll never see Tiffany again. Not alive, anyway, and not in one piece, I can assure you."

"So this is what your grand philosophy comes down to," I said exiting the elevator alongside him. "You get Havana's diary by threatening to torture and kill my daughter."

"That's about the size of it, Jack. Matter of fact, that's it exactly," he agreed, grabbing hold of my bicep and steering me toward a closed stainless steel door not thirty feet from the entrance to his office. "But just to show you we mean what we say, I want you to open that door," he said, pointing. "Go ahead, turn the handle, open it, and walk in."

Shockingly, I did what I was told, knowing I could rip him apart, limb-by-limb, yet understanding that Tiffany's only hope lay in the balance between the saturate hatred I held for him and his obsession with reclaiming Havana's diary.

I twisted the steel handle clock-wise. The door opened. I entered, and my heart sank.

Lying, stripped naked and pinioned to an operating table was Owen Ewing, a team of white-masked surgeons standing over his long muscular body, flesh flayed open, bones stripped bare, half-alive and sobbing.

"*Madson,*" he uttered. "*Tell my wife and daughters I love them,*" he pled. "*But not the rest, not any of this that's happening now, do you promise?*"

"Yeah, Owen," I swore to him, "I give you my word."

Then, my eyes shifted Dougherty. He was grinning, eyes gleaming, rapt in a glee reserved for the unabashedly insane.

"One thing you should know about the Kafka Society, Jack," he said over Ewing's screams as the surgeons went back to work on him. "*We don't fuck around.*"

Chapter Thirty-Three

B eing around Dougherty was like cohabitating with a disease, I decided, leaving the Starrett Building through its 26th Street exit and hailing a cab, I felt I'd already been tainted. Still, there was a force more powerful than revenge dragging me back to the hotel and on to the Angel's safe house where Havana and Savito waited, and that was the unimaginable prospect of losing my daughter forever unless I came up with a plan to save her!

As it stood, Dougherty had no problem acquitting me from his office-lair tethered as I was to the two alternatives he'd presented: turn over Havana's diary and save the Kafka Society from certain destruction or do nothing and allow my own flesh and blood to be slaughtered at the hands of his henchmen. *Was ever a man so torn between two prospects so totally repugnant to him? Was ever a man so certain as Dougherty that I would choose my daughter?* I asked myself, ever cognizant of the savage fact that it was my decision to pursue the Dougherty case that had put Tiffany's life in danger to begin with? *What kind of father was I?* I rued, watching from the cab window as New York life passed before me like a Tim Burton film, *What kind of man?* And for the first time I imagined that despite all of my adolescent vows, perhaps my father and I were not so unalike after all. Perhaps we were both foolish men, bound by the same desire to burrow at mountains whose girth we could not begin to conceive, which is to say, we were failures at most everything that really mattered in life.

Once at the Elysée, I ordered my car to the hotel's delivery dock pre-supposing Woods' agents were tailing me, then made my way south through the Queens Midtown Tunnel, the shock Tiffany's abduction had set raging tempered by the desperate need to conceive a strategy that somehow skirted the alternatives Dougherty had conscripted. *Why did the game have to be governed by his rules? Why did its result necessarily leave him untouched and me either inconsolable with grief or riddled with guilt?* There was a way. There had to be a way, and I prayed to God that I would find that path if it cost me everything I had, *if it cost me my life!*

I took the Grand Central Parkway onto Queens Boulevard, memories of my father swarming me like angry hornets, and it was as if the open wounds healed-over from the beatings, marathon arguments with my mother, and his loathsome suicide were back and bleeding freely again. Odd, but I'd always assumed one difference between my father and I was that at least I *tried* to be a good man, but lately my assumption that he *hadn't* seemed challenged by my own miserable existence. Who could say, after all? Maybe he'd tried harder than any man but, like St. Damian, simply had a heavier load to carry with whatever trestle of good he'd constructed collapsed under the strain of alcoholism and depression. And maybe that was the difference between my Dad and me, I was thinking as the Porsche glided down the Boulevard, crowded with people and cars and buses: I wasn't going to give up on life, or my mission to avenge Johnnie Giambi's murder, or—I swore to Christ!—saving my daughter because that was me, and these were the things I believed in, regardless of the odds against me.

I turned onto Jamaica Avenue, the "Ave" Savito called it, headed toward the New Canaan projects. All but deserted now with what was left of the two half-empty high-rises surrounded by a wasteland of vacant lots, I could understand why the Angels had chosen it for one of the dozen safe houses they maintained in the five boroughs. The idea, whether it was used to store guns and drugs, or a hideout for wanted men to lay low until the heat was off, was to have a girlfriend rent a place along with her mother, guard its parameters with electronic surveillance equipment, in-the-flesh guards, or both, board a pack of Doberman Pinchers there, and vanish from the face of the earth. Of course, this was not the Hells Angels way: there'd be no mother living there (the Angels would never abide an "old broad" hanging with them!), though the odds of having her name on the lease were good, with the odds of having a handful of "biker bitches" around for convenient sex better than that. Also, unlike Columbians, for example, the Angels didn't need long-fanged beasts protecting their interests—why would they? They had an HA security arm built into their org chart from day one, complete with a sergeant-at-arms and teams of D-bol junkies ready to pounce any gangbangers that happened on the place, along with a pre-designated plan to either make a stand or escape from an onslaught of local cops, ATF or FBI, as the case may be.

I spoke the words "call Havana" into the Porsche's Bluetooth as the two New Canaan buildings, ugly as high-security prisons, came into view. The phone rang but it wasn't Havana Spice who answered.

"Yeah?" a gravel-voice inquired.

"It's me, Madson. I'm here to see The Man."

There was a moment's silence during which a hand clamped over the receiver and a garbled discussion ensued.

"Okay," the voice came back. "260, Building Two, he'll be waiting."

I drove the Porsche into the entranceway, now in ruins with asphalt crumbling and weeds grown through it, past two teams of sentries who patrolled, guns concealed, around the entrance. If the two high-rises combined housed twenty-five hundred tenants in one thousand apartments during its heyday, I doubted it held more than one-hundred-fifty these days. Long story short, the Angels had chosen a ghost town with surveillance opportunities, stories one through twenty-four, spanning no fewer than twenty blocks.

A clean-shaven biker wearing wrap-around Wayfarers, jeans and boots with HA cuts and colors welcomed me.

"You can park here, no problemo," he grunted and looking at him and the security forces that enveloped the 911, I wondered, *who in their right mind would want to fuck with these guys?* the memory of the tat carved into his forehead still reverberating in my mind: **V.J.D.**, it read, the three things membership in the Hells Angels guaranteed, '**Violence. Jail. Death.**'

I entered what used to be the New Canaan projects, Building Two, lobby stripped now of copper plumbing, and anything else of value. An HA security detail gazed through me, eyes like X-rays, as I made my way to the staircase.

"Elevator," one of them rumbled.

"No, I'd rather..."

"*Elevator*," he said again, so I took the lift up one flight, exited, then stomped down the hallway, nerves raw, and agitated as ready to confront Sonny Coulter as I'd ever been.

When I arrived at 206, I didn't have to knock. The door opened. It was Chemo who stood in front of me, eye lids drooping as low as his room temperature IQ, "Hiya, Jack," he said dully. "Guess you didn't get blowed-up, after all."

I didn't bother to answer, just elbowed my way passed him to find Coulter sitting in an armchair, Havana and Savito standing on either side of him.

Havana came flying to me, shoeless and dressed in a N.J. Giants jersey, looking more beautiful than ever, "*Jack! I was afraid I'd never see you again!*" she gushed, throwing her arms around me and kissing my face as I stood stolid, staring at Coulter and the boy who, eyes wide with pupils dilated, looked frightened half-to-death.

"It's all right, baby," I whispered, drawing her tight to me with my right arm, my left hung loose at my side ready to defend myself.

"*They try to kill me ... the shot ... they ... *"

"I know, baby, I know," I assuaged, kissing her hair, black and shiny, eyes still riveted on the godfather biker. "Savito, you okay?"

The boy nodded a terse assent, "Yes, I think so," he answered, a response that set Coulter laughing like a jackal as he brought a can of Coors Light to his lips and chugged it.

"They're okay, for Christ's sake! Even you must know it wasn't us tried to kill 'em!"

"No, you just tried to kill me, then pimped-out the woman whose head they did blow off, that about right?"

Sonny shook his head, still laughing, "Madson, what the fuck is wrong with you?" he asked while Chemo took a step toward me from behind and five additional Angels emerged silent as wolves from the kitchen and bedrooms. "No, that ain't necessary," C4 laughed, waving them off. "Ol' Jack here's just got a case of the 'I-don't-know-who-I-been-fucked-bys.' See, Jack, we're the dudes saved Havana and her kid. It was your compadre, Dougherty, had that Sanchez broad greased. It was that fucker and his pack of faggot boy-fuckers killed Reicher and Amber; same with that washed-up punching bag pal of yours, Giambi. You, now that's a different story. Tight with Dougherty as we thought you was, seemed like you had somethin' to do with Ronnie's killin', but thanks to Havana now we know different. Fact is, that sandbox in underground Chelsea that Dougherty runs is filled with cat shit, Buddy, and we got to sift it clean."

"They kidnapped my daughter, Sonny," I blurted, Havana's embrace melting away as I stepped toward him. "They're going to kill her if I don't cough up Havana's diary. They say they're going to tear her body to pieces."

"And they will, Jack, they will," he agreed, swilling down another gulp of beer, "and, yeah, you might turn over that fucking diary, but that ain't the end of it 'cause that ain't the way we do things 'round here."

Coulter's grin disappeared sudden as a light switch flicking off and during that instant with green eyes narrowing, ashen face taut, and fingers stroking the gray-and-white goatee he sported, I could swear I was talking to

Satan, himself, bedecked in cuts and colors and bethroned on that worn-out armchair.

"You know anything about Hells Angels?" he inquired, crushing the empty beer can with one hand and tossing it into a corner of the room. "Hells Angels was members of the US Army's 11ᵗʰ Airborne Division back in WW Two. Elite paratroopers dropped behind Nazi lines to rain death down on the enemy from above." He pulled a cigarette from a pack of Marlboro Reds and lit it with a Zippo lighter. "Called themselves 'Hells Angels', HAs, for short, 'cause they flew on silk wings into Hell, itself, with twenty pounds of TNT strapped to each leg. The name Hells Angels was a badge of honor, a mark of invincibility, a wartime emblem worn by the toughest of the tough and soon it became more than a division of paratroopers, Jack, it became a fucking Brotherhood. And do you know what happened if one of 'em was wounded, stuck back there behind Nazi lines?" he asked, drawing his hand up slowly and pointing a column of cigarette ash in my direction. "They stay with 'im, Jack. Every brother that was dropped in was sworn to bring the others back with 'em, dead or alive, even if there wasn't but charred chunks of body left. That's the pedigree we derive from, Jack. So now let me ask you a question: Ronnie Reicher was one of our Brothers, and he was killed by Dougherty and that boy-fuckin' Society of twisted rich-fuck-foreigners, *do you think for one iota of one fucking second that life-long outlaws like us are gonna let 'em get away with that?* You come along with me, Madson," he said, popping up from his armchair like he was on his way to decimate a platoon of Nazis, "I got somethin' to show you!"

I followed Coulter through the kitchen and into one of

the four bedrooms, leaving Havana behind with Savito in her arms, horror-struck at the news of Tiffany's abduction. Devoid of beds or furniture, the room had been converted into a command center, empty save HA posters plastered on every wall with slogans like **"Step Down Or Aside For No Man!,"** **"Three Can Keep A Secret If Two Are Dead!,"** **"You Fuck With My Brother And You Fuck With Us All!,"** a table smothered in maps of underground Chelsea, and an arsenal of weapons such as I had never seen before: hand grenades, mortars, Sting anti-aircraft launchers, a crate filled with C4 plastic explosives, remote-control bombs and guns, foreign and American-made ranging from Rohm .22-caliber revolvers to Beretta .380s and AK-47s.

"When Angels are at their best, they embody everything an outlaw ought to: fight first, ask questions later. Take what you want: turf, pussy, beer, bikes, drugs, weapons. Fight back when attacked: retribution! Not an eye for an eye, but your life for an insult. Yeah, we worked with Dougherty and his boy-fuckers deliverin' drugs through our network of clubs New York to Berlin," he admitted, "but we never had nothin' to do with that sex-slavery shit. Too sick, even for us. And, yeah, we protected Havana, sold some prime pussy, hers and others, and made some good money doin' it, but when they smoked Ronnie, those foreign cunt-lappers crossed a line; a point of no return there ain't no way to get back across, now we're at war!"

I stood silent, whether impressed or just scared shitless, I could not determine. When I looked around me, one half dozen Angels seemed to have materialized from nowhere.

"I want you to meet some of the team you'll be workin' with, Jack; *us*, for revenge; *you*, to get your daughter back. This here's Davey "Bad Boy" Crockett." A round-shouldered

HA, wearing shades, and covered in tats, stepped forward. I shook his hand. "This here's Bobby "Elvis" Chacon," another man stepped up to me. I shook his hand. "This here's "Nomad," he ain't got no other name; and Johnnie "D-bol" Johnson; and Mickey "Li'l Rat" Diebold; and you already know Chemo," he added by way of introduction as I shook hands with each, every one of them changed totally in demeanor now that Sonny Coulter had vouched for me.

"We need to go over a couple of things," Coulter declared, marching toward the map-covered table, all business. "We got these blueprints from the sandhogs who work construction, underground Manhattan. Friends of ours goin' back to '06 when we joined their picket line after a union walkout. See here," he said, pointing to an area covering Chelsea piers down to 9th Avenue, "that's the length of the usable underground, the rest is filled with leaks or already flooded. Right here, we got the Starrett Building, 11th Avenue to 12th, between 26th and 27th. Directly beneath it, we got the Terminal," he noted, pointing. "Two blocks east of that, the Casanova Club. What's that mean to us? **Target One**: the Casanova Club is where the Society hangs out to get their drugs 'n pussy. **Target Two**: the Terminal's where they store their human cargo and ship it by freight car to the Chelsea piers. **Target Three**: the Starrett Building is where Dougherty and the other Feds play cops'n robbers every day," he said, straining to look up at me as he leaned over the table. "It's also where he's holding your daughter in a sound-proof bunker on the 29th floor, not a hundred-fifty feet from his office."

"Okay, you've got my attention," I retorted, pouring over the maps with him. "I know about the entrance here on 27th Street, the acupuncture clinic they use as a front, but there must be others."

"There are entrances to the underground all through Chelsea," he explained. "They're called manholes, brother, dozens of 'em! 'Course they don't have fancy elevators like the ones on 27th Street, but we don't care 'cause we're gonna take the steel stairs, same as the maintenance guys who inspect tunnel walls, and the industrial lifts the sandhogs use to carry drilling rigs and oxygen transfer pumps. Only this time, day after tomorrow, 5:30 pm, when an emergency siren sounds triggering an evacuation of Targets One, Two and Three, those elevators won't be carryin' sandhog drillin' rigs, Jack. They'll be carryin' an army of Hells Angels and a stash of C4 explosives that'll end the Kafka Society's underground playground, *now and for-fucking-ever.*"

"And how do I fit into all of this?" I asked.

"Easy," Coulter answered backing away from the table and collecting another Coors Light from Li'l Rat, "all you got to do is go see Dougherty and turn over the kid's IPad. 'Course he won't let you go after that, probably kill you and your daughter, but if you play 'im right it'll buy us the time we need to get an HA assault team down into the underground, free those kids, an' take care of some unfinished business."

"What about me and my daughter?"

"We'll send another team, maybe two, three Angels up after ya. By that time, your rat-ass buddy will have evacuated the place, shouldn't be too hard after that."

I mulled his plan over feeling like I'd just bit into a scrumptious eclair and a cockroach came swimming out of the cream, the image of Big O's innards laid bare on that operating table disrupting my thoughts like the burst of a thousand cameras flashing, knowing I couldn't trust Woods and his inept team of bureaucrats to save either Tiffany or me.

"Guess those are odds I'll have to accept, Sonny," I answered. "Sometime you just have to man-up and do it."

Coulter polished off the rest of his beer in a swallow and stepped toward me clasping my hands in both of his, "You're a stand up guy, Madson, and we ain't gonna let ya down," he vowed, *"not now, not never."*

Fair enough, I thought then, maybe Sonny was right. It was time to have a beer or two, celebrate our unholy alliance, and spend some time with Havana, but there was a phone call I had to make before I could think about any of that.

* * *

Post-Coulter discussion, I asked for a quiet place which Sonny 'okayed' without remark while he and the others discussed the finer points of Operation Stomp (a reference to cockroaches, I supposed) and Savito trounced Chemo one game after another playing the video game *Killing Floor 2.* It was time to reconnect with Woods, I decided, about some unanswered questions I could not divorce from my thoughts even with Havana escorting me to her bedroom to make the call.

"You're angry, Senor Jack, aren't you? Is it about me? Is it about your daughter?" she asked, taking hold of my hand and walking me into the room, furnished with just a mirror and a bed with a steamer trunk set at the foot of it.

"No, not you," I answered, squeezing her hand more tightly. "My daughter, yes, and one or two other 'disconnects' I need to discuss with a cop I know."

By the time we entered her bedroom, I was already dialing Woods' 'secure' line.

"Woods, Group 41," he picked up, gruff and ready.

"It's Madson."

"Jack," he said, suddenly animated, "where are you? We've been trying to get hold..."

"I already know. I saw Tiffany today via closed circuit TV monitor. It wasn't much of a visit."

"I see," he answered in precisely the opposite tone of seconds before. "Well, you know we're going to do everything we can to get your daughter back safely..."

"Like you did Ewing?"

"That," he countered, "was not our doing."

"Was he working for you?"

"Ewing was a precinct detective, Jack, he..."

"Was he fucking working for Group 41!"

"No, Jack, he wasn't, I swear to you," he answered throwing up a shield that he knew could never sustain the onslaught to come, "but you've got to stay the course. We've got someone on the inside who's penetrated the Society, one of our own, who we think can help find your daughter."

"I don't believe you! From the day we met, all I've got from you is misdirection and lies! Now Tiffany's been kidnapped and Ewing taken apart like some kind of laboratory experiment by these lunatics. I've had it with you, Woods. You, with your covert organizations within organizations and groups within groups! You wouldn't know the difference between lies and the truth if your own life depended on it, so why would I believe you now? No! You've lost credibility and now I'm taking this down my own path whether you and your spy agencies like it or not!"

"That's a mistake, Madson! What I told you before about Ewing is true. He wasn't with us or anyone. He wasn't in the Game, shit, he wasn't even in our League! Ewing was a day-trader who let curiosity get the better of him, pure and simple. Maybe he missed his glory days at Notre Dame; maybe he wanted to play 'hero' again, those are questions I can't answer, but one thing sure: *we had nothing to do with what happened!*"

I sat down on the edge of the bed, feeling the warmth of Havana's thighs as she locked her legs around me from behind stroking my temples gently with her fingertips to calm me.

"Don't do this, Jack," Woods tried to reason. "I know we haven't always seen eye-to-eye on things, but I'm asking you not to do anything rash. Take a moment to think things through and you'll see the best chance you have to save Tiffany's life is with us, helping us, like we talked about."

"Sorry, Woods," I uttered, the energy suddenly drained from me, "I just can't do that."

With conversation ended, I sat on the edge of the bed staring at the phone in silence, wondering if I'd just started down a path that would save or condemn my daughter. Quite simply, I did not know, but soon I would, I understood, surrendering to the tug Havana exerted as I fell backward and she wrestled herself atop me, face not six inches from mine.

"Will you make love to me tonight, Jack? Will you make love to me slow so I can feel your skin on mine and hear your heartbeat? I know you are in pain, so am I, so tonight let's take our time and comfort each other."

I nodded, a quiet smile crossing my lips as I stared into her ebony eyes, sparkling like gemstones.

"I want to kiss every part of you, Jack. I want you to talk to me while we make love. When you were gone, even when I could not remember what your face looked like," she confessed, "I could hear your voice, so soothing, talking to me, and it was like a drug, a wonderful drug that allowed me to sleep at night."

"I will, I promise," I said.

Then she giggled. It was sexy.

"You know that just sitting here with you now, I am wet, Senor Jack. So wet, I think I will need a diaper!"

"Not necessary," I pledged, rolling on top of her and staring, playful and ferocious, lost in the magnetism of those dancing ebony eyes, "I've got the cure for that."

Then, we made love and did all of the things she talked about.

Only better.

Chapter Thirty-Four

With ties severed between Group 41 and me, I was a free agent who'd supplanted 'laws' with 'outlaws.' No surprise there, I'd been veering in that direction for years now. *Out-Law.* Never before had I thought of the word that way before. In doing what I was about to do, I stood on the cusp of becoming not unlike the outlaws of bygone eras, Jesse James, Dillinger, and Bonanno, a man living outside society, I realized then, feverish with visions of freeing my daughter while going over the final details of our assault on the underground with Sonny and his boys. And, in truth, never had I felt so alone, even encircled by a platoon of Angels as I was, lost in my obsession to hunt down and kill the real and true monsters that prowled an unseen netherworld with Tiffany at its core.

I savored the sensation, the sonorous voices and words they carried buzzing around me like winged insects. In a world choking on hypocrisy, political correctness, and national grid lock, I was about to become a stranger to the empire in decline, an enemy of this Kafka society we had invented for ourselves, hell bent on saving my daughter's life and sending the most evil man I had ever encountered back to the Hell fire from whence he came!

At 5 pm, promptly, dressed in black blazer, turtleneck, and slacks, I abandoned the blustery streets of Manhattan for the Starrett Building lobby. I glanced skyward to the multiple surveillance cameras, then to the team of undercover cops playing out their roles as executives, panhandlers, and *haute couture* designers. I walked beyond the elevator bank to the unmarked door, the muscles in my body taut as coiled springs, then stared into the eye scanner covering the entry pad's dark glass with my palm. I listened for the click of the door lock, until I heard a voice I did not recognize say, "Come up."

I entered the deserted hallway and boarded the elevator, eyes darting to the face of the Omega watch I wore: **5:05 pm**, *twenty-five minutes to the Hells Angels assault on Dougherty's underground empire!*

The elevator doors opened at the 29th floor, command post for the Joint Terrorist Task Force. A man I assumed was Dougherty's bodyguard waited for me. Dressed in a black suit with black shirt and tie, sans Fu Man Chu mustache, with head shaved, and the letters K-I-L-L tattooed on the digits of his right hand and H-A-T-E on his left, there was no quantity of hand-crafted French soap that could take the stink of corruption or ape-like menace off him: it was Harold Fenderbass *aka* X Man, the former MMA champion whose fixed fight with Johnnie Giambi cost my friend his left eye and very nearly his life back in '08.

"Madson," he declared smiling, "you never seem to go away, do you?" he said, turning his broad, thick-muscled back to me. "Follow."

From there I trailed X-Man down the corridor to the

Starrett Building's east side, away from the JTTF nerve center, through a door that took us directly into the anterior of Dougherty's office, wondering what role he might have played in Johnnie's beheading.

I looked the room over with a raking glance as we entered. There Dougherty sat at his desk, Senator Jacob Mathias, Tony Coscarelli, Carlos Padilla, and Mohammad Tasserbehji seated before him, engaged in what appeared to be a heated discussion involving cash, banks, and the war in Afghanistan. Mathias, Tasserbehji, and Padilla craned their heads around to see the two of us as we entered. Coscarelli wouldn't have turned if we'd been accompanied by the Preservation Hall Jazz Band.

"Hiya, Jack!" Dougherty sang-out, rising from his chair, then remembering his audience of Society members turned back to them. "Excuse me for a moment, but before you do, understand that we can go only so far with all of this 'war' business, then we're going to have to find something else. After all, there've been no bridges burned with the Taliban. Tell them, Mohammad, explain to them, that these are men we can do business with..." Then, swinging around the desk, past the configuration of chairs, Dougherty approached me, hand extended. I shook it, weakly. "Stay available," he told X-Man and the two renegade FBI-types who joined him, one short with blunt bovine features, the other tall and refined looking, both dressed in dark suits. Then, flashing a winning grin, hand still clasped in mine, his eyes locked on my briefcase. "Finally seen the light, have we, Old Boy?"

I didn't answer; didn't have time since the meeting was all but over once Dougherty abandoned it.

"We're headin' out, Tom," Coscarelli declared,

standing up along with the others, donning their hats and overcoats. "The Senator here's gotta get back to D.C. for a vote and, frankly speaking, I gotta take a wicked shit," he quipped, turning to the others who faked nervous laughs at the rapier-like wit of Tony the Pimp.

"Yes, quite so," Mathias seconded, passing a curt nod to Dougherty and the others as he turned to leave. The wall door opened with an electric hum. "When you've got a good thing going like in Afghanistan, you stick with it! I've maintained that position from the beginning with George W. and goddammit I stand by it with Obama today," he blustered, slapping a pair of leather gloves into his palm for emphasis. "Tom, Mohammad, Anthony, I'll be seeing you when next we meet in Monte Carlo," he bade, exiting into the corridor headed for the underground.

I watched then, my hand shrinking out of Dougherty's grip, as the others left through that same door, until it was just the two of us, alone.

"Let's have it, Jack," Dougherty ordered, extending his palm out to me. "The kid's iPad, I want it *now*."

Eyes locked on him, I reached into my leather briefcase to retrieve it. Dougherty was wearing a pin-striped suit with a vest, the Windsor knot of his cerulean blue power-tie was immaculate, and I would have taken him for continental banker with an expensive mistress waiting in the wings but for the fact that his pallor was gray and he was sweating beneath his tan.

I handed the IPad over. He switched it on, "Password?"

"There is none. It's in 'Notes'."

He shook his head hopelessly, and touched the icon to bring it up, smiling as the header popped onto the screen. 'KAFKA SOCIETY: THE ORDER OF MOST FAVORED

GENTLEMEN', it read. I knew what he was seeing. I'd gone through Havana's diary Alpha to Omega the night before.

"Yes, yes," he muttered, scrolling screen-to-screen as the names, sexual preferences, and status of members within the organization rolled over each. "Right-O," he concluded, looking up from the device, eyes lit with an ardor sprung from what I recognized now as the dark wells of his spiraling madness, "That will do just fine."

"You know you're finished, don't you, Tom?" I said, gazing into his face, bright and shining, looking like some ill-conceived effigy of an iconic saint, rotting from within, cowled in a cap of snow white hair.

"I know nothing of the sort, but truth be told, I think it's you who should be worried, Old Friend. I bear no illusions when it comes to how you feel about the Kafka Society. Fact is, you'd never pass the muster anyway, don't have the balls for it." He raised an eyebrow, "Not a modicum of the imagination it takes to be one of us!'"

"Kill me, if you want, Tom, but not my daughter. Yeah, I can do you and your pals damage, but not her, not Tiffany. She's a civilian, wouldn't know Kafka from Max Schmeling."

He smiled. His gray eyes twinkled, "Afraid that won't do," he said lifting his index finger to his lips, "but you must have a lot of questions need answered before you and your daughter die. Come," he said, egging me along toward the far corner of his office where at the foot of a high-shelved bookcase stood a glass casement covered with a black velvet overlay. "I was just about to show the boys my collection before you came by and interrupted."

I approached the display. My eyes stole a furtive glance

at the watch jutting an inch and a half beyond the cuff of my shirt sleeve: **5:17**, *thirteen minutes more!* my mind raced, the Omega ticking like a time bomb on my wrist as I trundled behind Dougherty finally stopping at its edge, X-Man, and his two helpers, not five steps behind.

He studied the black overlay with a level of intensity that left me wondering if it was the coverlet, itself, we'd come to admire. The glass casement came waist-high on me, but might as well have fallen down from the sky onto my head for the sheer force of what I saw when Dougherty swept the cover away and the abomination on display leapt out at me from beneath the clear glass like ghouls unleashed from a gaping crevice sprung open to the netherworld. My eyes grew large, my stomach revolted. I staggered back a full step, repulsed by the grisly horror of what the rational part of me knew I was seeing, but the spiritual part could not bring itself to comprehend!

Heads. Severed heads. Perhaps fifteen of them. Skinned. Eyes, ears, nose, and lips removed. Each, preserved like the fifteen mangled faces of still living human beings so pink was the underlying tissue now exposed in Dougherty's office which to me had been transformed into the inner sanctum of Hell, itself!

I stumbled backward, body faltering, legs wobbling beneath its weight, and still the sight and smell of the heads remained, that same sickeningly sweet odor that had cascaded from the trunk of my car and the refrigerator from which I'd retrieved Johnnie Giambi's head at the Georgetown Inn. Breathless, my eyes flew down to my watch, a drill of hot bile sprouting up from the pit of my stomach: **5:23**, the world was cancerous! Life was a riddle turned inside out and I was on a roller coaster inside that riddle caroming like a bullet locked in a steel box, bouncing one impenetrable wall to another, I panicked, mind revolting at the very concept of time, *seven more interminable minutes!*

"Have you ever seen anything like them, Jack?" he proceeded, so totally immured I'd have thought him in communication with a parallel universe, and I was convinced then that Dougherty's real self had somehow been switched with the persona that he showed the world. After decades of living submerged, the real Tom Dougherty, *the one he dared not reveal,* had emerged triumphant, the stored up energy of all those lost decades radiating from out of him. "I always wondered how they did it. The incorruptible corpses?" he observed, lifting the casement's glass lid and taking one of the smaller heads into his hands. "Was it lead coffins sealed air-tight? A special arsenic solution? The skeptics could never explain it, but goddammit, I've tried every one of them: formaldehyde, Formalin. Even the "waterless" fixatives like glutaraldehyde will give you two, maybe, three years under the best conditions. No, I'll grant you those guineas at the Vatican know their embalming! This one here, *this rat-bitch,* sent to infiltrate our Society by Group 41," he ranted, staring into the empty sockets of the faceless head, "her name used to be Chok Por, a born again hooker from Macau. But, to me, these individuals no longer possess identities. Numbers, yes, because they're my experiments. This one, Chok Por, we had processed the old fashioned way: mummified, similar to the Egyptians. She'll be good for a thousand years inventoried down there in the tunnels with the others, but shriveled and emaciated, nothing approaching the quality of the so-called saints displayed under glass in Rome. The ones they call the

Incorruptibles? Well, goddammit, maybe they are a kind of 'miracle!'"

The watch! my brain cried-out as I stood silently listening, the sound of the Omega ticking pounding like timpani in my ears, until finally I succumbed, eyes drawn inexorably to my wrist, **5:20**: *by now dozens of machine gun-toting Angels were making their way into the depths of the underground through manholes, freight elevators, and heavy equipment lifts, 29ᵗʰ Street to the Chelsea piers, and soon it would it be over. Tiffany would be free, I'd see to that, I swore, the Kafka Society and its members crushed and the underground blown to oblivion this day and forevermore!*

"Have you ever been to the Vatican, Jack, you and Jennifer, prior to the divorce?" Dougherty asked, returning the head back into the casement. "I'm told Judge Crowley once had an audience with Pope John XXIII, a hell of a man! The two-hundred and sixty-first Pontiff of the world-wide Catholic Church, died 1963, but even upon close examination today most would believe he was still alive and simply sleeping. Same with the others," he noted, voice dropping an octave, "Saint Don Bosco, died 1888; Saint Silvan, died 350; Saint Vincent de Paul, 1660; Bernadette of Lourdes, 1879; on and on. I think a man of the world, like you, will understand this, Jack, but that is what so obsessed me! My failure, my inability, to prove that God, if there is one, has no interest in plunging his hand into the cesspool of human existence. No concern, much less love, for these pathetic creatures we call 'human', by duplicating the phenomenon of the Incorruptibles! Demonstrating, scientifically, that these physiological aberrations were never miracles at all! But I couldn't do it, Jack. Never quite got there…"

Time, time … Tiffany, Tiffany … The watch, the watch …

"Are you all right, Jack? You look like you're going to be ill. Why look at you! You're perspiring…" he said, stepping toward me, extending his hand toward my forehead. I slapped it away.

The watch, the watch … Tiffany, Tiffany … Time, time …

"Where is she, Tom!" I spat out, the contempt I held for him turned savage as the sullen water behind a dam on the verge of bursting beyond any semblance of constraint. "You're going to set my daughter free now or, I swear to Christ, I'm going to tear you limb from fucking limb!"

"Oh, yes, your daughter," he assuaged, motioning X-Man over. I watched the former MMA champ lurch forward, his two sidekicks in tow, Ruger SR9 with silencer trained purposefully on the imaginary bulls eye tattooed between my eyes. "I'll bet you're thinking you'll survive, aren't you?" Dougherty ventured, grinning. "I'll bet you think that like one of the heroes in those westerns you used to write back at St. Damian's, you'll somehow save your daughter, come out of this alive, and be the hero of your story! But you won't," he vowed with lethal certainty. "You see, that's the beauty of the Kafka Society. We see life as it is, without the veneer, minus the bullshit, you might say. It's only fools like you, Jack, that live their lives like they were in a dime store novel. But as you and your daughter shall see, your final moments will be anything but heroic because you," he said, stabbing a finger into my chest, "have been a terrible disappointment to me. Take him to his daughter," Dougherty told X-Man. "I want them dead. Erased from the face of the earth, like they never existed, understand? But the head, the girl's head," he said thinking better of it, "why don't you save that for me."

"You son of a bitch," I swore stepping toward him, about to take him down and out, permanent, when I felt the cold steel tip of X-Man's silencer shoved into the base of my skull.

"You can die now or die with your cunt daughter, it's all the same to me, Madson," X-Man threatened.

"All right," I nodded, swallowing a lump of anger, hot as nuclear waste, deep down into my gut so it would lay dormant, at least for now until I stalled a minute, two minutes, five minutes longer, for the Angels' assault to begin!

X-Man nudged me with the Ruger while his cohorts, the Cretin and the Intellectual, shepherded me toward the hidden door leading to the underground. Again, my eyes shot down obsessively to the face of my Omega: **5:30**, *where the fuck were they? What the fuck were they doing??* I anguished as sweat thick as hot tar formed at my temples and arm pits traveling in fiery streams down the sides of my face and over my rib cage. *Tiffany, I love you!* I was shouting as if from mountain tops echoing through vast stretches of canyons as far as the eye could see. *Hold on just a short while longer, Baby! I swear you're going to be all right! I swear to you God would never let anything happen to a young woman so lovely and promising as you! It would be unthinkable ... It would be...* Then, all at once, my thoughts short-circuited, the tenuous life line of hope severed, as the savage reality of our situation struck me like a kick to the groin. *This was not a dream; this was not some drug-induced nightmare; what was happening to Tiffany and me was real,* my mind raged as the doors to the underground slid open and the four of us entered the concrete and steel corridor, X-Man's weapon pointed not five inches from the posterior of my skull when sudden as a clap of thunder something inside my head snapped *and the fog lifted!*

The *occipital lobe* was responsible for interpretation of visual signals passed along from the retina, I remembered from my days at St. Damian's, but what I was seeing now was not coming from signals relayed retina-to-brain. No, this was something primitive and instinctual, I realized then, the grainy black and white film playing in the anterior of my mind was real: Sonny Coulter surrounded by an army of Angels, supplemented by sandhog workers, and mole people, the homeless men and women living in the bowels of the city, rising up against the para-military guards overseeing the Society's child slave operation, freeing the children from their cages, shooting dead their captors, burning the Casanova Club to the ground, the river that swept through the underground now an onslaught of roiling black water, alight with flames!

When we arrived at the chamber where Owen Ewing had been tortured to death, the heavy-gauge steel door opened with the touch of the Cretin's hand onto a security pad and there, pinioned arms and ankles to the wall of the concrete bunker, was Tiffany looking up to me, her father!

"Tiffany!" I gasped, eyes traveling to her, then to a second set of manacles, and the mechanical device Dougherty had described above them both. "I love you!" I swore, rushing to her.

And that's when I heard it. A deafening roar traveling at the speed of sound that seemed to grow in strength proportionate to the intricacies of the abandoned tunnels that slithered serpentine beneath the streets of New York, convulsing the foundations of the earth, itself!

Chapter Thirty-Five

The roar of the first explosion ruptured the wall of the bunker and I watched a long thin crack materialize along its north side where Tiffany stood helpless, the sound of sirens howling up and down the Starrett Building's twenty-nine floors like the vengeful spirits of a mass grave emptied.

"I'm so sorry, Daddy! I'm so sorry!!" Tiffany sobbed, eyes reaching out to me as her hands would have had they not been bound in steel sleeves.

I caressed her face, drenched with tears, "No, Baby, it wasn't you. It was never you! It was me who let us down!!"

"Get back against the fucking wall, Madson!" X-Man growled, slamming me into the concrete with his free hand as the cadenced voice of a woman echoed over speakers swirling like a cold wind through the corridor and into the bunker, '*A security breech has occurred—evacuate building now,*' she was repeating.

I glowered at X-Man, his expression now wary, darting to the chamber's entrance where the Cretin stood sentry, then glanced over my shoulder to my right where Dougherty's toy-for-torture protruded from the wall stark as a cobra: a polyvinyl ten gallon container filled with 70% pure hydrofluoric, flash heated by a Teflon coated coil, pressure fed to a fogging devise designed to project the vapor forward.

"You understand what's happening, don't you, Harold?" His eyes refocused on me and Tiffany. "There's been an explosion. It's all over for Dougherty and every one of you sons of bitches unless you get the fuck out of here now. This building's coming down!"

"Maybe it is, Mr. Madson," the Intellectual commented neutrally, "but not before you and your daughter take your medicine. Mr. Dougherty told us all about you, made you a special project, in fact. You and your outdated notions about honor and heroics, and how you squander your talents on whores and misfits. Is your whore worth your life and the life of your daughter?" He shook his head at the thought of it. "A man like you should wear a sign around his neck, **'Jack Madson public menace!'** But whatever you think you're doing, it won't change anything. You see, Mr. Madson, great men like Tom Dougherty don't die, they mutate," he lectured sounding more like his mentor, Dougherty, by the moment. "Bottom line, it's going to be fun watching you die," he smiled, seizing my wrist with both of his hands, then leaning his full weight down, forcing it toward the maw of the steel manacle!

I struggled against him, convinced that once my hand entered it would trigger an automatic lock that would pinion my wrist into its grip, while equally certain that X-Man would end it all with a bullet to my head if I emerged the winner.

"Do what he says, Daddy!" Tiffany pled eyes wide with terror. "Please don't make him shoot! Don't leave me alone with them!!".

And for me her words were like a razor's edge that divided real time from something akin to an opium dream because seconds later we were caught in the whirlwind of a second powerful explosion that ripped through the underground, rocking the Starrett Building at its foundation followed by the eerie groans of rebar contorting and concrete walls tearing apart, punctuated next by a far different sound, very near to us this time, cracking like a bull whip once and then once again.

It was then that I felt the inexorable pressure, wrist-toward-manacle, slacken and saw the Intellectual's hyper-focused eyes shift to the bunker door in time to watch his partner sink to the ground felled by a 9 mm bullet shot into his right eye. Puzzled at first, Dougherty's disciple gravitated like a sleepwalker toward the entrance, then realizing what had happened, pulled a Berretta semiautomatic from the shoulder holster he wore managing to get off three rapid-fire rounds, but it was too late, Don Woods, with gun already drawn, shouted a warning, then shot him dead through the heart.

X-Man, too, was disoriented and fell back a half step bracing himself against the force of the second explosion as it tore through the corridor and into the bunker. Then, call it luck or call it instinct, but instead of sucker punching him when I had the chance, I delivered a single piston-like blow with all the power in me to the back of his right hand sending the Ruger semiautomatic he held skating across the chamber's concrete floor. And this was my lucky break: instead of physically decimating me which he could easily have done as Woods, hit during the gunplay, lurched forward and a bevy of agents frantically worked the control panel trying to extricate Tiffany, *X-man went after the gun!*

I cannot tell you with certainty exactly what happened during the desperate moments that followed because for me reality became not unlike an old fashioned newsreel, sped up, with frames missing and me an actor playing my role oblivious of where it might lead, understanding that at that moment *I had to act!* **FRAME ONE**: *I turn to Tiffany. She is now free with manacles sprung open!* **FRAME TWO**: *I turn to Woods. He is collapsed, lying on the floor, unconscious!* **FRAME THREE**: *I turn to X-man. His back is to me and he is seconds away from retrieving the Ruger!* And just before those final missing frames, so difficult even now to recapture, I remember shouting *"Tiffany, get out of here now!"* Then, I reached up for the fogging device above us, took aim at the very moment X-man swung around, Ruger pointed at me, and easing my finger back on its trigger watched in morbid wonder as the vaporous cloud of hydrofluoric acid attached itself like a roiling suit of flesh-eating bacteria to every inch of X-man's body!

I didn't wait to hear the metallic sound of his gun when it dropped to the concrete floor or see the effect that Dougherty's insidious device had on him though agents later claimed X-man had clawed-out his own eyes as they disintegrated in their sockets and what was left of him afterward was no more than a pool of liquefied flesh. But for me then, body pulsing with adrenalin, there was no time to watch or even to think, I understood, racing toward Woods, dragging him feet first out of the bunker and into the corridor awash now with static-laden voices broadcast over NYPD two-ways and first response teams shouting commands as they treated burn victims and removed dead bodies. My eyes prowled the faces around me until finally I came upon Tiffany surrounded by a covey of paramedics.

"*Shut the door and lock it! That chemical is vaporized acid!*" I exhorted the agents nearest the entrance, dropping to my knees beside Woods protracted body like a marionette whose wires had been severed.

Woods had taken a bullet to the chest and was breathing shallow but steady. *He'll probably be okay*, I was thinking, *probably be fine* when I looked up to see Tiffany rushing toward me, arms outstretched, face pale and bloodless, as she fell into my arms.

"It's okay now, baby," I whispered, pressing her quaking body to me remembering what it was like to hold her as a small child. "It's over now, everything's going to be fine from now on, you'll see," I promised, eyes on fire as I glared over her shoulder watching paramedics, frantic to beat the building's collapse, loading Woods onto a stretcher.

"Dougherty?" I heard the blue-eyed SAC rasp. "Did we get him?"

"We collared eighteen…" one of the agents trailing alongside the stretcher started to answer.

"*Did-We-Fucking-Get-Him!!*" Woods roared, lifting his head off the stretcher, glowering into the faces of his subordinates.

"We think he may have escaped into the underground," a second agent volunteered breathlessly. "The entire area—25th Street to Chelsea Pier—is an inferno, Lieutenant, and this building's no better!"

"Radio Mendham police and have men posted at every airport in the tri-state area," Woods uttered weakly, head descending back onto the stretcher. "He may go home to collect his family before trying to leave the country."

I kissed Tiffany gently on the cheek, our eyes locked on one another's, Hemingway's phrase 'courage is grace under pressure' passing through my mind as Woods and his entourage disappeared through an emergency exit and paramedics eased her onto a stretcher knowing that if Dougherty had escaped into the underground he wasn't headed for Mendham or any place like it. They placed an oxygen mask over Tiffany's face and hastily set up a liquid valium IV and I was never more proud of her than at that moment. *This is truly a brave young woman*, I thought, our eyes still locked as they rushed her down the corridor on their way to the ground floor where emergency sirens howled and ambulances waited.

I was very much alone in the other-worldly quiet that followed the explosions and roaring fires that had begun to sprout up throughout the Starrett Building that night. I pocketed Woods' Glock 17, left behind in the rush to evacuate, and made my way to the elevator Dougherty and I had ridden just one day before. *Had he actually fled into the underground?* I could not know for certain but suspected, as Woods' men had probably deduced, that its network of connecting tunnels and exits leading back up to the streets was the only chance he had to escape the man trap Homeland Security and the FBI had set up in and around the Starrett Building. So, determined as God's avenging angel, I boarded the tiny cubicle hung by what was now super-heated steel cable feeling more like a man in a bathoscope descending into the depths of the ocean than an unlicensed private investigator.

Floor-by-tenuous-floor the elevator descended in fits and starts, the electric motor that tugged at its cables belching black smoke like the dilapidated diesel engine of an old tramp steamer. Down one fiery floor to the next it sank beyond the twenty-nine that led to ground level finally entering the surreal world the Kafka Society had created *one, three, six, eight stories* beneath the panicked streets of Chelsea where NYPD had already cordoned off twenty city blocks while civilians scrambled to safety behind concrete barriers and firefighters stood in anticipation of the building's imminent collapse.

Once arrived, I fled the elevator (a virtual oven at that point!) then trekked down the corridor to the driverless tram, still functioning like some bizarre Disney ride in the bowels of a bombed-out war zone. The upbeat announcer's voice listing stops and pick ups continued amid the flickering lights and clouds of sheet-white smoke pouring from the tunnels as if the Casanova Club and freight terminal had not been reduced to piles of rubble and the underground wasn't an inferno strewn with the charred bodies of what was left of Dougherty's security forces.

I stepped onto the first of six open cars, headed beyond the perimeters of what had decades ago been deemed unsafe for construction, out into no man's land where the icy Hudson penetrated eroding rock into the miles of unfinished subway tunnels. It was there, deep in the catacombs where Dougherty stored the corpses of his failed experiments, that I believed he'd run hoping to make his escape through a sewer or manhole far away from cops on the look out for him in the vicinity of the Starrett Building.

What I saw as the train lurched forward seemed too unreal to be adequately described, a dream or fragment of a nightmare: the last of the children being evacuated mostly by cops who, ignoring warnings blasted over emergency sound systems, carried those too weak to walk from their cages to makeshift pullies leading up to the street while like the ribald state of an army that had forgotten the patriotic premise of its war HAs like Li'l Rat, Elvis Chacon, and Coulter performed mop-up operations, AK47s blazing amidst the smoldering ruins, mowing down Dougherty's forces like dogs on the street as they ran, hid, or begged for mercy.

Riding the subway, ignored by predators, victims, the wounded and dying, made me feel more ghost than man, unnoticed and unseen, a tourist in Hell and I wondered, *could it be that I was already dead like in those movies where spirits carry on in a kind of purgatory oblivious to their fate?* Past bamboo cages, empty now with doors swung open like tenantless graves, fires flamed around me, some begun spontaneously from gas leaks and severed electrical cables wriggling along the river's edge like eels on a dry dock, others ignited by cables fallen from the ceiling, stretched half-hidden beneath the surface of the water where pools of floating oil glowed like mendicants' pyres and incinerated bodies were carried forward by the river's current.

My eyes strained to see beyond the spiraling clouds of white smoke billowing from wrecked structures, the ozone smell of arcing electricity filling my nostrils as the six-car-train slipped beyond what was left of the Casanova Club and terminal, away from the Starrett Building, its steel rebar and concrete walls set shrieking like a ward of anguished cancer patients crying out for morphine.

From the corner of my eye, I saw a maintenance door fly open and turned to see a solitary biker rush out into the station, eyes red-rimmed as if locked in their sockets with hot wires, screaming *"Hit the floor! Get down!!"* when suddenly the lights dimmed and a huge ball of fire leapt out at me like the lick of a dragon's tongue. The train of cars forged deeper into the tunnels as the fireball expended itself while the HA, still in flames, ran toward me hands raised in the air like a Baptist about to shout 'praise Jesus!' before he collapsed and died.

Finally I came to the end of the track. That is to say, the Kafka Society's subway track, but only the beginning of the stretch of stations and rails abandoned five decades ago. Water dripped from the ceiling and from out of the deteriorating walls with as many soot-stained white tiles missing as hung on them. I grabbed an emergency searchlight mounted on the console of the empty driver's car and turned it on. The stench of fungus made the air oppressive as, Glock in one hand and searchlight in the other, I exited the train and marched forward into the dark. Rats scurried away at the sound of my shoes sloshing through the steady stream of water that covered the steel track but I didn't care about any of that. It was Dougherty I'd come after. It was Dougherty I wanted, and I would not rest until I saw him dead.

"Dougherty," I called, the echo of my voice repeating 'Dougherty, Dougherty, Dougherty' like a ghostly chorus broadcast out into deep space. "I'm coming for you, Tom, you know that, don't you?"

"Is that you, Jack? I haven't got a searchlight like you, Old Boy. Can't see a thing."

"You know there's no way out of this. Why not make it easy on yourself, on Annie and the kids?"

"Exactly what is it you'd have me do?" the voice came back out of the shadows, louder then fainter, as he made his way through the deserted passageways.

I slogged further into the tunnel, the stream of water now up to my ankles.

"Come out with your hands over your head. I'll give you the chance you'd never give me. Do that and I'll let you surrender to the police."

"Oh, yes, Woods and his Group 41, must make you very proud to be a police informer. Is that part of a new western novel you're planning to write?" I heard him laugh over the roar of rushing water, shouts of oncoming police, and dogs barking. "You know, I could overlook all of this, Jack, it's not too late."

"Too late for what, Tom?" I asked, angling the searchlight, finally catching a glimpse of him dazzled by the light's piercing probe, then watching the long twisted shadow he cast skulking forward, back pressed against the wall into the darkness.

"There's plenty for two. I could still cut you in," his voice echoed through the tunnels as if he was bargaining in a boardroom and not the sewer we were in. "I know a place where no one would think to look for us. You know it, too. I've got money hidden there, Jack. Lots of money. You could marry Havana, if you wanted. Send her boy to a private school. You'd never have to work again. I could do that for you, Jack," he offered as I came to a fork in the system, both passageways flooded with water now nearly waist-high. "I'd even consider a fifty-fifty split if you'd drop all of this cops and robbers nonsense. You really never were much of a detective, but I guess you've figured that out by now, haven't you, Jack? Forget all of that and come along with me. Havana and the boy can join us later. I promise I'll make it worth your while."

"Come along where?"

"I can't tell you that now, can I? Not unless I knew we were going to be partners together in this."

"The FBI knows you're down here, Tom. You hear those dogs and the cops along with them? Those dogs don't give a shit about your money. The cops have you surrounded. No way out. Woods and the others have men hunting you down here and up above on the streets in every train station and airport New York to Boston."

"I know these tunnels and where they lead the way those city cops know Times Square. No, they won't be catching me any time soon. You have a gun, don't you, Jack?"

"Yeah, and I'm pointing it directly at you, Tom. Put your hands over your head and walk towards me or I will fucking shoot you dead on the spot."

"Afraid I can't see. I've told you that already. No lights where I am, Jack, but if you stop wagging that searchlight around and let me see where you are, I'll do as you say for Annie's sake, for the sake of the children."

I lowered the searchlights beam and directed it straight ahead, then thought better of it the instant it steadied. I flicked the shaft of light off. The tunnel went black simultaneous with Dougherty's first shot at me. His first round must have entered the water in front of me because I felt it strike my left thigh with an impact more like a karate chop than a gunshot wound. The second and third rounds hit the tunnel wall to my left traveling so close I could hear the bullets whistle as they passed.

There was no question from where the shots came so at least I knew which of the two passageways Dougherty had taken firing *one, two, three rounds* in his direction, not daring to flick the searchlight back on again. Eyes navigating through the dark as best I could, I edged closer to the wall and deeper into tunnel acutely aware that the man trackers and their dogs were closing in on us and that the sloshing sound of legs and feet moving through the water's current that allowed me to follow Dougherty had now stopped.

I considered that he may be laying for me around the bend or above the rails in one of the passengers' stations, *but why would he invest these last precious moments in killing me with his pursuers so close behind?* I asked myself. *No, the shots he fired had done what they were meant to do,* I decided, slogging ahead through the waist-deep black water spiked with headless corpses broken loose from Dougherty's collection during the blasts. *He didn't need or want to kill me. Those shots were meant to give him time enough to make his escape on to one of the still operational freight elevators he'd planned on using all along, then up to the street through a sewer or one of the maintenance crew entrances!*

Careful not to provide a visible target, back hugging the slime-covered wall, I lit the searchlight up again. Fifty feet later, its laser-like probe fell upon a gray door marked 'NYC TRANSIT' one-third submerged in the onrushing water. I struggled against the current and managed to force it open. Before me lay a curving iron staircase patched dark green with algae.

No longer afraid of an ambush, I lumbered up the stairs, then stood breathless perched on a rusty iron-grill landing staring dumbfounded at the 1928 Magnus elevator Dougherty had ridden to an inactive platform on the MTA's B line and freedom!

Chapter Thirty-Six

Onto the freight elevator I stormed, up to the subway platform abandoned save the nests of rats stirred by Dougherty and me, and out onto the street, fifteen blocks east of Chelsea. With the Porsche sequestered a mile away, I commandeered the first cab I could find at gunpoint. Out of service with police and ambulance sirens ripping through the cold December night, I ordered him back through the Holland Tunnel, eyes wide with panic as he, through the rearview, and I, through the back window, watched in awe as the Starrett Building toppled one quaking floor at a time starting with the twenty-ninth then descending to its center where amid a gigantic dark gray cloud the remaining thirteen floors collapsed like Colossus shot through the heart.

"*D'ya see dat, mahn,*" the East Indian driver asked, turning to me like an excited schoolboy. "*It's gone! Just like dat,*" he said snapping his fingers, "*disappeared!*"

I touched the Glock to the base of his skull, "You just look straight ahead and fucking drive."

"*Al Qaeda!*" he said suddenly, the enormity of what we'd just witnessed beginning to register. "*You tink dat? You tink it dem bastards done dis to us?*"

"Take Rt. 9 North," I instructed in a steady voice, nudging him with the gun. "Get off at McCarter Highway

and take that to Market Street. You know St. Damian's?"
He nodded eyes wide, still emotional. "Good, that's where
we're headed."

And indeed that was exactly where we were going
because like the signature to a rubric's cube one finally
masters during that instant of mental clarity when the
trappings of artifice drop off like scales and the truth waits
for you pristine as a newborn child, I knew that Dougherty
was headed to St. Ann's monastery.

Not unlike me five years earlier, desperate, with no place
to go and no one who'd have me, I'd sought refuge there.
But Dougherty's instinct to return ran far deeper than that.
He'd bought a new wing for the school — courtesy of the
Dougherty Foundation — to solidify his *bona fides* within
the Catholic Church, true, but for him there was a more
practical reason to have bought it and be returning there
today: it was there that he'd stashed his getaway money, a
fortune in cash and who knew what other currency to take
with him if ever forced to abandon the phony life he'd
been living and disappear "into the wind" like so many
high-profile criminals before him. Perhaps that cache was
hidden in the school, or in the church, or even the abbey,
itself, *but if the money was there, so was he,* I was convinced,
and this was my chance to nail him!

I handed the cabbie a one-hundred dollar bill, soggy
but intact, once we arrived, "It may not smell great, but it's
valid currency," I told him. "Now head back to the city and
forget you ever saw me."

He watched me march up the five stone stairs leading
to the heavy oak door that marked the entrance to St.
Ann's, gun in hand. I could hear his car speed away as
I pushed it open, the noise of traffic giving way to the

sound of men singing in Latin echoing through the narthex. It was the monks of St. Ann's performing their evening vespers, I realized, not a second before my eyes fell on Dougherty. A long shadow of a man, he was on his hands and knees, body half in and half out of an empty confessional, loading stacks of dollars, Euros, and diamonds into a black, leather carry-on from out of a section of false flooring within.

I raised the Glock waist high. Behind Dougherty, standing at the lip of a crimson apron leading to the altar where within a shimmering silver monstrance the Holy Eucharist was ensconced, thirty-five black-robed monks were chanting the *universalis*.

"Find what you're looking for?" I asked in a voice loud enough to penetrate the waves of Latin sweeping through the chapel.

Dougherty re-arranged himself to face me. He seemed bewildered whether by my presence or the futility of his situation I could not know, but in a matter of seconds he was himself again. Nodding, then smiling, he let out a deep breath and sat there on the floor outside the confessional, black bag brimming with treasure.

"Maybe you noticed the Lincoln town car out there? On my way to a private Lear jet, Jack. Off the grid to Buenos Aires, ever been there?"

"Can't say that I have, Tom," I answered pointing the Glock, held both hands out in front of me, directly at him.

"Magnificent city, German-built, you can count on that. A diesel truck can do a figure-eight in the streets downtown, that's how wide the boulevards run. Like Berlin in the 1930s, the construction of the city, I mean, just before the war when the Nazis *really were* something."

He shot a probing stare at me. "Mind if I stand? The floor is a little chilly this time of year. I must look ridiculous!"

"Go ahead," I answered, motioning with the gun. "You're either going to come with me to the police now or die where you stand."

"No need to go native on me, Old Chum. Lots of money here. Right in front of you. Ten million cash. At least that much in diamonds and securities. After all, it would only be you and I who know what arrangements we put together here this evening. Besides," he said, turning to reveal the Sig Sauer he was holding, "I've got a gun, too. Eight-shot semiautomatic and with my training at the Bureau, well, no brag, but I think I've got you dead to rights."

It was only then that I noticed a black-robed figure approaching Dougherty from behind. It was Fr. Jeremiah. "Tom? Jack? What are you two doing here?"

With those words, I watched Dougherty pivot in Jeremiah's direction, whether to address him or shoot him, I could not tell, but understanding that this was the only opportunity I'd have to overpower him, I decided to hang low, leap forward, and attack!

The distance between us must have been at least ten feet but seemed no more than a step or two judging by the time it took to close it and take hold of his right hand to wrest the Sig Sauer away. But Dougherty, schooled in jiu jitsu, was no cherry and proved it breaking the wrist lock I put on him with his free hand while driving a powerful knee upward into my balls as my Glock dropped to the floor! Not fun, I'll grant you, but if he was expecting me to double-over in pain so he could deliver a left uppercut to follow, I wasn't buying and instead came up with a thunderous right cross of my own that threw him backward toward Jeremiah, who stood paralyzed. *"No, no, son,"* the priest screamed watching the murder come to my face and the pupils in my eyes shrink to two black, shiny pools devoid of either reason or humanity.

Staggered back as he was, my path was obvious—attack and keep on attacking, fists blazing, using every combat move I'd ever learned during the course of the one hundred brawls I'd entered into in my life so far. But, like I said, Dougherty was nothing like cherry so with punches blocked and leg kicks rendered ineffective, we went at it *mano a mano*, me delivering short chopping blows to his face, his nose already smashed-in and spouting thick wads of blood and mucous, while he tried to finish me off with a choke hold, hands wrapped around my throat, still holding onto the Sig Sauer which moment-to-moment was shoved into my face as he clawed, and choked, using every tactic he knew trying to blow my fucking brains out!

It was during the height of that fierce struggle for dominance with a gaggle of monks rushing toward us from the front of the church that the first of two shots rang-out like an engine backfiring from the jerking, flame-stabbing 9mm semiautomatic Dougherty held. The first ricocheted off the chapel's side wall near a carved marble statue of the Virgin Mary blasting an ear off, the second hit Jeremiah just above the heart dropping him like a rock! The sight of Jeremiah fallen was enough to send my mind scrambling through a wizard's box of possibilities as I caught Dougherty with a leg sweep that sent him crashing downward while a torrent of thoughts swirled through my head with equal ferocity, *'Jeremiah dead' 'Jeremiah wounded' 'Hospital now'*

'Get ambulance', they clamored like conjuries set loose from another dimension.

Spurred by the seriousness of Jeremiah's condition as he convulsed on the floor, I swept the gun into my hand and locked its sights on Dougherty. Sprawled with arms and legs stretched out from his body he appeared the personification of his or some other secret society as he looked up to me with that boyish, conspiratorial smile I witnessed for the first time thirty years before. But in my eyes there was only one emotion, and that emotion was murder, black and cold as winter's night.

"I know you, Jack. You wouldn't shoot me, you must know that yourself, *couldn't*," he emphasized smiling, and breathing heavy, as if the twinkle in his eyes was enough to convince me and anyone else that everything was all right, no matter how far he'd drifted, no matter how far off the rails he'd taken it.

"You're poison," I swore, tightening my grip on the gun. "Everything you touch is poison."

"Getting a touch melodramatic, aren't we, Jack?" he asked, moving to his feet again. "You were never going to kill me or anybody. It's not in your nature so why not admit it?" He dusted himself off. "You see, unlike me, you really are a moral man, maybe even a Catholic, *deep inside*, and to kill a man, even a man like me, in cold blood? Well that, my friend, would be a mortal..."

But Dougherty never got to finish his treatise on the subject of Catholics, or mortal sin, or even Jack Madson because I pulled the trigger once, then again, firing directly into his face as nightmare remembrances of the decimated remains of Amber Starr, Ronnie Reicher, Chok Por, Johnnie Giambi, and the heads of those pathetic victims I had seen collected like museum exhibits in his office, swept through my mind unrelenting. The shots rang-out like the teeth-rattling retorts of a canon reverberating through the chapel, my own personal dissertation on the subject of simple justice in a world corrupted by corporate greed, mealy-mouthed lawyers and spineless politicians, for gods and demons, saints and sinners, and all of the men of indeterminate value like me to contemplate for all times to come.

"You are a mutant sent from Hell," I uttered standing over him, gun in hand, as a covey of Brothers tended to Jeremiah while others administered Last Rights to Dougherty who lie in a pool of blood, two bullets through his forehead, dead.

Chapter Thirty-Seven

Jimmy Bryant flicked off the Lanier tape recorder lying atop the gray-painted steel table that separated us. The crown of his bulldog head with curly hair sprouting like patches of rust-colored steel wool was all that he offered to gauge his reaction to my story. Finally, his ruddy face emerged up from the effort. He shot a drill of tobacco juice between his two front teeth drumming it into the bottom of a Styrofoam cup.

"It's got flare," he admitted after a moment's thought. "A media man's dream and bureaucrat's nightmare, but if you don't mind tellin' me, does it happen to be true?"

"Look, Jimmy, I just bared my fucking soul to you, told you everything I know, not just about Dougherty and the federal building attack, but about *me*, for Christ's sake. There's nothing more to tell and that's the truth!"

Bryant's oversized head, attached to his thick neck and barrel-chested torso, stuffed into the vested blue suit he wore, bobbed up and down ponderously.

"Your story sounds crazy but we're living in strange times, a peculiar civilization these days and so," he noted with a dramatist's panache, "I believe there are angles, viable possibilities let's call them, that can get these FLEAS off your back perhaps permanently since its scope is so broad and the people involved so prominent. You know what FLEAS are, don't you, Jack? Federal Law Enforcement Agencies," he explained, eyes narrowing as a high pitched laugh escaped from between his lips. "We can start with the fact that..."

But Bryant never got the chance to finish the *troupe l' oeil* he'd begun articulating, his eyes falling on the heavy-gauge steel door that he'd passed through himself four hours earlier to find Vicky Benson and my Georgetown pal Eddie Lawler marching into the visitors' room like grand marshals at the St. Patrick's Day parade, the faint sound of Nat King Cole's *Christmas Song* leaking like smoke through a key hole from the corridors behind them.

It was Lawler, miniature legs striding double-time toward us, who spoke first, "Mr. Bryant, a pleasure to meet you," he beamed, extending his hand, grinning ear-to-ear, "but I don't believe your services will be required any longer, at least not as they apply to Mr. Madson. Tell 'em, Vicky. Tell 'em everything that's happened."

"Eddie's right, Jack," she said turning over the paperwork to Bryant. "The U.S. District Court issued a court order dismissing your indictment based on exculpatory information provided in a motion by the prosecution. What that means is that effective 3:30 pm today, you're a free man."

"What time is it?" I asked.

Vicky glanced at her cell phone, "3:35 pm, the court order took effect five minutes ago."

"Jimmy?"

"Yes, indeed, the paperwork seems to be in order. All

the necessary signatures are here, but why?" he asked, his Irish brogue never more prominent. "What in God's blazing Hell has happened to turn all of this upside down since I arrived here this morning?"

"It's your priest friend, Jackie," Lawler chimed in. "You probably heard Jeremiah survived bein' shot like he was, but what the DA held back until late this morning was that Jeremiah swears that when you smoked Dougherty he had a gun pointed at you and it was self defense. Better 'n that, every goddamned monk present in the chapel that night told the same story, *zero deviation*. Self-defense! Self-defense!" Eddie sang-out dancing around in a circle, his right index finger pointed skyward like it was New Year's Eve and the clock had just struck midnight.

"And the second charge, conspiracy to commit terrorist acts?" Bryant asked pointedly. "The explosion brought down the Starrett Building?"

"That was Coulter. I'm defending him," Vicky shot back edging her long, lithe body toward him. "Sonny admitted to it, initial planning through final execution. Took federal agents to the Angels safe house in Brooklyn, himself, to show them the maps of the underground he used to mastermind the attack. He wants to take the rap. Says it gives the Angels the street cred they've been trying to re-establish for more than a decade now. Jack's name never came up except as an interloper who happened on the scene," she added passing Bryant a bright-eyed smile. "First, as a man trying to save Havana Spice and her son Savito Machado, then, as a father attempting to rescue his daughter after having been abducted."

"See? See the way it's all fallin' together? You're a hero, the way Vicky's been spinning it. Like a knight in shining armor come up from out of his man cave to rescue Havana, her son, and Tiffany. All three have already been interrogated by every agency they got and their testimonies go together better 'n dogs and dykes! Yeah, sure, there'll be questions. Lot's of 'em, you can count on that, but trust me, Jackie Boy, FBI, ATF, DEA, the whole alphabet soup gang and even your pal Don Woods at Homeland, are all singin' our song now that what was goin' down at the Casanova Club has, shall we say, seen the light of day!"

Bryant's wolfish blue eyes sharpened at the mention of the club's name, "The Kafka Society, is it? The boy, Savito, and his ubiquitous iPad," he ventured harkening back to my story. "His mother, Havana Spice, finally got it into the right hands and now the motherfuckers are scared. 'Time to circle the wagons, boys!' he called-out like he was John Wayne atop his mount giving orders to the 1st Calvary Division.' Time to protect the ever-vigilant government institutions and their keepers who guide this God-fearing nation of ours from the Director of the FBI to the Mayor of New York City and who knows how far up from there? I've seen it before and I'll see it again. There'll be no trial and there'll be no justice. Not today. Not in my lifetime. Does that about cover it, Mr. Lawler?"

"Indeed it does!" Eddie reveled raising his dwarf-length arms high into the air, Bryant's irony lost on him. "Indeed it does! By the time the music stops and everyone's sittin' in the right chairs, Dougherty's wife will be acceptin' a plaque and an American flag on behalf of her husband at Federal Plaza, and the Kafka Society morphed into some other secret society re-located to Brussels, or Stockholm, or Hong Kong; a figment of someone's imagination, probably yours, Jack-O! But if that's what it takes to keep you from servin' a hundred year stretch at Pelican Island, I don't think you're going to squawk much about it, are ya?"

I didn't answer immediately but waited to feel their eyes burning down on me, and their minds set wandering through the dark streets and hidden alley ways redolent with the stench of corruption and hypocrisy I'd been stalking for better than five years now. My eyes fell on a 2' tall Christmas tree constructed of steel wire and mylar put up by the guards in celebration of Christ's coming, and to me it could have been the logo for what passes for a justice system in this country.

"There was a French Jesuit back in the 1950s named Tielhard de Chardin," I finally answered. "When I was a kid over at St. Damian's in Newark, I read a quote from a book he wrote that sticks in my mind even today. 'It is the destiny of things real to destroy those that are artifice,' he wrote. 'In the end, only the truth will survive.' So let me answer your question this way. Yeah, sure, I'll play ball with the powers to be, Eddie," I said, watching a three-inch cockroach scurry beneath the bench were I sat and squashing it with my boot heel. "I'll play ball with the powers to be *for now.*"

Coming soon
From Barricade Books

Dark Angel

The next Jack Madson

Series crime thriller

By Ron Felber

(Turn the page)

Jack Madson investigates the suicide death of honor student Mary Linda Schumann on Princeton University campus. Satisfied there is no foul play, Jack is about to return to the West Coast when he witnesses adjunct professor, Dimitri Wilder, enter a local eatery wearing only a tattered trench coat and hi-top sneakers, an 18' machete dangling menacingly at his side. Methodically, Wilder stomps toward Princeton's star athlete, severs his right hand, then hops into his red Corvette intentionally running it into a concrete embankment during a high-speed police chase.

Two suicides related by just one clue: the phrase "the world is filled with Small Minds" carved by Schumann into a mahogany desktop before leaping to her death and the words "Small Mind" spat out like a gypsy curse by Wilder prior to his machete rampage.

Who could know that the serial killer that later emerges on Princeton campus is borne of radical evolution experiments carried out sixty years earlier by Nazi scientist Josef Mengele, Auschwitz' infamous "Angel of Death"?